Advance praise for

THE VALANCOURT BOOK OF WORLD HORROR STORIES

'This groundbreaking anthology of contemporary horror stories from around the world is an irrefutable testament to the international popularity of horror fiction as a form of literary expression . . . This book is a must for horror fans and the start of an exciting new series.'

—*Publishers Weekly* (starred review)

'This collection is stellar from top to bottom . . . this desperately needed anthology is meticulously researched and translated, offering stories from a variety of perspectives across five continents, and representing the broad range of storytelling styles and tropes that are used by all horror storytellers regardless of nationality.'

—*Library Journal*

'The rich variety of voices, angles, and attitudes exhibited in this globe-spanning anthology reminds us of all the wonderful things that horror literature can do – no passport required.'

—*Rue Morgue*

'This book is a gift. While the language of horror is universal, its means of expression necessarily varies from culture to culture. *The Valancourt Book of World Horror Stories* brings us a collection of tales by outstanding writers from all over the world. These stories are by turns unsettling, violent, strange, and beautiful – all the ingredients of great horror stories, from voices and perspectives we have lived too long without.'

—Nathan Ballingrud, award-winning author of
North American Lake Monsters and *Wounds*

THE VALANCOURT BOOK OF
WORLD HORROR STORIES

VOLUME ONE

Edited by
James D. Jenkins & Ryan Cagle

VALANCOURT BOOKS
Richmond, Virginia
MMXX

The Valancourt Book of World Horror Stories, Volume One
First published December 2020

All stories copyright by their respective authors.
This compilation copyright © 2020 by Valancourt Books, LLC
All translations copyright © 2020 by Valancourt Books, LLC, except
'The Time Remaining' © 2020 by Luca Karafiáth, 'Pale Toes' © 2020 by
Sanna Terho, and 'Mechanisms' © 2020 by Mara Faye Lethem.
The Acknowledgments pages on pp. 17-18 constitute an extension of
this copyright page.

Published by Valancourt Books, Richmond, Virginia
http://www.valancourtbooks.com

ISBN 978-1-948405-63-8 (limited hardcover)
ISBN 978-1-948405-64-5 (trade paperback)

Also available as an electronic book.

Set in Bembo Book MT

CONTENTS

Editors' Foreword

MOST HORROR READERS, to the extent they've thought about it at all, have probably always assumed that horror fiction is an Anglo-American phenomenon. From Horace Walpole and Ann Radcliffe to Edgar Allan Poe and M. R. James, to H. P. Lovecraft, Shirley Jackson and Stephen King, horror has always been first and foremost a product of the United States and the British Isles, right? Aside from a handful of 19th-century French or German or Russian stories that crop up every so often in an old anthology, or the occasional name bandied about by horror fiction connoisseurs, but whose works are largely unavailable and seldom read, such as the Belgian Jean Ray (1887-1964), there's not really much 'international horror fiction' to speak of. Everybody knows that, right?

But what if everybody was wrong? What if there were a whole world of great horror literature out there being produced by writers in distant lands, in books you couldn't access and languages you couldn't read? To an avid horror fan, what could be more horrifying than that?!

If you're still struggling to come up with the names of international horror writers, don't feel bad. You're not alone. Even in countries where fine horror fiction exists, it has often been ignored or forgotten. For example, in the introduction to his anthology of all-original Dutch horror fiction, editor Robert-Henk Zuidinga laments that 'few Dutch-language writers have ventured [to write in the field of the] literary horror story'[1], a judgment that neglects the psychological horror tales of Felix Timmermans (1886-1947) (recently published by Valancourt), the Aickman-style strange stories of Jacques Hamelink (b. 1939), and the elegant ghost stories of Kathinka Lannoy (1917-1996), to name a few. Similarly, the popular Norwegian thriller writer André Bjerke recounts that he was approached to edit an anthology of ghost stories from around the world and a separate anthology featuring only fantastic tales from Norway. In his response to the publisher, he warned that the Norwegian 'anthology is naturally leaner than [the international one], both in terms of quality and quantity' and wrote that, 'here I could wander like [explorer Henry Morton] Stanley in the undiscovered primeval forest – for no one has gone into this terrain before me'.[2] And yet, despite his initial misgivings, in the end Bjerke managed to compile an impressive volume of some two dozen fine Norwegian horror stories spanning 1840 to 1977, including one we've chosen for the present volume. To cite one more example, the Argentinian author of weird tales Mariana Enríquez recently declared that, 'There is no tradition of horror or weird writing in Spanish',[3] a debatable pronouncement that would no doubt come as a surprise to the Spanish writers featured in the present volume.

The moral of the story is that if one takes the trouble to look hard enough, there's a much larger body of world horror fiction out there than any of us would suspect. However, as Bjerke suggested, it often involves deep digging and venturing into uncharted waters.

1 Robert-Henk Zuidinga (ed.), *Uit den boze: Oorspronkelijke griezelverhalen* (Amsterdam: Sijthoff, 1984), p. 7. The translation is ours.
2 André Bjerke (ed.)., *Drømmen, draugen og dauingen: grøssere og selsomme historier i norsk prosa* (Oslo: Den norske Bokklubben, 1978), p. 5. The translation is ours.
3 Mariana Enríquez, 'Creating a New Tradition of Latin American Horror', https://lithub.com/creating-a-new-tradition-of-latin-american-horror/, Oct. 31, 2018 (accessed April 17, 2020).

In fact, international horror fiction has been around just about as long as it has existed in the English-speaking world. Not long after Horace Walpole kicked off the craze for Gothic fiction with *The Castle of Otranto* (1764), William Beckford published his masterpiece *Vathek* (1786), written in French and issued in Switzerland. And in the 1790s, while Ann Radcliffe's bestsellers like *The Mysteries of Udolpho* (1794) were flying off British circulating library shelves, the Polish Count Jan Potocki was writing, again in French, his own Gothic masterpiece, *The Manuscript Found in Saragossa*. Ukrainian-born Nikolai Gogol was writing tales in Russian that might be called 'Poe-esque' before Poe himself began publishing stories in America. During the Romantic era, while Gothic horror was popular in England and America, it also flourished in France, Germany,[4] Italy,[5] Sweden[6] and Spain[7], and throughout the 19th and early 20th centuries, many European countries, as well as places as far apart as Argentina[8] and Japan,[9] had a tradition of what might be termed horror or weird fiction. And, as you're about to find out from this book, horror fiction is alive and flourishing in nearly every corner of the world in the 21st century.

4 See, e.g., Daniel Hall, *French and German Gothic Fiction in the Late Eighteenth Century* (Bern: Peter Lang, 2005).

5 See Riccardo Reim (ed.), *Da uno spiraglio: Racconti neri e fantastici dell'Ottocento italiano*, (Roma: Newton Compton, 1992).

6 See the collections of rare 19th-century Swedish horror fiction published by Aleph, e.g., *Nattens paradis: Svenska sällsamheter*, ed. Rickard Berghorn (Stockaryd: Aleph, 2017).

7 See, e.g., Miriam López Santos, *La novela gótica en España (1788-1833)*, (Vigo: Editorial Academia del Hispanismo, 2010).

8 Probably more fairly termed 'weird' than outright 'horror', Argentine writers such as Jorge Luis Borges, Silvina Ocampo, and Julio Cortázar might be cited here, along with contemporary writer Mariana Enríquez, whose fine collection *Things We Lost in the Fire* (2016) was a rare international horror title to see wide release in English.

9 For example, Lafcadio Hearn's *Kwaidan: Stories and Studies of Strange Things* (1904), Edogawa Rampa's *Japanese Tales of Mystery and Imagination* (1954) or Koji Suzuki's *Ring* (1991) and its sequels.

The impulse towards horror appears to be a universal phenomenon, running through the literatures of a great many cultures over a very long period of time. If horror fiction as we think of it today is a relatively modern concept, the trappings of horror can be found in writing from all over the world throughout all of human history. From the witch Circe, murderous Sirens and man-eating Cyclops in Homer's *The Odyssey* to the Bible's stories of demons and devils, to the Roman writer Pliny the Elder's accounts of werewolves, it is not hard to find the precursors of modern-day horror in ancient texts from around the world.

But this isn't the place or time for a full exploration of horror throughout the ages or throughout the world.[10] The point we're trying to make is that horror is neither an exclusively modern phenomenon nor an exclusively Anglophone one, and moreover – and what might be most surprising – some of the world's best horror fiction has come (and continues to come) from elsewhere.

Yet although there is a lot of high-quality horror fiction continuing to be produced around the world, very little of it is being published for English-speaking readers. There have been a couple of encouraging exceptions in recent years – Dutch author Thomas Olde Heuvelt's internationally bestselling witch novel *Hex* (2016) and French writer Grégoire Courtois' harrowing *The Laws of the Skies* (2019) come to mind – but for the most part, on the rare occasions when foreign horror is published for an American or British audience, it's an isolated appearance of a short story in an obscure periodical, or publication online in some little-frequented corner of the web.

10 Such a book is yet to be written; however, Jess Nevins's recent scholarship, published in *Horror Needs No Passport: 20th Century Horror Literature Outside the U.S. and U.K.* (self-published, 2018) and *Horror Fiction in the 20th Century* (Santa Barbara, Calif.: Praeger, 2020), is probably the best place to start.

But even if not much foreign horror has made its way into U.S. bookshops, it's a big deal in its home countries. Did you know that in the tiny principality of Andorra, nestled in the Pyrenees between France and Spain, there is an annual government-sponsored competition open to all the country's residents, with the writer of the best horror story earning 600 euros? Or that Bulgaria and Denmark have active horror writers' associations? (In Denmark there's so much horror fiction being published that they even give out annual awards for the best; one of the winners is featured in this book.) In tiny Iceland, and in the Spanish region of Galicia, publishers have launched versions of the seminal *Weird Tales* magazine in their local languages. In Catalonia, one small publisher annually chooses four prominent Catalan authors to lock up in a reputedly haunted castle for a weekend to write horror tales, then publishes the results in a yearly volume. In recent years, horror anthologies have even begun to crop up in languages most people have never heard of, like Western Frisian and Corsican.[11] The closer you look, the more you find that horror fiction really is everywhere.

So why isn't more of it being made available to English-speaking readers?

Well, it's pretty simple really. For starters, most horror these days is published – both here and abroad – by small presses. Small American and British presses probably don't have someone on staff who can read and evaluate the quality of Romanian, or Swedish, or Afrikaans horror stories, while conversely the small Romanian, Swedish, and Afrikaans publishers might not have the financial wherewithal to commission English translations of their books and send them out to potential U.S. or U.K. publishers. So in many cases

11 We are presently working on a companion volume to the present one, to include a selection of horror stories from minority and endangered languages.

the material remains appreciated only by the comparatively small audience able to read it.

The idea of compiling a volume of world horror fiction is one we've been kicking around for a while, but although the idea seemed a good one, it immediately gave rise to all kinds of questions and problems. Should the book focus on classic stories from the 19th and 20th centuries, present-day writing, or a combination of the two? If we were to exclude American and British work, what about other English-language stories (e.g., from Australia, New Zealand, or India)? Would we collect previously translated material or concentrate on stories that had never before appeared in English? And if the latter, how were we to find them?

Ultimately we decided to feature contemporary writing in this first volume and save older and classic material for a potential future project. We also chose to focus primarily on non-English-language fiction, and specifically on material that had never before been translated. Recognizing, however, that many countries – some of them significantly under-represented in American publishing – use English widely (for example the Philippines, featured in this volume), we ended up excluding only English-language contributions from the U.S., U.K., Canada, Ireland, Australia and New Zealand. On the other hand, authors from those countries writing in another language were eligible for inclusion (such as Spanish-language writers from Puerto Rico, Franco-phone writers from Quebec, or an author writing in Irish or another indigenous language).

We posted a call for submissions on our website and social media accounts in early 2019, inviting submissions for this volume. Stories written in one of the fifteen or so languages we were able to read could be sent in their original language; others had to be accompanied by some sort of synopsis or rough translation to give us an idea of what the story was about and whether it seemed like the sort of thing we might like to commission a professional translation of. Though the call for submissions did not result in a large number of entries, it did bring in several very high-quality tales, including two ultimately chosen for this volume, by Attila Veres (Hungary) and Marko Hautala (Finland).

The process of finding the rest of the stories mostly involved a great deal of research. In a few cases our jobs were made easier by foreign editors who had compiled anthologies of the best horror stories from their countries. But when all else failed, we went to Google and ran searches like '*mejores escritores de terror mexicanos*' and '*skräckberättelser på svenska*', and spent months poring over books, articles, websites, reviews, etc., to learn who were the preeminent horror writers in those different countries and languages. Then we sought out those authors' works – sometimes with a fair amount of difficulty – and spent countless hours reading through them to find the very best ones. In the end, we read more than 200 stories from around 40 countries, originally written in around 20 different languages, narrowing it down to the ones we thought were the best and most interesting for this book.

A book like this one has obvious limitations. First, in terms of space: with nearly 200 countries in the world and some 7,000 living languages, there is no way to include a comprehensive selection of all the world's horror fiction in just one volume. And then of course there's the matter of language: having decided to focus primarily on stories that haven't previously appeared in English, we were limited to stories in languages we could understand (though fortunately some of these, like French and Spanish, have a broad international reach) or ones that were submitted to us with accompanying translations. To the reader who is disappointed her favorite country – China, Russia, Turkey, or wherever it may be – was not included, we can only say that this is the first in a projected series of similar volumes and we hope that the success of this book will lead to an even wider geographical selection of submissions for future books.

In terms of the stories we did choose, we aimed for as diverse a group of entries as possible, both in terms of geographical diversity (North, Central, and South America, the Caribbean, Europe, Africa, and Asia are all represented in the book), a wide range of themes and content, and a diverse lineup of authors that ensured a high rate of inclusion of women writers, authors of color, and LGBT-interest material. We also made a specific effort to seek out contributions from countries whose literatures are less well known to American readers, like Ecuador, Senegal, and Martinique. Finally, we aimed to find stories that used horror in interesting and novel ways, such as Flavius Ardelean's 'Down, in Their World', in which the author incorporates age-old superstitions from his native Transylvania, or Bathie Ngoye Thiam's 'The House of Leuk Dawour', which updates oral Senegalese folklore traditions into a modern-day horror tale, or Flore Hazoumé's 'Menopause', which manages to be both an unsettling horror story and a clever piece of social commentary on women's roles in Ivory Coast society. The resulting selection of stories is an eclectic mix that we hope horror readers will enjoy as much as we did.

There's an oft-cited statistic that only 3% of the books published in the U.S. are translated works. As you're about to see from the following stories, the reason for this is not a lack of high-quality foreign language material. The primary reason is almost certainly cost: professional translation services are extremely expensive and cost-prohibitive for all but the largest publishers. For that reason, we translated all but three of the stories in this volume in-house, in consultation with the authors, for whose edits and suggestions we're very grateful. We welcome comments and feedback from readers about the translations or the book as a whole. Let us know which stories you liked best, which of these authors you'd love to read more from, and what you'd like to see in a potential second volume.

Whether you call them horror stories, *griezelverhalen*, *historias de terror*, *skräckberättelser*, *racconti dell'orrore*, or (perhaps our favorite) *spookstories*, there's something universal about the telling and reading of a good, creepy tale. A whole new world of horror is awaiting your discovery. Turn the page and encounter the international side of horror . . .

James D. Jenkins & Ryan Cagle
Valancourt Books
April 2020

JAMES D. JENKINS and RYAN CAGLE founded Valancourt Books in 2004 and since that time have republished over 500 lost and neglected texts, primarily in the fields of Gothic, supernatural, and horror literature, with an aim to making these books available in affordable editions for modern readers. They are also the co-editors of the four volumes of the acclaimed *The Valancourt Book of Horror Stories* series. James holds a BA in French and an MA in Romance Languages and Literatures and also studied Dutch and Italian at university; he has since learned over a dozen more languages and took advantage of his language studies in translating many of the stories for this volume.

Acknowledgments

The editors would like to thank first and foremost all the authors who submitted stories for our consideration, both those we ultimately selected for this volume and those we didn't have room to include. It was a delight reading each and every one of them.

We acknowledge our debt to editors who preceded us and whose work made our own easier, including but not limited to Teresa López-Pelliza and Ricard Ruiz Garzón's anthology of fantastic literature in Spanish by women writers, *Insólitas* (2019); Antonio Rómar and Pablo Mazo Agüero's compilation of contemporary horror stories from Spain, *Aquelarre* (2010); Martijn Lindeboom's anthology of new Dutch horror tales, *Halloween Horror Verhalen* (2016); André Bjerke's excellent Norwegian anthology *Drømmen, draugen og dauingen* (1978); and Lelani Fourie's anthology of contemporary Afrikaans horror stories, *Skadustemme* (2016).

We are particularly grateful to Ramon Mas and Ricard Planas at Editorial Males Herbes for having shared with us a number of Catalan texts, including the one selected for this volume; to Laura Sestri for kindly sharing a variety of Italian horror stories with us and taking the time to respond to our questions; to Erica Couto for her kind suggestions and information on Spanish and Galician horror; to Jette Holst for her invaluable information on modern Danish horror fiction; to Luis Pérez Ochando for his help with translation questions; and to everyone else who provided guidance, suggestions, or feedback on the volume. Thank you!

THE VALANCOURT BOOK OF
WORLD HORROR STORIES

Luigi Musolino

Uironda

Horror literature is nothing new in Italy: it dates back at least to the first half of the 19th century. And the contemporary horror scene in Italy is particularly robust, including a number of authors whose works have appeared in English translations, like Samuel Marolla and Nicola Lombardi, and others still awaiting international discovery, such as Eraldo Baldini, Claudio Vergnani and Danilo Arona. But our favorite current Italian horror writer — and in our opinion one of the best young horror writers in the world right now — is LUIGI MUSOLINO *(b. 1982), a native of Turin. In his masterful two-volume collection* Oscure Regioni *[Dark Regions] (2014-15), which still lacks a complete English translation, Musolino presents twenty horror tales — one for each of Italy's regions — all inspired by local folklore. In his stories, the idea of Italy as a country of sun and sea is merely a façade for tourists: in reality, it is a country filled with witches, monstrous creatures, and dark caverns, where madness and unease lurk behind the veil of everyday normality. We're pleased to kick this volume off with the title story from his most recent collection,* Uironda *(2018). We think you'll agree with us that Musolino is an author we'll be hearing much more from in the future.*

E RMES LENZI COULDN'T TAKE IT ANYMORE.
   After fifteen years as a truck driver, after hundreds of thousands of kilometers traveled, he felt like a needle that was always running over the same vinyl record. A disc of tar, whose grooves were the highways devoured by the

old Scania, the only songs the roar of the motor and the dull throbbing of his back pain.

Whose sad, bleary eyes were studying him from the rear-view mirror? No, they couldn't be his.

When you no longer recognize your own reflection, you'd better start worrying, my friend, he mused, noticing a movement in his lower abdomen, as if someone were stirring his bowels and his conscience with a red-hot ladle.

'Fuck,' he murmured, his voice weary from an eternity of truck stop sandwiches, burnt coffee, and smog. 'Fuck these streets that are always the same. This goddamn backache. Daniela. Everything.'

From the sun visor on the passenger side his seven-year-old son Simone looked on, hugging a headless woman. The photo had been taken one sunny morning, one of those days when the sky is so blue it hurts your eyes. Ermes remembered that moment well, a piece from a period in which he had been happy and which now seemed to belong to another life, another puzzle.

In the background of the image some trees stood out, an emerald-green field, and the gentle curves of two hills.

The woman's fingernails were manicured, painted fluorescent yellow. Simone's hair was so red that it recalled a violent sunset, his cerulean blue eyes seemed to rival the sky.

Ermes had torn his wife's face off the snapshot in a fit of rage, crying and swearing. A year had already passed since she left him, taking along with her the house, his son, and a good part of his dignity.

'You're never here, Ermes. I can't raise Simone on my own. We're not a family anymore . . . I don't know what we are. I . . . don't think I love you anymore.'

Daniela's farewell could be summarized like that. A few words to tear out his heart, throw it on the ground and dance a jig on it.

His protests hadn't done any good, his promise to reduce the hours spent in his truck, his tears, his excuses, their son who was drifting in a cloud of apathy as the days passed and the arguments grew more heated.

She wanted a divorce.

'When a woman makes a decision, you'd better believe it's hard to get her to change her mind. Always remember that,' his father, a truck driver like him, had told him once. But Ermes had never given too much weight to the old man's words, and the hope of winning Daniela back had become an obsession. Then he had discovered that she was seeing someone else, the elderly manager of a small firm in Turin.

It was like he went crazy.

In the course of a few weeks the pleas turned into telephone calls in the middle of the night, surveillance, scenes.

One evening he had intercepted the dandy who was screwing Daniela and had fractured two of his ribs and a cheekbone. If passers-by hadn't intervened, he would have kept on punching and kicking him until he killed him.

At that point the stalking and assault charges had come simultaneously, and his wife's top-notch attorney had massacred him, leaving him high and dry.

Basically he was working now so he could cover his legal expenses and pay support to Daniela and Simone, whom he could see only one weekend a month. He lived in the rear cabin of the truck: a bed, a fridge, a television the size of a postage stamp, and two electric burners. Like a vagabond, a gypsy.

There had been panic attacks, alcoholic blackouts, a long break from work. The situation had settled down little by little. He had stayed on his feet, but he could no longer see the point in anything.

Joyful images from the past attacked him like starving beasts, sucking the marrow from his bones and reducing him to a state of perpetual exhaustion. His existence had become a journey without a destination, a succession of streets leading nowhere. Stinking truck stops, packaged cookies, urinals, high-beam headlights, cigarettes, showers, anti-wart slip-on shoes, pitiful meals, dismal thoughts, Little Trees air freshener, rest areas. He was forty-two years old, had few friends, and the only things he managed to accumulate were debts, kilos on his waist, and X-rays that told him: 'Well, you've spent the better part of the last twenty years with your ass on a seat, you'll have to have surgery on that herniated disc sooner or later.'

He felt alone. A wanderer on life's road. So fucking desperately alone.

More and more often when he shot across an overpass he would entertain the idea of pulling over to the shoulder, getting out of the truck, and throwing himself off. A simple leap to leave all his problems, his anxiety, behind him. If it weren't for Simone, maybe . . . When had he seen him last? He didn't remember. But he hadn't been well. Gaunt, dark circles under his eyes, his spirit crushed by his parents' separation.

A horn honking from somewhere brought him back to reality. The sound waned away, the cry of a dying person in a hospital ward.

Ermes struck the steering wheel with a weak, resigned fist, slipped a Camel between his lips and tried to concentrate on the road that would bring him to a warehouse located on the outskirts of Krakow for yet another delivery of Made in Italy furniture.

There were still too many hours left.

The digital tachograph, the contraption installed in the truck to monitor speed, length of stops, and kilometers traveled, informed him that in half an hour he would have to take his first break. The rules for road safety for commercial vehicles were ironclad: forty-five minutes of rest every four-and-a-half hours of driving, a maximum of nine hours a day, never more than fifty-six hours a week. He had colleagues who circumvented the system by attaching expensive devices to the tachograph, but Ermes had never yielded to the temptation. If he were discovered, he could kiss his driver's license goodbye for a couple of months.

He was somewhere on the A4, around fifty kilometers from the Verona exit. Another eleven, twelve hours of driving awaited him. He had left at four from Turin and the rising sun, a fiery ball low on the horizon, cast a blinding glare on the guardrails. He weighed the idea of turning on the CB radio and talking with some fellow driver traveling the same stretch, but decided against it. The conversations were always the same. They wouldn't help him.

The traffic began to intensify. Enclosed in their little metal boxes, hundreds of individuals rushed towards the usual tasks, factory, office, routine; expressionless faces behind the windshields, pale and rigid hands on the steering wheel like those of mannequins in a shopping center.

Lenzi first focused on the wheels of a truck identical to his that was passing him, then brought his eyes back to the road: about three hundred meters away, a little group of crows hopped around some roadkill on the shoulder, plunging their beaks into soft, yielding tissue, tearing strips of flesh with famished determination.

He eased up a little on the gas pedal, curious: there was something wrong about the upside-down shape on the ground over which the birds were going into a frenzy. It was too large to belong to a cat or a dog, and it seemed to still be moving.

'What the hell . . . ?'

Coming up to where the crows were, Ermes stuck his head out the passenger's side to see better, and the cigarette nearly slid out of his mouth.

In the flutter of black wings, in the disorderly plunging of heads and beaks, he glimpsed a hand lying on the asphalt, a hand covered in clotted blood which might have belonged to a small woman or a child. The rest of the figure was covered by the shapes of the large birds, their feathers glistening like tar.

It was a question of moments.

Having passed the scene, Ermes looked in the rearview mirror: there were only the crows, intently pecking the asphalt, then taking flight towards a sad rest area overgrown with weeds. No carcass. No hand. He rubbed his eyes, crushed out the cigarette in the ashtray.

Yes, he needed a break and some coffee. The umpteenth stop in those glistening non-places, the umpteenth espresso, the umpteenth heartburn.

Ten minutes later he got off the highway and parked the Scania in the area reserved for trucks.

He would have given anything to get rid of the back pain, to erase the image of the crows with their idiotic eyes scampering around that helpless little hand.

Too much butter. There was always too much butter in the truck stop croissants. Even so, he couldn't stop eating them because they somehow gave him a sense of familiarity, of security. That mushy taste on the back of his tongue was always the same, it never changed.

He chugged the coffee, thanked the fat woman with the colorless eyes who was squeezing oranges behind the counter and dragged himself to the bathroom.

He was assaulted by the smell of stale urine and cleaning products. Without any particular reason, he thought of his ex-wife and his son; it took him a few seconds to be able to remember their facial features, the way they laughed or pronounced his name.

Yellow-painted nails, carrot-colored hair.

In front of the mirror he rinsed his face with water and dry-swallowed some aspirin. His backache gave him no reprieve, extending in hot rays of pain a little above his buttocks.

There was no one in the restroom. Letting out a long hissing fart, he headed towards the nearest toilet without looking at his own reflection.

Eat, shit, sleep, suffer, die. What a strange, repulsive contraption a human being is, he mused, surprising himself with the gloominess of his thoughts.

After cleaning the toilet seat with a large handful of toilet paper, he made himself comfortable; while he defecated, he occupied his mind by reading the writing that dozens of travelers had scrawled on the bathroom walls. Another certainty in his uncertain life. However far he might go in his Scania, whichever truck stop he might choose to stop at, the bathrooms always contained those written testimonials of a passage. Absences made into presences through words, scratched into the particleboard panels or traced with permanent markers.

As usual, a good ninety percent of the writings were obscene, for the most part offers or requests for sexual services accompanied by a telephone number.

Ermes stopped on

YOUNG COUPLE SEEKS HAIRY TRUCK DRIVERS FOR MEETUPS

and

GAIA THE WHORE, CALL/FUCK

He started to laugh, a bitter disgusted laugh. Then, as he let his eyes run along the door of the stall, the heartbroken mirth caught in his throat. In the riot of obscenity and stylized male members, his attention was captured by some angular writing in fluorescent yellow that stood out from the rest.

And not only because of its color.

He read aloud:

> *There is no escape from the road*
> *of black whirlpools that swallow tar,*
> *take the junction, get to Uironda,*
> *become part of this realm!*

Uironda. It had been that name which had startled him, which had pressed a memory switch in his brain, triggering a scene he had experienced . . . how many years earlier? At least thirteen or fourteen, when he was little more than a novice at the job, a young man filled with hopes and good intentions, for whom the road hadn't yet become a bore.

Uironda. He had heard the sound of the word, and now it was in front of him, written down. Memory is a strange thing. A meaningless term linked to a stupid little story told to him by a stranger. He had heard it uttered only once, at a truck stop in the Rho Fiera area near Milan, where he had stopped to take a little nap, and now those moments were returning to the surface as if by magic, with extreme clarity.

After a siesta in the rear cabin he had climbed down from the vehicle to get a coffee and phone Daniela, who was his girlfriend at the time. He had come across three truck drivers, between forty and sixty years old, seated at the edge of a flowerbed, drinking and talking; a tattoo-covered guy with a long beard resting on his chubby belly gestured to him, holding out a can of beer fished from a cooler full of water and ice.

'Have a seat with us here where it's cool, boy,' he had invited him with a smile, showing two rows of nicotine-stained teeth. 'The highway's not going anywhere, don't worry.'

Ermes had obeyed, had introduced himself under the comradely gaze of his three colleagues, and had taken part in a discussion that was surreal to say the least.

'A pleasure, Ermes. I'm Massimo, and that's Vittorio and Roby. We were talking about weird stuff,' the tattooed man had explained, including the other two with a wave of his hand. 'When you spend a good part of your life on the road, all sorts of things happen to you, for sure.'

'Oh, yes,' had replied Vittorio, a wiry man with the skin of an iguana and eyes overrun with capillaries. In his dilated pupils you could read his urge to speak. 'I was just telling about that time when I was on the CB with a fellow trucker from Bari, Amos. Amos was his handle. We often crossed paths on the Turin-Milan stretch, and we would talk for a few minutes, as long as the signal lasted. Anyway. It's night, a shitty night, one of those where you're running behind schedule and you can't stop and you can't wait to crack open a beer and have a shower and some undisturbed sleep. Amos and I have been tuned into channel five for a few seconds, we've hardly greeted each other and exchanged a couple of words, but I can barely hear him. Amos sounds strange to me, his voice is tired, but most of all it's *far away*. I tell him a couple of times: "Amos, is your radio working, is your CB all right, are you already out of range? Because you sound far away." And he goes: "Vittorio, I am far away, yes. This is the last time we'll speak. I just wanted to say goodbye. Safe travels." Then the communication freezes suddenly and it's like my CB is going crazy. Static, weird sounds, I think I hear screams . . . then . . . silence.'

Vittorio had run the beer can along his sweaty brow, interrupting himself and fixing his gaze on the eyes of the others with a mysterious smile. Scratching his long beard,

Massimo had invited him to go on, with the look of someone who has already heard a story dozens of times. Roby, the other driver, the oldest and quietest, with only a few thinning hairs and sad eyes, held his head down, smoking a stinking cigar. Vittorio had resumed the story, this time looking Ermes straight in the eyes.

'So, I try to reestablish contact with Amos, but nothing. After a few minutes I catch another fellow on that frequency, we start to chat about this and that. And then at some point he goes, "Have you heard about Amos?" He knew him too. I get a chill at the base of my spine, you know, like when you have the feeling you're about to listen to something you don't want to listen to, and I respond, "Heard what? We talked a few minutes ago on the CB, the signal was bad. He said some odd stuff to me." My colleague is silent for a few seconds on the other end, and then he bursts out: "What the fuck are you saying? It's impossible, Vittò. You must be mistaken. Amos died yesterday morning. He ran off the road on the Gambetti viaduct and went flying off. I thought you knew. It looks like . . . it looks like he fell asleep at the wheel. There's no way you could have talked to him." I swear, I got goosebumps, my legs started to tremble and I had to pull off onto the shoulder to catch my breath. And suddenly I recalled Amos's words: "*I am far away, yes. This is the last time we'll speak. I wanted to say goodbye. Safe travels.*" And that's the strangest thing that's happened to me in thirty years of driving a truck,' Vittorio had concluded, winking at Ermes, who had listened to the tale with a mixture of fascination and disbelief.

It had been then that Roby, the third trucker, had broken in. It had been then that he'd heard the word which now, traced in yellow lettering on the door of a stinking lavatory, was once more before his eyes: *Uironda*.

The man had begun to speak in a submissive, almost infantile voice. The spirals of smoke from his cigar softened his features, which were wrinkled with grooves, his fingers gnarled and twisted from gripping the wheel and maneuvering the gearshift.

'Yours is a curious story, Vittorio,' he had begun, squashing the butt of his cigar under his boot, 'but I have a better one. Well, really I don't know if it's better, but it's certainly more interesting than some lame highway ghost.'

Despite his feeble voice and melancholy eyes, the old man had given Ermes a feeling of wisdom and authority.

'Have you ever heard of Uironda?'

They hadn't done more than shake their heads and fetch a second beer from the cooler, disregarding the soundtrack of horns and engines beyond the glass and cement outline of the truck stop.

Roby had scratched his bristly chin and had opened his mouth a couple of times silently as if he couldn't manage to find the words. 'Uironda is a highway exit that doesn't exist but is there, which takes you to a town or a city that doesn't exist but is there. Or rather, it exists, but not on this plane. As if it were an overlap, an interference. Uironda is a mirage. It's a story that goes around among those older than us, a kind of urban legend. A Romanian trucker told it to me when I was first starting out.'

'I don't understand,' the tattooed guy had interrupted him. 'Never heard of this Vironda.'

'*Uironda.*'

'Tell us more.'

'Well, the Romanian who told me about it wasn't very clear. According to this guy, Uironda is a place that you can reach or glimpse when you've spent too many years on the road and the continuous headlights on your retina, the repetition of certain structures and habits, has set your mind in the right way. When you've been driving for hours and the view is always the same, and the guardrails, the architecture, the road, are repeated in an identical way for kilometers, sometimes you seem to be hypnotized, have you ever noticed? And that's the moment when it's like you're in a trance, when you're driving while your mind is somewhere else, and when you're most liable to doze off. And it's in that moment when the highway exit leading to Uironda can be seen: when you're at the limit, desperate and confused, when you're dead inside and the road has taken away too many hours of your sleep and too many moments of your life. You can see the exit for Uironda and in some way . . . take it. That's how it was explained to me.'

'What the hell kind of story is that?'

'It's a sort of word-of-mouth myth that goes around in our narrow circle. I've been sitting on my ass on that truck seat for forty years, and I've happened to hear that name other times too. Whispered in a truck stop bathroom, shouted by a drunken whore in a parking lot, crackled from a truck's CB radio . . .'

Ermes, who had listened to the story with extreme attention, had leaned forward. In those days during his breaks he usually bought pulp sci-fi novels and read them before sleep, and Roby's story had captivated him.

'So this Uironda would be a kind of parallel reality, if I understand right? Another dimension, like you read about sometimes in science fiction books?'

'Yes, boy, something like that. Have you ever thought about the life we truckers lead? We live as though in an alternate reality with regard to common people. The highway, the truck stops, the parking lots, are all non-places, places people pass through and immediately forget . . . We're the ones who know them best, who live them the most. Uironda is supposed to be a kind of alternative reality in an alternate dimension. Something like that, boy, indeed.'

'And what's supposed to be in this Uironda, if I might ask,

Professor Roby? And why that name?' Vittorio had mocked, concluding the question with a vulgar sneer.

'The man who told me the story was very vague on that point too . . . First he said that the dead are in Uironda. Those who died on the road. Who go there to spend eternity, in a kingdom of metal and cement. Then he muttered that in Uironda there's something that none of us would ever want to see but which at the same time we would want to contemplate with all our might. The most atrocious and unspeakable desires, the deepest fears, the darkest hopes, the atrocities one has committed. As for the name . . . well, I couldn't tell you. *Uironda*. It's a name like any other, for a place *like no other.'*

'And someone . . . in short, does someone claim to have been there? Have you ever met someone who says he's been to . . . Uironda?' Lenzi had asked, before draining the last of his beer.

'Uironda doesn't exist, boy. It's a highway legend,' the man had cut him off, spitting a yellowish gob on the asphalt. 'And if someone claims to have been there, well . . . they're either full of shit or out of their mind.'

Ermes remained seated on the toilet a few moments longer, staring at the yellow writing without seeing it, the memory of the first time he had heard of Uironda unraveling in his mind, then he wiped himself, got to his feet and took the cell phone from his jeans pocket.

He snapped a couple of photos of the poetry, read the words aloud,

> *There is no escape from the road*
> *of black whirlpools that swallow tar,*
> *take the junction, get to Uironda,*
> *become part of this realm!*

uncertain why he was doing it.

Maybe to have proof.

To remember.

And maybe to spread the absurd legend of Uironda, recounting it to some fellow driver to kill boredom.

After washing his hands and rinsing his face, he headed once more to the café area. He ordered a second coffee. His eyelids felt heavy, as if they were encrusted with dirt. The chubby barista had disappeared, replaced by an elderly dwarf with a bristly moustache doing its best to hide an enormous harelip. The convenience store chain cap lowered on his head conferred a ridiculous, clownish touch.

Ermes observed him captivated while he made the coffee, his insect-like movements, the skin of his neck a desert of wrinkles and ugly spots. His age could be anywhere between seventy and a full century.

'Here's your espresso, Signor Lenzi,' he croaked, pushing the little cup towards him with a smirk. He had too many teeth. Too many tiny teeth.

'Thanks a lot,' responded Ermes, reaching for a packet of sugar. The movement stopped in mid-air. A tightening in his lower abdomen. 'How do you know my name?'

The old man looked at him with a perplexed air, bending his dinosaur neck a little to the side. 'Sorry, what did you say?' His harelip was trembling.

'My surname. You said: "Here's your espresso, Signor Lenzi". How did you know it?'

'You're mistaken,' squeaked the old man. Now his face was deadly serious, molded wax over pale skin. 'You must have heard wrong.'

Ermes tried to think of something to say, but all he did was swallow air like a fish out of water. All of a sudden he felt very tired, uneasy, *scared*. When he managed to speak, the words didn't coincide with his thoughts.

'Say, have you ever heard the story of Uironda?'

What the hell are you saying? his mind shouted. He looked around as if to make sure that no one had heard him. Only then did he realize the truck stop was empty. Not a soul. The stagnant smell of burnt toast lingered in the air, mixed with the stench of exhaust fumes.

The old barista started to laugh, the tired chuckle of a derelict. He slipped off his cap and put it on the counter, rocking his head from side to side, his skull full of dents, as though someone had taken a hammer to it.

'No. I've never heard of Uironda.' His amused expression suggested exactly the opposite. 'But let me tell you one thing . . . There are two kinds of death: sometimes the body remains, other times it vanishes along with the spirit. This usually happens in solitude, and, not seeing the end, we say that the person disappeared, or left on a long journey. Do you catch my drift, Signor Lenzi?'

Once again he showed his smile of microscopic sharp teeth, and Ermes couldn't help taking a step back.

'How do you know my name?' This time he had shouted.

The old man remained motionless beside the coffee machine, staring at him and laughing.

Ermes turned around and rushed out of the deserted truck stop. The last thing he heard before sprinting across the parking lot straight for the Scania was the crow-like voice of the barista, who yelled, 'The espresso is on the house, Signor Lenzi! We hope to see you again soon!'

Half an hour after he'd started driving again, Ermes began to seriously doubt his own mental faculties. The more he thought about the business with the old man at the truck stop, about the little hand among the crows, about Uironda, the more he convinced himself that depression and failure had once more gotten the better of his judgment.

And yet the poetry was still there, in the photo taken with his smartphone. He hadn't dreamed that.

His only desire was to return home. Rest. Spend the weekend with his son, at the sea, in the mountains, any place other than the road, the nothingness of a pointless journey. He cast a glance at the photo of Simone hugging Daniela's headless body.

He turned on the radio, but no matter how much he fiddled with the dial he only managed to catch some static discharges and a strange chanting. Radio Maria, probably. He hoped he hadn't lost his antenna, promising himself to have it checked at the next stop.

He gave up on music and put his mind on autopilot.

At 11:57 he realized that the traffic was thinning out in a strange way. It was almost lunchtime, and that stretch of bypass lined with monstrous coal-stained factories was usually so congested that you could count yourself lucky if you managed to get past it without wasting more than ten minutes. Now, on the other hand, the Scania marched on without a hitch as the sky filled with clouds that were assuming a worrying yellowish tint as they advanced along the horizon.

Ermes turned his eyes towards a ramshackle Multipla that was passing him at a steady speed. It seemed to him that there was something out of place with its occupants: the driver's head looked squashed, featureless, dangling on a too-thin neck, while the woman in the passenger seat had her hands on the dashboard and her head bowed as though she were preparing for a violent impact. On the back seat, nestled in a car seat, something shuddered that was more like an enormous hunk of flesh than a baby. Ermes accelerated to match the Multipla's speed, but it shot by, leaving a puff of yellowish smoke behind it; before it disappeared around a wide curve, Lenzi thought he glimpsed some bizarre shapes tapping on the vehicle's rear windshield, shiny black figures that reminded him of the jaws of a stag beetle, the exoskeleton of some exotic insect.

Could they be going to Uironda? he wondered, astounded. He couldn't manage to get that little story out of his head.

He rubbed his eyes, filled with a sensation of bewildered detachment, trying to keep his thoughts on driving, on driving and nothing else, and after having tackled another twenty kilometers with his heart beating in his chest like a bass drum, he had to accept the absurd fact that he was alone.

Alone.

There were no other vehicles on the highway. Only the old Scania with its now lusterless chromework and the tractor trailer squeaking like an old rocking chair. He slowed down, looking out the windows as if he had been marooned on a desolate, alien land.

There must be an explanation.

You were distracted and took the wrong road, you didn't see a road work detour and you continued along a stretch of closed highway . . .

The cloud front, a catarrhous cascade of ochre fog, rolled in his direction, crackling with pink lightning, feeding his sense of bewilderment. The words of the old barista at the truck stop came back to him and he felt goosebumps running up his arms.

There are two kinds of death: sometimes the body remains, other times it vanishes along with the spirit. This usually happens in solitude, and, not seeing the end, we say that the person disappeared, or left on a long journey.

Nor were any vehicles to be seen in the lanes traveling in the opposite direction, beyond the dividing barrier. The landscape along the sides of the bypass seemed the result of a sloppy copy-and-paste: factories, water towers, lopsided cement high rises, all the same, gray, depressing. Ermes couldn't pick out a single recognizable building in a stretch he had driven thousands of times. On the top floor of a gloomy apartment building, behind broken windows that recalled chipped teeth, he caught sight of two figures looking out, possibly a woman and a little boy. He wondered what they were doing in that crumbling structure.

Soon it would start raining. Maybe hailing. A vague smell of iron and electricity in the air foretold it, an odor that smelled of urgency, as the storm front rushed on. Too yellow, too bulbous, too *tangible*.

Ermes Lenzi's umpteenth work trip was assuming the features of a nightmare.

He couldn't tear his gaze away from the horizon. Some frothy offshoots of cumulonimbus began to coagulate under the action of the wind, and for several moments they recalled a titanic face silhouetted in the sky, a bald head with white eyes, without a nose, its mouth curved in a sardonic sneer of disapproval. An explosion of low-timbred, guttural thunder cancelled out its features and Ermes was assailed by fear.

A primal, irrational fear, like he had never experienced before.

And you could say he'd had plenty of fear in his life. He had experienced frequent panic attacks after the breakup with Daniela. On a couple of occasions he had thought he was dying. But now it was different. As if every cell of his organism, every recess of his mind, was vibrating with a terror that had nothing to do with death, with annihilation.

His first idea, dictated by instinct, was to turn around. Stop the Scania and put the throttle in reverse, anything to put distance between him and those angry clouds, that deserted highway. He had to go back where he'd come from, maybe reach the truck stop with its strange harelipped barista and the disturbing yellow writing in the bathroom stall.

He had to come across cars, people, someone.

He lit a cigarette with parkinsonian movements, ordering himself to think rationally.

A U-turn was out of the question. He would risk prison and lose his job for what in all probability would turn out to be nothing but a flight of fancy, an illogical alteration in his mind, which had been chewed up by the stress of the past months.

'Fuck!' he swore. 'Breathe. Breathe.'

He had to proceed towards the next exit, the next junction. There was no other option, and he couldn't be very far. How much time had passed since his last stop?

He directed a questioning gaze at the digital tachograph and was hit by a wave of nausea. It should have shown the kilometers traveled, the time elapsed since his break at the truck stop, but the digital numbers had been replaced by seven simple characters, which fluttered on the display like a crazed sign:

UIRONDA

The cigarette slid from his lips onto his lap. He brushed it away with an irritated swipe of his hand, pulling the truck over to the shoulder.

And descending from the cab so he no longer had to see that writing, his chest squeezed in a clamp, Ermes Lenzi realized he had stopped the Scania about ten meters from a road sign indicating a junction. The sheet metal sign was a dark yellow color, stained with rusty streaks. The writing, in an elegant and out-of-place cursive, left no room for logic.

Next Exit – Uironda

He remained standing there observing the sign, his arms hanging slack at his sides. The world – which world? – was cloaked in a terrifying, unnatural silence. Lenzi knelt down on the warm asphalt, bringing his hands to his face, a tormented statue of flesh erected to challenge the road and the imminent storm.

After having tried to phone his ex-wife and a couple of friends – no signal – Ermes climbed into the cab of the truck like a fat caterpillar. The pain had returned to gnaw at the base of his spine with the tenacity of a mastiff. Somehow the excruciating throbbing that tormented him brought him to a state of quiet resignation. Slumped in the seat, his hands on the wheel, he practiced the breathing exercises to treat panic attacks, trying to find a sense in the madness that he was living.

Hadn't there perhaps been days when he had wished to be the last man on Earth? Days in which the desire to disappear, to be alone, far away from problems, from anxiety, had become an obsession, a necessity?

You've got your wish. No traffic, nobody to interact with, no nothing. Just you and the road, just you and a goal, finally: Uironda.

He smiled, rummaging in his shirt pocket. There was one half-crushed Camel left in the packet. He decided to save it for a better occasion. Then he turned the key, shifted into first, and advanced at a crawl, passing the road sign that had so greatly disturbed him.

He would drive until he reached the next exit. No, he couldn't turn back. And if that exit really led to Uironda, well . . . he would take it, enter the territory of superstition, of urban legend. Deep down he was only looking for a way to shake up his dull life, a distraction, a spark that would ignite anew his will to live, his curiosity. This could be his chance.

Uironda.

The storm had caught up with him. Carried on the wind,

the first raindrops beat down on the Scania's windshield. It was a dirty, yellowish rain that the windshield wipers struggled to sweep away, smearing the glass with greasy gunk. Maybe the storm was coming from Africa, loaded with sand and dirt. Ermes rolled up his window and accelerated, launching the truck into the fury of the elements.

It was like entering a tunnel filled with liquid dust. The vehicle's headlights could barely cut through the rain to illuminate the center line.

The digital tachograph went completely mad, showing sequences of figures and numbers apparently devoid of meaning. Every so often, like the flash of a strobe light, the name of the mirage junction appeared on the display, the non-place that old truckers whispered about, men like Roby, the first – and last – person to pronounce Uironda in his presence.

Ermes clenched his teeth and squinted his eyes, concentrating on driving, praying to get out of this storm as soon as possible. Violent gusts of wind assailed the trailer, making it swing on its suspensions. He had never driven in similar weather conditions. He was dealing with a freak storm that reduced visibility almost to zero. The wind's cries were like the howls of a dying beast, and very soon in the overwhelming yellow clouds Ermes noticed some dark shapes outlined beside the windows, in front of the windshield.

Disembodied shadows. Twisted hands that stretched towards him in an attitude of supplication. He tried to ignore them. And he decided to turn on the CB radio, tuned to channel five.

'Is . . . is anyone listening? Over,' he whispered into the receiver. He hardly recognized the sound of his own voice, a gritty rasp. 'This is Ermes, is anyone there?'

The radio crackled, a hiccup of static discharge and chopped-up syllables.

'If . . . if there's someone there, listen, I think I'm lost. There's no one on the road and I've ended up in the middle of this storm that came out of nowhere and . . .' Ermes swallowed saliva. He didn't like the cracking in his voice. The tears at the corners of his eyes. He was about to give in to panic, to start crying and shouting like a child who has lost his mother in the supermarket. He pulled himself together. 'If there's someone there, respond please. I don't know where I am. Over.'

And finally someone spoke. A friendly, familiar voice. And just because it was so familiar, it was frightening.

'*Daddy?*'

'Si-Simone?'

It was his son. The words were faint, barely audible, coming from an unfathomable distance, but without a doubt from Simone's vocal chords.

'Yes, Daddy. When are you coming home, Daddy? I miss you.'

Ermes Lenzi gave in to the irrational. He tried to calm the sobs that threatened to shake his chest. 'Simo, Daddy's coming soon, all right? Daddy's coming soon and he'll take you to the movies, okay? Daddy's coming as quickly as he can.'

The realization that he was lying came over him. The terrible certainty that he would never see his child again.

'Mommy and I are waiting for you,' Simone crackled through the receiver, and now the voice was his *and yet not his*. Altered by a liquid gurgling, more like the sound of a flooded engine than a human voice. 'Mommy and I are waiting for you at home. *In Uironda*. Come.'

'I'm coming. I'm on my way. Daddy's coming, Simo.'

On the other end, silence.

Ermes Lenzi put his foot down on the gas pedal, his face disfigured by a mad grin.

'*There's no escape from the road, the black whirlpools that swallow tar, take the junction, reach Uironda, become part of this realm!*' he began to murmur.

He continued thus until, after an interminable while, he found himself outside the storm once more, greeted by a night without stars, black and cold like damnation.

A viaduct towards nothing, a strip of tar hurled towards a ghostly horizon. A one-way asphalt road with no guardrails, suspended over the Abyss, on a dark blanket without reflections. This is what Ermes' reality was reduced to. Everywhere he looked there was only impenetrable blackness. The Scania's headlights barely lit up the asphalt.

He proceeded at thirty per hour because if he made a single error, if he ran off the road, he was sure he would be precipitated into an eternal void of no return, like an astronaut lost in outer space. A sci-fi movie he had seen with Daniela came to mind, a film whose title he didn't remember. There was a spaceship, a metal colossus that moved thanks to propulsion from an artificially created black hole inside it, and there were nightmares that took form to drive the passengers to madness. How did that film end? Not well. Not well. Ermes told himself that happy endings are for the weak. That in real life happy endings were nothing but an illusion.

Far off, on the right side of the road, a point of light materialized. Red. Perhaps a streetlight, or the emergence of a planet or a star.

No.

Advancing, other crimson flowers blossomed in the darkness, reminding him of a swarm of fireflies on the motionless surface of a lake.

They seemed to be the lights of a village, of a small town.

Ermes felt he had almost arrived. He perceived it in a dull vibration in his chest, in his bones. His back pain had disappeared. He kept his eyes fixed on the bright beads that were taking shape on the horizon.

Uironda?

Without thinking, he rolled down his window and was struck by a warm wind that smelled of decay. He gasped for breath. He wondered what the all-pervading darkness outside the cab would have whispered to him if only that darkness could talk. Would it have told him the story of Uironda, its genesis, its why? He hoped soon to have an answer to the swarm of questions buzzing in his skull.

The street began to climb. At first gently, a false plain that made the old Scania's motor rev up; then still more, still more, until Ermes had the sensation of proceeding vertically.

Maybe he was.

Lost in that ditch of darkness, he wondered if concepts like direction and gravity still had any meaning. The only thing he had to do was follow the road. Go with it, like he had always done.

The lights were still there. Clearer now, closer. Red lights that cast a scarlet glow on a river or a road.

He couldn't wait to reach his destination. He sped up.

And it was then that a noise worked its way through the awkward grumbling of the motor. It was coming from the rear cabin, the narrow space which for the past few months had been his home. Dull thuds, as if someone were throwing punches at the dividing wall or a violent struggle was being enacted. The blows ceased with a screech, a muffled wheeze, a shout.

'Don't do it. Ermes, stop, pleeeeeasehelpusssssss!'

Ermes was about to stop the truck when the headlights illuminated a road sign, the first he'd seen since he had emerged from the storm.

WELCOME TO UIRONDA

A hundred meters further on the street forked to the left. The Scania, as if impelled by an invisible force, took the junction without Ermes' having to turn the steering wheel. The wheels started to vibrate as the truck tackled a sharp bend overlooking a sea of darkness; for a moment it seemed that the vehicle had tilted forty-five degrees toward the passenger side, so much that Ermes had to hang on to the wheel with all his strength. Finally, with a jolt, the old Scania stabilized and emerged from the curve spitting smoke in a deafening scream of pistons.

And it appeared.

Beyond the windshield.

Ermes found it before him all of a sudden.

Glistening, ruthless, dead.

Uironda.

The tires whistled on the asphalt, and the truck came to a stop a few hundred meters from the city walls.

Immense pinkish walls, from which a tepid wind of death blew.

The trucker got down from the cab, advancing towards the outskirts of the city-mirage with watery eyes and gaping mouth.

It wasn't like Roby, the old trucker, had described it so many years earlier.

No one who had died on the road, no architecture of sheet metal and cement.

At least, not for him.

For him, Uironda was flesh and torment. A colossal error – the final one – born of obsession, of the disintegration of that little he had managed to create in his existence.

It took him long minutes to be able to embrace and comprehend the vastness and complexity of the vision, to identify the individual parts of it.

From enormous, heinous acts derive enormous, heinous hells.

At first he took in the minor details, if you could say that about thresholds and structures that were dozens of meters high: a nostril, a lip like a slimy snail, an ear. Afterwards, stepping back, trying to observe the panorama in its entirety, like an explorer who for the first time finds himself before an immense mountain chain, he had a fleeting view of the whole.

Buttocks and legs, bellies and ribs, forearms and hands turned into plains, plateaus, hills, mountains. Hairs like alien trees, wrinkles like streets, blood like rivers.

Everywhere, in the skin, destruction. Bare structures of tormented, lacerated epidermis, torn muscles, disarticulated joints. Immense wounds that had become doorways, gashes made into windows, bluish bruises like the mosaics of archaic, forgotten temples.

His Uironda.

Two colossal bodies entwined in a last embrace of blood, disbelief and pain, a frozen anatomical city on the autopsy table of final understanding.

The bodies of a woman and a child.

Ermes screamed. That scream did not express fear or remorse. Simply astonishment, as every doubt left him, as he understood and remembered. He distinguished a hand the size of a cathedral raised towards the sky, manicured yellow-painted nails the size of whales. Pinkish hills of battered breasts, the dark portal of a navel.

Far off blazed what at first had seemed to him a surreal field of red-tinted grain. The stems waved in the hot wind, pungent with decay.

Hair so red that it called to mind a violent sunset.

The childish mouth half-closed in a vain attempt to escape the crushing asphyxiation.

Simone.

Ermes wandered a long time in the territories of Uironda.

He considered the gigantic rosette of a neck without a head, separated from the body in a rage of senseless violence and thirst for vengeance.

Daniela. Oh, Daniela, I'm sorry.

The two windows of cerulean blue eyes in a face as large as Notre Dame.

He slipped into each of the city's orifices, under teeth archways and eyebrow columns; he passed through aisles of mucous membranes and caverns encrusted with earwax, his feet making squishy sounds in the ever-present crimson puddles.

He smelled the wounds and the cuts, where the knife had performed the martyrdom that no father and husband should ever carry out, he passed his trembling hands over the unusable tubes of the severed veins, stared crying at the buttresses of the vagina surmounted by the unusable altar of the clitoris. He heard the death rattle of nerve endings beyond repair.

When he was too tired to go on, Ermes Lenzi lay down under the shadow cast by Daniela's severed head, on a mattress of hair half-covered in brain matter, contemplating the dark sky that was lit up by the blood of Uironda.

He lit the last remaining Camel. It smelled of smog and bodily fluids.

Simone's glassy eyes, immense like only a child's can be, studied him accusingly from the western extremity of the city-mirage that had revealed the truth to him.

My God, what did you do? My God my God my God . . .

His back sent him a lash of perverse pain.

The same pain experienced when he had crashed down on the rocks a few seconds after having jumped off the viaduct.

The rotten wind ceased to blow.

The bloody fluorescence of Uironda dimmed like embers from a forgotten bonfire.

Not much time passed before Ermes Lenzi plunged into a dreamless sleep, the last Camel still clenched between his fingers.

And as his eyelids closed, while the motionless Uironda embraced him like an authoritarian and terrible mother, the trucker knew that the city, with its load of hells and remorse, would be there waiting for him when he awoke.

Glistening, ruthless, dead.

For eternity.

Translated from the Italian by James D. Jenkins

Pilar Pedraza

Mater Tenebrarum

When we asked horror fans from Spain which Spanish writers should be included in an anthology of the world's best horror stories, one name came up again and again: PILAR PEDRAZA. Pedraza (b. 1951) is a film professor at the University of Valencia, who over the past 35 years has also produced an impressive oeuvre of fiction, including both novels and short stories. Curiously, although Pedraza is well known to horror readers in her own country, where she frequently features in anthologies, and though there exists a book-length study in English of her work, Kay Pritchett's Dark Assemblages: Pilar Pedraza and the Gothic Story of Development *(2015), none of the author's work has previously appeared in an English translation. 'Mater Tenebrarum' (the title is Latin for 'Mother of Darkness') is probably Pedraza's best-known story; like much of her work it is a very Gothic tale, peopled with horror fiction mainstays like witches and vampires, and featuring her trademark blend of horror and macabre humor.*

T HE GRAVEDIGGER BASTIÁN emerged from the night-mare that had tormented him during the few hours of sleep he managed to get after his drinking binge the night before and opened his eyes to the light of an unpleasant day. His mouth was thick. A burning sourness rose from his belly to his throat. The efforts he made to belch brought on a fit of coughing. Remembering the work he had left not even half done, he muttered some blasphemies that didn't give him the slightest relief. He was on the verge of yielding to the temptation to roll over and go back to sleep, but one of the voices in his head told him that he had to finish digging the grave if he didn't want the people from the day's first burial to arrive and find no hole for their deceased. The local council was so poor that he couldn't afford an assistant to help with the hardest work, although sometimes the coal merchant's son, the red-headed Candido, who had devils in him, would lend him a hand in exchange for some tobacco.

Lupo came out to meet him, wagging his tail. His drooling tongue hung out between his fangs and he was panting, choking with servile passion. He slept in the tool shed on a pile of empty sacks. All the mud in the cemetery seemed to have stuck to his hairy coat. On his back he had some reddish scabs that never managed to heal. And far from lessening his ugliness, the tenderness of his expression accentuated it. But he was a good dog. He happily joined the gravedigger in the rain: they would not leave each other's side all day long. Since old age had made them retire from the world, all they had was each other. Their mutual company was enough for them, along with the proximity of the dead people, who were no bother, absorbed as they were in musing on their nothingness. At most they gnawed discreetly at their shrouds if Bastián had drunk a lot, or they drummed with their bony fingers on the wood of their coffins, not to cause a fuss and have someone open them, but only for fun. Bastián felt an immense tolerance towards them.

When they were near the half-dug tomb, Lupo lowered his ears and began to tremble, scratching at the muddy earth with his paws and recoiling. But Bastián knew the animal was no coward. He was never frightened by the will o' the wisps of decomposition, nor the strolls of the lost souls in the blackness of moonless nights, nor the boys who threw rocks at him when he prowled outside the walls of the cemetery seeking relief for his masculine urges in the bellies of the female dogs. This, however . . .

'Bloody hell! What is this?'

In the grave he had begun to open last night, before getting so drunk he couldn't even see where he was putting his shovel, there lay a dark and suspicious lump.

'What the dickens is this corpse doing here?' Although he hadn't checked whether it *was* a cadaver, for him any body in that position had to be. Bastián's world was made up of those who were dead and those who weren't yet. And he went on planting them, a devout gardener, in order to fertilize the world.

With the handle of his shovel he moved the lump, which stretched and let out a groan. From the pile of old rags a thin little face and small hands, bony, bluish like diluted milk, filthy with red mud, emerged into the ashy light of the rainy morning. This wasn't a corpse, it was hard but not stiff, and beneath the blue and mauve whiteness of cold there were purple transparencies that announced the bloody warmth of life.

'Well, well! Good morning, girl!' the straw-hearted man exclaimed with thick irony.

She sat up. She sat there at the bottom of the hole, looking at him balefully with her green little eyes. She was a girl as old as the world, scrawny and pale, bleary. A mop of unkempt red hair stuck out from between the creases of the thick garment covering her, which appeared to be a military cloak.

'Come on, get out of there! I have to finish the grave.'

He offered his callused hand to the girl, who spurned it and climbed out like a spider, gripping the soft walls of the hole, at whose edge she sat down without saying anything.

'Better hope you haven't caught cold or damp or anything, if you slept in this hole.'

She didn't open her mouth. After a while, Lupo, who at first had growled, scrunching up his muzzle and showing his fangs, approached her. In his pupils strange fires burned. The spirit of the old dog in him was working for the first time in a long time, and it did so painfully since up until then happiness for him had consisted in the cultivation of apathy. Something simultaneously sweet and bitter was taking hold of him, flowing towards the deepest fibers of his canine insides like a love potion, or a death one, at the same time as he felt something tighten around his neck, pulling him towards the girl who had risen up from the earth.

Bastián began his work, making sure to pay no heed to the girl, who didn't stop looking at him with her bleary little eyes, whose dark circles underneath, like the marks of a beating, seemed on the verge of spreading across her face. She had a large mouth, lipless like a snake's, and she was graceful as a kitten, but there was something about her that was disturbing, insect-like.

The man got out of the hole and sat down to rest beside her.

'I don't know you, girl. You're not from around here, huh? What's your name?' he asked as he chewed a piece of tobacco, looking out into infinity.

'My name is Ángela, and I'm not from anywhere. I have to go now.'

She rose and, bundled up in the rain-soaked cloak, she started to walk without turning back. She slipped between the tombs and the cypresses like a shadow. Lupo followed her for a moment with his eyes. When he was about to lose sight of her, he got up and ran barking after her with the happy energy of one who has finally found his reason to live.

But the job was not a comfortable one. There was a lot of walking and not much eating. All day they traversed vacant lots, following paths that didn't seem to lead anywhere, skirting walls furtively. Lupo missed the slop and scraps Bastián gave him, the warmth of the fireplace, and even the sounds the dead people made when they stretched their bones.

Ángela and Lupo advanced along silent streets. In the city everyone was asleep except the cats in heat and a mare who was miscarrying in the southern suburbs. Her moans were carried on the breeze. The night would have been lovely, had there been eyes to see it. When the moon peeked out between the clouds, the world turned gray and black, every detail sharp as in an engraving. And when it appeared in the middle of a clearing, it was terrifying. Beams of white light filtered through the treetops and traced a changing lacework on the ground, turning the rough brick arches and well parapets into marble and the tears seeping from the stones into diamonds. A mercuric cloak had fallen over the world. It was not possible to imagine hearts beating beneath that frozen platinum veil, nor love, nor warm limbs entwining on feather mattresses. Perhaps, yes, snowy bodies trembling with impotent love between crisp starched sheets.

Ángela used the stars to calculate whether it was a propitious moment for what she was planning. The Star of Bitterness was in the exact center of the night. In the darkness evil swelled, ripe, about to fall in one's hands like a fruit. It was time.

The old door of the charnelhouse opened at a push from her little hands. The spectacle offered to her view in the moonlight didn't make the slightest impression on her. She was used to it. They were familiar to her, the stiff corpses of the condemned that hung from the beams in the courtyard like hams, those who lay piled up on the ground, those stacked up rotting under the porticos.

Lupo, believing he'd figured out his new mistress's intentions, walked ahead, ripped off a corpse's left hand with bites and tugs and dropped it at her feet like an offering.

'This mutt must be an idiot!' the girl exclaimed in a low voice. 'That's not what we're here for, you silly fool. Why are you in such a hurry?'

Lupo, whose greatest misfortune was understanding human language, which made him an object of scorn to dogs and cats, felt something like the desperation of an aging lover for his girlfriend, although neither he nor Ángela knew that, both being creatures little inclined towards love. But anyway his rheumy eyes filled with tears that ran down his muzzle, and his heart shrank.

Unconcerned about the movements of the beast's soul, she headed with decisive steps towards the corpse of one of the hanged. Stiff and lifeless, it swung in the night's quiet air because a bird that had nested in its belly had come flying out at the sound of footsteps. The cadaver's face was handsome in the moonlight; in it there was a definitive quietude.

'How lucky you are, you dead bastards, not having to run around trying to earn a living.'

But remembering that her father, shut up in a deep dungeon, wouldn't be long in joining them in the same club of those who danced at the end of a rope, she fell silent out of respect and went to work.

He had a good set of teeth, a shame about the incisors that had been broken by a blow, perhaps from a rock, which had also cut the upper lip. Ángela rose up on tiptoes but couldn't reach. She looked around and found only a block of stone long detached from the wall and black with moss. Faced with the effort that awaited her, she gave a kick of impatience.

'Damn you, you son of a bitch!' she rebuked the hanged man. 'They could have hung you lower!'

The stone was porous and light like a rotten tooth, but

for the girl's bird-like strength it meant pain if she lifted anything weighing more than the folds of her cloak. She managed to drag it, however, and climbing up on it she reached the scarecrow's mouth, from which she pulled out several molars with skilled and vigorous little tugs, paying no heed to the stench coming from the black hole and the blue tongue.

In the western part of the ramparts there stood an abandoned turret, in whose damp ruins old Crisanta, a third-rate witch and sorceress, lived all by herself. She had seen better days, but too much tippling had made her lose many of the gifts she had received from her female bloodline, which had passed down from mothers to daughters the pact with Satan, ratified with a drop of blood. If she appeared to be a beggar, it wasn't from poverty but from the worst of miseries: avarice, which left her uncomfortable, dying of hunger and dressed in rags, although she was sitting on treasures that she hid in her magpie's nest.

She received Ángela with a grunt and invited her to sit beside her on a bench in front of the fireplace, where a charred log was burning out and about to disintegrate into ashes. The girl remained standing, took a packet from a pocket of her cloak and set it noisily on the table, saying with the dry voice of a little despot:

'I brought you this, Crisanta. Let's see what it's worth.'

Without looking at her again, Crisanta stirred the fire with an iron fire shovel, her eyes fixed on the embers which shone for a moment like rubies.

'What is it?' she asked, feigning indifference.

'Molars freshly pulled from a hanged man.'

'Molars from a hanged man! Right!' mocked the sorceress. 'And how do *I* know they're from a hanged man and not waste from the barber's?'

Ángela didn't respond. Crisanta turned towards her and fixed her dust-irritated eyes on the girl's, which reflected the purest and most innocent evil in their greenish waters. In all the days of her life, she had never seen eyes like those. It was whispered at the sabbath that they were the devil's eyes, but she had never been permitted to see those. How come this little brat just happened to have them? What had she done to deserve them? When the women's glances met, it poisoned the air to the point that Lupo raised his head, anxious as though he scented danger.

'If I say they're from a hanged man,' the youngster muttered between her teeth, her face pale with rage and her throat swollen, 'then they're from a hanged man.'

Her eyes had hardened like stones. Some dark spots on her irises painted figures of black toads on the green water.

'I'm not interested,' replied the old woman, turning her glance away towards the fire, which had gone out again. 'Right now I'm mixed up in something big.'

'Big? What do you mean, big? Spoiling some woman's love affair or making her miscarry. Beyond that, I don't know what you're capable of.'

'A hand of glory. You don't happen to have a hand?'

'There's a loose one in the charnelhouse. If you want, I'll bring it to you. My dog tore it off, but I didn't know it was good for anything.'

'It's no good, girl, it's no good. I need a fresh hand, with blood in its veins, not the dried-up rotten things you're in the habit of carrying about.'

'Fresh!' Ángela remarked in a falsetto voice. 'Is it to eat or what?'

The old woman explained to her what a hand of glory was and how to make it. To begin with, she needed the hand of a hanged person, not like those rotting in the charnelhouse, but rather a fresh one.

'From a man or a woman?'

The girl's question caught the sorceress by surprise. She didn't know.

'Doesn't your guide show you?'

She was referring to an enormous book Crisanta had, which was called *Great and Universal Elucidarium*, an inheritance from those who had preceded her in the art and the source of most of her knowledge. It was so large that to finish reading a line, she had to take a couple of steps in front of the lectern. It was written in black ink that was so corrosive it had eaten through the paper in many places, and in spiky handwriting like the devil's own.

'It just says a hanged man's hand,' the old woman responded with a sigh of impatience.

'Well then, it has to be a man's,' the girl judged. 'It's a shame because in the city a few days from now they're going to hang the coal cellar murderess. The one who killed her three children and hid them in the coal in the kitchen.'

'We can try. We have nothing to lose. With what they'll give us for a hand of glory we won't be poor anymore.'

'Why are you talking in plural like the bishops?'

'Because I'm referring to you too. If you help me, we'll share it. I'm no longer up to jaunts through cemeteries and you have a knack for getting into tricky places. Go on, girl, bring me a fresh piece and you won't regret it. Don't waste time with this crap,' she said, sending the hanged man's molars into the fire with a sweep of her hand. A thick but ephemeral smoke rose up, as if from the other world or in a theater.

Ángela had remained thoughtful, with Lupo nestled up at her feet. She seemed to be attentive to the sound of the wind which, crashing against the tower, howled furiously in search of other paths between the holes in the rocks and the thorny shrubbery.

At dawn, lost among the crowd, she attended the execution of the infanticide in the market square. When the fury of the storm provoked by the departure of the condemned woman's soul dispersed the people and there remained only two guards watching over the corpse, which would hang from the gibbet a couple of days as a warning and lesson to bad mothers, Ángela took shelter from the rain with Lupo in the vestibule of the Church of St. Justa. From there she could observe all that happened at the gallows and its surroundings.

Not even she herself knew for certain what she was going to do. She counted vaguely on the guards' getting drunk that night and sleeping like logs. She trusted in the dark force that seemed to have been hovering over the city for some time. Caught up in her plans, she remained motionless all day, curled up like a cat. She was cold and hungry, and she knew there was no use in staying there while it was daylight, but she was bound by a leaden laziness that had been overpowering her to the point where she was unable to move.

Her presence made the woman who usually begged in the doorway cower in her spot as if she wanted to disappear. She was a young blond woman with no arms, but with the beautiful legs of a tightrope walker, an idiot angel fallen from the archivolt. Passing in front of her, a lay sister who was coming out of the temple stopped and tossed some coins in her lap. The girl raised her ingenuous iris-blue eyes and smiled kindly and gratefully. Ángela, who was watching the scene a few steps away, let out a mocking chuckle. The old woman fled in terror. For a moment the two girls had seemed to be one, and that one, the devil.

The hours passed like those in a feverish dream, sometimes slowly and at others so fast that she would have said the tower clock had gone mad. Its clapper sounded not like bronze but iron. The dampness of the stones had gotten into the girl's soul and, arriving at her frozen heart, had turned to frost. Lupo shivered along with her.

The dead woman's long hair fluttered against the inclement sky like a black flag. Wrapped up in their cloaks, the guards paced around in circles without neglecting their watch, but when that time of night arrived when there is a wrinkle in the fabric of the world and senses and natural laws cease to reign, they fell asleep, and Ángela prepared to take advantage of their slumber.

But a troop of silent shadows overtook her, emerging from the corners of the square and flowing together like a river. Surrounding the gallows, they lowered the hanged woman without delay. They were her relatives, fed up with so much scandal. They weren't inclined to have shame brought on them for a single minute more. They had come to an agreement and they were carrying her off. This was unknown to Ángela, who in her capacity as an innocent though diabolical child saw only the skin and guts of the world, but not the schemes of men. She followed them like one more shadow through the maze of the upper-class neighborhood, with which she was unfamiliar, passed in front of the Casa de las Rocas where they kept the elephant given by the sultan of Egypt, which trumpeted at the sound of people. Lupo stifled a panicked bark, cut short by a kick from his mistress that instantly made him keep quiet. Then they crossed the river and headed to Los Cigarrales, entered the estate and deposited the dead woman in the crypt after they had put her in a coffin and the curate had said a funeral prayer at top speed.

When everyone had left, Ángela opened the coffin, grabbed one of the dead woman's arms and pulled on it until the hand was outside, with the wrist on the edge of the wall of the box. There was something in the air just then, barely an icy breeze circulating through the black and gloomy dampness of the crypt. But the girl was used to the groans of the souls who resist leaving their bodies for good and the murmur of those that remain stuck to the flesh. She knew she didn't have to pay any attention to those phantasms, smoke from a bonfire that has gone out and a siren's songs carried on the wind from the region of shadows. She took a firm grip with both hands on the hatchet Crisanta had lent her, raised it as high as she could, and, collecting her scant strength, unleashed it again and again on the dead woman's stiff left wrist until the hand came loose. She then groped with her own hands until she found it and put it in a pocket of her cloak.

Then a hair-raising creak made Lupo's fur stand on end. The door flew open. In its opening, silhouetted in the paleness of the sky, which was beginning to be tinged with pink, there appeared a tall, white figure. Something dark oozed from its mouth and its clawlike hands opened and closed like those of an automaton. Ángela squeezed the murderess's hand in her pocket and gulped. Her fright was giving way to awe. Because she was beginning to realize who the woman was who, for her part, was looking at her with relief.

'Señora . . .'

'None of that señora stuff. I'm calling it a night. Can't I be left alone in my own house?'

She sniffed.

'There were people here.'

'Yes, señora. The hanged woman's relatives stole her from the gallows and brought her here to bury her. They left her in this coffin.'

'And what are you doing here?'

'I came for a hand to cast a spell.'

'Well then, if you've finished, get lost.'

When the vampire returns to her lair, she won't be happy at finding you there, Ángela remembered from a song from her childhood.

*

'Good, girl, good. We can make use of this. It's not too spoiled yet,' Crisanta said, palpating the pale severed limb and squeezing the horrid wound with expert fingers. Her beady eyes gleamed with satisfaction and willfulness. 'Someone,' she remarked, 'should have given this broad a reading before it was too late. It's obvious from these lines that she was going to come to a bad end,' and she traced them with her index finger on the dead flesh. 'They look like flies' legs. Now we have to make the brine of glory.'

'How?' asked Ángela.

'The brine of glory,' the old woman said slowly and solemnly, as if she were reading, 'is made with salt, saltpeter and pepper, and a pinch of gunpowder if you have some, all mixed together. You put the hand in it in a clay jar and leave it there fifteen nights. It says so in the book.'

The witch carried out her schemes in the presence of the girl, who didn't miss a detail. She absorbed the knowledge with the cold avidity of the disciple who knows she will betray her teacher and neither feels any scruples nor anticipates any remorse.

'Look how lovely, my dear,' said Crisanta with giddy enthusiasm when the salting time had passed. 'Dry and clean, it doesn't even seem to be from a cadaver. Like the hand of a virgin at the altar.'

Ángela assented earnestly, although the thing reminded her more of a hen's foot.

'The nails are broken,' she pointed out.

'So what?' replied the other, annoyed. 'It doesn't matter. Now I just have to grease it and it'll be ready to burn for hours.'

'What do you make the grease out of?'

'With fat from a hanged man or a cat, it's all the same. We'll use some from a cat. There are women who have qualms about killing cats because they think they're guardians of the home, but I have no such scruples, nor do I believe in superstitions. Cats are cats, they can't do anything to us.'

'Which one should we kill? A black one? Or the neutered tabby, which will have more fat than any of them, with that belly of his hanging down to the ground?'

'It can't be a neutered one,' the old woman said. 'Fat from a castrated cat is easy to get, since they let you cut their throats without fighting back, but it has less power than fat from an intact male. Go and see if you can find the striped one with the yellow eyes. He's probably sleeping on the steps in the sun.'

Lupo went out with her into the splendor of the blue morning. Soon they found the cat, curled up into a ball between two rocks. He awoke at hearing them, cast a sleepy golden glance and yawned, showing the beautiful teeth of a miniature wild animal.

'Come on, mutt, time to earn your keep.'

The dog obeyed to the letter. After a brief skirmish full of sound and fury, from which he emerged bleeding, he deposited the soft palpitating prey at his mistress's feet.

With no small difficulty, Ángela was reading her way through the *Elucidarium* during the old woman's absences, sneaking a peek whenever she was alone in the tower, feigning fatigue or menstrual pains, which had come to her for the first time on the day when Lupo killed the cat so they could extract its fat. She learned from the book that the hand of glory was a tool used by robbers in their exploits, since it had the virtue of making all the inhabitants of a house, masters and servants, fall into a profound sleep, and opening all the doors and locks for as long as the fingers of the hand were lit like candles. She fantasized about what she could get for herself with the help of the hand Crisanta was preparing, and she dreamed of getting hold of the book. It contained many other invaluable secrets and it would help her make her way in life and go from being a scavenger to someone with real power. But before she had the chance to carry out the plans she was concocting in her imagination to make off with those treasures, the people who had ordered the talisman showed up.

They came enveloped in a cloud of dust, two men and a woman. The men entered the house, but the lady remained in her saddle, her head covered in a wide-brimmed black hat that permitted only the gleam of two eyes like embers and the tip of a haughty nose to be seen. She wore a dirty but elegant black and green dress that brought out her good looks. She must have been very young and arrogant.

Crisanta took the dead woman's stiff hand from a fine crystal cheese dish where she kept it and, setting it atop a cloth on the table, showed it to her clients, exaggerating its virtues and the efforts it had cost her to acquire it.

But with a sweep of his hand, the younger and more quarrelsome of the two men threw both cheese dish and carrion to the ground, where they smashed with the sound of broken glass.

'It cost you a great deal to get hold of this rubbish, old woman? And you had us come here for that?'

'What's the idea? You know more than I do about how these things have to be made!'

'I won't say anything about making it, but you're not going to deny that this is a female hand. You're a lazy good-for-nothing.'

And to show that no one made fools of them, and also as a warning to incompetent witches, they cut off Crisanta's left pinky and took it with them, saying it was a good talisman against senile old women who tried to con them. The girl and the dog trembled when they heard the young lady in the black hat laughing.

'I told you so,' mumbled Ángela again and again while the old woman, howling in pain, applied a poultice to the wound.

After chewing some henbane leaves, she fell into a doze. She appeared greatly relieved. Before losing consciousness, she said to the girl:

'Get out of here. Since you started hanging around this house I've had nothing but hassles. I want to be alone.'

Ángela set out walking and, followed by Lupo, headed towards the nearest cemetery, Santa Rufina, in search of a night's lodging in the mausoleum of the Mira Valdesúa family, which could be opened easily, but then she thought better of it and hurried her pace towards Los Cigarrales. She felt an irrepressible desire to see the inhabitant of the crypt again. What's more, since the vampire wouldn't return until dawn, she had time to sleep for a while.

There, hidden between two old caskets, she overheard an entertaining and instructive conversation between the two women, who had become friends. The vampire was dripping with blood, the other was a melancholy, one-handed ghost. When the monsters had set off on their nocturnal errands, she threw herself into the infanticide's coffin, which being new was the most comfortable, and she slept divinely until dawn.

That night Ángela conceived the idea of getting hold of a hanged man's hand and using it to escape from poverty.

The storm raged, surrounding the turret in lightning and thunder. The smoke from the fireplace seemed possessed: it came in instead of going out. Shadows not justified by the candles' light danced on the walls. Ángela had stopped what she was doing and watched them with furrowed brow as though she found some flaw in their movements. The skull she was polishing with a piece of agate rested forgotten in her lap. Now and then Lupo sniffed at it apathetically.

Pilar Pedraza

Suddenly Crisanta leaned against the kitchen sink, raising her hands to her chest. She was turning blue. When she fell to the floor emitting terrible spluttering sounds, Ángela was on the verge of running away. She had to get out of there because if that old hag died, the devil would surely come for her soul and she didn't want to be around when that happened.

'Help me,' panted the old woman. 'Help me or I'll curse you with my dying breath!'

Lupo had taken shelter trembling in a corner. A hissing wind crept through the chimney, which besides smoke also scattered ashes from the hearth across the room. The pale lightning flashes lit and then extinguished the light of the world. Each time it thundered it seemed the turret would come tumbling down. Ángela dragged the old woman's body to the bedroom, pulling her by the feet. It cost her a painful effort to lift her up and put her in the bed. When she had managed it, she remained seated on the floor for a moment without moving, recovering her breath, while the old woman wheezed in a pure death rattle.

'The pact! The pact must be undone!' she exclaimed all of a sudden with a voice that didn't seem to be hers, stretching one hand towards the girl. Ángela got to her feet and approached her. Both were terrified. 'In the dresser drawer ... the parchment ... take it out and burn it, and help me to make the act of contrition.'

In that wobbly and dilapidated piece of furniture, enormous as a mausoleum, there were all kinds of rubbish, mixed with the very finest linen, silverware, and objects of value. Ángela rummaged frantically until coming upon a roll tied with a black ribbon. Her excitement was such that she didn't realize she had poked herself with the tine of a fork. A drop of blood stained the parchment.

The heaviest thing, she told herself, was going to be the

Elucidarium, because as for the rest of it, she only planned to grab the highest-priced objects, which were small. At first she intended to put it all in a sack, but then she considered that if she used a very fine damask pillowcase she had seen in the depths of the dresser to pack the things in, she would kill two birds with one stone, so she took it out of the drawer and laid it out on the floor.

'What are you doing, my child?' asked the old woman, sitting up again, with a firm and clear voice little in keeping with her deathbed condition.

The girl did not answer. She put half her body under the bed and dragged forth a little coffer, which she placed in the center of the pillowcase.

'No way, not that,' shouted Crisanta angrily. 'It's taken me a lifetime to acquire it!'

'Shut up, grandma, you're going to make yourself worse. What does it matter to you anymore? It won't do you any good now . . . It's better if I take it, since after all I've been the one who's taken care of you . . .'

'You'll bury me at least? Look, if you leave me here, I'll rot, and my soul will be furious, and I'll bring harm to you and . . .'

'Yes, woman. Calm down.'

But when the old woman breathed her last breath, resembling a belch, and remained quiet for good, Ángela no longer thought of anything but getting out of there as quickly as possible. She finished making a bundle with the pillowcase, put the book in it, and left the turret dragging it like the ant drags its booty against wind and tide.

Although she no longer needed to yank molars out of corpses to earn small change, wealth didn't go to Ángela's head nor cause her to abandon her habits or her work. She studied the *Elucidarium* with eagerness day and night, until her head was bursting and her eyes were filled with grit. There were things she didn't understand, but she made great progress. And when they condemned Pedro Madruga, who was said to be her own father, she saw the perfect opportunity to get hold of a good hand with which to make a powerful talisman. This time she wasn't going to sell it cheap to some young gentlemen like Cristina did with her work. She would use it herself to her own benefit. Thus she used all her astuteness, patience, and ability to slip through the cracks like lizards do, until she managed to get hold of that magnificent member, strong from having come from a son of the village and at the same time with skin soft like silk from not having worked in the rough and vile jobs that destroy body and soul. And she started marinating it in the brine of glory.

At the same time, she learned from the *Elucidarium* that leaving a sorceress's corpse uninterred brings bad luck. Remembering that Crisanta was rotting unburied in the turret, she felt a great cold rise up from her belly to her throat while sweat pearled on her forehead.

'That's just stuff and nonsense, right, mutt?' but this time the dog didn't agree with her. The book didn't lie.

'Fine, even if that's how it is,' she said, reading his thoughts, which she could do because she was the one who made them up, 'I burned the pact the old woman had with Old Nick, and thus she was off the list of sorceresses. So it's all the same whether she's buried or not.'

But, unable to deceive herself with that argument, she finally decided to return to the fortress and take care of the corpse. And one night she went out from the river mill with Lupo, took the rough road along the walls and circumvented the ditch on the western side, climbing the embankment covered in nettles, which cruelly punished her audacity by breaking the crystalline capsules of their poison on her skin like Bolognese tears breaking at Carnival. The old mutt was no longer up for adventures. He gasped for breath on the way up, but followed his mistress indefatigably. The cancer of love had grown until it completely took over his heart, turning him into a gooey emblem of fidelity.

Ángela was scared. She had learned from the book that a dead person's hatred was a poison worse than a viper's venom. She had supplied herself with a crucifix and some branches from a white hawthorn, a good remedy against bloodthirsty spirits. Around her neck she wore a silver choker with a sapphire stolen from Crisanta, and a jet amulet a pilgrim had given her in exchange for letting him touch the budding firmness of her breasts. But the terror of the serene night was so great that it flooded her spirit, opening ulcers in it for which there was no cure.

The turret rose in the middle of an ocean of silence, enveloped in the scent of the wild fig that grew in the ditch, fed by the putrefaction of the corpse of a large animal that had fallen to its death. Ángela was surprised there was no smoke coming from the heights of the fortress like before, when the old woman kept the hearth fire lit. The door was neither closed nor open: it was now no more than a dried-out piece of wood, the wind's plaything. She fumbled for the table in search of the candle, but her hand found only dust and some small dry objects. Finally she came upon a stub of a candle. She lit it and stuck it to the dirty table with wax drippings. In the doorway leading to the old woman's bedroom she thought she saw eyes like coals watching her malevolently.

'It doesn't smell of death here,' she said aloud, and Lupo appreciated the information, since he no longer had a sense of smell.

In the bedroom there was nothing. No bed, no corpse, no dresser, no trunk. Only the bare walls, which were beginning to crumble from dampness and neglect.

The heat of the night was beginning to give way to the

coolness of dawn. The girl shivered as she leaned against the door jamb, staring like a madwoman at the empty bedroom, inhabited only by uneasy echoes.

One day the hand of glory was ready. Large, well cured, shiny with grease, its fingers seemed candles capable of burning for a long time. She made a little base for it so she could stand it on its wrist like a five-armed candelabra. She felt that the hand loved her, could imagine it caressing her hair or giving her pats on the shoulder. It kept her company. She remembered that she had met Madruga once at a crossroads and the bandit had given her a handful of nuts and spoken to her kindly, calling her daughter. But she didn't know if that had happened in her dreams or in reality.

She chose as her victim a usurer named Catuja who was as rich as a queen. She was said to have great treasures, guarded with the help of three very ferocious mastiffs. No one went near her house without being invited. When a peddler tried to, they ate him up on the front steps.

The day recommended by the stars arrived. The girl had gotten a sack for the plunder and carried the hand of glory in a pocket of her cloak. She had thought about leaving Lupo locked up so he wouldn't bother her, but the mutt was obstinate. He stuck by her, assumed the bearing of a greyhound to hide the fact that his lungs were destroyed, that he could hardly see, that he stayed alive only through force of will. She brought him with her, not out of pity but out of habit.

There wasn't the slightest breath of wind. She could light the talisman outdoors in front of the garden gate. It was like Madruga's hand was impatient to go into action. The fingernails caught fire with a cheerful crackling, five perfect, serene little flames arising from them, whose light, at first bluish-gold and then orange, filled her soul with confidence. Scarcely had the light started to shine when Catuja's garden gate opened without a sound, as if it had recently been oiled. The garden was a tangled mess of confused plants, whose life seemed to be in their center, like animals, and not spread out through cells and fibers. Rose bushes and nettles embraced. In a bed of lilies a poisonous oleander bush grew. In the back the house rose up, silent and unlit, like a mausoleum.

Hearing the sound of steps on the gravel path, the mastiffs came. They were enormous and so similar to each another that one would have said it was just a single dog that had inexplicably multiplied, like a Cerberus duplicated beyond just the heads. Their eyes shone in the darkness, their butchering fangs, their drool. But when Ángela held out towards them the lit hand that she held in hers, they dropped drowsily to the ground. Lupo, who had been terrified at seeing them approach, stood still with his ears perked up, looking at them incredulously. Then he approached them with great caution, with movements more of a cat than a dog, and seeing them so docile, he dared to confront them, showing his teeth and growling.

Black like the night thanks to her cloak and light as a breeze, Ángela headed for the door of the house. The dogs followed her, wagging their tails. And this time too the dark door opened soundlessly, slow and solemn, leaving an open passage towards the shadows of the hall. Everything was perfectly calm and in darkness. Lighting her way with only the light of her bandit father's hand, she ascended the stairs to the bedrooms of the upper floor, where Catuja's chamber was.

It is bad to let a sorceress rot away alone, sounded an echo in the girl's head. She couldn't allow herself to be scared, but fear comes whenever it wants. It had entered the house like a breeze and it was in her heart and in her legs. Lupo felt it too. He trembled and was wary of the other dogs, although they remained docile and behaved with Ángela like loving pets.

The old usurer's door opened, at first so slowly that

Ángela feared the talisman was failing. But it ended up opening all the way, revealing the immense room, whose size made it seem an attic or a barn. There were dozens of candles burning in it, whose light cast a glimmer on the objects placed on the furniture. On one rough and peeling wall hung many floor-to-ceiling mirrors that cried out for a return to reflecting scenes from palace ballrooms, and paintings and tapestries dulled by dust, in which the gold threads gleamed and the silver ones were turning black. On a sideboard there was a little coffer with the appearance of containing jewels.

Catuja was sleeping in a bed that was somewhere between a straw mattress and a nest. One would have said she was dead if it weren't for her breathing, which though not quite a snore, was at least a happy snorting. She must have been dreaming of something pleasant, for in her face was reflected a happiness that came from within.

Ángela had placed the hand of glory on a nightstand and took the coffer in her hands. It was small but very heavy. When she opened it, she was dazzled. Diamonds like raindrops wounded by the sun and a bleeding ruby necklace sparkled in the light of Madruga's fingers. *Let's go, don't get bewitched now*, said a man's voice, and another: *There's no need to rush, kid, you did enough of that when you left the sorceress unburied*. The girl looked around. She didn't know what to grab. Everything was within reach and everything was tempting. The fingers of the talisman had burned down halfway. *There is time*. But when she was putting a handful of beautiful, worthless necklaces that she had found in a drawer into the bag, she heard a loud noise behind her. Lupo had stumbled against the nightstand that was serving as a pedestal for the hand, which had fallen to the ground. *Bad, very bad*. Three fingers had gone out, and on the others the little flames were in their death throes. They didn't take long to go out.

All of a sudden, the mastiffs recovered their ferocity. As

if they were coming out of a dream, they shook themselves, stretched, and turned fierce again. Their barks awakened the whole house. Catuja shot up in bed as if propelled by a spring, yelling:

'Burglars, burglars, burglars!'

The hunt began.

Lupo and the girl flew down the corridors, descended the stairs in the blink of an eye, crossed the hall, went out into the garden like in a dream. They carried the mastiffs with them, fastened to their bodies. They felt their fangs tearing their flesh, cracking their bones. In the night, sweet with blood and noisy like a celebration, shouts were heard and lights were lit. The thorns of the rose bushes caught in the folds of the cloak, feet tripped over paws, hands groped desperately at the garden gate until managing to open it.

No one had ever been able to catch Ángela, who knew how to scurry through cracks like a little viper and knew all the city's labyrinths. Though she was injured now, they weren't going to catch her this time either. She hid in a doorway. She descended stairs to forgotten basements, sneaked like a rat, coughing bloody froth, through damp passages, then along tunnels, through sewers, until she emerged at the surface, very far away.

Finding herself once more under the stars in the serene night, without shouts or commotion, or any other danger now that death was nesting in her wounds, she sighed with relief. Lupo had followed her. He was missing an ear, he was limping so much that he was really just dragging himself along on his stomach. He was black with blood in the moonlight. *How much blood it costs to reach the end.*

'Stupid fucking mutt . . .' she murmured with something vibrating in her voice, perhaps a little tenderness.

What shone in front of her like a white ribbon wasn't the river but the wall of the cemetery.

'Look! We were always meant to wind up here!'

The next morning when Bastián neared the pit he had left half dug the previous night, he knew that something was going on. It wasn't merely a feeling: a trail of blood, coming out of a bush, came to a stop at the hole.

'Damn it! Now the dead are coming on their own two feet and putting themselves in the hole all alone,' he said aloud to relieve himself from the sudden terror that had gotten the better of him.

He leaned over and cast a fearful glance: for the moment, he didn't want to notice too many details of whatever was there, he only wanted a general idea. The first thing he saw was a wrinkled cloak that seemed familiar to him. He forgot the blood and felt better.

'Eh, girl! Having a free sleep in my inn again?'

She didn't move. Nor did the shapeless and dirty lump that lay curled up in her lap.

'Oh, Lupo, you senile old bastard! I knew things weren't going to go well for you out there! Why did you need to suffer hardships at your age?'

And although prudence didn't advise it, he filled the pit with dirt, planted a white rose bush on top, and kept that little secret in his old heart.

Translated from the Spanish by James D. Jenkins

Attila Veres

The Time Remaining

Hungary, a relatively small country of fewer than 10 million people, has always had an outsized literary and artistic production, but horror fiction seems to be a relatively recent phenomenon there. One author working to put Hungary on the horror map is ATTILA VERES *(b. 1985), a novelist, short story writer and screenwriter. His first novel,* Odakint sötétebb [Darker Outside] (2017) *was a surprise success in his native country and was followed by the story collection* Éjféli iskolák [Midnight Schools] *in 2018. 'The Time Remaining' is one of his most recent stories, first appearing in the anthology* Aether Atrox (2019), *a volume that features a lineup of Hungary's best contemporary horror authors. We think he's a writer to keep an eye on and whose work we're confident will continue to make its way to English readers.*

M Y THERAPIST URGES ME to picture a different story, a story in which Vili doesn't die, or at least not like that. But before I can rewrite my past, first I need to face it — recount everything that happened exactly as it happened, up to the point when I lost control.

Vili's death struggle started on a Friday. It was pouring outside, giving the perfect melodramatic tone for announcing bad news. The three of us, my mother, Vili and I, were sitting in the kitchen.

Vili was given to me by my maternal grandmother on the 1st of May. I remember this because I was desperately trying to decipher the meaning of this celebration, but no one was able to give me a satisfactory answer. In a way, the 1st of May celebration continues to be a mystery for me to this day.

We were going to the festivity, the whole family, my father, my mother, and my grandmother, to enjoy the company of other families, watch the performers on the main stage, and indulge ourselves with the purchase of unnecessary objects at the vendors' row. Early on during the festivity a great storm materialized out of nowhere, devastating the marketplace. My grandmother ran back at the last minute to buy Vili from a seller who was desperately trying to save his hut from destruction. My grandmother grabbed Vili, not even bothering to wait for the change, while the seller was defying the torrential wind.

Grandmother slipped the gift into my hand, and she yelled – and this was the first time she yelled at me, though it was driven only by the need to be heard over the raging wind – to take care of Vili and always remember her. I could not make sense of that request at the time, for she was my grandmother, how could I ever forget her? Standing in the windstorm, I suddenly had an eerie vision. I felt like the world was about to fall to pieces, the wind would soon rip through the field and tear apart people and the past and the future, and I would fall into a dark abyss beyond time. I embraced Vili, and I found his touch rather comforting. He was soft and warm, and he made me feel that together we were solid enough to withstand the violent force of the wind. Vili's charm rested in his smile; not a clumsy grin, nor a condescending half-smile, not even the downward-facing, bitter grimace that so often featured on his fellow toys. Vili had a friend's smile, empathetic, approving, animating, but also with a touch of adult-like solemnity.

The sense of apocalypse ceased in the car. I clutched Vili in the back seat, and I knew that everything was all right.

Grandmother was sitting next to me. I saw tears blurring her eyes, but she smiled at me, assuring me it was only sand. My mother turned back and looked at grandmother with that stern look I thought she exclusively reserved for me when I did something wrong or when she assumed I had done something wrong, which were basically the same after all. I didn't think she could give that look to others, especially not to her own mother. They did not say a word to each other, and I soon fell asleep, grasping Vili.

After that, I saw grandmother very rarely, until one day my parents explained that she had gone to Australia on a family visit and would not return for a while. They showed me where Australia was on a world map to address my confusion, and they also showed me kangaroos and other peculiar animals in a book, which intrigued me. I hoped we would soon visit grandmother so we could maybe watch kangaroos together. My father and my mother agreed that if I behaved well enough throughout the year, this wish of mine might become reality and sooner or later we could visit grandmother.

I was a kid, surely that's the reason why I was so blind to the truth, although they say that children have heightened sensitivity to the minor changes in their environment. Perhaps I am the exception, or my mother was especially skilled at lying, even to herself. What is important to note is that I was not in possession of that information then: I did not know that my grandmother had passed away during that year. My mother asked her not to visit us, and we did not visit her either. My mother did not want me to remember my grandmother as a sick old woman, as her illness had consumed her body little by little, though I only know this from my father's account. He told me when he was drunk, decades later. I know that my mother wanted to protect me when she decided to lie. I know that she wanted the best for me: what else could a parent possibly wish for her offspring but the very best? My father, inebriated, made wise by long years of experience, thought otherwise – he believed that my mother was scared to pronounce the words, she was scared to verbalize that her own mother was dead. In any case, for me my grandmother was a living person for years to come, even though she had long been buried under the ground at the time when Vili started dying.

I only understood this later, in adulthood, partially due to my therapist's help. My mother thought I was too attached to Vili. She wanted me to be the best, the most successful, the most confident. In her view, life was an ice-cold forest, children being wolves in it, who think they form a pack, but at the end of the day they will all aim for the same job, same house and same female. Emotional overreliance on the false sense of security bestowed by a plush toy weakens one's character in the long term, and the weak fall prey to wolves.

We were sitting in the kitchen – two cups of tea steaming on the table, one for her and one for me. Chamomile, I feel sick at the smell of it to this day, yet my mother made this tea to soothe the emotional impact. She didn't make any tea for Vili, from which I deduced that something terrible must be coming.

My mother looked at me, very seriously, as seriously as when I broke expensive things, or when I ran out in the road chasing my ball. In retrospect, and I told this to my therapist as well, I suppose that in those very seconds, before articulating those words, she was thinking of my grandmother, her own mother. *I am going to be straight with you*, she said. *There is something wrong with Vili. Vili is sick, and sadly the odds are against him.*

She went on. *Unfortunately, even plush toys can get sick. Maybe it's genetic, the illness might remain latent for years before it manifests. Vili was manufactured in China, and it's very easy to catch all sorts of nasty diseases in those factories. Vili has been examined by doctors, and the prognosis is clear as day: Vili is going to die.*

I looked at Vili, who was lying on the marble kitchen table resting his friendly eyes on us, and only then did I realize Vili's inherent nudity, which made my heart ache. I wanted to cover his little body to protect him from the coldness of the world. I grabbed Vili and squeezed him against my chest. As I glanced at my mother, I could just catch a smile on her face. *You look so nice together*, she said. *I wish I could always remember you like this.*

Vili has two months left, she continued. *Take care of all his needs in the time remaining. The most important thing is to make sure Vili lives out his final days in dignity. Drink up your tea*, my mother said finally, and she wouldn't let me go to my room until I finished my tea to the last drop. That was the last time I drank chamomile tea in my life.

I retreated to my room with Vili. I sat down on the edge of my bed with him, and I felt like the world had shrunk around me, like I was locked in a cage from which there was no escape. I could have talked to my father, but I was perfectly aware of the household dynamic. My mother took care of my upbringing, while my father gave her financial stability. I knew that it would be a waste of time talking to him. In a normal situation, I would have turned to my mother to ask for her help in curing Vili – but she had just assured me that she was unable to help my plush toy.

I laid Vili on the bed, and I swept my hand over his body, not looking this time for warmth or safety, but for the symptoms of his disease. I had no idea what these symptoms could look like – Vili's body temperature seemed just fine. I searched and searched, and I could feel that Vili was avoiding my gaze, just as I was avoiding his. In that moment he became actually naked, not for his lack of clothing – he became naked because my fingers were searching for the end of his life.

I finally found the first rupture in his armpit. The thread had started to loosen, allowing Vili's insides to be seen through a small hole, the white stuffing that was his blood, his flesh. I knew right away that my mother's doctors were telling the truth. Vili's body was sick. I felt like my chest was too small for my lungs, that my brain was swelling and boiling in my skull. The world seemed darker, not in a metaphorical sense, but literally, the edge of my eyesight went black, I felt I could faint at any moment.

I knew with absolute certainty that death was real.

I grabbed Vili and threw him into the corner with all my strength. Vili bounced back from the wall, knocked his head against a shelf, and fell behind my backpack. I couldn't explain to myself the cause of my rage back then, and it took years even for my therapist to convince me that it was a normal reaction to what had happened to me. I tried to rationalize my behavior by thinking that I only wanted to save Vili: I had to hate him because he wasn't alive – and if he wasn't alive, he couldn't possibly die. Perhaps I wanted to save his life by admitting that he wasn't actually alive.

So many years have passed since then that it's time to be honest with myself now. My therapist also encourages me and tells me these things are completely normal until a certain age. I could talk to Vili, and he often talked to me as well – in my head. I believe this phenomenon is often referred to as an imaginary friend, when certain segments of a child's developing personality manifest as a voice or a character. That was Vili to me. He always guided me to do the right thing, to choose the harder path. I often imagined that Vili was a superhero and he saved others, my parents included, from some perilous situation like a burning car after an accident.

That night I lay in my bed and Vili was still in the corner. I found it hard to fall asleep though I was exhausted by anger and grief. And then I heard it, I heard Vili's cry. Most likely it was all in my head, but I could clearly hear the voice coming from the corner – he was crying, not out of fear or due to his illness, but because he had let me down: he was not a good enough plush toy, so I had had to punish him. Then I realized that I was the one who had failed him, my anger was unreasonable, rather an indication of my own stupidity. I jumped out of the bed crying and I ran to the corner to hug Vili. I promised him I would never ever let him down again, I would be by his side for the time remaining.

When I finally fell asleep, Vili wasn't crying anymore.

My mother and other mothers in the neighborhood often socialized, primarily to discuss useful tips regarding the everyday issues of raising children. Thus it is not surprising in retrospect that soon enough other plush toys at school got sick. I felt relieved, because I was not alone in this fight – others had to face the same dread as me, and we quickly found each other. I can't recall their names, although they were my friends. My therapist says it's one of the mind's defense mechanisms. Apart from their names I remember everything about my friends, so if it's a mechanism, it's not working very efficiently.

The four of us formed a gang, developing a kind of friendship, even if the vast majority of our time together was spent discussing the practical aspects of our toys' dying process. There were two boys and one girl in the group besides me. The fact that our mothers wanted their boys to set aside their plush toys at a certain age was more or less understandable, but I have the impression that parents are less strict with girls in this respect. A girl can play with plush toys for a longer period of time, my therapist agrees with me in this – it is socially acceptable for a girl to keep her plush toys even into adulthood. Still, the girl's plush toy, Ferkó, got infected with the sickness all the same.

Vili more or less stagnated the first two weeks; only the rupture in his armpit had apparently been growing bigger, and the thread had started to loosen in other areas as well – at his foot, at the edge of his hand where he had black claws made of cotton. By the end of the second weekend his fur started to fade. During this period Vili's voice in my head was calming. He kept my spirits up, as if I were the sick one, not him. I often fell asleep listening to his voice.

During this time I unfortunately sometimes peed in my bed again. My therapist says that's normal, it's called regression, an emotional reaction which entails going back to a former stage of development. After a while, I stopped sleeping with Vili because I didn't want to stain his fur. My mother was not very happy with the bedwetting, and I was well aware that it was a sign of weakness. My mother would shake her head impatiently and sigh heavily to express her discontent, and I would stand in the middle of my room in shame, shaking in the coldness of dawn, but Vili's voice gave me comfort even then.

Then things took a turn for the worse.

One day I came home from school and found Vili on the floor, the thread broken on his side and the white stuffing pouring out of him. My heart sank. I thought Vili had died while I was at school. But I could hear his voice, very quiet, weary with pain, but still clear. Vili was alive. I took him carefully in my shaking hands, which only caused him to lose even more stuffing, my throat went dry from panic, I could hardly breathe. I laid Vili on my bed and tried to hold his wound together. I couldn't sew, and I despised myself for that. Eventually, I applied super glue to the edges of the wound and held the material together while I whispered to Vili that everything was going to be all right, although I knew that nothing was ever going to be all right.

The next day it turned out that the others had had similar experiences as well. One of my friends, the boy who always wore black-framed glasses, told us about the deterioration of his plush toy named Nyinyi. My bespectacled friend's thinking was a bit slow and dim – a year or two later he was sent to another school because his learning difficulties had become too severe.

There is a chance – but not a certainty, because I didn't stop to talk to him, I simply walked by as if he was a thrown-away soda can or a cigarette butt on the cold concrete – that I passed by my friend a couple of years ago, now an adult. My friend apparently lived on the streets, he had a thick blanket wrapped around his waist. There was a tin can by his feet with some coins in it. My friend kept staring straight ahead like someone who had stopped counting the minutes and days long ago and let time flow effortlessly through him. He was still wearing the black-framed glasses, which he kept sparkling clean just like in his childhood. I didn't turn towards him, and I didn't give him money. I wanted to get this miserable man out of my sight as quickly as possible. Maybe it wasn't even my friend, just someone who looked like him.

When my friend was still a kid, he told me how Nyinyi's condition took a turn for the worse. Under Nyinyi's tiny, fluffy tail a hole opened up – it was not even the thread but the fabric itself that loosened, allowing Nyinyi's freshly torn anus to eject thick red fiber onto the floor. My friend tried to push the yarn back, but he only made the hole bigger. My other two friends, the boy and the girl, listened in shock first to the account of my bespectacled friend, and then to mine. Later that week their own plush toys started to deteriorate as well. One morning the girl found her toy Ferkó with a severed arm – his right arm had detached from his body during the night. The other boy's plush toy, Egyes, went into paralysis. We didn't quite understand what this meant, since we all knew that plush toys don't move by themselves, only when we move them or imagine them to be moving. Well, my friend's toy didn't move anymore. He didn't die, my friend told me; he was one hundred percent alive, only disabled. Soon after, the stuffing started to pour out of Egyes' mouth – the sickness made him vomit up his own guts.

We were all faced with the situation that our plush toys were losing their vital filling, and our knowledge taken from movies made it clear to us that such an excessive loss leads to certain death. We needed a transfusion to keep our toys alive, and for this we had to find other, still living plush toys.

I fished out some of my old toys from the toybox, those I hadn't played with for a long time – Szilvio, a plush bunny who was given to me by distant relatives for a Christmas years past (I didn't give him this name, it was written on the funny bow he was wearing); a Disney-franchise plush based on one of their current movie's side characters, which I named Gyuri for reasons unknown, and finally a female fox, Anni, who used to be my favorite toy for a long time, until I didn't find her fur soft enough anymore, so upon mutual agreement I had retired her into the toybox. Now I spread them out one by one on the floor. I could hear their voices as well, those old voices they used to talk to me in when I still played with them. But Vili's voice drowned theirs out. He was begging me not to do this, that these toys didn't deserve it – but by then Vili had another hole in his body and the stuffing needed urgent replacement. I also knew that no matter how brave Vili wanted me to see him, he was terrified; I felt it. At this time Vili often talked to me in his sleep. I don't think he was conscious, his words were too confused, too out of character – he was whining in his sleep, often mumbling obscenities; every word reeked of fear.

I smuggled a knife and a pair of scissors from the kitchen and I started with Gyuri, the Disney toy. I never considered him to be too clever, nor very sensitive; on the other hand he was made of an excellent material manufactured somewhere in China. He didn't get sick though, and I was angry at him for this. He didn't deserve to be so lucky. I made an incision with the knife on Gyuri's abdomen – I could hear him screaming in pain, then begging for his life. But at that point there was no turning back. I slipped the scissors into his wound and cut through his skin. Gyuri was screaming, and I was screaming with him, or instead of him because he didn't have a mouth or throat to scream out loud. I wanted to give him an actual voice in his final minutes.

My mother asked me during dinner why I was shouting in my room. I told her I was doing surgeries, dissections in order to prolong Vili's life expectancy. My mother was drinking red wine, I recall this because her teeth were black when she smiled. *Good*, she said, *I'm glad that you're taking responsibility.*

That made me happy. My therapist says this is normal, children always want to live up to their parents' expectations, and my mother's expectations were always quite high. She took out a box of ice cream from the freezer and carved out a slice of the delicacy for me. This happened very rarely, only on festive occasions. She placed the bowl full of ice cream in front of me and took another sip of the red wine. She kissed the top of my head, another evident sign of motherly love, which nonetheless scared me at that moment. My hair got sticky from drool and wine. *It's important*, she said, *that we take care of our loved ones, that we're by their side even in times of hardship.*

I didn't notice it as a child, but my father says my mother was drinking too much in that period, usually right before bedtime. This made my father unwilling to share the bed with her, bothered by the smell of alcohol. Now he drinks too, of course. Apart from that night I still remember my mother as a sober person though.

My father later also told me, and this gives a special context to my mother's behavior that night, that my mother had abandoned her own mother in the final hours of the latter's life. Or final days. Or final weeks. All in all, my mother kept her distance in the physical, geographical, and emotional sense as well. My grandmother died alone. That night my mother obviously projected her desire to have done it differently onto me. I was, of course, not aware of this at that time. I ate my ice cream and in the following days I butchered my remaining plush toys, screaming and whimpering to vocalize their death throes under the edge of my scissors.

There were times when I would scream for hours, because I didn't finish Anni off right away. We figured that only freshly transfused stuffing was optimal for our plush toys. There could not be more than half an hour between the moment of transfusion and the donor's death, otherwise the stuffing would coagulate – it would turn useless and poisonous. But if we only took a handful of stuffing from our donor at a time the donor wouldn't necessarily die; on the contrary, we could keep them alive at our will in order to extract a second and third portion from them, this way prolonging the lives of our favorite plush toys. I extracted three portions from Anni, and I gave voice to her suffering all the way to the end. I didn't enjoy killing the toys. I hid their remains shamefully in the corners of my room, and early one morning I sneaked out to the street and threw the carcasses into a distant trash can. Then I spent days in terror fearing that someone would knock on my door and confront me with the murder of the three plush toys.

Naturally this never occurred, but my therapist agrees with me that such a fear is an indication of my lack of sociopathic tendencies. I didn't find joy in this kind of torture, and my mind feared retaliation – for I regarded my actions as sinful.

Sometimes I wish I had enjoyed it. Then everything would have been so much easier.

I carefully stuffed the fresh filling into Vili. I knew this was a painful, demanding procedure for him as well, so I sedated him in my imagination. He breathed in anesthetic gas from an old carnival mask made of papier mâché – obviously this mask was turned into an anesthetic mask only in my mind, but the trick worked. Vili fell asleep; I could hear his rhythmic breathing in my thoughts, but not his voice. Why I didn't do this with the toys I killed I cannot say for certain, but on some primordial level I felt that pain was a necessary element of the process.

I carefully stuffed the fresh, hot filling under his skin with my fingers. I used an office stapler for the stitches. One of my friends, the one without glasses, managed to get a stapler for each of us. His parents were rich and successful. They had some sort of company, and maybe a restaurant too, but I'm not entirely sure about that. Everyone was a little scared of him because his family was so wealthy, and the power of money can be sensed even as a child. I met him once as an adult. He didn't recognize me, although he was staring right at me – or maybe he did but chose not to talk to me. He quickly looked away and rushed off, perhaps holding the handle of his briefcase a tiny bit tighter. He had an expensive suit, an expensive briefcase, and an expensive pair of shoes. It hurt me a bit that he didn't recognize me, just like I didn't recognize my friend with the glasses.

Anyway, as a child he stole the equipment for us from one of their offices. This speeded up the stitching procedure, which was crucial for me because Vili's sewing loosened more and more every day. No matter how quickly I stuffed in the new filling, when I came home from school or woke up at dawn, he had lost just as much or even more in the meantime.

When we ran out of plush toys at home we had to look elsewhere for resupply. Since we were kids, we didn't have much to spend, except for our rich friend. He was able to purchase new toys and gave us some spare coins now and then, but never enough. With my other two friends I would go through the charity shops in the hope of finding some discounted plush toys. Sometimes we would steal toys from these shops and run through the streets like hyenas with our prey, hoping that no one was following us. These stolen toys smelled like poverty, but they fulfilled the purpose we needed them for. We eviscerated them and stuffed their filling into our own toys. The girl's older sister advised us to mix fresh blood into the cotton wool so our plush toys would get stronger. We followed her advice and collected lizards from our school's sunny playground. They were easier to kill than the plush toys because we didn't need to imitate their suffering, they were inherently alive. We slushed their blood onto the cotton wool, but this method didn't bring any visible results.

Not then at least.

The situation soon turned more dire. Vili's skin burst in several places, but not along the stitching like before: the plush itself had worn so much that the wear eventually became a hole, through which the life-giving filling flowed out. These parts were harder to staple because the fabric would often burst or grow precariously thin. Vili's friendly eyes also became blurred. They were covered in some kind of fog, as if his plastic eyes had faded from the inside. One afternoon, as I was trying to close up his recent wounds, Vili's left eye fell out of its place and hit the floor with a thud. I felt like I was going to vomit. Vili was blindly looking at me with his one eye, while where his other eye should have been there was only plush and filling. I wanted to scream, but I bit my arm instead. I didn't dare hug Vili because I was scared his other eye would fall out as well. I tried to glue the fallen eye back, but my efforts were clearly in vain. The eye had nothing to stick to anymore, it would only fall out together with the filling again. I knew that Vili's time remaining would soon be up.

At that point Vili was no longer able to sleep from the pain. I would listen to his groaning all night long, his begging, swearing, and cursing. This was not the Vili I knew – my Vili always knew what was right, even if the harder path was the right one. But at night the dying Vili loathed the world that doomed him to suffer – he would either insult everyone and everything with spite, or moan out of terror like a lunatic. He did his best to hold it together by day, but he spoke less and less. He became remote, and sometimes I could hear him cursing in the daytime as well.

After a while, his other eye went blurry and eventually fell out. I put red tape in the place of his eyes, so Vili spent his last days with two red X's on his face. The scattered limbs, eyes, and fluffy insides were starting to cause us more trouble. The boys complained that the scattered filling was infecting their other toys with sickness – the wheels detached from their Matchbox cars, their plastic soldiers fell apart, and their LEGO pieces didn't fit together anymore. The girl attempted to work out the meticulous protocol of our plush toys' dying process because her parents were doctors. Hence, following the girl's advice, we started to collect the potentially infectious plush body parts in resealable plastic bags – we painted the universal biohazard symbol onto the bags with black markers. I placed Vili's eyes, stuffing, and one of his legs that had detached in the meantime into one of these bags.

I was scared to stay alone in my room, especially after I woke up one night to the gaze of Vili's red X eyes. Vili was lying on my pillow and stared right at me, even though at night I would always put him into a warm, cozy nest on the floor, firstly in order to protect him from potential bed-wetting and secondly because I could barely stand his smell anymore. He smelled of death, and I would choke from it at night. *My eyes*, Vili shouted at me. *Where are my eyes?* I screamed and tossed Vili away, causing him to fall on the floor with a painful groan. For the first time I peed my bed while I was awake. Vili was whimpering quietly on the floor, so I got out of bed, carefully slipped my hands under his head, and placed him back in his nest. Although I was scared, I wasn't angry at him. He was only a sick, demented plush toy. He didn't mean to hurt me, not consciously at least.

Not yet.

The others reported similar experiences about their plush toys' disturbed minds. Our rich friend claimed that Egyes had been whispering terrible things in his ear all night about the endless, bleak darkness that swallows everyone like an insane father, and about the Black Emperor who ruled in its guts. The girl stated that Ferkó had attempted to sneak out the window – whether he wanted to escape or kill himself was not entirely clear, but after she thwarted his plan she could feel him pinching her feet and thighs so as to prevent her from falling asleep. Since then she would sometimes wake up to find her plush toy lying on her chest with his mouth attached to her skin, as if he was trying to suck the life and flesh out of her. Our friend with the glasses recounted that his plush toy walked in circles around the room, cursing and swearing and listing the names of those who had offended him, those who ought to be ended, whose heads should be pinned onto the wall of the LEGO castle, whose blood should be used to sully the television screens.

My therapist maintains that these episodes are no more than violent fantasies, the products of a child's imagination, which we brought to life in order to confront the unbearable stress and confusion we were faced with. Still, after a while I had to tie Vili up at night because he would often crawl into my bed, nauseating me with his filthy breath, his burning gaze pointed at me and clutching a tiny plastic sword in his hand. If I tied him up, nothing of that sort would happen; then I would only hear his painful groaning, his whining that overflowed with his terrible fear of death, and his cursing of life. He cursed the one who brought him to life, who forced him to live and die, for otherwise he had existed in lifeless unconsciousness until then.

He was cursing me.

Our friend with the glasses was first. One day he found Nyinyi lifeless on the floor. Nyinyi had passed away in his sleep. Our friend's parents threw Nyinyi's corpse in the trash, and when the body disappeared from the trash can leaving dirty traces behind on the floor, they resorted to corporal punishment against their son. Despite our friend's firm insistence that he hadn't touched Nyinyi's corpse. The second night after Nyinyi's disappearance our friend saw him from his window. The deceased toy was dragging a dead cat through the street, disappearing under a garbage bin with his victim. The next day our friend examined the bin and its surroundings but found nothing but used stuffing.

Vili talked less and less; he would instead broadcast a sort of feeling, like a radio station. *I'm ready*, he broadcast to me, *I'm ready to die*. He had suffered enough; his eyes couldn't see anything but red, every single breath was an agony. He asked me both verbally and nonverbally to end all of this.

Naturally, I resisted for a long time. Though I killed off many other plush toys just so Vili could live, killing Vili was a different matter. On the other hand I also knew that Vili had to die. My mother's prophecy had to be fulfilled, otherwise all this suffering would have been in vain.

Meanwhile, the girl's plush toy died as well – she found him in the middle of her room upon returning from school. The filling was still pouring out of his emaciated body, his hands stretched forward as if he was still trying to reach something. The girl read up on the topic, and she found that the only way to prevent our plush toys from resurrecting was to bury them together with an onion – at least that's how I understood it at that time.

She acted according to her theory: she placed the corpse into a resealable plastic bag and poured some onion around it. The plush toy didn't return. We all felt relieved by learning that, except for our friend with the glasses, since Nyinyi was still haunting around his house. Several dogs and cats went missing, and one night someone tried to break into the apartment through one of the ground floor windows. The policemen who arrived on the scene found only cotton wool.

Vili was incessantly begging to die, night after night and morning after morning, hardly allowing me a moment of rest. At the same time a new theory started to circulate among my friends, prompted by the increasingly aggressive activity of Nyinyi – that our plush toys crave death because it breaks the bond between them and humans so they don't have to serve us children anymore, and they can roam the world equipped with the power of the grave, equipped with the power of the Black Emperor. We deduced that there must be more plush toys like Nyinyi out there, they might be gathering in the canals and at the bottom of forgotten cardboard boxes, scheming viciously, planning their revenge on us who created them, gave them voice and life, only to eventually take it away from them.

Vili's odor became unbearable, and he couldn't articulate his words anymore. His voice was like a slightly open door through which the coldness of the grave could reach me. I couldn't stand watching him suffer anymore, and I couldn't bear my own exhaustion either.

I used the knife and the scissors. I feel ashamed recalling this – I stood over him for hours with the blades in my hand and I cried. My hands shook; whatever I had done before didn't matter now, only this one act of murder. Vili begged me incessantly to do it, he tried to catch my eyes with his red, blind ones. At last I did it, I forced myself to cut him open as meticulously as I did with the other toys. After the first cut, for a brief moment, he was his old self again, the old Vili. I chose the harder path, and this made the ensuing hours somewhat easier; the silence in my head, the complete absence of Vili. I howled loudly over Vili's body until my mother found me upon her return from the shop. She caressed my head while I hugged her legs, seeking safety and compassion. She soothed me, and then she said that one sentence, which I think made me hate her forever.

Don't cry, it was just a plush toy.

My mother explained to me that you have to make the cadaver resemble its living counterpart as best as you can – you can't bury a person with their insides and limbs scattered all over in the coffin. We reassembled Vili's body, pushing back as much stuffing as possible, stapling his skin together so he would resemble his old self again. He didn't – his body was the most horrible sight; his face was a deformity, his friendly smile now a cut-up grin of insanity. We placed the body in a plastic bag. I demanded that we put some onion into the bag as well – my mother gave in, chopped a bit of red onion and sprinkled it beside Vili. Then we buried the bag in the back yard – I also placed a small cross on the grave. My mother offered me sweets again, then ordered me to tidy my room.

The next morning, I found the cross fallen over, and the

grave disturbed, as if the earth had been moved from below. The school bag dropped from my hands because I knew that Vili had returned.

Of course, I had alternative theories as well. It could have been an animal that dug up the body, or even a person, a poor child who could only afford dead toys. Perhaps it was Nyinyi who had come for Vili so as to take his distorted body and present it at a gathering of the undead: *Look, this is what mankind does to us.*

The girl explained to me how it happened, not then, but years later, as an adult.

We met in a shopping center. My cart contained only two bottles of vodka and a six-pack of beer. She was the one to notice me and called my name in a tone which implied she was happy to see me, as if I was a good old friend, a link to a carefree period of the past. When she called my name I trembled as if she had struck me, and I felt ashamed for not recalling hers. I smiled at her as best I could to camouflage my embarrassment. The girl had become a mother, her daughter standing by the basket with her head down and a plush toy in her hands – Vili. My throat went dry when I saw Vili; of course I knew it was not my Vili, just another, similar plush toy.

I saw a tiny lesion on the neck of the toy. The girl, who was now a mother, was smiling at me. *It's like yours was*, she said and leaned closer to me so she could whisper in my ear. *Sadly*, she whispered, and I could smell chamomile on her breath, *sadly, she got infected with some kind of disease. This plush toy is dying, and my daughter has to accept it.*

I dropped the basket, the bottles of vodka smashed against each other, pouring their contents all over the floor, and I felt the urge to throw myself to the ground and lick it all up. *I know why yours came back, I figured it out*, she continued and I wanted to run but my body didn't obey. I listened carefully to what she had to say, and we agreed to have coffee or tea some time, but we didn't exchange numbers, and I vomited in the restroom for hours until the security guards kicked the door in.

I should have used garlic, whereas my mother used onions, which didn't possess any spiritual or symbolic power. Onions are unfit for keeping the dead on the other side, apparently.

I was not aware of this as a child. I was weary and exhausted after finding the disturbed grave. I felt sick, and for a while I had a serious wish to die and have this whole thing over with.

It only struck me at night that Vili might not return in the shape I remembered him. That he might resemble Nyinyi – and I started to be scared. For he swore to come back for me, didn't he? Didn't he plan to take revenge on the one who gave him life and death? I was certain then that he would return for me to drag me with him into the hole I dug for him in the back yard with my bare two hands.

I was not wrong.

The house went dark at midnight – the lights went out on the street as well. Power outage. Darkness surrounded me like thick cotton wool. I was paralyzed. My mother was asleep, my father on a business trip. I started to whimper, but I didn't feel ashamed even back then, for this was the whimper of an animal in the mouth of the predator.

I heard a noise from downstairs, then the voice of something heading up the stairs. The house was filled with the smell of the grave. Some hours earlier I had considered death to be a momentary blessing, but now I felt that death was not the end – something much worse was waiting, and it was coming for me.

I could hear Vili's voice again, louder and louder as he approached.

Only it was not Vili anymore; wherever he was after I'd killed him and before he returned, he brought a piece of that place with him. His voice was the voice of death, like the munching of a thousand worms, it meant nothing but itself, emptiness – but to my terror, beyond the sound of maggots and decay it was the voice of my grandmother.

Hail the Black Prince! Vili said. *Hail the Black Emperor!* he shouted, and showed me what the Black Prince was, what the Black Emperors were, for it was impossible to express their nature with words, only with dreams and images; and I fell on my knees and prayed to them, the Black Lords. I was ready to worship anything just to prevent Vili from taking me to the bottom of the grave, as fodder to the Lords, as fodder to my grandmother who, at this time, I didn't even know was dead.

By then, I could hear Vili dragging himself towards my door. He smelled of rot and onion, and he tried to speak with a real voice, but whatever he meant to say, death and the earth he was choking on impeded him from doing so. He only growled quietly.

He stopped in front of my room; the odor of death became insupportable. I was struck by the waves of genuine hate from under the doorstep. I knew that Vili would take me to where he had come from, and something changed in me.

I'll give you anything, just let me live, I whispered because I couldn't even speak, *you can take anything, you can take anyone, anyone but me! Please!*

I wasn't taking the harder path then. Vili wouldn't have approved were he alive. Alas, he was not.

Vili waited a few seconds, then he went down the hall-way, and I crawled under my bed and trembled until the morning came. I thought I wouldn't sleep, but exhaustion got the better of me.

When I woke up, in the daylight I thought it had only been a bad dream. Actually, nothing had happened. According to my therapist, everything I experienced or perceived as an experience that night was completely normal, a child's mind struggling with the inconceivable. In the morning, I thought I would go to school as usual, but I wouldn't talk to my friends anymore. I would leave all this plush toy stuff behind, after all it was indeed time for me to grow up. I crept out from under the bed and went to the kitchen to have breakfast.

She was drinking chamomile tea, I could already smell it from afar. My mother was standing by the counter with a teacup in front of her. I stepped into the kitchen and greeted her, but she didn't reply. The odd smile on her face, some sort of an idiotic grin, scared me to death. She gazed at one spot, senseless and emotionless, and I felt a knot forming in my throat. I called for her, but she didn't react. Her hand rested on the mug, but she wouldn't say a word, wouldn't move, and I got furious, since everything was her fault, everything; that I was there, that I was alive, that she killed my toy, killed my childhood, and now she was not even able to say *Good morning*! Something snapped inside me, and I did the unimaginable. I stepped up to her and shook her as if I was shaking a tree to make its crop fall down.

My mother's teeth fell out of her mouth, her glass eyes dropped and clattered on the counter. Her skin opened up because there was no sewing to hold her together, her hair fell off her head.

Her body unraveled, and there was nothing left in my hands but a handful of cotton wool.

Translated from the Hungarian by Luca Karafiáth

Cristina Fernández Cubas

The Angle of Horror

CRISTINA FERNÁNDEZ CUBAS (*b.* 1945) *has been called one of the most important Spanish writers to emerge since the end of the Franco dictatorship and has been credited with inaugurating 'a renaissance in the short story genre in Spain'. She is the author of novels, short stories, drama, memoirs and biography, and in 2016 won the National Literature Prize for Narrative and the Premio de la Crítica Española for her collection* Nona's Room. *Reviewing that book for* The New York Times, *critic Terrence Rafferty wrote that Cubas is 'most interested in the ambiguities and periodic disturbances that plague the imagination, and reports on them with the appropriate sense of awe, even of dread. In the territory of the imagination, the threat of madness is never too far away, a dark cloud hovering', a judgment equally applicable to the following story. 'The Angle of Horror', first published in 1996, is by now considered a classic of Spanish horror fiction and is often reprinted in Spanish-language anthologies, although mysteriously it has never previously appeared in English.*

NOW, WHEN SHE KNOCKED ON THE DOOR for the third time, looked through the keyhole without seeing anything, or paced angrily along the rooftop terrace, Julia realized she should have acted days ago, the very moment she discovered that her brother was hiding a secret, before the family took matters into their own hands and built up a fence of interrogations and reprimands. Because Carlos was still there. Locked in a dark room, feigning a slight indisposition, abandoning the solitude of the attic only to eat, always reluctantly, hidden behind opaque sunglasses, taking refuge in an unusual and exasperating silence. 'He's in love,' their mother had said. But Julia knew that his strange attitude had nothing to do with the vicissitudes of love or disappointment. That's why she had decided to stand guard on the top floor, next to the bedroom door, scrutinizing the slightest sign of movement through the keyhole, waiting for the summer heat to force him to open the window that looked out on the rooftop. A long and narrow window, through which she would leap in a single bound, like a pursued cat or the shadow of one of the sheets drying in the sun, an appearance so rapid and unexpected that Carlos, overcome by surprise, would have no other choice but to speak, at least to ask her, 'Who gave you permission to burst in like that?' Or else: 'Get lost! Don't you see I'm busy?' And she would see. Would finally see what her brother's mysterious activities consisted of, would understand his extreme paleness and would rush to offer him her help. But she had been keeping a close watch for over two hours and was starting to feel ridiculous and humiliated. She abandoned her lookout post by the door, went out onto the rooftop and once again counted, as she had done so many times over the course of the afternoon, the defective and broken tiles, the plastic clothespins and the wooden ones, the exact number of steps that separated her from the long, narrow window. She knocked on the window glass and heard herself say in a tired voice: 'It's me, Julia.' Really she should have said, 'It's still me, Julia.' But what did it matter now? This time, however, she pricked up her ears. She thought she heard a distant groan, the creaking of the bed's rusty springs, some shuffling steps, a metallic sound, again a creak, and a clear and unexpected: 'Come in. It's open.' And at that moment Julia felt a shudder very similar to the strange tremor that ran through her body days earlier, when she realized, suddenly, that *something* was happening to her brother.

It had already been a couple of weeks since Carlos had returned from his first study trip. The second of September, the date she had colored in red on the calendar in her bedroom and which now appeared increasingly remote and impossible. She remembered him at the foot of the stairs of the British Airlines jumbo jet, waving his arm, and she saw herself jumping enthusiastically on the airport terrace, amazed that at eighteen he could still have grown even taller, returning his kisses and greetings, pushing her way through the crowd to welcome him in the lobby. Carlos had returned. A little thinner, quite a bit taller, and noticeably pale. But Julia found him even more handsome than when he left and paid no attention to her mother's comments about the poor English food or the unmatched excellence of the Mediterranean climate. Nor, when they'd gotten in the car and her brother seemed happy at the prospect of enjoying a few weeks in the beach house and their father pestered him with innocent questions about the little blond girls of Brighton, did Julia laugh at the family's wisecracks. She was too excited, and her head was buzzing with plans and projects. The following day, when her parents stopped overwhelming him with questions, she and Carlos would recount the summer's events to each other in secret, on the roof like always, their swinging legs hanging over the eaves, just like when they were little and Carlos used to teach her how to draw and she used to show him her sticker collection. When they got to the garden, Marta came out to meet them, giving little jumps, and Julia marveled a second time at how much her brother had grown. 'At eighteen,' she thought, 'how absurd!' But she didn't say a word.

Carlos had remained lost in thought, contemplating the house's exterior as though he were seeing it for the first time.

He held his head tilted toward the right, his brow furrowed, his lips contracted in a strange grimace that Julia could not interpret. He remained motionless for a few moments, looking toward the housefront with the eyes of one who is hypnotized, oblivious to the movements of the family, the hustle and bustle of suitcases, the proximity of Julia herself. Afterwards, without hardly changing his position, he leaned his head on his left shoulder, his eyes reflected astonishment, the strange grimace of his mouth gave way to an unequivocal expression of fatigue and depression, he ran his hand along his forehead and, concentrating his gaze on the ground, he dejectedly crossed the paved garden path.

During dinner, their father continued to take an interest in his conquests, and their mother went on worrying about his bad complexion. Marta told a couple of jokes that Carlos received with a smile. He seemed tired and sleepy. The journey, perhaps. He kissed his family goodnight and retired to bed.

The following day Julia awoke very early, reviewed the list of reading recommendations Carlos had given her when he left, gathered up the notebooks in which she had jotted down her impressions, and climbed up to the roof. After a while, tired of waiting, she jumped down to the rooftop terrace. Her brother's window was half closed but it didn't appear there was anyone inside the room. She leaned out over the balustrade and looked towards the garden.

Carlos was there, in the same position as the night before, contemplating the house with a mixture of astonishment and dismay, leaning his head first to the right, then to the left, fixing his gaze on the ground and dejectedly crossing the paved path that separated him from the house. It was then that Julia understood, all of a sudden, that *something* was happening to her brother.

The 'doomed love' hypothesis was gaining ground at the

tense household lunches. A blond, pale young English girl from Brighton. The melancholy of first love, the sadness of long distance, the apathy with which youths of his age usually regard everything unconnected to the object of their passion. But that was at first. When Carlos was merely sullen and aloof, being startled by any question whatsoever, diverting his eyes, refusing little Marta's cuddles. Maybe she should have acted decisively then. But now Carlos had just said, 'Come in. It's open,' and, plucking up her courage, she had no alternative but to push open the door.

At first she couldn't discern anything but a suffocating heat and a labored, plaintive breathing. After a while she was able to distinguish between the shadows: Carlos was seated at the foot of the bed and the only glimmers of light that had been able to penetrate his fortress seemed to be concentrated in his eyes. Or were they his eyes? Julia opened one of the window shutters slightly and gave a relieved sigh. Yes, that despondent boy, hidden behind impregnable sunglasses, his forehead sprinkled with gleaming droplets of sweat, was her brother. Except that she now found his paleness too alarming, his attitude too inexplicable, to go on justifying him in the eyes of the family.

'They're going to call a doctor,' she said.

Carlos was unfazed. He went on for several minutes with his head bent toward the floor, knocking his knees together, playing with his fingers as if he were performing a children's song on the keyboard of a nonexistent piano.

'They want to force you to eat . . . to leave this filthy room for good.'

Julia thought her brother shuddered. 'This room,' she thought, 'what is it that's making him stay in this room so long?' She looked around and was surprised that it was not as untidy as she might have expected. Carlos, from the bed, was breathing heavily. 'He's going to speak,' she told herself, and, suffocated by the stifling atmosphere, she timidly pushed open one of the shutters and half opened the window.

'Julia,' she heard, 'I know you're not going to understand anything of what I might tell you. But I have to talk with someone.'

A glint of pride lit up her eyes. As in times past, Carlos was going to make her a party to his secrets, turn her into his most faithful ally, ask her for help that she would rush to give him. Now she understood that she had acted rightly in standing guard beside that shadowy room, acting like a ridiculous amateur spy, enduring silences, measuring the dimensions of the lonely, scorching hot rooftop over and over again. Because Carlos had said: 'I have to talk with someone ...' And she was there, beside the half-opened window, ready to attentively take note of everything he might decide to confide to her, not daring to interrupt, not caring that he spoke in a low voice, difficult to make out, as if he feared to hear his own lips utter the secret reason for his unease. 'It all comes down to a question of ...' Julia could not make out the final word muttered in a whisper, but she preferred not to interrupt. She took a crumpled cigarette from her pocket and offered it to her brother. Carlos, without looking up, refused it.

'It all started in Brighton, on a day like so many others,' he continued. 'I lay down in bed, closed the window to forget about the rain, and I slept. That was in Brighton ... Did I already say that?'

Julia assented by clearing her throat.

'I dreamt that I had passed my exams with flying colors, that they loaded me down with diplomas and medals, that all of a sudden I wanted to be here with all of you and, without thinking twice, decided to show up unannounced. Then I got on a train, an incredibly long and narrow train,

and arrived here almost without realizing it. "It's a dream,"
I told myself and, extremely pleased, I did everything possible not to wake up. I got off the train and set off towards
the house, singing as I went. It was the early hours of the
morning and the streets were deserted. Suddenly I realized
that I had forgotten my suitcase in the compartment, the
gifts I had bought for you all, the diplomas and medals, and
I had to return to the station before the train left again for
Brighton. "It's a dream," I told myself again. "Imagine that
I've sent the baggage by mail. Let's not waste time. Worst
case scenario, the plot will thicken later." And I stop in front
of the house.'

Julia had to make an effort not to cut in. These things
happened to her too and she had never considered them the
least bit important. Since she was little she had been able to
control some of her dreams, to know suddenly in the middle
of the worst nightmare that she, and only she, was in absolute control of this magical series of images and that just by
deciding to, she could get rid of certain characters, summon
others, or speed up the pace of what was happening. It
wasn't always successful – for that she had to be conscious
of ownership over the dream – and, what's more, she didn't
find it especially fun. She preferred to let herself get involved
in the strange stories as if they were really happening and
she were simply the protagonist, but not the owner, of
those unpredictable adventures. One time her sister Marta,
despite her young age, told her something similar. 'Today
in my dream I was in charge,' she had said. And now she
suddenly remembered certain conversations on the subject
with her classmates and she even thought she had read something similar in the memoirs of a baroness or countess that
a friend had lent her. She lit the rumpled cigarette she was
still holding in her hand, inhaled a mouthful of smoke and
felt something rough and hot that burned her throat. When

she heard her own cough, she realized that the most absolute silence reigned in the room and that it must have already been a while since Carlos had stopped speaking and she had given herself up to stupid fantasies.

'Go on, please,' she said finally.

Carlos, after hesitating, proceeded:

'It was the house, the house where we are now, you and I, the house where we've spent all our summers since we were born. And yet there was something very strange about it. Something tremendously disagreeable and distressing that at first I couldn't put my finger on. Because it was exactly *this house,* except that by a strange gift or punishment I could see it from an unusual visual angle. I awoke sweating and shaken and tried to calm myself by remembering that it had only been a dream.'

Carlos covered his face with his hands and stifled a groan. His sister thought he mumbled an unnecessary 'until coming here' and she relived, with a sense of disappointment, the transformation she had witnessed days earlier at the garden gate. 'So that's what it was,' she was going to say, 'just that.' But she didn't say a word this time either. Carlos had gotten to his feet.

'It's an angle,' he continued. 'A strange angle which, for all the horror it evokes in me, is nonetheless real . . . And the worst part is there's no escape. I know that for the rest of my life I'll never be able to free myself from it.'

The final sobs made her look away towards the rooftop. Suddenly it made her uncomfortable to be there, not understanding much of what she was hearing, feeling definitely alarmed in the face of the breakdown of someone she had always believed to be so strong, healthy, and enviable. Maybe her parents were right and Carlos's problems couldn't be solved by kindness or by listening to his secrets. He needed a doctor. And her job was going to involve something as simple as getting out of that suffocating bedroom as soon as possible and joining in the rest of the family's worry. 'Well,' she said decisively, 'I had promised to bring Marta to the movies ...' But then she noticed that her facial expression belied her feigned calmness. In Carlos's sunglasses she saw her own face reflected twice. Two heads with disheveled hair and very frightened, wide-open eyes. That must be how he was seeing her: a girl caught in an ogre's den, inventing excuses to quietly leave the room, awaiting the moment she could cross the threshold, take a deep breath, and take off running downstairs. And now, moreover, Carlos, from the other side of the dark lenses, seemed to have become spellbound scrutinizing her, and she felt below those two heads with disheveled hair and frightened eyes two pairs of legs that were beginning to tremble too much for her to be able to go on talking about Marta or the movies, as if this were just an ordinary afternoon when Marta or the vague promise of taking her to the movies mattered. The shadow cast by a windblown sheet deprived her of the sight of her brother for a few moments. When the light returned again, Julia noticed that Carlos had approached even closer. He held the glasses in one hand; his eyelids were swollen and he had a delirious expression. 'It's amazing,' he said in a faint voice. 'You, Julia, I can still look at you.' And again that preference, that uniqueness that he accorded her for the second time that afternoon put an end to her intentions with an unbelievable speed. 'He's in love,' she said during dinner, and without appetite she ate a plate of tasteless vegetables that she forgot to salt and season.

It was not long before she realized she had acted stupidly. That night and those that followed the first visit to the attic. When she set herself up as go-between between her brother and the world, when she took charge of making his untouched plates disappear from his bedroom; when, like the loyal ally she had always been, she revealed to Carlos the doctor's diagnosis – acute depression – and the family's decision to hospitalize him in a rest home. But now it was too late to go back. Carlos received the news of his imminent hospitalization with a surprisingly relaxed attitude. He put on his sunglasses – those impenetrable glasses he only dared to remove in her presence – declared his desire to leave the attic, walked arm in arm with Julia through some of the rooms of the house, greeted the family, answered their questions with reassuring phrases. Yes, he was fine, much better, the worst was past now, there was no need for them to worry. He locked himself for several minutes in his parents' bathroom. Julia, through the door, heard the click-clack of the metal cabinet, the crackling of paper, the dripping of eau de cologne. When he emerged, she found him neat and well-groomed, and he seemed much more tranquil and serene. She accompanied him to his bedroom, helped him get into bed and went down to the dining room.

It was somewhat later when Julia suddenly felt frightened. She remembered the attic door's lock, torn off by her father several days ago, her mother's concern, the doctor's meaningful gesture as he declared himself powerless against the pains of the soul, the click-clack of the metal cabinet . . . A white, tidy cabinet in which it had never occurred to her to nose around, the medicine chest, her mother's pride, no one else could gather such a quantity of medicines for any situation in such a small space. She ascended the stairs two at a time, panting like a greyhound, terrified at the possibility of giving a name to what was unnameable. Arriving at the bedroom, she pushed open the door, opened the shutters and rushed to the bed. Carlos was sleeping peacefully, without his inseparable sunglasses, unmindful of anxieties and torments. Neither the torrents of sun from the rooftop filtering in through the window, nor Julia's efforts to wake him, got him to move a muscle. She surprised herself by wailing, yelling, leaning over the staircase and calling the names of the family. Afterwards everything happened unbelievably quickly. Carlos's breathing was becoming weak, almost imperceptible, his face recovered at moments the quiet and tranquil beauty of other times, his mouth sketched a beatific and peaceful half-smile. The evidence could now no longer be denied: Carlos was sleeping for the first time since he returned from Brighton, that second of September, the date she had colored red on her calendar.

She didn't have time to regret her stupid behavior, nor to wish with all her strength that time could turn backwards, that it could still be August and she would be sitting on the rooftop eaves beside a pile of notebooks awaiting the arrival of her brother. But she closed her eyes and tried to convince herself that she was still little, a girl who during the day played with dolls and collected stickers and who, sometimes, at night, suffered terrible nightmares. 'I am the master of the dream,' she told herself. 'It's only a dream.' But when she opened her eyes she didn't feel capable of going on with the deception. That terrible nightmare wasn't a dream, nor did she possess any power to rewind images, alter situations, or even make that handsome and peaceful face regain the anguish of illness. Again the shadow of a windblown sheet took possession of the room for some moments. Julia turned her gaze again toward her brother. For the first time in her life she understood what death was. Inexplicable, incomprehensible, hidden behind an appearance of feigned rest. She saw Death, its horror and destruction, its putrefaction and abyss. Because it was no longer Carlos who was lying in the bed, but Death, the great thief, crudely disguised in another's features, roaring with laughter between those red, swollen eyelids, revealing to all the deception of life, proclaiming her dark kingdom, her capricious will, her cruel and unshakeable designs. Julia rubbed her eyes and looked at her father. It was her father. That man seated at the head of the bed was her father. But there was something immensely disagreeable in his features. As if a skull had been made up with globs of wax, powdered and colored with theater makeup. A clown, she thought, a clown of the worst type . . . She grabbed her mother's arm, and a sudden repulsion forced her to move away. Why was her skin suddenly so pale, so slimy to the touch? She ran out to the rooftop and leaned on the balustrade.

'The angle,' she groaned. 'My God . . . I've discovered the angle!'

And it was then that she noticed Marta was beside her, with one of her dolls in her arms and a nibbled candy between her fingers. Marta went on being a lovely child. 'You, Marta,' she thought, 'I can still look at you.' And although the phrase struck her brain with another voice, with another intonation, with the memory of a loved one she would never again see alive, it was not that which jolted her the most, nor which made her cast herself on the ground and beat the tiles with her fists. She had seen Marta, Marta's expectant gaze, and in the depths of her dark eyes the sudden understanding that *something* was happening to Julia.

Translated from the Spanish by James D. Jenkins

Michael Roch

The Illogical Investigations of Inspector André Despérine

Supernatural sleuths and occult investigators might not be anything new in the horror genre, but we've never come across one quite like MICHAEL ROCH's *André Despérine. Posted to a remote region that no one, including he, has ever heard of, the incompetent and shamelessly opportunistic policeman Despérine somehow manages to find himself involved in one paranormal case after another. Roch (b. 1987), who lives in Martinique — a Caribbean island whose tropical forests and beautiful white sand beaches seem to make it an unlikely wellspring of horror fiction — primarily writes in the fields of science fiction and Afrofuturism, but fortunately for us also occasionally dabbles in horror. This trio of interlinked tales — you'll have to read all three to see how they fit together — first appeared in 2012 and marks the author's English-language debut.*

I.

ANDRÉ DESPÉRINE'S FIRST GLORY

AUTUMN HAD DESCENDED OVER VALDECÈZE like a heavy cloak falling on a pair of shoulders. It had smothered the small French *département* under a cover of gray clouds through which the sunlight barely filtered, rendering the houses of the town of Sacqueroy drab and lifeless. All week it had rained and the summer's heat was gone for good.

André Despérine was just out of the police academy and for a start his superiors had sent him to buy coffee and croissants at the bistro on the corner of rue Lesoule. He strode along the sidewalk with a certain awkwardness, three coffee cups squeezed between his fingers and a paper bag filled with pastries clenched between his teeth. He zigzagged between the puddles, walking with hurried little steps so that the coffee wouldn't get cold while at the same time making sure not to spill a single drop. He arrived very quickly at number 21 only to discover, after having traversed the small garden, that he was incapable of knocking on the door or ringing the bell.

'Bloody hell,' he murmured.

He hesitated a moment, staring at the threshold of the doorway with a perplexed expression, then kicked three times, leaving traces of mud on the red-painted wood. Inspector Hébiart opened the door instantly.

'You took your time, Despérine.'

Hébiart didn't help relieve him of the coffee cups or the bag of croissants. He returned directly to the living room, where he settled in, after a slight hesitation, in a mauve velvet armchair, beside Inspector Mélion and the chief inspector, M. Gontan, who were sitting on a spinach green sofa. They were all three questioning the woman who owned the house: a little old lady with curly hair who, hunched up on a wobbly stool, appeared ill at ease.

Cadet Inspector Despérine entered the room still taking small steps, placed the three cups and the croissants on the low table and went back to close the front door under the oppressive looks of his silent colleagues, who were waiting for him to stop bustling around so they could resume the course of their interrogation.

'All right, Mme Morille, where were we? You had indicated to us that you weren't in the vicinity of the Saint-Ange

School last Thursday at the time class was dismissed,' Gontan said. 'You claim to have an alibi for the kidnapping of young Théo Juvignan, seven years old.'

The old woman hiccuped. With her left hand brought up to her neck, she fiddled with a heavy-knit red wool scarf. Her other hand was rumpling her dress at knee-level, the fabric riding up as she clutched at it, allowing a glimpse of her bare ankles above small slippers.

'I was at the park.'

'Montcalm Park?'

'The one downtown, yes. With those truly lovely tall trees.'

'What do they matter?' Gontan interrupted.

He jotted some lines in his notebook before shaking his thick moustache with an adroit movement of his nose, as he was in the habit of doing whenever he wasn't convinced.

'And what were you doing at Montcalm?'

'I was picking some herbs: among the trees I find plants to use in my infusions.'

Gontan took a deep breath. To his right, Mélion was staring at Mme Morille without moving a muscle. Hébiart was lost in contemplation of a stuffed owl sitting proudly atop a pedestal table.

'Does that have to do with your . . . professional activities?' Gontan went on.

'As a healer, I often advise my clients to drink infusions of medicinal plants . . .'

'Which you pick under the plane trees in Montcalm Park.'

The chief inspector made an imperceptible movement of his eyelids: he didn't believe in this charlatanry. He tucked his notebook into the inner pocket of his raincoat and stood up abruptly.

'Well! I think we're finished with you for the moment.'

'And the coffee?' said Mélion, astonished all of a sudden.

'Shit, yes: the coffee.'

Gontan sat down again, pulled a cup towards him, took a croissant from the sack and dipped the end twice in the hot beverage. He cast a quick glance at his cadet inspector, standing ramrod straight in a corner of the living room.

'Hey, Despérine, don't just stand there. Sit down!'

André Despérine looked all around him; there were no more chairs available and it would have been rude in his view to squeeze in on the sofa between his two superiors. With a timid smile, old Mme Morille pointed to a little stuffed cushion pushed against the wall. He sat down and found himself with his chin in his knees, but kept his arms crossed as he watched the others eat their breakfast. While they were stuffing down their first mouthfuls, the healer of Sacqueroy stood up, suddenly looking down at them from above, her eyes half closed and her face solemn.

'Eat well, for you too shall be eaten! All of you here, it is your destiny.'

She prophesied these words with an otherworldly voice that was not her own. Gontan, nonplussed, stopped chewing mid-bite; Hébiart, almost choking, swallowed his coffee with difficulty, and Mme Morille, once more taking on a lucid expression, resumed the submissive and hunched posture she had displayed a few seconds earlier. Mélion put down his cup with a calculated slowness, then addressed a nod to the chief inspector. The latter hesitated.

'Well, well, well ... We have to question some other suspects. Meanwhile, I would ask you to please stay here in your lovely home.'

The officers got up and made their way back to the threshold. Mme Morille remained alone at the low living-room table, apparently overwhelmed by events. André Despérine was preparing to cross the doorstep when Gontan pushed him back inside. The chief inspector addressed him in the patronizing tone he used with all new recruits while he looked disdainfully at the enormous beige raincoat Despérine was floating in.

'No, not you. *You* stay here. I have serious doubts about that loony there' – Gontan twitched his moustache – 'so you stay. You're not coming.'

André Despérine leaned forward slightly and ended by catching his superior's glance in his. Gontan then summarized the gist of his instructions.

'You stay here to watch her, but if you have a moment this afternoon – yes, it's already past noon – you'll take the coffee cups back to the corner bistro.'

Believing the chief inspector was finished with him, Despérine went to close the door, but Gontan stopped him again.

'Oh! And one question, Cadet Despérine: do you know what the advantage of living in Sacqueroy is?'

The young inspector, still wet between the ears, didn't know what to answer.

'Valdecèze is the smallest *département* in France; so small that it contains only one town, three hamlets, and some cows. This isn't Paris: here, everything gets found out quickly. The incompetent are fired very quickly, just as the best are very quickly rewarded. So I say this to you frankly: don't get smart with us, and do your share of the work. Can you manage that?'

André Despérine nodded three times in agreement. Gontan's moustache twitched excitedly under his swollen nostrils, then the old fellow went off to join his subordinates on the other side of the street, where they awaited him in a police car. After the door had closed, Despérine was startled at feeling Mme Morille's hand slip into his. She had gotten up from her little stool without his noticing it and was now huddled close to him, pressing her chest firmly, but with a certain gentleness, against the cadet inspector's back.

'You're staying?'

Despérine moved away brusquely, nearly knocking a picture frame off the wall.

'I'm staying, on the chief inspector's orders.' *Good God, what is she doing?*

'You have a hunch?'

Mme Morille caressed his palm. *Good heavens . . .*

'You take me for the person who kidnapped little Théo? I didn't do it, but there is a lot of nasty gossip. I know the town considers me a witch: I treat, I cure, I heal . . . Sometimes I make predictions with my tarot cards and read palms. But people don't like that. They are quick to blame me for their misfortunes. You have a feeling about me?'

'No!' exclaimed Despérine.

Mme Morille had kept the young inspector's hand in hers and had again trapped him against the wall. He was unable to get loose except by resorting to violence against her. The little old woman mumbled, her nose in the neck of his overly large raincoat.

'I have a feeling about you.'

'About what you said a minute ago?'

'About the infusions?'

'No, about the . . .'

The inspector stammered. Mme Morille looked at him with a diffident expression, with eyes that hadn't grasped the meaning of his question. Her head full of white hair swayed from left to right.

'What did I say a minute ago?'

'That doesn't matter. What feeling did you have about me?'

'You are a good person. That is why you stayed. It's after the bustle of work, when you are alone, that you think the best and you succeed.'

'Where are you going with this?'

'I feel your heart as though I was holding it still warm between my hands.'

André Despérine wanted to flee the premises at top speed, but his legs didn't respond. *Good God, what is she saying?*

'What are you saying?'

'I sense your goodness and the innocence you keep deep inside you. I would love to help you in your search! But for that, you would first have to grant me that favor.'

The inspector stammered before the absurdity of the situation: grant Mme Morille the favor of assisting in the investigation? Despérine shrugged his shoulders, scratched the back of his head, tapped the tip of his shoe on the wood floor and finally pulled his hand away from the woman's.

'Yes, yes, I tell you yes! Help me?'

'Then come! Follow me!'

When she invited him to follow her, she pushed him through the living room to the kitchen. There was a little wooden door painted in a hideous manner, white with sky-blue trim, squeezed between the stove and the refrigerator. Mme Morille hung her aprons from it.

André Despérine was forced to open this little door in order not to be crushed by the healing woman's shoves. The panel opened onto a narrow stairway that led down into the darkness. The inspector hurtled down the several steps faster than he would have expected; he no longer felt Mme Morille's palms on his back. She had remained upstairs and for a second he thought he saw her eyes penetrating the backlit silhouette.

'Wait,' she said. 'I'll turn on the light!'

The yellow glare of a bare bulb illuminated the little cellar, done up as a reception area for Mme Morille's 'business'. A round table covered in a checkered cloth was framed by four varnished wood chairs. The cellar walls must not have been well kept – you could smell an odor of mustiness and dust – for they were entirely covered by dark-colored curtains. In one corner, on a console table, languished a voice recorder and underneath, an empty cat basket.

'He left without warning,' explained Mme Morille with a stab of sadness in her throat. 'Poupi never came back.'

She had taken hold of the inspector's left hand again. He was pulled towards the table and sat down, happy to be at a comfortable height. Mme Morille leaned towards him, her white curls falling over her face. She had a wide smile, like a little girl excited at the idea of going into a doll store.

'I have a wondrous power!'

Despérine smiled to hide his unease.

'Really?'

'I can bring Théo back, make him reappear here. Just like that, investigation over! But it is dangerous, you must not move.'

André Despérine had a hard time understanding what the healer's game was, but his mother had always advised him never to stop someone carried away by their own momentum. He let her proceed. From a camouflaged drawer under the tablecloth she took out a candle stuck into a bronze holder. She lit the candle and placed it in the center of the table. Then she took the inspector's hand once more and with a gesture of her index finger asked him to give her his other palm as well. He gave it to her a little reluctantly.

Entirely caught in the witch's trap, André Despérine thus attended a spiritualistic séance for the first time in his life. Mme Morille intoned a psalmody barely whispered between her teeth. The young man seemed to recognize the words, but he couldn't have said what they were – an indigenous language perhaps, smooth and flowing, but strangely incisive. The arcane chant lasted several minutes, which passed very quickly for the bewitched Despérine. The healer softened the sound of her voice, her lips still moved, but the esoteric phrases became inaudible.

Without forewarning, Mme Morille's grip on Despérine's palms tightened again at the same time as the artificial light from the ceiling flickered. The inspector stifled a little cry of surprise. The old woman held him too tightly for him to get free. Little by little the light dimmed; it became subdued without Despérine's being able to identify the cause. He knew he was toppling into a world outside his control when he felt a slight draft of air at the nape of his neck.

Despérine raised his eyes towards the staircase and the door leading to the kitchen. It was closed. The curtains moved imperceptibly and a dark emptiness settled in around them. There was only the light of the candle to illuminate the room when Mme Morille gave an enormous start.

This time, the cadet inspector really cried out. *Good God!* The seer didn't seem to notice, plunged in her trance, her lips animated by a faint monody, her closed eyes suddenly rolling upwards, wide open. Despérine wanted to let himself slide down underneath his chair, but a superhuman force holding his arms kept him at the table. He kept his eyes wide open, seized with a great terror. He thought he would vomit when the ghostly faces began to appear, a thousand decapitated heads turning around them faster and faster, they too monotonously reciting an unknown poem.

Then, in the center of the tornado, above the flame from the candlestick, a complete silhouette formed. Smoke spread out from the candle like incense, the hazy outlines of a child's body materialized before the inspector. Mme Morille was still in a mystical ecstasy, disembodied or possessed. The force she was exerting on the young man was almost enough to break his bones, but the pain was so deafening Despérine felt incapable of crying out; it climbed up his arms all the way to his ears, squeezing his cranium like a gigantic vise.

André Despertine witnessed, powerless, the inexplicable apparition of little Théo, who, judging from his green tint, seemed terrified at having materialized floating in the center of a spectral whirlwind. He was suspended with his arms folded and, starting to shout, he drowned out the deafening silence that filled the cellar. From the other side of the round table, Mme Morille was suddenly racked with convulsions. She shook her head in every direction with movements so sudden that André Despérine expected to see her neck break. But the witch opened her mouth wide, a thick and viscous drool at the corners of her lips.

'You will be eaten! Eaten, Despérine! Eaten!'

She threw herself at him, her hands reaching out for his throat, but he was faster than her and dropped to the ground. Getting back up, he grabbed the bronze candlestick, which had rolled away, and before the witch could pick herself up, he smashed her curly-haired skull repeatedly, spreading a bloody mush on the checkered tablecloth. The tempest of poltergeists ceased immediately, and when his fit of madness had subsided, Despérine was speechless, almost forgetting the young boy who was curled up at his feet on the stone floor.

The door at the top of the stairs flew open, and Mélion and Hébiart, preceded by Chief Inspector Gontan, rushed into the basement. The kitchen lights were on; night must have fallen.

'Good heavens, what's going on here?' Gontan shouted.

He jumped the few remaining steps and rushed towards the cadet inspector and the young boy.

'Explain yourself, Despérine!'

In his superior's eye, instead of the black pupil, André Despérine perceived the reflection of a glorious medal of honor. The best are very quickly rewarded, Gontan had said. Despérine weighed carefully each word he said then.

'I simply heard a noise, little Théo was in the cellar, Mme Morille tried to intervene, it was self-defense,' he said.

II.

ANDRE DESPERINE VS. THE CATS

Valdecèze was without a doubt the smallest of France's *départements*; so small that very few people could pinpoint it on a map. André Despérine himself was ignorant of its existence until he was appointed to the post of cadet inspector in the little town of Sacqueroy.

Located several kilometers to the north of Dijon, the territory of Valdecèze included, besides Sacqueroy, three hamlets, a little more than five thousand inhabitants and several hundred cows; an eighteen-wheeler could cross it in less than an hour, it was devoid of tourism. The population lived there secluded, piled on top of one other in the vicinity of Sacqueroy. The outrageous proximity of the residents – Despérine had noticed – encouraged a climate of constant criminality. That didn't bother the inspector he had become, since it was his job to arrest the murderers and rapists.

Yet André Despérine was astonished by the supernatural turn taken by the investigations in which he participated. Sometimes he didn't understand any of it – paranormal phenomena quite simply surpassed his comprehension, although he wondered whether he wouldn't do better to think up some reasons for being scared. Despérine wasn't scared, his mother had taught him to hold onto his courage with both hands and clench it like a little bird ready to fly away. And it was no doubt his sangfroid, he remembered, which had won him his first medal: he had found little Théo Juvignan locked up in a madwoman's cellar.

A lot of water had flowed under the bridge since that day. He had ascended in rank, but he wasn't more respected by his colleagues. Mélion and Hébiart relied on their years of experience to assign to Despérine as many futile, idiotic, or ridiculous activities as possible. Chasing down coffee in the morning, taming the copy machines, or giving his cheek-bones a workout at the victims' reception desk were his daily lot. Inspector André Despérine held out hope, however, for the situation had every chance of changing very soon: the number of medals of honor hanging above his desk grew each month.

It was however on an order from Mélion that André Despérine had found himself on the picket line at three a.m., a few meters from the hamlet of Branolin – which consisted of only two houses and a small shed at the bend in a wooded path. On a stakeout in the underbrush, the inspector had the impression of being frozen from head to toe. Several days earlier he had finally managed to have his overly large rain-coat changed for another one exactly his size. But this new raincoat didn't allow him to wear a thick sweater as a liner; in the end, Despérine regretted his recent acquisition. He was cold.

The inspector was standing against a tree, shivering slightly in the dark and under the watchful eyes of – he thought – an owl; he had heard it moving among the tree's branches, but he hadn't been able to see it, for it was a moon-less night. Despérine was cold and would have liked to pour himself a cup of the coffee he was keeping warm in a ther-mos, but Mélion and Hébiart were supposed to arrive in a few seconds and wouldn't have liked him to drink without them.

Indeed it was when this idea dissipated that the police car arrived noiselessly on the outskirts of the hamlet. Hébiart had let the car glide in neutral the last fifty meters, controlling the speed with only the brake. They stopped with precision under the trees; Mélion got out first and came to greet Despérine.

For three days now Mélion had been the new chief inspector of the Sacqueroy police department: Inspector Gontan had taken a leave of absence to take part in an African safari and hadn't returned. Shaking his colleague's hand, André Despérine hesitated whether to present a face distorted by sadness or a complaisant smile congratulating Mélion on his new promotion. The grimace he sketched left his new superior unmoved.

'It's awful . . . That animal must have been a hell of a beast to drag down M. Gontan by its teeth.'

'You always have to beware of felines,' Mélion had responded.

Despérine offered him the thermos of coffee and while he was greeting Hébiart, Mélion drank the first cup, then passed it on.

'All right! Gentlemen, this will be a delicate operation, I fear. Our gang of burglars is definitely using this hamlet to move jewels and bundles of counterfeit bills between Dijon and Sacqueroy. We don't know if the place is guarded, but we'll surely be able to seize some of the goods.'

Mélion pulled a sheet of paper rolled in a rubber band from the inside pocket of his raincoat. He handed it to Hébiart without looking at him; Mélion was staring strangely at the hamlet, as if he had been hypnotized by the three buildings of wood and stone.

'The warrant, Hébiart! The warrant! Keep it safe!'

Then the chief inspector set forth at a determined pace towards the village. Despérine and Hébiart followed him hesitantly, fearing to be noticed by its occupants. Both had the feeling they were being watched. In the heavy silence only the sound of their shoes on the gravel road marked the rhythm of their progress, and Despérine wished the owl would hoot once or twice. But nothing happened until they were all in the courtyard of the first house. Mélion opened the door by turning a brass handle in the shape of a cat's head; it wasn't bolted and that didn't bode well.

The dwelling was empty: no furniture, a tapestry in shreds, some spiders weaving their webs and, on the ground, scattered rat droppings. Mélion pulled out his firearm from under his armpit, then took out a flashlight, which he lit.

'Let's take a look around. We'll see what we find.'

They surveyed the different rooms of the house with an exaggerated slowness. Despérine hadn't had time to taste the coffee, but the slight tension hovering around them was warming him up little by little.

'Monsieur Mélion,' he murmured, 'there's nothing here. Let's try the other house!'

'Shush!'

Mélion raised his arm. With the beam of the flashlight he indicated a door which, half open, led to the bathroom.

'Hébiart, go look in there!'

Inspector Hébiart slowly approached the panel, which he pushed with his fingertips. The bathroom had been deboned of its sink and bathtub. There was nothing on the walls but several cracked white ceramic tiles. Yet he took a step back.

'That stinks! Damn, that really reeks!'

'Go in!' Mélion ordered, illuminating the small room.

'It's like a corpse decomposed in here. Light up the ceiling for me, there's a trap door!'

Hébiart leaned against a wall and, leaping, caught the handle of the trap door. The flap broke under his weight, the slab of rotten wood came crashing down, the odor of death was suddenly unbearable and a cat, very much alive, fell onto the inspector's face. In the flashlight beam, Mélion and Despérine saw the animal slash Inspector Hébiart's cheeks.

The latter tried to get out of the ambush, but found himself huddled on the floor, in a corner of the little bathroom. The cat hissed, leapt, and yowled all around him. It ended by flinging itself on Hébiart, planting its claws in his scalp.

Hébiart's cry was a howl of pain.

'He ate my ear!'

The cat made a quick getaway between Mélion's legs. Hébiart made a move to catch it, it or his ear, but finally remained hunched over, one bloody hand stuck to his temple.

'He ate my ear, fuck!'

'Let's get out of here!' Mélion ordered.

The chief inspector took a step forward to lift him by his armpit. Helped by Despérine, he dragged him five meters to what used to be the living room. In their haste, the flashlight slipped out of Mélion's hands and rolled across the dusty floor. In front of them, barring access to the front door, and all around them, about twenty cats observed them in silence. Mélion lifted his subordinate up and they all unholstered their revolvers. In the semi-darkness, Hébiart thought he recognized the ear-ripper and fired. The bullet missed its target, but, alerted by the detonation, all the cats swooped in on the inspectors like a single wave crashing on a reef.

It was a stampede. Mélion dived to the floor to recover the flashlight and got up whipping the empty air with his arms. Despérine was using his legs, kicking the felines like footballs as soon as one got too close and avoiding those that leapt at him by making little sidesteps. In a fleeting movement of the flashlight beam he thought he saw Hébiart with three cats at his throat. Mélion was two steps from him, worked up like a devil, beating his arms like a baby bird jumping from its nest. With a clumsy gesture, the chief inspector hit Hébiart's head with his flashlight. The light went out in a sound of broken glass. Despérine considered the situation a lost cause and jumped through the first window opening he saw. He found himself face down on a lawn damp with the night's coolness.

André Despérine crawled on all fours for several meters and as quickly as possible, with the sole desire of escaping that army of cats. He found refuge in the barn on the other side of the little lawn and hid behind an old tractor that stank of diesel, incapable of thinking up a plan for getting out of this trouble. He had dropped his gun on the grass. For several minutes he heard only Hébiart's inhuman cries. And then silence fell once more with the dull stamping of a thousand paws disappearing into the night. Despérine took a deep breath. He swore inwardly, his heart wouldn't stop pounding. And Mélion called him.

'Despérine, where are you?'

'In the barn!'

'Don't move!'

The stamping of feet resumed: a horde was moving in the dark around the barn. Mélion was walking in the middle of it.

'Poor fool! You still don't understand?'

Despérine frowned. No, he didn't understand. He didn't understand what the new chief inspector meant.

'Understand what, Mélion?'

'I'm going to kill you, Despérine! Like I killed Gontan, like I killed Hébiart. It's your turn!'

The gate to the shed turned heavily on its hinges. André Despérine discerned Mélion's silhouette in the center of the opening and those of the cats, who, furtively, made their way into the wooden building.

'Good heavens! Are you joking? Gontan died in Africa!'

Despérine was looking for a way to flee, his fingers inadvertently touched the sharp edge of a harrow positioned at the front of the farm vehicle.

'I was the lion!' retorted Inspector Mélion. 'These cats are mine! You must always beware of felines, I told you. There can be only one inspector in Sacqueroy and you're the last obstacle to my success. You understand?'

'That's ridiculous.'

'You're the ridiculous one, Despérine! Since your arrival in Valdecèze, there's never been anyone more incompetent and opportunistic than you!'

Mélion advanced slowly and Despérine felt like he was being squeezed in a vise; he sensed the cats' breath at the nape of his neck. He had to react fast and decided to charge full speed ahead. He ran straight forward, ignoring the assaults of the cats that scratched and bit him, and collided head-on with Mélion. He would have liked to knock him backwards – he would have had a small chance of being the first one out of the barn – but the chief inspector was steady on his legs and he absorbed the shock with a disconcerting ease. He sent Despérine sprawling to the floor, throwing him to the back of the nearest nook shrouded in darkness, by the wooden gate.

'Quit crawling, Despérine. I see you with my cat eyes. You can't escape.'

Mélion approached again, the felines marching at his heels. Despérine tried again to knock his superior down. The leap was so sudden that it surprised Mélion. The chief inspector stumbled backward over one of the cats. Off balance, he took several recoiling steps and ended by falling heavily on the tractor harrow. It perforated his pelvis straight through.

Surprised at his own action, Inspector André Despérine almost forgot the oppressive presence of the cats. But seeing Mélion on the ground, they turned towards him and rushed forward to devour him.

Despérine left the premises as quickly as he could. It was only when he had returned to the wheel of the police car that he vomited the contents of his stomach on the passenger seat. The Branolin hamlet operation had gone terribly wrong, bringing about the deaths of his two colleagues. But, for the first time in his life, André Despérine found himself in sole command, chief inspector of the Sacqueroy police department.

III.

ANDRÉ DESPÉRINE'S FINAL INVESTIGATION

Police inspector André Despérine was a forewarned man. A witch had predicted his death, he had seen his superiors die, but he had always managed to thwart the Grim Reaper's plans. And because forewarned is forearmed, Despérine took his work very much to heart. From arrest to arrest and from medal to medal, he had ended by finding himself, on this autumn afternoon, holding a simple scrap of a torn blouse in his right hand. It was here, under this tree, on the edge of Montcalm Park, that everything had finished for the girl, and it was here that Despérine's investigation had begun. A murky affair like hundreds of others he had been through.

Despite being exactly the right person for the case, Despérine felt there was nothing he could do. His legendary logic was stalled. The kidnapping – if it had been one – had been perfectly orchestrated. No sign of struggle, no tracks, no blood . . . Nothing. Thus no clue, no lead. Only a pointless bit of cloth from one of the victim's garments. Poor girl. She had been seen for the last time three days ago in front of this beech tree. It was the last place she had known, her final destination, here, under these branches, before disappearing. *Bloody hell.*

The past two days, the victim's relatives had become more and more insistent. Nay, demanding. They had realized that in the small county of Valdecèze the only lawful authority who could find their daughter was Chief Inspector Despérine. That, no doubt, is why they got it into their heads to harass him with telephone calls and visits to the police station. *No, we're not making any progress, ma'am. Yes, we're doing our best, sir.* Tears and protests, or even outrage, seemed to be the common character trait of every member of that family. At first sympathetic, Despérine had quickly found himself experiencing pity, then indifference for those people. *No, ma'am. Yes, sir.* Could one of them have been behind it all? Was one of them the abductor of young Catherine? If that was the case, it had been perfect acting. Or maybe they were all the killers. But why would they have killed her? What was the motive? Despérine found no logic in it. His brain was empty.

No idea of what could have happened wanted to take root in his mind. So he had no explanation and thus would have no tolerance for the killer. Just as the family would have none for him if he failed. He felt truly disarmed facing this investigation and facing the others' looks. However, he persisted in just standing there, even if all his subordinates had left again after yet another day of investigation. He felt obligated, liable for some moral debt. He had to stay longer and take time to reflect. Around the tree there remained only some yellow plastic banners: DO NOT CROSS. It was forbidden to the public to go any further, but of course he, Chief Inspector of the Sacqueroy police department, could do it. And Despérine wanted to cross the barrier. He had to know, to discover the truth. He felt that the secret wasn't far. Not very far from this tree. This beech. Alone among all the plane trees in the park.

The inspector walked around the tree. The scrap of blouse had been found stuck between two pieces of bark. *Here, precisely.* He put the tip of his index finger in the hollow of the vertical crease. A grim story. And the family shouting their heads off and his colleagues who were starting to think that yes, *You'd be better off retiring*. What a fucking story.

The sharp clap of a gate was heard. Despérine turned around. About twenty meters downhill, a little old man had come out of his cabin. Despérine knew him, he was the only witness. Anyway, the last one to have seen the victim.

'Your Catherine used to come this way to relax, read, or draw little sketches,' he had squeaked, stretching his time-worn fingers towards the large beech. 'The tree's roots were her favorite place, I guess.' At the presumed moment of the tragedy, M. Beauligneux was gossiping with a neighbor woman, exchanging fruits and vegetables from his garden behind the little hovel. His alibi had been verified. He wasn't the culprit.

The old man mumbled some inaudible words into his reddish beard and sat down on a rocking chair. He began to rock, making the chair crack like an old stump and looking at the inspector, his eyes round like marbles and surrounded by wrinkles. Despérine gave him a wave, which the octo-genarian didn't return. He simply took out a pipe, lit the bowl, then rubbed his thighs with one hand, like someone patiently waiting for his dinner.

The sun was setting. Night was coming and Despérine's stomach was already growling. It was dinner time, but this business – bloody hell! – couldn't go on any longer. He had to resolve it.

A squawking surprised Despérine in the midst of his worries. He raised his head. Perched on a little branch, a baby bird sang in an imaginary language. The man smiled at it. It was true that this place breathed the beauty of perfect nature. Catherine was quite right to come here and reflect. The grass under his feet seemed soft and welcoming and the gnarled tree roots offered a natural armchair. *Sit on my lap*, thought

Despérine, with a honeyed voice that wasn't his. There was also that business about the pedophile that he'd have to finish later. Another fucking story. He chased the vision from his brain.

Emptying his mind. In fact, that was what really mattered at the current moment. The inspector breathed deeply and surprised himself when he encircled the tree with his long arms. They went almost all the way around the trunk. He thought he had lost that kind of childish impulse long ago. Nose against bark, Despérine sniffed the beech, which gave off a sugary smell, with a little peppery aftertaste. Exquisite. A spicy candy. Gingerbread and a playground. *Good God, what's happening to me?* Despérine relaxed his embrace and ran a hand over his face, letting go at the same moment of the torn fabric that had suddenly become too heavy. He was fine! There. He sat down with his back against the trunk and smiled at the breeze that had risen. Transformed into a chill, it ran down his spine like a shiver as brief as a little laugh. The beech stretched its branches above him. Despérine observed them – had they moved? They had grown slightly and pro-tected Despérine from an ever darker sky. He closed his eyes and he heard. The tree vibrated to the rhythm of a heart of sap. The inspector breathed deeply. *It's in your head.* When he opened his eyes again, several branches had added themselves to the others. And other birds had come to complete the first one's warbling. A fantastic idea awoke in him, of a marve-lous creature of which he could perceive only a vague shape, a fuzzy outline behind opaque glass. Despérine rose calmly. He felt deep down that he had nothing to fear. Something told him to let himself be guided by his senses. His surprised smile grew, and he caressed the tree's bark. The beech crack-led slightly with pleasure, a renewed sensation. If the tree had a secret, it would give it to him.

The sweetened scent of this miraculous plant suddenly

overwhelmed Despérine's bronchial tubes. He grew a little dizzy, staggered, caught himself on a branch that was offering him a hand. Its colleagues had now bent down to the ground, and the light of the setting sun filtered through their leaves. They danced, carried away in a fairy dance, addressing joyous giggles to their guest. In its autumnal shell, Despérine found once more the sensations of a forgotten maternal womb. A thousand and one birds, blackbirds, jays, or robins, flew whirling around him. Their thousand and one colors, autumnal orange, poppy red, or tulip yellow, sparkled in a luminous concert. *How beautiful it is!* Caresses of wings on Despérine's outstretched arms, kisses of beaks on his cheeks, and branches with a divine feminine sensuality filled him with happiness. *God how good it is!* Despérine was already laughing softly under the overpowering aromas, carried away by the flight of the birds; he kept his balance on the lowest branches. His hands came to meet the bark which twisted, crackled, reached out towards his touches. *My tree!* It was a secret that couldn't be betrayed, nor even shared. It was his alone now! Euphoria. Transcendent joy. Despérine wanted to take it once more in his arms, but the trunk split in two to unveil an inhuman abyss.

The scent in his nostrils became atrociously delicious and the inspector, anesthetized, broke out in a great fit of laughter. The broken bark evoked a myriad of compact wooden teeth, an enormous mouth opened below him whose perfumed breath enthralled his spirit. You couldn't see the bottom of it. Despérine couldn't see its hunger. *My tree . . .* The inspector leaned over to give it a deep kiss, at the height of his pleasure. Unknowingly he put his foot in that wolf trap, and the wooden mouth began a slow and determined chewing, closing a first time. Then a second. The beech crushed his feet little by little, going up the length of his legs. Tears of joy flowed down Despérine's cheeks, his thundering laughter became painful. He still saw those reddish colors like a young girl's cheeks. He still felt those brief and inexperienced caresses. And that rare and delicate fragrance, better than a garden of jasmine and roses. Despérine couldn't help touching, caressing the body within his grasp; or was it the branches which held him by the hands? The beech's teeth reached his rib cage, which cracked as it pierced his flesh and the torrent of hemoglobin flowed well beyond the bowels of the earth. But that smell *of God!* easily overcame that of fresh blood. Laughter changed suddenly into a cry of madness, just before Despérine's reddened head disappeared between the wooden teeth, exploding like the final burst of a fireworks show.

Twenty meters away, in front of the hut on the edge of the park, the little old man was still seated on his chair. He massaged his stomach, looking full. The beech had resumed its initial position; there remained only a piece of shirt, stuck between two sections of bark.

Translated from the French by James D. Jenkins

Tanya Tynjälä

The Collector

Peru does not seem to produce a great deal of horror literature. Indeed, in his recent book on 20th-century horror fiction, Jess Nevins identifies only two Peruvian writers, both of them rather obscure, and we were unable to locate others. TANYA TYNJÄLÄ (*b.* 1963), *whose works include novels, short stories, and works for young readers, describes herself as a writer of fantasy and science fiction, but the following story seemed to us a perfect fit for a volume of unsettling tales. 'The Collector' — the original Spanish title, 'La coleccionista', makes it clear that the titular character is a woman — is a creepy modern-day updating of the Calypso myth from Greek mythology. First published in 2017 in the author's collection* (Ir)Realidades, *it was recently selected for inclusion in an anthology of the best speculative fiction by women writers from Latin America and Spain, and we're pleased to be able to make it available to English-speaking readers as well.*

JULIAN HEADED HURRIEDLY TO HIS DATE. Two months ago he had met the most beautiful woman in the world. All his friends would have envied his luck, were it not for the fact that he couldn't tell anyone about his relationship. That was one of the many conditions that Diana imposed. Another was that she refused to spend the night with him. She never explained why, but he assumed she had strong religious convictions.

Thus Julian hadn't yet enjoyed intimate relations with the young woman. But he didn't care much about that. She was so beautiful that he felt satisfied just looking at her, and what's more they got along perfectly, they liked the same music, the same writers, the same films. It had in fact been this that had recently made him start to question the relationship. How much longer would such a 'perfect' relationship survive? Sometimes it's so boring to agree on absolutely everything. Not that he wanted a stormy relationship, he'd had those in the past and knew that they were destructive in the end. He enjoyed the peace he felt with Diana, but a little jealous scene every so often might have spiced things up a little.

As if she sensed what he was thinking, Diana decided all of a sudden to agree to spend an entire weekend with him. In light of her proposal, Julian resolved to put aside his doubts for now. Mysterious like always, she asked him to pick her up at a roadside café. From there they would go to a place she knew well and which she was sure he would love.

Since he met her, Diana had seemed more than mysterious; secretive would be the right word. He didn't even know for certain what kind of work she did. She had told him she was a professional collector and that the nature of her activity required the utmost discretion. Discarding the possibility that such a sweet and intelligent woman could be involved in any illicit business, Julian came to the conclusion that Diana bought pieces of various kinds at auctions for millionaires who didn't want their identities known. And that explanation left him satisfied. Why think any more about it?

Julian arrived at the appointed place half an hour before their scheduled rendezvous. The café was logically located next to a gas station that was more than dilapidated. There were two old men there working as attendants; Julian wondered how much longer they could go on working. They looked tired, decrepit.

He stopped the car and asked them to fill up the tank. One

of the old men looked at him with amusement and started laughing like a madman. Shaking his head, he entered the disorderly room that served as their office. The other man slowly approached.

'Don't mind him, he has a screw loose from being here so long.'

'Well . . . he was a little rude, wasn't he?'

The old man began filling the tank without saying anything. He seemed to be on the lookout for something; he cast fearful, sneaking glances at the café. He gave Julian the impression of someone who is being watched.

'Do many people come this way?'

'Those come who have to come. If you don't have a date, it's not worth the trouble of coming all the way here. That's what brought me, and here I've stayed.'

The coincidence of talking about a 'date' seemed more than strange to Julian. But he said nothing, only smiled.

'How much do I owe you?' he asked when the old man finished his work.

'You'll pay later, on the way out. Because I'm sure you're going in the café, right?'

Julian couldn't help feeling uncomfortable with what the old man was saying. First the reference to the date, then to the café. It was as if he knew exactly what Julian was going to do. It could be just a coincidence; in the end, if the place Diana had spoken to him about was nearby, surely many couples passed by the gas station on the way to their destination. On the other hand, the journey from the city to that place was long, so it was perfectly natural after so much traveling to decide to have a coffee at the only available place in sight. However, deep down Julian felt a certain unease that signaled to him that something wasn't right.

'Take this, I've written down how much you owe. Don't forget to check it before you go in, please,' he said, taking

Julian's hand desperately and looking around in all directions.

Julian pulled his hand back nervously. The other old man came out of the office and shouted between laughs:

'Don't forget to try the pie!'

The man who was attending to Julian looked wild-eyed at his companion as he shook his head no.

Julian could barely stop himself from running towards the café. He didn't want to spend any more time with those old men, who were obviously disturbed. As he walked away, he could hear them both discussing in whispers.

Once inside the café he was surprised to see that the place contrasted with the condition of the gas station. Everything was immaculately clean and tidy. There were several men there of different ages, all of them looking as if they were spending a weekend in the country: hand luggage, comfortable clothing. Apparently the place Diana had spoken to him about was very popular. He sat down at the counter.

'What can I get you?' The woman waiting on him was middle-aged, neither pretty nor ugly, quite friendly and neat.

'Just a coffee, please.'

'Are you sure you don't want to try my apple pie? I make it myself every morning. It's very popular.'

'So it seems. At the gas station they recommended that I try it.'

'That's right, everybody here likes my pie.'

'But no, thanks. I'm not very hungry, maybe another time. I'll be in the area all weekend.'

The woman served him the coffee and retired with a smile.

Julian looked at his watch. There were still several minutes left until the agreed-upon time. He took a sip of the coffee, which turned out to be quite good and fresh. He looked around. He noticed that all the customers were men. It struck him as odd. Suddenly he realized he hadn't seen any cars parked outside and he wondered if these might be locals? But they all had hand luggage . . .

The woman approached him with a slice of pie.

'On the house. Don't turn me down – look, I've only given you a little, you won't regret it.'

Julian thought she must be one of those women who feel proud of the one thing they're good at and insist that everyone try it. Out of politeness, he took a mouthful. The pie melted in his mouth, it had just the perfect amount of sugar. They say that even the most insignificant small town has its hidden gems, and this one's was the gas station's pie.

'It's really delicious!'

'I told you, it'll make you forget your cares, you'll see.'

Julian took another greedy mouthful. Suddenly he noticed there was no one in the kitchen.

'You don't have a cook?'

'I don't need one. I prepare everything very early, before opening.'

'Then I congratulate you, the coffee is more than fresh, the pie is a delicacy . . .'

'Thank you very much,' she said, smiling again.

He continued eating that magnificent pie. He looked at his watch. Diana would arrive at any moment. He wanted to ask for the check, but the woman wasn't there, she'd probably gone into the kitchen. He took out his wallet and opened the paper the old man had given him to see how much he had to pay. There wasn't a single number on it, only scrawled in nervous handwriting: 'Whatever you do, leave this place. And don't eat the pie.'

Julian froze. He looked around. All men, all with hand luggage, like someone going away for a weekend, and all of them eating the same pie as him. He eavesdropped on their conversations: they were all talking about the magnificent woman they had met. The descriptions varied; for one she was blond, for another brunette, further on she was tall and thin and for the person beside him she was small and chubby, but to all of them she was the perfect woman. They were all there waiting for her, for she had made a date with them in that remote place.

Julian thought about getting up, but it was already very late. All of a sudden he only wished to stay there, eating that delicious pie. What's more, he had to wait for Diana, who would surely be arriving soon.

The woman approached him again at seeing his plate empty.

'Here's another slice. I'm sure you want it, isn't that right, Julian?'

He looked her in the eyes and found himself looking into Diana's gaze.

Translated from the Spanish by James D. Jenkins

Bernardo Esquinca

Señor Ligotti

It probably shouldn't surprise anyone that the same country that gave us Día de Muertos and the films of Guillermo del Toro should have an active horror literature scene, but for some reason we don't seem to hear much about it. A partial list of important contemporary Mexican writers in the genre would have to include names like Amparo Dávila, Alberto Chimal, and Raquel Castro, all of whom have had work published in English, and F. G. Haghenbeck and Cecilia Eudave, whose horror fiction seems only to be available in Spanish. But there was one name in particular we kept coming across on every list of the best Mexican horror writers: BERNARDO ESQUINCA. *Esquinca (b. 1972) is a prolific author of horror novels and short stories and has also co-edited two volumes of fantastic tales from Mexico City. His works often blend the genres of horror or weird fiction with the crime novel, a formula that has proved successful with both readers and critics (he was awarded the Premio Nacional de Novela Negra in 2017). If you've ever been frustrated that people in other countries get to read things before you do because of the long lag time to translate and publish them in English, you're about to get a little bit of revenge. The following story, taken from the author's forthcoming collection* El libro de los dioses (The Book of the Gods), *hasn't even appeared in Spanish yet, meaning this is its first appearance anywhere.*

S EÑOR LIGOTTI SHOWED UP AT THE END OF A CONFER-
ENCE. As usual, Esteban signed some books, listened to his readers with studied politeness and gave quick, concise

tips to the ones aspiring to become writers. When he was preparing to leave the auditorium, with that mixture of satisfaction and emptiness he felt after every presentation – yes, he had readers, but he always wanted more – he saw him seated in the last row, with his red canvas bag, the bowtie in place of a necktie, the snow-white beard, with the tips of his mustache ending in points, in the style of some figures from the Revolution, and a walking stick with a silver-plated handle.

Señor Ligotti rose to his feet with an unexpected agility, extended his hand in a vigorous manner – Esteban could feel the hardness of several rings pressing against his skin – and spoke to him without beating about the bush.

'I'd like to make you a business proposition. Will you let me buy you a coffee?'

Normally Esteban would have refused. He didn't like chatting with people from the audience beyond what was necessary; talking with strangers was something that made him uncomfortable. He would often receive invitations to workshops, reading groups, and even to bars, which he rejected while trying to hide his irritation. This time he had the perfect excuse: his wife was in the final stage of pregnancy and he had to get home as soon as possible. Maybe that's what made him accept, the need to distract himself from the stress of the imminent childbirth, from the anxiety that didn't let him concentrate to read or write.

Esteban soon found himself seated in a private booth at a Vips cafeteria with this elderly eccentric, who seemed plucked off a theater stage and who at the same time had an impeccable bearing and an overwhelming dignity. He was spending time with a stranger. *Having kids changes you*, was the phrase he'd gotten used to hearing since Adela had gotten pregnant.

Señor Ligotti fixed him with an inquisitive look.

'How are things going? Does one make a good living writing?'

A typical question. Before responding, Esteban glanced at the book display stands next to the cash register, filled with bestsellers. Every time he went in a Vips, he lamented that his novels didn't form part of that club: the books that were sold in bookstores, but also in supermarkets, shops, restaurants.

'I make a living from what I write, but it could be better.'

'For all of us it could be better. Worse too. It's all about knowing how to take advantage of opportunities. Do you own your own home?'

'No. No matter how much I save, I never have enough.'

Señor Ligotti took a sip of his coffee and set it back down on the table. Then he moved his ring-filled fingers, making them chime against the mug.

'Si non oscillas, noli tintinnare . . .'

'What?'

'It's an old saying, as old as I am. If you don't swing, you don't ring, like bells. I've been one of your readers for a while: I think you're a talented writer, that you deserve better luck. I know you're obsessed with the Colonia Juárez neighborhood, since many of your stories take place there. I own an apartment in the Berlín building, which I'm putting up for sale. Are you interested?'

Esteban looked at his beer: he had hardly touched it. On the other hand, Señor Ligotti was going for his third coffee. Maybe he didn't sleep?

'I've rented my whole life. I dream of buying a house . . .'

'How much do you have?'

'Not even a million pesos.'

Señor Ligotti stroked his beard with his ring-laden hand. The one on his pinky finger had the logo of the National University: a shield borne by two birds of prey.

'Give me what you have and it's yours. I'd rather that someone who values old buildings live there and care for it. I have a great fondness for that apartment.'

Señor Ligotti's eyes glazed over. He paused to let out a long sigh.

'I lived there with my wife. She died last year.'

'I'm sorry.'

'The money isn't an issue for me. It's a sentimental thing: I can't leave all those memories to just anyone.'

The old man stood up and placed a card on the table. Before leaving, he said:

'Come and see me at my office. And bring your lawyer, if that makes you feel more comfortable.'

Esteban was thoughtful. It was the type of offer he fantasized about getting, but he didn't want to take advantage of a melancholy old man. He looked out the window: a luxury car pulled up to collect Señor Ligotti. The chauffeur got out and opened the back door for him.

He went to the cash register. The bill had already been paid.

Adela was suspicious. Sitting at the kitchen table with her hands on her belly to feel the baby when it moved, she had listened to the story Esteban told her as he walked back and forth, more and more euphoric. She asked him to be cautious. Things didn't happen so easily. Not to them. Nor did she believe in coincidences. Everything had a reason, a consequence.

'It smells like fraud.'

Esteban opened the refrigerator. He looked inside, took out a slice of ham and closed it again.

'Why would a rich old man commit a fraud? It's absurd.'

'We don't know anything about him. He could be a decoy, the tip of the iceberg of something we can't even imagine.'

'Do you hear yourself? We should write a suspense novel together. You're more paranoid than I am.'

'I'm suspicious, which is different. And more intuitive than you. Let's suppose that he really is a rich, lonely widower. An eccentric man who commits frauds in order to . . .'

'In order to what?'

'. . . amuse himself.'

Esteban knelt down beside Adela. He put his hands on her belly in an attempt to reassure her.

'Some of our friends have had similar opportunities. People who make them a good offer. And we always say, "What a lucky devil!" Well, now it's our turn. Don't they say that babies bring good luck?'

'That money is all we have. And we're on the verge of being parents. At least bring a lawyer to the meeting, someone to advise you.'

'Lawyers are expensive. I have experience with contracts, remember that I've signed lots of them for my books. Trust me.'

Adela felt exhausted. For eight months she'd had something living inside her that she couldn't see but that she could feel moving within her, growing, feeding. She slept little and badly. She didn't want to go on arguing; she got up and went silently to bed.

Esteban remained in the kitchen. He looked out the window to contemplate the pitch-dark night, barely illuminated by the poor lighting of Colonia Juárez.

In the middle of that darkness was their new home, waiting for them.

Esteban entered the lobby of a luxurious building that housed various offices. He saw from the wall directory that the office of Ligotti Industries shared a floor with the corporate offices of Grau Press, an important transnational imprint that had rejected his work on several occasions. That coincidence upset him, stirring up old frustrations. What was wrong with his writing that made it unworthy of being included in their catalog? Grau Press published renowned authors, but also a lot of rubbish. Esteban didn't fool himself: he knew he'd never win a prestigious award – he wrote thrillers, a genre scorned by critics – but at the same time he knew that his books had quality. And what's more, they sold. So what was the problem? He was thinking about that when he got off the elevator on the top floor and was still considering it when, after a short wait, the secretary told him to go in.

Señor Ligotti's office impressed him: marble floor, mahogany furniture, leather chairs, cut glass ashtrays, and books: the walls were covered with shelves. As he sat down in front of the desk and Señor Ligotti handed him the sale contract to review, he realized that a good part of that library consisted of Grau Press titles. Curiosity got the better of him and he asked his host why.

'I know the owner, we're good friends. Every time a new title comes out, he gives me a copy. By the way, you should publish there: it's an important publishing house, it would get your name out there.'

'I've tried, but I haven't had any luck.'

'Talent isn't a question of luck. It's all about getting a push in the right direction. I can help you.'

Esteban's eyes shone with intensity. He began to flip through the pages of the contract and signed them without paying any attention.

'Really? I wouldn't dream of asking you for that favor . . .'

Señor Ligotti moved his ring-laden fingers over the glass ashtray, producing a sound similar to the one he had made with the mug at Vips. For a moment, Esteban felt that time had stopped, that nothing else existed but that rhythmic, hypnotic tapping.

Si non oscillas, noli tintinnare.

Señor Ligotti's voice brought him back to reality.

'You're not asking, I'm offering. It's in your best interest: several of the titles you see here were published thanks to my opportune intervention. And with great success. I have a good eye, my neighbor knows it.'

'I should sit down to write. Lately things haven't been easy for me. Pregnancy brings a lot of worries and complications with it. For example . . .'

He was on the point of affixing his signature to the final page, but Señor Ligotti interrupted him:

'Wait. Before we finish with this, I want us to make a verbal pact, a gentleman's agreement.'

Esteban's mind remained overrun with the worries he hadn't managed to express: diapers, ultrasounds, the birth.

'Yes?'

The old man was now holding his cane in his hands and stroking the silver handle. When had he picked it up?

'That you let me visit you in the apartment. It's the only condition I impose. We can talk about books, drink coffee, and discuss the progress of the work I'll be proposing to Grau Press.'

Esteban smiled, relieved. For a moment he thought that the agreement was going to slip through his fingers.

'Of course.'

He signed, sealing the pact.

The move happened a week later. To celebrate, Esteban organized a party attended by his writer friends and some ex-colleagues from when he used to work in the cultural bureaucracy. He drank one beer after another as he showed the flat to each guest who arrived. The Berlín building was an old edifice, well maintained. Just the type of place he liked. The apartment had high ceilings, thick walls, hardwood flooring. Three bedrooms, two full bathrooms. There was a fireplace in the living room, which gave a touch of elegance. And the best part: it was located on the building's ground floor, which would save him from having to climb the stairs with the stroller.

At some point that night he went up to Clemente, an author of crime novels whom he'd known for many years and with whom he had the kind of friendship that usually develops between writers: not very honest, self-serving, based more on gossip than a genuine interest in each other's work.

Clemente was drinking mezcal from a mug: there weren't enough glasses.

'This apartment is amazing. How did you manage to pay for it?'

'I got a loan. There's no other way except going into debt.'

'And the down payment? Through the roof, I'm guessing.'

'My mother-in-law helped us.'

'And how are the neighbors? Have you gone to ask them for sugar?'

Esteban was carrying two beers in his hand. One of them was for somebody else, but now he didn't remember who. This time he responded truthfully:

'I haven't come across anyone. I haven't heard them either. The good thing about old buildings is you don't hear anything.'

'If I were you I'd find out right away who I'm going to be surrounded by for the rest of my days.'

A couple approached to say goodbye. Esteban took advantage of the opportunity to free himself from Clemente. Their conversation was starting to bother him. He decided to avoid him the rest of the night. He was a negative guy whose paranoia was usually contagious.

Another thing Esteban made it a point to show his friends

was the answering machine. A relic that he found amusing. He enjoyed showing people something that had gone obsolete. He found it appealing to think of the time when answering machines were in vogue, all those voices being recorded, being listened to within lonely houses. Ghosts talking to ghosts.

The last guest left at six in the morning. Esteban managed to get his shoes off and collapsed beside Adela, who was in a deep sleep. He embraced her and gave in to the warmth emanating from her body, to the fog of alcohol, to sleep.

The buzzer rang at seven in the morning. Esteban heard it between dreams, incapable of getting up. Adela woke him, shaking him.

'He's asking for you.'

With his eyelids still shut, Esteban asked, 'Who?'

'Señor Ligotti.'

His eyes opened in surprise.

'What does he want? Tell him I'm sleeping.'

Adela sat down on the bed.

'I already told him. But he insists on seeing you. He says the two of you agreed on it.'

'We agreed?'

'That you would see each other. Go talk to him. It gives me the creeps thinking of him out there waiting.'

Esteban got up reluctantly and put on his shoes. He didn't splash water on his face nor comb his hair, hoping that his appearance would dissuade the inopportune visitor.

He opened the apartment door. Señor Ligotti was waiting in the hallway, resting on his walking stick.

'It's about time.'

Although he was half asleep, Esteban recognized the anomaly.

'How did you get in the building?'

'A neighbor was going out. Everyone here knows me.'

'I haven't seen anyone in days . . .'

Señor Ligotti came closer.

'Aren't you going to invite me in?'

Esteban hesitated. The old man's visit was ill-timed, but he couldn't be rude to him. After all, he had helped him to buy the place. He stepped to one side and with a wave of his hand invited him to enter.

'Of course, come in.'

He added in an ironic tone:

'Make yourself at home.'

The visit was hell. Señor Ligotti chattered indefatigably and seemed to have no intention of leaving quickly. Esteban's head ached from the hammering of his hangover. He could hardly follow the old man's chit-chat, which passed from one theme to another that was no less meaningless. Despite his discomfort, he realized something: he had idealized him. When he met him, he seemed to him a humanist, a philanthropist, an extinct species that he had had the luck to run across. Now he saw him clearly: he was a guy who was arrogant, maniacal, presumptuous. Why the hell had he come? And so early. That's how loners were: they weren't conscious of other people's time. They required as much attention as an only child. On top of everything, Adela had fled, on the pretext that she had to visit her mother, leaving him at the mercy of his 'guest'.

Esteban dozed off at times. Every time he opened his eyes, he saw that Señor Ligotti was continuing his infinite monologue. He caught some phrases that troubled him, questions that the old man made without waiting for a response: *'How's the new book going? What's it about? I suppose you haven't got very far. Something will have to be done so that you make progress, so that you swing, so that you ring . . .'*

In the end he fell asleep. When he awoke, shaken again by Adela, it was already night. When had Ligotti left? He thought the visit had been a bad dream, a nightmare brought about by his hangover. But on the living room table he saw the ring with the National University logo.

Adela picked it up and said sarcastically:

'Now your *friend* has an excuse to come back.'

Señor Ligotti turned into a problem. He would appear at any day and time, with an attitude that bordered on demanding. Besides being annoyed, Esteban was worried: this wasn't a question of indiscretion but of obsession. The old man returned on the day following his first visit. Esteban gave him back the ring, thinking that would keep him away for a while, but he kept coming back. Sometimes he rang the buzzer outside the building, other times he rang directly at the apartment door. What was most disturbing was his way of ringing, insistently, as if he were there to deliver an urgent package.

Esteban began to avoid him. If Señor Ligotti came to the door, he would open it saying he had an important appointment and, after excusing himself, would set off down the street at a rapid pace. He would also pretend there was no one home until the old man left. One time when he was returning from the store, he saw him at a distance, standing in front of the building's door. He immediately turned around, took a taxi and went to see a movie. At first this game of cat and mouse seemed funny. Adela spent most of her time at her mother's; dodging the old man became a source of entertainment for Esteban. A kind of challenge: to see who wore out first. The old man won't hold out longer than me, he told himself. Several days passed in this way, until the episode with the answering machine.

It was on an afternoon that was gray with rain-charged

clouds. Esteban was reading Clemente's recently published novel in his study. He was curious whether it would prove to be as bad as the previous ones. The intercom buzzer sounded. He peeked through the kitchen window, which looked out onto the street. It was polarized glass, which allowed him to look without being seen. He discovered it was Señor Ligotti and returned to his chair. After a few minutes, the buzzer stopped ringing. Esteban could go back to concentrating on his reading. He could hear thunder, a downpour was starting to fall.

Something distracted him from the book. A strange feeling: he wasn't alone. There was a presence, not within the house, but outside. Through the kitchen window he saw an image that disconcerted him: Señor Ligotti was still outside, in the rain, staring at the building. The old man took a cell phone from the inner pocket of his bag and dialed a number.

The apartment's telephone rang.

Esteban let it ring. He felt the muscles in his body twitch, as if they were shrinking. The answering machine switched on. Señor Ligotti's irritated voice boomed:

'I know you're there. Open up.'

He tried to recall: had he given him his number?

'You must let me in. Fulfill your part of the bargain.'

He had an absurd, unsettling thought: the old man could see him, his gaze penetrated the polarized glass. He didn't dare to move, like a cockroach surprised when a light is turned on.

Señor Ligotti didn't say anything more. He remained there with the telephone to his ear, getting soaked. The rain could be heard outside and through the answering machine as well. It was an unreal sound effect, the echo of a nightmare. The machine's tape reached the end and the recording cut off, breaking the spell. Esteban reacted by going to his bedroom. He got in bed, hiding under the covers like when he was a child.

Adela suggested they go on vacation. You're very tense, she told him, it would do you good to get out of the city. The next morning they got in the car and took the highway. When the first cows appeared, Esteban started to feel better. They stayed at a resort with thermal baths. They were sunny days, with a lot of reading. Clemente's novel was rubbish, and that contributed towards improving his state of mind. It had too many legalistic details that dragged down the plot. A lot of knowledge about the judicial system, not much of a story.

Adela and Esteban devoted themselves to the vacation. They swam. They ate excessively. They made love slowly so they wouldn't hurt the baby.

A week later, Esteban felt back to normal. He thought about his behavior the preceding days, the irrational fear that the old man had awakened in him. Now he knew what to do. He would confront him. He would put a stop to the situation. If necessary, he would shout the truth at him. He was nothing more than a senile old coot, finished, pathetic. On the way home his confidence grew. The end of the problem was nearing, the solution was in his hands.

He never imagined what would be waiting for him at home.

He opened the apartment door. Señor Ligotti was inside, clinking his rings against a steaming cup of coffee.

After the initial shock came the anger. Adela looked at Esteban, blurted out a *Get him out of here, I don't ever want to see him here again*, and shut herself up in the bedroom. Señor Ligotti sipped his coffee with a carefree air, as if his presence were the most natural thing in the world, something which infuriated Esteban even more. He stood in front of him, containing his desire to hit him.

'This time you've gone too far. How did you get in? The neighbors helped you with that too?'

The old man shook his head no. Then he smiled, amused.

'I have a set of keys. And since you didn't want to fulfill your part of the bargain, I felt obliged to use them.'

'What bargain?'

'We agreed that I would visit you. It was the pact we made before signing the contract.'

'You're crazy. Don't you get it? Nobody wants you here. Get lost or I'll call the police.'

'That's no way to treat a guest.'

Señor Ligotti stood up, but instead of going to the exit he headed towards the kitchen, where he served himself another cup of the coffee he had made.

Esteban went after him, furious.

'Get out of here! I'll have you thrown in jail, I swear it!'

The old man rested his hip against the kitchen sink; he took a sip of his beverage while he looked at him challengingly.

Esteban turned around, went to the telephone and dialed the emergency number. 'Home invasion,' he said, raising his voice so that the elderly man would hear him.

He went back to the kitchen. Señor Ligotti gave a cackling laugh.

'Home invasion? Seriously? That's the problem with not writing. Writing is like a muscle, and if it's not used, the language atrophies. I urge you to get back to your keyboard. What's more, it would do you good to write longhand: the sentences flow better that way.'

The doorbell interrupted his discourse. The police had arrived quickly.

Esteban looked at the old man cruelly.

'You won't be laughing about this.'

He went to open the door. He led the officers to the kitchen. There was nobody inside, only the steaming cup. They searched the rest of the house: nothing.

Señor Ligotti had vanished. Just like a ghost.

The next person to ring was the locksmith. Esteban asked him for a new, high-security lock. He also thought about changing the one on the building's front door, but first he had to consult the neighbors. Where the hell were they hiding? He was overrun with a mixture of feelings. On the one hand, rage; on the other, embarrassment. He had made a fool of himself with the police. The officers looked at him with suspicion, no doubt they considered him paranoid, even a prankster. Adela was no help. Instead of serving as a witness, she turned against him: it hadn't been a good idea to buy that apartment. I TOLD YOU SO. The police finally left without taking their statements.

The following days were even stranger. Esteban slept fitfully, awakened by nightmares in the early morning hours. On one occasion he opened his eyes in the midst of the darkness, overcome by a feeling of anxiety. It was raining. He lay there listening to the sound the drops made striking the window glass. Suddenly he made out a silhouette sitting in a chair at the foot of the bed. A flash of lightning lit up the room, allowing him to recognize Señor Ligotti. He realized that the sound he heard was produced by the old man's rings tapping the cup he held between his hands.

Si non oscillas, noli tintinnare.

He awoke with a stifled scream. It was morning. Adela was in the bathroom. The sound of the shower could be heard through the door.

The certainty grew that he was losing his mind. That dream had been too real; he was starting to have problems telling whether he was awake. Things got worse days later, when he found Señor Ligotti's ring on the desk. The birds on the National University logo spreading their wings like a menace. Adela tried to calm him down: surely he left it the day he let himself in with his keys and you hadn't realized it. Despite his confusion, Esteban had one certainty: he couldn't count on his wife. She was only thinking about the baby, she refused any additional worries. He opted not to tell her anything for now. He kept silent about each new discovery, each message – he was sure that's what they were – that the old man was leaving him: a visiting card (he gave it to you when you met him, don't be paranoid, Adela would have said), a little glass bell that he had never seen in the house, more rings . . .

Señor Ligotti was a demiurge, there was no other explanation. A demiurge or a demon, and the solution was to call a priest to exorcize the house. His mind was made up to go to the neighborhood church to explore the possibility when he made another disturbing find.

He was trying to read in the living room without being able to concentrate. He felt a cold draft coming from the floor. Esteban crouched down and approached the fireplace on all fours. The frozen air hit him in the face. He stretched out his hand to touch the back and it gave way, revealing an opening behind it. The fireplace had a metal plate the same color as the wall, an effective camouflage. Esteban went through the hole. It turned out to be a passage, full of leaves and branches, which led to the building's side courtyard. There was another removable plate there through which it was possible to exit to the exterior.

Señor Ligotti was not a specter. He was something worse: a dangerous madman.

A mason took care of covering the hole in the fireplace. He laid bricks and mortar and afterwards added a coat of paint. Meanwhile, Esteban decided to go over the house inch by inch in search of more passages. He checked closets, the flooring, under the sink. Also doors and windows: he wanted to close off any possibility whatsoever of intrusion. Adela waited patiently while he did all this and then said they needed to talk. She didn't want to fight or argue, she told him. Things had gotten out of control. She wanted to get out of there as soon as possible . . .

A sound coming from the door interrupted them. With a gesture of his hand, Esteban asked his wife to wait. He went towards the entrance armed with a kitchen knife. On the floor he saw an envelope. He bent down to pick it up and opened it with trembling hands.

It was an eviction order.

Esteban had a moment of clarity. One where the events of the past few days fit perfectly, where his stupidity and indolence played a central role. In the desk drawers he found the contract that he had signed with Señor Ligotti. He tried to read it, but he couldn't: the letters became blurry, wobbly. He scanned it, emailed it to Clemente and urgently asked him to review it. You're the expert in legal questions, he told him in the message.

The telephone rang minutes later. His friend's first sentence disturbed him even more:

'You sent the wrong document.'

'What?'

'The purchase contract you sent me is incomplete and therefore invalid. The last sheet is a different contract, to publish a book.'

Esteban took the document he had scanned: it was that one, there was no question. In the first paragraph he could read: 'Ligotti Industries declares that . . .' He felt nauseous, on the verge of fainting.

'It's the one I signed.'

'The old man screwed you. For legal purposes, you didn't acquire an apartment: you promised to write a book within one year.'

'He's very clever. He got me to sign without my noticing the trick . . .'

Esteban summarized the recent happenings for his friend.

'What am I going to do? I'm ruined.'

Clemente tried to calm him:

'I'll investigate Ligotti with my court contacts. I'm sure we'll find something shady in his past, something that could help you. Meanwhile, don't leave your home or you'll lose it.'

When he hung up, Adela already had her suitcase ready. She was going to her mother's house. Esteban agreed: it was the best thing to do. For her to be safe while he sorted out the serious mistake he had made. He would barricade himself in the apartment. It was his home. He had poured all the money he had into it.

To take it away from him, they would have to kill him.

When he was young, Esteban lived through something similar. His parents spent years saving with the goal of buying a house. After great sacrifices they collected enough for the down payment. The family moved from the small apartment where they were living to a two story house with a garage and a yard. To celebrate, they organized a meal attended by relatives and friends: everyone hugged them, congratulating them on their new lifestyle. Esteban met the neighbor kids his own age, soon he was playing football and hide and seek with them.

That phase didn't last. The expenses smothered his parents; they stopped making the monthly payments on the house, they ended up losing it. Esteban never forgot the day they moved out: the neighbors looking out their doors and windows with sympathetic faces, the feeling of profound shame at the public exhibition, the defeat in his father's tired expression, his mother's tears, his older brothers' silence.

Now the story was repeating itself. The family curse that condemned them to be eternal renters. However, there was a difference: with his parents it had been a poor financial calculation. On the other hand, he had let himself be tricked like a child. And what was at risk wasn't only the apartment.

He could lose Adela. He could lose his sanity.

He remained sitting on the living room sofa for hours, watching the closed hole in the fireplace as if he expected to see Señor Ligotti come out of it, until night fell. He put his thoughts aside, got up, and flipped the light switch.

It didn't work.

He went through the house pressing the other switches, with the same result. Just what he needed: the power had gone out. He didn't have a flashlight, nor candles. The time had come to ask the neighbors for a favor. Maybe he could even get some information out of them about Señor Ligotti.

He went out to the hall. It was illuminated by a milky white bulb, the outage had occurred only in his apartment. He knocked on the door next to his and realized it was half open. He didn't want to be taken for an intruder, so he said loudly:

'Hello . . .'

There was no response. He knocked again, this time louder, and then added:

'I'm your neighbor, my power's out.'

As no one responded, he pushed the door a little and stuck his head in. The hall light allowed him to see that the apartment was empty. It smelled damp, musty. The floor was bulging, rotten. It was obvious it had been abandoned for a long time.

He headed for the adjacent apartment. Its door was also ajar; he knocked and waited several seconds, then opened it slowly, as if he wanted to delay the moment of revelation.

There was nothing inside except for a forgotten paint can.

Was it a coincidence? There was only one more apartment, at the end of the hallway. If he found it empty he would go up to the next floor and the next, until he found someone.

He walked, listening to the amplified echo of his steps. He felt like the ghost of a lonely castle. A lost soul in eternal search of companionship.

The door was closed. He put his ear against it: silence. Nothing seemed to be moving inside. He put his hand on the knob; it wasn't locked, so he could turn it, producing the grinding sound made by rusty objects. He was going to enter, but he was stopped by the ringing of a telephone behind him. He remained frozen for a few seconds until he realized it was his. He ran to his apartment and answered it, panting.

He heard Clemente's voice.

'Get out of there right now!'

Esteban caught his breath and asked:

'What are you saying? Why?'

'I found out some things about Ligotti. Get your things and get out! There's no time for explanations.'

Esteban had left his apartment door open. He saw that the hall light was going out. Then he heard someone unlocking the front door of the building.

Before the line went dead, Clemente managed to say:

'Ligotti owns the whole building.'

That day in his childhood when Esteban and his family moved from the house they had lost to a minuscule apartment, something strange occurred. He woke up thirsty in the early morning hours, he felt feverish, claustrophobic. His older brothers snored in their bunks, resigned to the overcrowding. He went to the kitchen for a glass of water. He wanted a little air too, some space.

A glow coming from the living room caught his attention. The television was on. The screen showed colored bars indicating the channel was off air. They had always seemed enigmatic to Esteban: a signal, the key to an encoded message. He saw his father's silhouette outlined against the light. He had fallen asleep in the chair. He went up to him to wake him; he was surprised to discover his eyes open, fixed on the screen.

'What are you doing, Daddy?'

His father didn't notice his presence. Esteban was going to talk to him again but something stopped him. In that moment he didn't know it; now, as he held the telephone in his hand, as he listened to the emptiness of the line that had gone dead, taking Clemente's voice along with it, he understood what it had been.

Señor Ligotti's figure appeared in the doorway. He recognized him despite the darkness: in one hand he gripped his walking stick.

He hadn't said anything more to his father because his empty gaze contained a warning. Something sinister was living inside him and if he broke the trance it would emerge with all its power. The bars on the television kept it at bay. It was better to leave it like that.

Underneath people's skin there were monsters, like the one he now had to face.

Energized by the whiplash of adrenaline, Esteban looked around for things that could help him hurt his attacker. The darkness only let him make out the largest objects: a chair, a dresser, a plant, nothing he could use as a weapon. He weighed his chances. Señor Ligotti was crazy but he was an old man. It would be easy to subdue him. Various images passed through his head: he would knock him down with a shove, he would straddle him, he would humiliate him with slaps. He wanted to see him break, listen to him sob. The rage built up in recent days overflowed. Opening his mouth, Esteban let out a sharp, primitive, animal cry and sprang at his rival.

He didn't manage to topple him.

Señor Ligotti easily sidestepped his attack, then struck his cane across his face, breaking his nose. Esteban fell to the ground, bleeding profusely. The old man bent down, grabbed him by one foot and began to drag him down the hallway.

While he was being hauled like a sack, Esteban wondered: where did the old man draw such strength from? He saw a flash of lightning and heard the rain start to come down. Where was he taking him? He tried to escape, but his strength failed him. The darkness became thicker, he lost consciousness.

The cold water of the rain woke him. The world had gone upside down, the buildings hung from an asphalt sky. It took him a moment to understand that he was upside down on the building's rooftop terrace, that his body was hanging over the edge. He looked towards his feet and saw that Señor Ligotti was holding him by one leg. How had he gotten him all the way up there?

The old man began to swing him. Slowly, from left to right, moving his body like a pendulum.

Overcoming his fear, Esteban sought answers:

'Why are you doing this to me? What do you want? Answer me!'

A lightning flash illuminated the old man's face. In that final moment, Esteban understood. Señor Ligotti looked at him with a mixture of curiosity and impatience, the same way a human observes the slow movements of a mollusk.

He wasn't a madman: he was a higher being. A god who was toying with him just like a boy playing with ants.

The old man's voice rose above the sound of the wind and rain:

'Si non oscillas, noli tintinnare.'

Esteban felt him let go, the vertigo of the fall, the abyss sucking him towards a certain death. He closed his eyes and hugged himself, anticipating the position of his body in its shroud.

But he didn't fall. Señor Ligotti held him once more by the leg and then dragged his body over the edge of the terrace until he placed him safely on the roof. Esteban remained curled up in a ball, trembling and crying like a newborn baby. The old man leaned over him. He brushed the wet hair back from his face and positioned it behind his ears. Then he kissed him on the forehead.

Esteban closed his eyes, fearing the real denouement: his rival's hands strangling him or disemboweling him with a knife.

He opened them seconds later. Señor Ligotti had disappeared.

When the police visited him in the hospital where he was recovering from an inevitable rhinoplasty, Esteban decided that he wouldn't press charges against Señor Ligotti. He was terrified to face him again, to have a confrontation with him. He stated that because of the darkness he hadn't been able to see his attacker's face; that he had no enemies nor the slightest idea of who had been responsible for the assault.

While this was going on, Clemente supervised the moving of everything from the apartment in Calle de Berlín to Adela's mother's house. Esteban didn't want to set foot in that place again. He would await the imminent birth of his child sheltered under his mother-in-law's roof.

Afterwards, calmly, he would seek a new home for his family.

The birth and the first month of infancy kept his mind busy. However, it didn't take long before he fell into a deep depression. He started therapy with a psychologist who, after hearing his terrifying story about Señor Ligotti, suggested he commit it to paper.

'You could try writing a novel. It would help you. Isn't that what you writers do all the time? Exorcize your traumas through literature . . .'

Esteban was reluctant at first but wound up accepting the advice. After a slow, painful start, when he was on the verge of abandoning the project, he entered an inspired catharsis: the ideas flowed at a dizzying rhythm, the plot fit together with a coherency he had never before experienced. Four months later he finished the novel, which he entitled *Señor Ligotti*. He sent it to several publishers with the certainty that he had just written his best book.

The first offer didn't take long to arrive. To his delight, it came from Grau Press. The novel, retitled by some genius in the marketing department as *Sinister Stalking*, was an immediate success. His bank account grew with equal speed and he was able to get a modest apartment on the outskirts of the city. This time he hired a lawyer to deal with the contract.

Fortune smiled on him. But by now Esteban wasn't naive, he couldn't be after recent events.

Everything had a price. It was just a matter of waiting for the bill collector to show up.

His son turned two. During all this time, Esteban didn't write anything. *Sinister Stalking* continued to be reprinted; the royalties it generated were enough for them to live well and he preferred to devote himself to his family. He didn't miss creative work and even stayed away from public events. He started to think of retiring, of the possibility of remaining connected to literature through teaching. A couple of universities showed interest in hiring him. Maybe, he sometimes mused in the early morning hours when suffering from insomnia, he had written everything he had to write.

There was also another possibility: that he was paralyzed by the fear of not being able to surpass *Sinister Stalking*'s success.

As if he divined his thoughts, the director of Grau Press called one morning to invite him to the office. We have to talk, he said. Esteban accepted out of politeness: they were his publisher, he lived off them, he couldn't say no. He saw it as a courtesy visit.

As he checked in at the lobby, he was relieved not to see Ligotti Industries in the directory. He relaxed even more when he got off the elevator on the top floor and discovered that his old enemy's offices were for rent. Where had he gone? Had he died? What did it matter? The truth was that he was glad to avoid him.

The director received him with forced enthusiasm. He was an executive who didn't know much about books; on the other hand, he mastered numbers and accounts to perfection. They made small talk for a long while. Esteban's discomfort was growing. He began to look for an excuse to get out of there.

Suddenly, the director took his arm and led him down a hallway.

'Actually, it's the owner who wants to speak with you.'

Esteban was surprised. He had never dealt with him.

'And to what do I owe the honor?'

'He's concerned because you haven't sent in anything new . . .'

They arrived in front of an enormous wood door. It was

old, with elegant carvings. On the upper part, in the middle, a phrase was inscribed:

SI NON OSCILLAS, NOLI TINTINNARE

Esteban's back went stiff. His vision clouded and he felt the urge to vomit.

The director put his hand on the doorknob.

'. . . and when an author gets writer's block, he likes to help. He knows different methods for stimulating the imagination.'

The door opened, the director pushed him inside. Esteban was petrified, incapable of opening his eyes, until he heard a voice:

'Welcome. Sit down.'

It belonged to a young man. Esteban raised his eyelids. Behind the desk he saw a blond-haired fellow, clean-shaven, with horn-rimmed glasses. He felt ridiculous. His paranoia had gotten carried away again. The answer was obvious: Señor Ligotti knew this office; surely this was where he'd gotten the phrase from.

He approached the desk, still nauseous from the shock, and sat down.

'Sorry, I don't feel well.'

He closed his eyes again. The air in the office was thick, hot; Esteban felt he was suffocating.

With excessive familiarity, the owner asked him:

'Are you drunk?'

Then, changing the subject, he added:

'I have something for you . . .'

Esteban heard him open a drawer. Then he heard something that terrified him, a sound that confirmed what he already feared: that his nightmare was really just beginning.

'. . . it's the contract for a new book.'

Behind him, from some corner of the office, the sound continued to be heard.

The jingling of a hand loaded with rings.

Translated from the Spanish by James D. Jenkins

Flavius Ardelean

Down, in Their World

Bram Stoker's choice of Romania as the setting of Dracula *was not accidental. The country has a rich folkloric tradition, full of terrifying creatures and legends. Yet Romanian horror fiction is a relatively modern phenomenon. Its origins can probably be traced to the 'fantastic tales' of writers like Mircea Eliade, author of the literary vampire novel* Domnişoara Christina [Miss Christina] (1936), *and its contemporary practitioners include Marian Coman, some of whose work has appeared in English, and Oliviu Crâznic, credited with the first modern Gothic novel in Romanian. But perhaps the most significant is* FLAVIUS ARDELEAN (b. 1985), *who has published three collections of macabre fiction, some of which might be likened to Robert Aickman's strange stories. The following tale, which appeared in* Acluofobia (2013), *is set among the peasants of rural Transylvania. For many in that region, even today, the boundary between the natural and supernatural worlds is not clear-cut. Encounters with fairies or ghosts are not seen as out of the ordinary, and the notion of 'bad places' where one mustn't venture is firmly ingrained. Transylvania's aura of mystery and the supernatural pervades this story, in which several legendary creatures appear, including the* ielele (fairies), ştima (spirit of the waters), *and the* vâlva, *an entity that inhabits mines and comes in two varieties — good ones who lead you to buried treasure and evil ones who punish you for removing it. To complete the glossary of terms used in the story,* ţuică *is a potent home-brewed brandy, the equivalent of Romanian moonshine, and* mămăligă *is a dish made of corn meal, not unlike Italian polenta.*

H E HAD HAD A FOREBODING, but he had drowned it in a gram of tobacco and shot of *țuică*. For courage.

The sun had not yet come out from behind the mountains when the four men got their cart out on the street and bridled the horse in whispers, each of them chewing a cigarette stump between his teeth – four fireflies floating between the houses. They did not talk to one another, they knew it from their fathers and *their* fathers and *their* fathers: when they set out before dawn they did not speak because sharp are the claws that guard the treasures of the depths, fiery are the eyes of the *știma*, cursed is the voice of the fairies. So they were silent and took puffs from their cigarettes, three in the cart and one pulling the harness to the left and to the right, leaving the village and setting out towards the forests, towards the black chaos from which they would take the scrap iron that would allow them to live for another month.

They were kinsfolk – brothers, cousins. Stelică, the youngest, wasn't responsible for raising any children, as the others were, but it didn't matter, money is money, his wife wakes up tomorrow or the next day knocked up and what then? What then? he thought and put out the unfiltered cigarette against the wood of the cart before throwing it into the surrounding darkness. He took out a chunk of *mămăligă*, broke some off and passed the rest on. The others, fumbling in the darkness for the *mămăligă*, threw their butts away as well and spit several times to clear the bits of tobacco off their tongues. Then silence (only the horse's hooves and the men's munching). From time to time, Nicu lit the lantern and illuminated around them and only then could the men look into one another's eyes and their looks all masked the same thought: the fire in the stove last night, just a few hours earlier, when Stere awoke from a nap and secretly told them that he had dreamed about his grandma telling them not to go there if their lives were dear to them, that Piele would get hold of them, and their women would never see them again . . . Insufferable women! the men thought, swallowing their *mămăligă*. They had no choice. Where would they get money? Eh? Where would they get money? The women usually kept quiet and didn't gather in the doorways when they left to steal the old iron, but just knelt down before the icons throughout the house and whispered prayers. But this time they had not said anything to the women. They had no business knowing that they were headed toward the Turk's Mouth, that accursed place, maligned by many, but whose riches were sought after by even more. But fear is fear, as grandfather Tache, dead now these forty years, used to say, and each of them had a morsel of fear in his pocket when he set off.

Stelică couldn't bear the silence, which was casting him even deeper into black thoughts, and he cleared his throat to whisper:

'Say, didn't that guy Piele live around here?'

'Shut up,' Nicu's voice was heard.

He lit the lantern, then put it out.

He couldn't bear the silence, but what bothered him even more were the old men's superstitions. They had kept him far away from the Turk's Mouth for so long, but Stelică had decided to change things. If there was one thing he was good at, it was talking. Stelică could manage to convince anyone of anything, anytime, and any way. He had a gift, his mother said. He was a 'hustler', he said. So too he convinced the men to go to the Turk's Mouth. The riches were said to be significant, and they were fair game; the entire structure had been left in disrepair after the decommission order, untouched by outsiders because of the curse of the bad place, in which the entire region seemed to believe since the story of old Piele.

Their lit cigarettes could be glimpsed in the night as the men entered the forest. The horse snorted, trod on rocks, somewhere a stream flowed. The men smoked and thought about their wives.

Stelică fell asleep and was awakened by Stere.

'Get ready,' he said. 'Time to wake up – we're there.'

It was growing light. The horse was agitated.

'Come on, giddyup! What's wrong with you! This way!' said Nicu.

The horse took several steps back, the men held on to one another.

'Hey!' they all yelled and then they decided to jump off the cart and take the horse by the harness to calm him. The horse kicked and snorted, tried to flee, but the men led it aside and tied it to a tree.

'Stelică, see what there is for him to eat. If anyone passes by, tell them they sent you from the town hall to do some cleaning up.'

'Come on Nicu, what the hell! And stand here like an idiot, waiting for you all day? I was the one who told you that we should come here.'

'What did you tell us?'

'I came with . . . I said . . .'

'Stelică, if you think that you led us here, you are mistaken,' said Nicu sharply.

'Then who, Nicu?' asked Stelică.

'Hunger,' Nicu responded curtly and turned around.

'And I can't come in with the rest of you?'

'No,' said Nicu, going toward the mouth of the mine. 'Next time.'

'That's what you said last time, at the other mine,' Stelică

said in a whisper, then louder: 'At least leave me some cigarettes.'

'Wait until the others come back, I don't have any more,'
said Nicu, getting down once more from the cart, after which
he performed a short inspection of the mine's entrance.

The horse, still snorting thick steam, turned its glance
towards the village. The men returned from the bushes.
Vasile raised his arms towards the others and said:

'Come on, over here.'

They knew what was coming. Vasile was the oldest,
Auntie Valeria's husband, as wizened as he was intelligent and
God-fearing, imbued with the mists of the place as a cellar is
imbued with mold. He whispered a prayer for those who dig
in the earth's core. Vasile had gone down into many mines
and since he had lost his brother in one of them, many, many
years ago, he had never gone down to dig without whispering a prayer first. 'God defends you from the pixies, but you
have to want it. You have to tell him, since otherwise how is
God going to know, if you don't say it to him? Do you think
he has nothing better to do than take care of you?' That's
what he always said and then he would stammer a prayer that
nobody understood. Stelică made a 'tsk' sound and gestured
to them to give him a cigarette. He didn't believe in God.
Nor in pixies, nor in good places and bad places. He had to
steal the iron in order to get money. If he could find work,
he would work, no question, but there was nothing to be
found in the whole region, so all that was left for him to do
was get his hands on some 'business', as he called it when he
talked with the guys at the dance club every Friday. So now
he took the cigarette between his teeth, made a sign that they
should give him some more – how was he supposed to stand
outside in the cold with only one cigarette? – and walked to
the cart.

'Stelică, come here!' yelled Vasile, calling him to prayer.

'Leave me alone,' Stelică responded with irritation.

'When the whirlwind comes and chases you around here, you'll be sorry you didn't listen to me.'

'All right,' said Stelică with his back to them. 'Come on, faster, the sun's coming up.'

Vasile finished whispering the prayer and the men took their tools and climbed up the hill towards the decommissioned mine, a black cave in the snow, with rusted signs indicating the danger of death awaiting whoever dared to go down into it. Signs, that's all. The town hall hadn't set up fences, hadn't installed locks, and guards were out of the question. A sign. But the stomach is more powerful than the brain and hunger is stronger than a good guard, so the men climbed toward the mine, went up in order to go down.

It was said that there was still old iron to be removed from the Turk's Mouth mine. It was not a large mine, it did not belong to a complex, it had perhaps been an unsuccessful exploitation attempt, or, rather, nobody really knew what had been wrong with it or why it had fallen into disrepair. And yet, despite the riches it was suspected to contain, there were not many who penetrated into its depths. The reason was one that made Stelică laugh. He too had heard the story: that the fairies of the earth roamed in those parts, and when it was decided to construct a mine, many people died before it was even opened. And then many more met their end after the exploitation began, until it was decided to call an end to the activities on the grounds of 'high risk of accidents'. And then there was the other story, the one about Piele, who led seven children from the community into the mine and undressed them and laid down beside them. Stelică had been told when he was a child: 'Don't play with old Piele, he comes from a wicked family!' He had a wife and two children, but his mind was shot from drinking, and he led youths and girls from the neighboring villages into the mine and kept them there. It went on more than a year until they found them, but they were all dead, only Piele was living, he slept covered in rags, with a hand on one of the unfortunate children. The first ones taken were already decomposed, but Piele paid no heed, he slept and ate with them there, then went down from time to time to the village to his family. He told no one where he spent his days and nights. Stelică shook off a shiver when he remembered the words of his brother, now a professor in the city, how he told him when they were younger: 'There was this guy Piele – well, you don't know him, 'cos they've taken him away now – and this Piele stunk of death like one of the undead.'

Stelică lit a cigarette and looked around: the white of the snow was streaked with the gray of the trees. Then he looked at the mine's entrance and imagined Piele sleeping alongside the children's corpses, Piele who escaped the people's fury only to be killed in Jilava prison by his cellmate. Apparently even in prison there's justice for child rapists.

He spat in the snow and took a drag from the cigarette.

The three men lit the lanterns and went into the mine. The snow had remained behind them, it was warmer in the narrow tunnel. They walked on the rails, their steps slid on the stones. The smell was no longer at all like that of fresh snow, of sleeping forest. Other things had slept an eternal sleep in the mine. The men knew what carcasses smelled like and here, at the entrance to the mine, somewhere in the darkness, there were surely some rotting cadavers of small animals.

'This way,' Nicu's voice was heard.

They followed him to where the rails turned to the right, and they entered a room dug in the walls of the tunnel. A table, two chairs. Nothing else. Something moved in a corner and the men directed their lanterns that way. Nothing.

'Rats?' asked Stere, but no one responded.

'Follow the rails, they'll lead us to a gallery,' said Nicu and the men started off.

There was still plenty of oxygen around, so they didn't have to worry, and they breathed easily when they reached the main gallery and saw the metallic structures.

'All right, we stop here,' said Vasile. 'Let's take as much as we can and leave. Further on there's no air, we're not going there.'

The men did not respond and were reconciled to what Vasile had said. Vasile was a wise man. Everyone knew that. They wedged their pliers and crowbars in hinges, cut through pipes, lifted iron bars, put them in the wheelbarrow. Then once more: bend over, stand up, sit down. And so on.

Stere suddenly felt a warm breeze at the nape of his neck. He turned around and pointed his lantern toward the darkness opposite him, but he didn't find anything there. He had just turned back once more to his work when he again felt something – this time like a soft touch on his elbow.

'Hey!' he said.

His heart was pounding. Even there, where it was possible to breathe, he had to catch his breath every few minutes and wipe away the sweat that was dripping in his eyes.

'What's wrong?' asked Nicu.

'Nothing,' said Stere and illuminated the walls alongside him from one end to the other. He saw an entrance into a side gallery and headed towards it. In the darkness within he thought he saw a movement – short, like a thought (or a blink). He stopped, turned towards the men, but they hadn't noticed anything, neither the movement nor that Stere had gone off away from them. They were lifting up chunks of rail and putting them in the three wheelbarrows they had brought with them.

Stere went in through the entrance and lit up the darkness of the gallery. It was a room similar to the others they had been in, only perhaps with a lower ceiling, in which there were stacks of beams and several very large metallic containers. Stere was going to see what was in them when he heard movement to his left, and, when he directed his lantern that way, he could have sworn he saw a leg disappearing around a corner – perhaps another gallery, perhaps a tunnel. Stere hurried towards that spot, but made it only three steps before he felt as if he were submerged in darkness – not the darkness in front of him, but rather that behind him, beneath him. His feet had pierced the rotted wood covering a well, and Stere plunged several meters into the darkness. His lantern struck against the walls of the well and went out.

The men heard the wood cracking and, a second later, the dry sound of Stere's body hitting the ground.

'Hey!' yelled Nicu. 'Where are you? What'd you do, eh?'

They both ran towards the spot from which the sound had come and cast their light over the pit.

Stere was curled up at the bottom of the well with his eyes closed and his legs in an unnatural position, like branches broken after a storm.

'Hey!' yelled Nicu. 'Hey, do you hear me?'

'Oh no!' Vasile wrung his hands. 'Oh no!'

'Stere! Hey, Stere!' Nicu continued to yell, but Stere didn't say anything.

'Is he still breathing?' asked Vasile.

'I don't know. Keep quiet now!'

And there was silence. Nicu directed his lantern towards Stere's face and tried to listen carefully. From the darkness behind them came the weak echo of dripping water rhythmically hitting a plank. The wind whistled distantly through the galleries, and, below, from the well, Stere gasped softly.

'Yes, he's alive,' said Nicu. 'He's breathing.'

'Oh, God help him!' said Vasile and made the sign of the cross in the air in front of him.

'Vasile, we have no way of getting him out. Go to Stelică and tell him to run to the village and bring a long rope.'

'Fine, Nicu, but keep him talking and let him know we'll be getting him out, because if he dies here, we're in for it.'

He sighed and left quickly through the tunnel towards the light.

Auntie Valeria was standing in the middle of the courtyard with her hands on her hips, looking towards the mountains. Ana was sweeping around her as though she were a statue, gathering up the rocks that had collected under the snow, which she had just pushed up along the fence.

'Watch out, you're in my way!'

But Valeria was looking into the void and said nothing.

'My gosh, only the – I won't even mention his name – can get through to you, God forgive me!' Ana got angry and made the sign of the cross.

'Ana,' said Valeria.

'What is it, auntie?'

'Ana, this is not good.'

'What's not good, auntie? Are you starting up with that again?'

'Ana, this is not good, I can feel it.'

Ana let the broom fall and asked:

'What do you feel?'

'Where are our husbands, Ana?'

'In town.'

'Are you sure?'

'They're in town. Selling iron to somebody.'

'I don't believe it, Ana.'

'What do you mean, you don't believe it? Didn't they tell you so last night?'

'Ana, the iron is still in the barn, in its usual place.'

'What are you saying?'

But a shiver had already gone down Ana's spine. She remembered how he had whispered to her last night that she was his 'sweetheart'. It had been a long time since he had said anything like that. A shudder passed through her whole body and she turned her back on Valeria and headed towards the barn. She entered and went to the back, where the stolen iron from the Dominiţa mine was piled up.

She turned and looked into Valeria's eyes, still lost among the mountains.

'Where are our husbands, Valeria?'

'I fear they've gone to the Turk's Mouth, Ana.'

'But they're not crazy!'

'Yes . . . Crazy from hunger, Ana. Crazy from hunger.'

Vasile was still several steps away from the mine's exit when he heard a muffled giggle echoing from behind him. He turned and saw a woman – a girl, rather – with long hair that was red like fire, dressed in long, white robes. She was barefoot and her grin was covered by the palms of her hands. Vasile looked straight into her large eyes and made the sign of the cross. He couldn't move, he was fixed to the spot, looking at the girl and whispering the Lord's Prayer endlessly, until the first tear flowed unexpectedly down his left cheek. Then the girl turned and started towards the central gallery. Vasile wiped his tears and took flight away from the mine as fast as his aged bones could carry him.

Stelică was in the cart, smoking. When he heard the footsteps, he raised himself up to his full height and saw Vasile, pale and weak, coming down from the mine, saying something, gesturing.

'What is it? What happened to you?'

'It's Stere.'

'What's wrong with him?'

'Stere fell in a well. Go and fetch a strong rope. A long one.'

'But how did he fall? What did you do in there?'

'Shut up and run, didn't you hear me?'

'I'm going now.'

'And be sure not to come back alone, but don't bring the whole village with you either.'

'OK, who then?'

'I don't know.'

'Ion?'

'Ion's good. But tell him to keep quiet.'

'OK, I'll keep him quiet.'

'Hurry.'

'I'll hurry.'

The two of them untied the horse and Stelică mounted it and, without looking back, he urged the horse on and set off towards the village.

'Stere! Hey, Stere, do you hear me?' yelled Nicu.

Stere murmured something from the bottom of the well.

'Stay just like that, okay, they're coming right away with the rope to get you out of there. Don't be scared, you're all right.'

But he knew that wasn't the case, however much he might try to reassure him: fear had crept in under Nicu's skin. His brother was dying at the bottom of a well in a decommissioned mine, he was alone, pouring his lantern's light into the well and all around, old Vasile had left and was never coming back. It was silent and only Stere's voice could be heard from the depths of the earth, groaning slowly and melodically as he came back to his senses and felt the pain coursing through the veins in every corner of his broken body.

It was a repulsive sight, but he had to keep his light trained on Stere, had to talk to him, to try to keep him awake, not to let him slip into the soft sleep of . . . He knew it was his only chance of escape. He and Vasile and Stelică and, if Vasile had thought of it, maybe even Ion. A good man. Only them. He couldn't trust anyone else, and the police . . . well, they couldn't call the police. They would all be arrested and even more misfortune would fall on their houses than . . . But he must stop thinking like that. It was neither the time nor the place for dark thoughts.

'Stere, hey, look up here, Stere! You hear me?'

He would have liked to cry. Why not? To run to his wife now and throw himself at her knees, to tell her he had lied to her, that his work wasn't in the city but at that damned Turk's Mouth, the scourge of the earth, the hole to hell. To be a young man once more, to love each other, to hold hands and roll in the hay, to take her palms in his, listening to her with blushing cheeks: 'Listen to what Mama says, Nicu, she knows what she's talking about. She's lived three times longer than you and her eyes have seen many things, and her ears have heard many things. The Turk's Mouth is cursed.' But how to tell her the truth . . . They were flat broke, there was no money to send the child to school in the fall, the furnace was growing colder. Yes, he would have really liked to let it all out and cry.

'Stere, just a bit longer, okay.'

He decided to go to the tunnel, to leave that narrow room and watch for Vasile. In fact, he hated it there, in the darkness of the earth. So he left. He stopped at the entrance to the main gallery and looked towards the exit. At the end of the tunnel the white light was totally undisturbed. Not a silhouette, not a sound, nothing.

'Where are you, Vasile? God damn you!' he sighed and remembered Stere.

He cast his lantern's light towards the well.

'Look, Stere, I'm here, stay calm, I'm not leaving.'

He stood with one foot in the room in which his brother had been swallowed up and the other in the main gallery, peering along the length of the tunnel and directing his lantern beam from time to time towards the edge of the well.

'I'm here, my brother. I'm not leaving you.'

The warmth was flowing out of his body, leaving him, making way for the cold and the darkness and the stench of wet and rancid earth. In the blackness above, lights floated and then disappeared. It was cold and dark again. The pain jabbed at him in the darkness, from below, where his legs should have been, jabbed and bit, tormenting the flesh and scratching the bone. Light, once again. In the distance he heard a voice, softly, as if in a dream. But it wasn't a dream, and if it had been, it would have been a nightmare. He recognized the voice, it was Nicu's, his brother's, it was coming from above, from wherever the light was coming from, from time to time through the fog. The pain rose to his arm and his hearing focused. He could clearly hear Nicu, how he was trying to reassure him. It's all right, he was saying from the darkness, it's all right. Yes, Nicu, it's all right, thought Stere, but I can't move and I can't scream. It's all right, you say.

Again the darkness.

Now light.

Darkness.

Nicu's voice.

Something moved above him. Clods of earth broke loose from the walls of the well, struck him. Something was descending towards him. He would have liked to yell for Nicu, to tell him to come, to get him out of there, to shine his light down below, into the abyss where he lay broken. But he couldn't . . .

Something was descending, sliding along the walls of the

pit, the dirt crumbled, a loud scuffling sound, then nothing more.

Silence.

The fog returned. The warmth banished the pains of flesh and bone, the torpor dripped on his skin like warm honey. He was sleepy. He closed his eyes, but the darkness was just as black as outside, as in the world. He no longer felt pain. Now he was warm. There was something beside him, he knew it, but it didn't matter, he was warm and fine, he no longer felt his legs. Whatever was beside him drew nearer and sat on his chest. He felt the burning skin of its thighs and buttocks on his chest and abdomen. He felt the rough hair swooshing down over his face, the fingers caressing his throat, his ears, his temples, his hair. He felt the warmth of the stranger's body heating him and flowing through him towards his legs, down there where his body had become darkness, felt it catch fire in the small of his back, he groaned, writhed. He rose to embrace the creature and to caress its sweaty skin, his palms slid down, all the way down towards the edge of the world, into the darkness, he groaned and cried and knew that he was dying.

Stelică burst into the house and looked at the women kneeling before the icons, their heads covered in scarves, sighing, weeping. But he said nothing and left to search for rope.

'How did the horse act?' Valeria's voice was heard.

Stelică stopped and turned around.

'When you arrived there, how did the horse act?' the woman repeated.

'I don't know.'

'Think.'

'I don't know, he struggled.'

He was ashamed to look the woman in the eyes. He

looked somewhere above her, through the small window in the wall, through the small curtain, through the small garden, through the world that all of a sudden was too small.

'It was the *vâlva* of the mines,' said the woman. 'The horse saw the bad place and he did not want to stay there.'

'Come on, cut it out! There's no time for fairy tales!'

'Are our husbands dying, Stelică?' asked Ana in a weeping voice.

Stelică didn't know how to respond, so he turned around and entered the other room.

'Well, boy,' said Valeria, 'you do not want to believe. You are young and believe yourself safe from the darkness of our ancestors. You walk through the town, you drink and you eat, and you think what we old people say is just fairy tales. But they're not fairy tales, Stelică. It is the way of things for us. And for you, whether you like it or not.'

Valeria was talking alone, but she knew that Stelică was eavesdropping from the next room. He was listening, but he didn't want her to know.

'My granny took me by the hand when I was little,' the woman continued, 'and led me to the back of the courtyard. And do you know what was there, Stelică? Do you know?'

Ana was trembling and crying beneath the icon.

'It was the *măiestre*, Stelică. They were playing there in a circle, under the moon. My eyes were heavy with sleep, I thought I was dreaming. But the next morning when I went to the back of the garden, behold the grass was all trampled down. My granny said then that I should never go out alone to look at the fairies, for alone we are weak, Stelică, there is only strength in numbers. God help us, for alone we can do nothing. Have you said a prayer?'

'I have,' Stelică's voice was heard on the other side.

'Are you listening to what I'm saying, Stelică?'

'I'm listening, since you never keep your mouth shut,'

said Stelică, coming out of the room with a long rope wound around his left arm.

He went out into the courtyard and yelled towards the neighboring house.

'Ion! Hey, Ion!'

'What is it?' could be heard from behind the fence.

'Do you have work?'

'I don't.'

'Let me give you some.'

'OK,' said Ion and started towards the gate, happy as could be because he could leave the yard for a little while.

Valeria crept up behind Stelică's back and put her hand on his shoulder.

'Stelică, you have killed our husbands,' she whispered. 'You have pushed them to do what should not be done. Stupid men! How could they have listened to you, you silly fool . . . Sins were committed there, boy: a man slept with children, may God forgive me! A place is not made bad only through magic or fairies, but also through crime, and crime is what Piele did there. There is war waging in the pits of the earth, and you had better pray hard that you can bring our men out of that darkness.'

The woman's threat stung him like a cold slap across his cheek. He blushed and lowered his head.

'God grant that place does not harm you,' the woman went on, and then withdrew slowly into the house, from which Ana's stifled sobs could be heard.

Ion entered the courtyard and asked him, 'What is it?'

'Will you come with me to the Turk's Mouth?'

'No way, man, get out of here!'

But Stelică didn't say anything more, he just looked him straight in the eyes, deep, really deep, and in his eyes Ion saw the abyss, the precipice and the wind, and he understood that it was bad, very bad, that something had become twisted in the world, and that he would find out soon whether it could be put back into place or not.

'Stere, they'll be coming any time now,' yelled Nicu so that he would hear him from the well, but saying it was one thing and feeling it was another.

He was a full-grown man, middle-aged but sturdy, tough and powerful, and yet he felt fear, as if something were circling around him and blowing on his skin, but there was nothing; he saw it too, when he pointed his lantern around and thought about grandfather Tache and how right he had been. From time to time he lit up the edge of the well in order to reassure Stere, or at least that's what he hoped.

'Stere, keep your eyes open! After we get you out of there, well, we'll have food and drinks and dance, and have the biggest party anybody's ever seen. You hear me?'

He was trying to keep him awake somehow, but only through words. It seemed he no longer dared go near the edge of the pit, it was horrible there, seeing Stere bent over backwards with his legs broken in all directions, with reddened eyes and an empty gaze, groaning absently in his pain. But it seemed as though the groans had increased recently, thought Nicu, yes, that's how it seems, he told himself. They were longer, more slippery, like fish in spring, deeper, like the groans in the darkened streets at night, when the young girls sleep badly and the young men don't sleep at all. And so he fell silent, listened, and directed his lantern towards the well. Stere groaned longer and more often, his wheezy breath heaving in blood-filled gasps. Nicu felt a shiver and suddenly imagined himself descending on a rope to hoist up a corpse, cold and purple, its hair full of dried blood.

'Hey, don't you even think about dy—' he said and took the three, four long steps that were necessary to reach the edge of the well and shine light into the pit.

But he couldn't finish what he was saying. The lantern cast waves of light on Stere, but Stere was not alone in the pit. On top of him was seated a pale woman, with red, disheveled hair, naked and filthy with dirt. She was crouched up on Stere's chest, with her head thrown back, looking at Nicu with a crooked smile on a chipped face. A loud hissing rose up from the woman's throat and her black pupils slid upward, disappearing into her head, leaving visible only the total whiteness of a pair of dead eyes.

'What . . .' Nicu said, but he didn't have time to say anything more, because the woman shot out towards him and in three movements had arrived up beside him.

One: her right hand embedded in one of the walls of the well.

Two: her left hand embedded in the opposite wall, higher up, lifting herself, hurling herself towards Nicu.

Three: her right hand caught the edge of the well and the woman leapt toward Nicu, taking him by the T-shirt and dragging him furiously into the well, throwing him alongside Stere.

As he fell, Nicu saw the lantern hitting the sides of the well, and then darkness all around, before the great darkness from within his head, in the moment in which his skull shattered, his neck dislocated, and the blood shot out of his mouth.

Stere felt the shock. Nicu's body was lying breathless beside him, his head crushed in the impact with the ground. He was terrified at the woman's strength and his fear sent a wave of blood to his head and his limbs, waking him. He couldn't see anything, but he was beginning to understand what was happening. He was at the bottom of a well and Nicu was beside him. Probably dead. Someone had been next to him, a woman. Now she was no longer there. She had dragged Nicu, well no, she had thrown him headlong into one of the walls of the well. Probably. Then the woman had gone. It was quiet. They were alone. Probably. He tried to move, but the pain stung him in both legs. He tried to shout. He choked. Coughed. Tried once more and a weak sound issued from his throat. He tried again. Louder. He gave free rein to his voice, fighting against the pain, and screamed. The echo traversed the galleries. He fumbled in the darkness to his left and wet the tips of his fingers in something warm and sticky, thick, pasty. Stere then prodded the indentation in Nicu's skull, from which a steaming broth was flowing. His hairline descended into a little valley filled with liquid and bone chips, then rose again and descended at the back of his head. Stere was gripped with a feeling of powerlessness and tried to stop his tears, clenching his teeth and hitting the ground under him with his fist.

He cried out. The echo was broken by the walls. A cry of fear. A cry of fury, of impotence. A cry of death.

No one responded, there was only the echo striking the walls then dying away.

Crying, he began to sing, softly, in a whisper:

> *I saw my dear lover,*
> *Five demons were beating her,*
> *Red blood flowing like a river . . .*

And then he heard footsteps. He was quiet and listened: the scuffling of dragging footsteps above. The steps stopped at the well's edge. He heard breathing – heavy like the wind through the valleys of his childhood. A snarl, then silence. His heart pumped blood, too much and too quickly, and Stere felt that all that blood must be flowing out of unknown orifices in his body, somewhere in the darkness, into the black earth beneath him. Another snarl and Stere heard clumps of dirt breaking loose from the walls of the well as the creature slid slowly into the pit.

A thud and the creature was beside him. Stere wanted to scream, but he no longer could; his jaws were clenched with fear, so he began to cry and squeezed his eyelids shut, but in vain: the darkness in his head was just as black as the darkness outside.

The creature bent over him and emitted a disgusting stench from its open mouth. Then it left Stere and went over to Nicu. Stere listened in the darkness: a sound of ripping – Nicu's T-shirt was torn in one motion. Then a powerful blow and Stere could hear Nicu's ribs crack noisily. The creature dug around in Nicu's innards and Stere could almost imagine it all and vomited. He smelled the scent of warm, fresh blood, and that of urine and feces almost made him faint. He turned around part way, dragging his legs and whispering through his sobs, no no, please, no . . .

He felt a hand, a human hand, twisting his back around. The creature had taken his shoulders with both hands. Stere raised his arms and groped at the body: human back, chest, hips. The creature sat on him and Stere felt its thighs around his hips. The creature let go of his shoulders and after a moment of silence pounced with both fists in his chest. Stere let out a broken sound, emitted from his mouth at the same time as a gush of blood.

In his last instants of life, Stere felt a dull pain in his chest, heard his ribs cracking, and felt the flesh tearing beneath the creature's fists, heard a loud ringing in his ears and felt something warm flowing from his ears. The creature burrowed its head into Stere's body and began to tear at his flesh with its teeth. With the last of his strength, the man raised his arm and set his hand on the head of what was devouring his body, a head covered in short hair, with large, sharp ears, with a bloody muzzle and big round eyes: the head of a dog.

★

Stelică jumped off the cart first and rushed towards Vasile. He found him pale and trembling.

'Vasile, you didn't go back in? What are they doing in there alone?'

The five men untied the horse from the cart and started off towards the mine's entrance with ropes and shovels, with long boards and lanterns. Stelică and Ion had gathered them from among the neighbors, whispering through the doors so that the women would not hear, careful not to be seen by too many people on their way towards the mine.

Vasile didn't respond, he was ashamed to say anything, to confess his cowardliness, to tell them what he had seen in the tunnel.

Stelică wanted to rush towards the entrance, but Vasile stopped him, without saying anything more. Stelică looked at him and understood all. Something had happened in his absence, Vasile had seen or heard something, the earth had caved in, or gas had come to the surface and exploded. Something had happened there, at the entrance to that hell, but Stelică was too afraid to ask anything, or even to say anything, so he was silent and turned towards the Turk's Mouth mine. The Devil's Mouth, as he had heard Valeria saying, when he departed through the gate accompanied by Ion and left the women alone in the house, crying and clutching at their scarves under the icons.

Stelică made a sign to the men not to enter the mine. They stopped and looked at him dumbfounded.

'Hey, there's men dying in there, isn't that what you said?' one of them said.

But Stelică didn't look at him and didn't answer him. He climbed the hill with his left hand raised to the right side of his chest, forgotten there after he had made the sign to them to stay where they were. Like that he arrived at the mine's entrance, where he stopped and let his hand fall limp at his side. He stopped there, looking into the distance, into the blackness of the tunnel, and his glance received a response: a pair of eyes looked at him from the darkness. There was no life in those eyes and yet they moved – the creature took several steps towards him and Stelică observed what it was: a white ram with milky eyes looked at him and blew out thick steam like smoke.

Stelică didn't take another step, he turned around and looked at the men. He wanted to signal to them to leave, to go back to their own world, but he stopped with his hand in mid-air, the gesture cut off as if in forgetfulness.

It began to rain. Somewhere, in the forest, there was the sound of a woodpecker drumming at a tree.

Translated from the Romanian by James D. Jenkins

Flore Hazoumé

Menopause

The daughter of a Beninese father and a Congolese mother, Flore Hazoumé grew up in France but has long lived in Ivory Coast. She is the author of ten books, including one of relevance to the horror genre, a collection of short stories entitled Cauchemars [Nightmares] *(1994). The title is appropriate: in Hazoumé's stories, the everyday quickly takes a turn for the bizarre or nightmarish. 'Menopause' is our favorite of her stories, and the author's favorite as well; she has since adapted it for a play version. The story is set in an unspecified African land not unlike Ivory Coast, in a male-dominated society where marriages between older men and much younger females are the norm. For the narrator, then, her approaching menopause represents more than just a physical alteration in her body; it is also a reminder that as an older, unmarried woman no longer capable of bearing children, she will lack a clear place in society. Hazoumé uses the framework of a horror story both to make a comment on African society and to tell an unsettling tale in which the narrator's midlife change may be even more terrible than she at first suspected . . .*

I'VE ONLY JUST RETURNED from a two-month vacation to Cape Lake when I rush to the phone and dial Clémence's number. I need her so much. Only she will be able to comfort me. When a young girl's voice responds that Clémence no longer lives at that address, I'm gripped by a senseless fear.

'It's not possible! No, it's not possible.'

The voice on the other end hesitates.

'Wait a moment, I'll get my husband.'

I hang up. I slip on a jacket and get in my car. I shiver. Could Clémence already have . . . ? No, it's not possible, she's only six months older than I am.

Nervously, I bring my hand to my throat. I feel the soft skin flee from my fingers. I park my car in front of Clémence's house. I ring. The sound of steps on the gravel. Flipper, the dog, barks. The door opens halfway, a young woman smiles at me. She looks like a twenty year younger version of me. She looks like my two daughters too.

'You're the one who called just now? My husband was sure you would come. He's waiting for you in the living room.'

She signals me to follow her. I observe her. Women in our world have always been lively, young, and beautiful. I've never seen a woman grow old, but next to this young girl, I feel withered, rough like a piece of burlap. I follow her anxiously down the corridor, Flipper at my heels. Clémence's favorite paintings are still hanging on the wall. The notes of our theme song, the hard-to-find original version of 'Afrikan Krystal' sung by Daya Smith, are coming from the living room. Clémence had promised to give it to me for my birthday in a few days. I look around. I understand everything now, I feel like laughing. Clémence is playing a joke on me. Nothing has happened to her. She hasn't changed. She's still the same. She's waiting for me, smiling, in the living room in front of a cup of tea. I walk with a more assured step.

The young woman opens the door for me. Clémence is sitting with her back to me in an armchair facing the window. I see only her dark hair where, to my great surprise, some white strands have blended in. My anxiety vanishes. I can confide in her without fear, explain without shame what's happening inside me.

'Clémence! I was so worried; you really scared me, it's really bad of you to . . .'

She turns around slowly, I can see half of her face. The

end of my sentence hangs in the air. A cry of horror escapes me. There, in Clémence's armchair, a middle-aged man looks at me with a calm expression.

'What's wrong? Do you feel ill? Why don't you sit down.'

'I . . . I'm looking for my friend Clémence, she lives here, she lived here, I . . . I don't know anymore.'

I collapse into a chair. My head is all muddled. The man puts his hand gently on mine.

'Your friend no longer lives here. She is gone.'

'Gone? No, it's impossible, a person can't just go without taking anything with them, leave everything behind. The photo of her husband, the one of her wedding, of her daughters, a person can't just leave like that! No one can change to that extent,' I say under my breath, scrutinizing for a moment the stranger's impassive face.

I cast a disoriented glance around the whole room. Flipper has come up to the old man and is licking his hands, how strange! They act as though they've known each other forever. A mad thought crosses my mind; but I don't want to believe it. Could Clémence . . . ? I reject that idea. And yet, that way of running his hands through his hair, of stroking his chin with a dreamy look. So many details remind me of Clémence. I stand up, in the grip of a great agitation. At the doorstep, the man places his hand affectionately on my shoulder and murmurs in a comforting voice:

'There are many ways of leaving.'

As he says these words, he plunges his clear gaze into mine. For a fleeting moment I have the strange sensation of having always known him, of finding a friend I thought I'd lost.

That evening, Claude and Pascale, my two daughters, Frédéric and Joël, their husbands, as well as my two granddaughters come to my house for dinner. This familial interlude is good for me and forces me to take my mind off things. I have just enough time to fix dinner and get dressed. I choose a skirt that covers my calves, a long-sleeved blouse. I prefer outfits that are lighter and less covering, but for the past few weeks . . . Let's not think about it any more!

At 8 p.m. the doorbell rings. I assume a calm expression. My two daughters kiss me, my granddaughters Emmanuelle and Paule hop around me. I stroke their curly hair as they pass by. My two sons-in-law, so alike with their timeworn faces, shake my hand. I seem to sense an unusual warmth, a complicity, in the smiles they give me. Claude, my eldest daughter, joins me in the kitchen where I'm arranging some glasses on a tray.

She looks at me insistently. Is it that noticeable?

'You look tired, Mom!'

My lips pursed, I don't say anything. She takes a couple steps. I anticipate her gesture. I start to take a step back, too late! She has already run her hands through my hair.

'You're losing your hair, Mom! Look!'

Do I need to look? I know that trivial spectacle only too well. Every morning on my pillow I gather up handfuls of hair. With every passing day my hair grows more and more sparse.

I manage to stammer a response.

'I . . . I went to the doctor. Apparently it's menopause; I'm following a treatment. Everything will go back to normal. Come on, it's late, let's sit down at the table.'

During the meal only my daughters and I speak. My sons-in-law say almost nothing. Men, in our world, speak little. They look out on existence with an expression that reflects all of mankind's wisdom.

Is it their function that surrounds them with this inde-finable aura? Here, men make up a separate clan, an inaccessible caste. Beneath their idle appearance, they hold power, wisdom, knowledge. The very balance of our society is in their hands. The women, simultaneously the ants and the grasshoppers, are the lifeblood of our world. They are the future and they beget the future. For those aging sphinxes, stuck in the wanderings of their thoughts, women are a kind of short-lived turbulence that barely disrupts the order and functioning of the society they have skillfully built.

For the first time in my life, I find myself admiring them. I feel close to them. I feel like talking to them, learning their opinions, their thoughts, and thus having a foretaste of what perhaps awaits me ... I turn towards them. Our glances meet. One of them slides his hand towards mine and squeezes it with emotion. I read the profoundest respect in their eyes.

When dinner is finished, we make ourselves comfortable in the little sitting room. My sons-in-law smoke their cigars with a vacant look. My daughters have a discussion, carefree. My granddaughters sit on footstools, playing at my feet. I relax and softly hum 'Afrikan Krystal', my favorite song. I think of Clémence. Without noticing, I've crossed my legs. My skirt has slid up, revealing my ankles. Paule, my younger granddaughter, caresses my legs. Unsuspecting, I indulge myself in that soft contact.

'Oh, Granny, your legs, they're like a cat's back!' she yells, pulling on the long, hard hairs.

'No, more like a black rabbit,' retorts Emmanuelle.

With a brusque movement, I fold my skirt back over my legs. Instinctively, I turn towards my sons-in-law, as if only they could come to my aid. There's an awkward silence.

'It's getting late,' they say finally in a single voice. 'It's time to leave.'

My daughters, uncomfortable, remain silent. Have they guessed? They won't say anything, I won't say anything. It's the law, this stage of life is lived alone, far from the gaze of others, with courage, with modesty. I had almost forgotten.

Once I'm alone, I go up to my room. Tonight I have the courage to face my own image, this strange body which yet is mine.

I stand before the large mirror, completely naked. I close my eyes, unable to bear this horrible vision, this grotesque reflection of myself. Yet, I must! I open my eyes. I can't help flinching in repulsion. With horror, I notice the extent of the illness that's devouring me. My breasts are completely covered in short, bushy hairs. Is this arm mine, this hairy chest? These arms, these legs, made up in a long, hideous down? Is this really me, this hermaphrodite, this unnatural thing?

My eyes wander for a moment over the bedside table where the photo of my husband is. At least he would have helped me to get through this stage of my life. Only today do I realize how I miss his silent presence and what a void his death has left. Exhausted, I swallow two sleeping pills.

For several days I don't notice anything abnormal. My transformation seems to have stopped, the growth of my body hair seems to have balanced out. Only the forerunner symptoms of menopause persist and reassure me: dizziness, hot flashes, bloating.

On the other hand, my skin worries me. Some already existing wrinkles have become accentuated; others have appeared on my forehead. Bags have formed under my eyes. Now I look like a middle-aged woman. After all, maybe that's what getting old is, maybe that's the menopause the medical books talk too briefly about. I suddenly realize I'm the first woman to see herself grow old. In our world, women never reach old age, what becomes of them? I know the answer. I refuse to believe it. But can one struggle against the order of things?

In the street, no one notices me. The couples are all alike: young women in the arms of their middle-aged husbands, families built on the same model: young girls holding the hands of their mother and their worthy father, in the prime of his life. They all pass close by me without noticing anything. Maybe people take me for what I'm not. The other day, coming out of a store, a young woman bumped into me and said: 'Oh! Sorry, sir!' It's true that I was wearing pants.

So I've decided to shave my legs and arms and wear dresses again. What a pleasure to see those vile hairs drowned in the bathtub! I'm finally going to put on an elegant dress. Who cares if my face is marked with age, my legs are still respectable. I take a dress from the wardrobe and slip it on. I have the impression that it used to fit a little tighter at the hips. The anxiety of the past few weeks must have made me lose weight. So much the better! There, all done.

I turn towards the large mirror. I look at myself, I burst out laughing. I laugh until it hurts, no, it's not me, this miserable clown. I laugh harder and harder, no, it's not me, this grotesque creature, this transvestite, this weirdly attired caricature in a dress that hangs everywhere, this woman with no breasts, no hips, no curves. And I laugh over and over without realizing that my laughter ends in tears.

I got up early this morning. A sort of intuition forced me to get out of bed. I feel that something irreversible happened last night. I avoid the large mirror. I run my hand over my face. Under my fingers my skin is as rough as that of a man who hasn't shaved in several days. The mirror behind me mocks me. I won't look at myself. I already know what I'll see.

I take off my nightgown unhurriedly. All the hairs have grown back, my breasts have totally disappeared. I hold my breath. My heart beats harder and harder, faster and faster. Gently, slowly, I lower my eyes towards the only feminine symbol I have left. I can hardly breathe, my vision goes blurry, I put my hand between my thighs, I'm reeling, I'm losing my mind. Under my fingers, an unambiguous growth. In a final cry of horror I lose consciousness.

It's dark, I must have slept a long time. My memories are confused. I have the impression of living a second life, in a new skin. I'm sitting in the living room, in an armchair. An appetizing smell is coming from the kitchen. I get up, I light my pipe. I am very elegant tonight in my three-piece suit. Dominique told me that we'll be receiving guests. An old friend, it seems. Here she is. She smiles at me, young and radiant.

'Did you sleep well, darling? Clément and his wife won't be long.'

A ring at the door. They're here. Standing on the doorstep are the young woman and the man who are living in Clémence's house. He looks at me in silence and hands me a record: 'Afrikan Krystal'.

'Happy birthday,' he says to me, with an attitude of complicity.

Translated from the French by James D. Jenkins

Christien Boomsma

The Bones in Her Eyes

It's commonly claimed – even by the Dutch – that the Netherlands has no real tradition of horror fiction, but Dutch literature does contain some hidden gems in the genre, like the often horror-tinged 'fantastic' tales of Ferdinand Bordewijk and Belcampo, Kathinka Lannoy's volumes of ghost stories, and the bizarre and unsettling stories of Jacques Hamelink. And in more recent years, the Dutch horror scene has shown increasing signs of life. The works of Paul van Loon and CHRISTIEN BOOMSMA *have proven extremely popular with younger audiences, while Thomas Olde Heuvelt scored an international success with his 2016 novel* Hex. *Both Olde Heuvelt and Boomsma were featured alongside a number of other emerging horror writers in a pioneering 2016 anthology of new Dutch horror fiction, from which the following tale, 'The Bones in Her Eyes', is taken. The story came to Boomsma after she accidentally hit a cat with her car: the look in the animal's eyes haunted her in her dreams, though we doubt those dreams were quite as nightmarish as this tale they inspired.*

I T'S THE EYES I JUST CAN'T GET OUT OF MY SYSTEM, glowing yellow-green in the darkness when they were caught in the glare of my headlights. Some people would call such a sight demonic, but they're haters, and why should I pay any attention to what they say? No, to me they were mirrors that showed with an unsettling sharpness a truth that I didn't seem to grasp. I knew it was important for me to see it, to understand it. But it eluded me, and it eludes me still.

Matt – my boyfriend – always said there was nothing you could do about it when it happens, but I never believed him. I considered those rural roads full of carelessly murdered hedgehogs, flattened frogs, squashed rabbits, and bleeding ducks to be a typical expression of human inability to treat the world with respect. Getting home in time to watch *Farmer Wants a Wife* is more important than a creature that breathes, that feels. That dies.

But that evening I discovered that things could be different. I had had a long day because I go – no, went – once a month to the drawing academy in Rotterdam. Quite a drive if you live as far north as I do. So when I drove back into the village I could already taste the night in the day. It was the time when animals leave their holes and lairs and slip into the world. A dangerous time.

So I drove slowly, scanning the roadside where the grass was already withered because autumn was on its way. And I saw them: a cat's eyes, like small glowing lamps in the falling dusk.

What was perhaps more frustrating: the cat saw me too. It sat motionless waiting along the side of the road and watched as I approached.

And this is what's so infinitely difficult to accept: I wasn't careless and I wasn't speeding, although naturally I wanted to get home, plop down on the couch, and close my eyes while Matt poured me a glass of port.

In the end, the animal did it itself. And there was nothing I could do.

One moment it was still there. I saw the ears – a little too short – and the tail, which looked as if it had once been longer and had an odd kink in it. I even imagine seeing the whiskers, a blend of black and white, although that is highly unlikely. But in my head, where I keep the memory, I do see them.

I don't think I was going much faster than 50 km per hour. Maybe even 30. But in the split second it should have taken to pass the animal, it moved.

I saw it. A quick leap, perfectly timed as if the cat had chosen its own death – but animals can't do that – and it stood right in front of me on the road.

I braked with everything I had. The wheels jammed, screeching over the cobblestones. There was a 'thump' that made me queasy. Then: silence.

'Oh God,' I whispered to the dashboard. 'Oh shit.'

My hands were trembling when I switched off the ignition. They were shaking when I opened the door. The warning sound began to beep, but I left the lights on while I let my feet drop onto the deck of the tossing ship the road seemed to have turned into.

I stumbled to the front of my car and knelt down beside the cat. The short ears with a piece missing, the tattered fur and the half-black, half-white whiskers. Mouth open – was the lower jaw shorter than the upper? Blood was streaming out, and the head had been scraped by the pavement. And that was the good scenario because it could also have a skull fracture. Its paw lay at an odd angle, definitely broken. And still more blood, which looked brown rather than red in the glow of the headlights.

Its eyes were open, but those weren't damaged. The pupils were enormous and hardly left room for the yellow-green reflection around them. And then it looked at me. Bleeding and dying, the cat looked at me.

Was there reproach? They say animals can't feel human emotions, but if elephants can mourn and dolphins can love, why couldn't a cat blame you for what you've done?

'Stupid cat. Why didn't you just stay put?' I whispered. I brought my trembling finger to its head and petted carefully between its ears. 'I'm so sorry.'

Blood stuck to my fingers and while I tried to think of where to wipe it off, I noticed the thin yellow collar around the animal's neck. The little silver address tag.

Of course. The accident hadn't only affected the cat that was now lying here dying in the street. Somewhere there was an owner, maybe a whole family, who would be devastated by the loss of this animal. My fault.

But I've never walked away from my responsibilities. Not even now, with a stranger's voice in my head and glass splinters from an attic window at my feet.

I reached for the collar to remove the tag. I must have been hurting the cat because it suddenly lashed out and drove sharp claws deep into my wrist.

'Shit!'

Lightning fast I pulled my hand back. The cat had stuck its nails deep in my skin and thick drops of blood dripped down and mixed with the even thicker cat blood. Just what I needed, I thought. I brought my wrist to my mouth and sucked. It was just what I deserved.

Just pick it up, very carefully, and don't look at the nauseating spots left behind on the road. There was a grocery box in the trunk of my car and I put the cat in it, after which I set it next to me on the passenger seat. I wished I could talk to it because it must be suffering horrible pain. Fortunately it didn't scratch me again.

It lived on Appelstraat. Number 79.

How do you do that kind of thing? What do you say when you ring someone's doorbell with their housemate dying in a cardboard box? And you're the one responsible?

The garden path that would bring me to the front door of number 79 seemed endless. It was a rather small detached house that screamed 'overdue maintenance'. Roof shingles that had slid into the gutter, chipping paint on the window frames, a break in the glass of a skylight high above, a wild confusion of bushes in the garden. A bramble caught its thorns in my jacket as if it wanted to prevent me from reaching the front door. And then there was the cat, motionless in its little cardboard box, looking at me with those reflecting eyes. The deep scratch on my wrist throbbed and ached as only cat scratches can.

What was I going to say in one minute,

fifty seconds,

thirty seconds,

ten . . . ?

'*Good evening. I'm terribly sorry, but . . .*'

It was not a good evening, and it was about to get much worse.

'*Hello. I realize this comes as a shock, but I accidentally . . .*'

What good would 'accidentally' do them?

'*Your cat suddenly jumped in front of my car and I didn't have time to brake. I . . .*'

That sounded as though I was blaming the cat.

When I had finally reached the end of the path and put my finger on the doorbell, my brain was nearly bursting with possible apologies and tears that I kept holding back in my weary head.

And then the door opened, and I suddenly realized there was an even worse possible scenario than the one about the inconsolable toddler who'd lost her dearest pet: that of a lonely old granny who had no one else but the cat, which she loved like a child.

And I had killed that child.

So when I saw the thin, gray tufts of hair on the skull of the woman who opened the door, the wrinkles like crinkled paper, the liver spots on her forehead, one of those synthetic beige skirts that no one under eighty dares to wear anymore, and the walker with which she had patiently made her way to the door, I could hardly get a word out. I began to sniffle helplessly and held the box out towards her. 'I'm so sorry . . .'

That was the moment when the woman should have broken out crying herself, or gotten angry. The moment when she should have chased me off with her cane or had a heart attack from the shock. But none of that happened.

She took the box from me calmly and looked inside with a kind of absent curiosity.

That was the moment when I really should have known that something wasn't right. And I don't mean because of the accident or the dying animal in the box. Something was *off*. But I was tired and shaken up and didn't notice it.

She bent over the box, shaking her head, and stuck her hand inside. 'What have you been up to, Dante? What on earth got into that silly cat head of yours!'

I sniffled. 'I'm so terribly sorry, ma'am. I couldn't avoid him and I hit him with my car. I'm well insured, we can call the vet. I want to take care of everything.'

She looked up. 'Aw, what a nice girl you are. He does that sometimes, you know? He just takes off and does stupid things. I'm always telling him: don't do that, be careful now, but he is *so* stubborn.'

She turned her attention back to the animal in the box. 'Shame on you, Dante! Now look what you've done. You've made this nice girl cry. Shame, shame, shame.'

I tried again. 'Shall we drive together to a vet's office? I'll gladly pay.'

But the woman shook her head resolutely. Maybe she wasn't as fragile as I had initially thought. 'Not necessary, dearie, not necessary. He's a tough one, my Dante.' A sharp look at me. 'But you look a little peaked. I bet you'd like a cup of tea. For the fright.'

I didn't want any tea. What I wanted was to go home and

take a bath and forget all of this had happened. But how could I tell her no?

'I never hear from my children, you see? And Dante here isn't very talkative either. A nice cup of tea would do us both good,' she went on.

I hesitated. My sense of guilt was huge, but so was my headache. And I wanted to say no, I wanted . . .

'It's just the two of us, my husband and I, you see. And Dante of course. Oh, and I mustn't forget Frits. That's our canary, but he doesn't really sing anymore. Too old, I think. Just like my husband. He's ninety-four. He's not so well anymore. We used to play little games, he and I. We would play Halma or Parcheesi on Sunday evenings. It's the Parkinson's. He knocks all the little pieces over. That's how it goes, he can't help it of course, but still . . .'

'I'm sorry, ma'am,' I managed to say. 'Matt, my boyfriend, will wonder where I am, so if you're sure there's nothing more I can do for you . . .'

It went totally quiet and I heard only the rasping sound of a dying cat from the box that she had placed on her walker.

She looked at me with an unspoken accusation in her eyes and nodded. 'If you'd rather go home, dearie, then I'll manage on my own. Alone.'

I know. I may have turned my back a million times on my parents' faith and decided that whatever is up there ruling the universe, in any case it's not the sexist, unimaginative, and vengeful old man my parents' church made it out to be. But I'll never be able to shake off that impression. Not entirely.

The church had gotten its claws of sin, duty, and an endless awareness of not-enough in me when I was so small that I didn't know the difference between the words 'mercy' and 'jersey'. Now that I'm an adult, my only defense is my refusal to let myself be controlled by it.

And Matt.

I would go crazy if Matt weren't there to scrape the burning coals off my head every so often.

'I should have stayed,' I told him later that evening. 'I mean: why couldn't I bring myself to drink a cup of tea with her? I killed her cat! And now she's there all alone with her husband, who can't do anything either. Did I already tell you that he's 94, her husband? That means he must have fought in the war, that he saw the Wall go up and then fall again, that he saw radio and the newspaper make way for television and the internet. Everything!'

'Impressive,' Matt said calmly. He bent over and refilled my glass with port. Tawny and fairly old, just the way I like it. He has always known exactly what I needed, and thus that tonight a cheapie from the supermarket wasn't going to cut it.

'She used to play games with him. But now his Parkinson's is so bad that he always knocks the pieces over, she says. Is that our future? Together in a dilapidated little house on the edge of the inhabited world with a canary and a cat? And then I come along and destroy even that.'

Matt came and sat beside me, and through the soft fabric of my bathrobe I felt the warmth of his thigh against mine. Upon seeing the look in my eyes when I came home, he had first run a full bath and then guided me with a gentle hand towards the bathroom to relax in the warmth of the water. Now he listened to me as only he can: sweet, loving, clever, and above all without judgment.

His hand glided towards my leg, pushed the flap of the robe aside and caressed my warm skin. The sudden intimacy brought me almost to tears because I knew that she – that little old woman – that maybe she had also had it once, but no longer.

He saw it, stopped, and brought his hand to my face. He stroked my cheek with the back side of his ring finger. I felt the callus there and the hardness of his knuckle and sighed. 'Sorry, I'm rattling on.'

'And that's exactly why I love you so much,' he muttered. 'Because things like that affect you. That makes you unique.' He grinned. 'Tender Tara.'

He always used that pet name when I got emotional over abandoned shelter dogs, refugees in trouble on the borders of Europe, or yet another cutback in social services under the guise of 'efficiency'. I hate that no one calls it by its right name: economizing on the weakest.

'I feel guilty,' I whispered. 'Dante . . .' I saw the lack of understanding in his eyes and quickly added: 'The cat. I hit him hard, Matt, really hard. All that blood! And she totally didn't get what was really happening. She thought he'd just get better. That when she wakes up tomorrow and goes to the kitchen, then . . .'

'A person can't do everything,' Matt said, and he kissed my forehead softly. 'Not even my Tender Tara.'

His fingers stroked my hair. 'Otherwise just go back later and check on how the beast is. Then you can still have a cup of tea with her and maybe even play a game. She'll like that better than if you had stayed this evening.'

He was right, of course. That's how Matt is. He always knows how to guide me so that it feels good and safe.

So when his lips touched mine, I finally dared to surrender myself. I kissed him back and welcomed the warmth. I had a plan. And everything would work out fine in the end.

Naive, right? To think you can make up for taking a life with a belated cup of tea?

I should have known it wouldn't be so easy. Especially when the night, which had begun in a heated intoxication of oblivion, passed into something else.

I hadn't yet slipped deep into the sleep I so desperately

needed when it began. An endless falling as images flashed by: the dark cobblestone road, only lit up here and there by a single nostalgic streetlamp, the glowing eyes on the side of the road, the screeching brakes that drowned out the sound of my car stereo. The cat's mirror eyes that wanted to tell me something I couldn't see, couldn't hear.

My eyes flew open. Sweat on my skin. I stared at the ceiling without seeing anything.

A dream. It was only a dream.

Soft scratching from the darkness. The cat? But . . .

I reached my hand towards the still figure beside me. I longed for the reassuring warmth of his sleeping body. His security.

But when my fingers stroked his skin, they felt not the rough hairs of a man's arm but something plush, soft. And immediately afterwards . . . sticky, wet, as if . . .

'Shh,' Matt whispered in my hair. And I forced myself to relax.

You're imagining things.

Only there was something sticking to my fingers when I woke up the following morning. Something I was certain I had washed away hours earlier in the hot water of the bath.

It couldn't be blood.

It just couldn't.

I was standing in front of the mirror when Matt gave me a quick good morning kiss. 'Be a little kind to yourself,' he whispered in my ear. 'Don't make yourself crazy, promise me that?'

I nodded obediently while I washed my hands and watched as a thin stream of red was caught in the water and sucked down the drain.

'For real, ok?' he insisted. He pulled on his jacket in the hallway. I saw how he patted his pocket to check if he had his cell phone with him.

'For real,' I promised again.

The door shut behind him with a bang that sounded more definitive than usual and a shiver went down my spine.

Only then did I let go of my right wrist, which I had been holding in my left hand, and look at the deep scratch the cat had made. It was fiery red and the edges were open a little. In between yellowish-white pus glistened. I wiped it away carefully with a tissue, but immediately thereafter more blood and pus welled up. At around a centimeter distance from the wound, all around, I saw that small, shiny blisters were forming.

I frowned. Matt had bent over the spot the night before. He had disinfected it, but I was better off letting it air-dry, he had said. Now it looked as though it were infected.

I put some new gauze on it – clumsily, with only my left hand – and got dressed. No matter what I'd promised Matt, I had no intention of sitting around the house all day. Not after that night.

The cat eyes pursued me, even now that my eyes were open and the morning sun was coming in through the high windows of our apartment. If I looked away from the mirror, they seemed to pop up in the corners of the glass, only to disappear again when I turned my gaze toward them. They wanted to tell me something, ask something perhaps, but I still didn't know what.

The scratch on my wrist throbbed. Slower than my heartbeat and deep inside. I shut my eyes, shook off the unease, because that second promise – that I wouldn't let myself go crazy – that one I intended to keep.

And so I ate a container of yogurt with granola and drank cappuccino from the far too expensive coffee machine Matt had given me last year for my birthday.

My car still smelled of a strange mixture of wet fur, blood, and panic from the night before. I saw the wet place where the animal had lain; the blood had leaked through the cardboard box. Under the trees too, just before the turnoff onto Appelstraat, I saw the evidence of the previous night's events: black tracks that my car tires had left on the cobblestones.

I braked and drove slowly on towards number 79. Stepped out. Lead in my shoes. Repeated the greeting I had thought up: *'Hello ma'am! I just wanted to see if you were doing all right. And if you still needed help with Dante.'* Saw the movement of the crocheted curtains behind the window next to the front door. The hint of dark fur between the folds. A cat that popped up behind the grimy glass.

My heart skipped a beat.

It couldn't be him. Not *that* cat, not those too-short ears, that kink in the tail and that bloody crust over his eye where the cobblestones had scraped away his skin and fur. Even if he had in some miraculous way or other survived the accident, he couldn't just be there . . . *sitting.*

And yet he was.

The animal came a little closer to the windowpane until the black hairs on its flanks splayed out against the glass like little spiders. He turned his head in my direction and looked at me. I looked back and I shouted at him wordlessly: *What?!*

He squeezed his eyes shut against the bright light.

What do you want from me?

No answer, of course. In a cat's eyes you can read everything. Love, arrogance, affection, egoism. Hope. Accusation. You find what you need, or perhaps what you fear.

The scratch on my wrist had resumed its slow throbbing. I took a step back, stumbled a little when the heel of my shoe landed in the space between two tiles. And saw the door open.

I couldn't remember pressing the bell – in fact I was certain I hadn't – but clearly the old woman had no intention of letting the chance of a visitor slip away and kept a lookout on the street. 'Dearie! You again? How nice!' she greeted me.

Hastily I stuck my hand out. 'Hello, ma'am!' I said, and the words I had practiced rolled out of my mouth. 'I couldn't stop thinking about you. And Dante. Is that him, behind the window? I thought . . .'

'You've got that right, young lady,' the old woman said. 'Just as I was saying. He's a tough rascal! He won't get away from me so easily.'

My glance glided back to the window. The cat had not moved.

'Now, child. Come inside. I take it that today you have time for tea?'

That wasn't a rebuke, I decided. This was an open, friendly invitation.

'Of course I have time,' I answered. 'Mrs. . . . .'

'Gottlieb,' she said. And then, in a confidential tone: 'My family comes from Germany, but after our marriage we lived for a long time in India. Lovely country, you know.'

'Pleasure to make your acquaintance, ma'am,' I said politely as I followed her over the threshold. 'I'm Tara. And once again, I'm terribly sorry about yesterday.'

Was that the moment the trap snapped shut? Or had that already happened when I ran the cat over?

Was it really I who made the choice to go in?

'Go on into the living room, dearie. I'll be right in with the tea,' Mrs. Gottlieb said kindly.

'Are you sure?' I asked. 'Wouldn't it be easier if I helped?'

'Not necessary,' she waved me off. 'But nice of you to offer. I'll let you know when I need your help.'

And so I did what she asked and opened the door to the living room. On a chest against the wall there stood little statues of Indian gods: I recognized Ganesha with the elephant head, Brahma with the four faces, and a little one I wasn't sure about: a chubby type with a pot of gold in one hand and a bludgeon in the other. Something to do with wealth? Even Kali was there with her blood-dripping tongue.

Not my taste in room decorations, I decided, but the old lady was naturally devoted to her past.

The sagging green wingback chairs by the window fit better with the image of an elderly woman, just like the sanseverrias on the window ledge. The thick leaves stuck up sharply and I couldn't help but touch them. They're obstinate plants that refuse to die, however hard you try to forget them.

The cat was still sitting beside the plants. 'Hey,' I said, as I stuck my hand out to pet him. 'Hi Dante. How are you?'

Never stick your hand out to a cat you barely know. And definitely not when that cat probably has dubious memories of you. Of your car. Dante hissed, fiercely and vindictively, and lashed out.

'Damn!'

I reached for my wrist and pushed the sleeve a little further up. The discharge from the first wound was already penetrating the gauze, but this second lash had torn open some itching blisters and there too the yellowish-white liquid was coming out. It smelled sweetish, but not in a good way.

'Gross,' I mumbled, while I irritatedly began dabbing my arm dry with a rumpled paper tissue I dug out of my pocket. It was clearly not enough. I needed a new bandage, or in any case Band-Aids.

I went to go look for the old woman in the kitchen. She must have a first aid kit or something? After all, Band-Aids don't expire, so I didn't have to worry about that, and . . .

I heard something.

Maybe it was there earlier and I just hadn't noticed. It was a soft rasping that sometimes stopped, only to start again tremblingly a few seconds later.

I held my breath. I didn't know precisely what I was hearing, but it sounded unreal, almost unearthly.

The cat, who had watched me suspiciously for a little while from the windowsill, leapt onto the ground. With his tail in the air like a tour guide's umbrella, he walked towards the sliding doors that separated the living room from another room behind it.

The sound was coming from there, I realized. And with a queasy feeling in my stomach I recognized it now too.

It was the sound my grandmother had made in the final moments before she died. When she was gasping for the air that her body could no longer process. When she'd had it. Finished. But not quite, because no one wanted to help her go.

On the other side of the sliding doors was the sound of death.

Why did I go to look?

I was in a stranger's house, a guest. It wasn't my place to go investigating, to open doors. I could have waited until Mrs. Gottlieb came back with the tea. I could have gone to her and asked her for a Band-Aid. But I didn't.

I think it was because of what I had experienced with my grandma. A woman who had tried her whole life to fulfill the requirements God had imposed on her – although she didn't know exactly what those were, the instruction manual is after all subject to debate. A woman who always fell short because of that, just like my mother after her. Just like me. And who was crushingly forsaken in the very moment when she most needed help.

I closed my eyes and once more saw that fragile body in the hospital room, chilly despite the bright colors on the wall, flowers on the windowsill, and the cheerful voices of the nursing staff. Heard how her lungs compulsively filled with air, while less and less oxygen reached her blood and all that time the sickness festered in her bones and organs.

No one who wanted to help her during that endless waiting for a cruel death which, with every step closer it crept, took half a one back. They mustn't, they couldn't, it wasn't their place . . .

And because of that, I couldn't bear for anyone, even a stranger, to suffer without someone holding his hand and making it clear that he wasn't alone.

The sliding doors were stiff – the mechanism had seen better days – but finally they lurched open and I landed in the back room.

A heavy, waxy, sweet odor struck me – an odor that I recognized from the wound in my arm, although that was much less pervasive. Thick curtains of dirty yellow velour let only a small strip of daylight in. The wheezy rasping had stopped, and I looked around hesitantly.

And then . . . Rustling. Fluttering.

I turned to the left and saw a round birdcage on an old-fashioned stand. Vintage, hipsters would call it, but a hell for the bird, who was condemned to lifelong solitary confinement in a far too cramped cell.

The canary's feathers must have been yellow once, but now they were faded to an off-white. They stuck up in all directions as though they had fallen out and were subsequently stuck back in at random. The head was crooked, as if a taxidermist had missed the mark in his attempt to model a dead animal into a live one.

Only the eyes sparkled: black pinheads that glistened in the dusky light. The animal – Frits, she had called it Frits – opened its beak and I almost expected it to start singing. Instead I heard a sort of ticking that sounded wrong and distorted.

I stepped back. Hand over my mouth.

It was a reflex, perhaps. An instinctive attempt to protect myself. As if the evil – did it already feel that way then? – would force its way through my mouth into my body.

But I forgot even that when I saw the bed in the corner and the pitiful figure in it. The hospital bed – one with those white metal bars – was slightly elevated, so that whoever was lying in it had a view of the crack in the curtains. He was covered by nothing more than a grayish-white sheet, but under it I saw the sharp outline of a decrepit body.

Thin legs, gnarled joints. A sunken pelvis and a hollow under the rib cage as if he consisted of nothing but bones.

My glance slid upwards, towards the arms on top of the sheet. I saw scabs and sores and a sickly color. His throat was sunken, the flesh around the mouth rotted away, and I saw far too many teeth, like the grin of a skeleton.

And once more it was the eyes that frightened me the most. They were almost nothing but pupil, with hardly any white, and they shone in the semi-darkness.

My grandmother's eyes, my grandmother's body, my grandmother's death, but times a hundred. I stared at the ruined body that breathed, kept breathing. At the mouth that opened and then spoke.

'Please.'

How long had that wreck of a man lain here in the twilight of the back room? Weeks, months?

Deep down I knew that it must have been years. The way in which the skin was corroded to a leathery membrane draped over the bones, the gums that were receded to past the bare roots, even the way the sores had become ensconced until they formed part of his being, was a long-term process.

I swallowed with difficulty. However much I wanted to,

I couldn't seem to take my eyes off the figure before me. Or away from the hand which lay palm upwards on the sheet and whose index finger moved, as if he were gesturing to me.

The movement was minimal, but a cloud of cloying sweetness broke from his body and stuck in my nose. I retched.

This man was dead, I realized, or he should have been. Just like the bird, which I only now realized was as undead as the man. *Her* husband.

Just as undead as Dante.

Dante, who had tried to kill himself by throwing himself in front of my car, after which I had brought him back to this house where death is stretched out to a neverending dying.

Again that almost imperceptible finger movement. Again a blast of poisonous sweetness in my nose, while the bird fluttered with lifeless wings against the bars of its cage.

'Help . . .'

He fell silent, tormentedly gasping for air, while I could see that he wanted nothing so much as to stop breathing.

How long? My God . . . how long?

'Oh! You've met my husband!' Mrs. Gottlieb's voice.

I turned around. She stood on the threshold of the back room, just between the sliding doors. On the walker stood a pot of tea with two cups beside it. The liquid was brewed so strong that it was almost black.

'Yes,' I managed to utter. 'But . . . he needs help.'

Home care, a hospital, a hospice. Gentle hands, a place – any place – that wasn't here, where his pain could be stilled and he could go in peace.

'Is there someone who helps you?' I asked, after an uncomfortable silence. And when she gave me no answer but just kept looking at me with a look that was somewhere between mildly critical and – I can't call it anything else – eager, I went on talking. Though only because I didn't want to hear the rasping sound of death. 'Shall I call someone? The doctor maybe?'

My words felt laughably practical, an echo of the equally laughable words of the previous day. But what else could I say to keep the doom that threatened to close in on me at bay?

Because *she* smiled.

'You're still here, aren't you, sweetie?' she said. 'Didn't you say you wanted to help?'

I swallowed down a new wave of nausea. 'Yes, but this . . . I can't do this.'

'Of course you can help. Especially you. You brought Dante back to us. You have power, life. You're as good as immortal! Don't you see how desperate he is? How much we need you? And you'll hardly miss it.'

'But . . .'

'Come on! It's no big deal.'

She stepped forward, away from her walker. It seemed as though she was less wobbly than earlier. More energetic. Her right hand closed around the edge of the hospital bed. The man's eyes bulged in pure panic.

'Come on, Antonie. Don't be silly,' she said.

She came closer. Took my hand. Her skin was dry and wrinkle-smooth, the grip many times stronger than I had expected. She turned my arm over with a quick movement, so that my wounded wrist was visible. The yellowish moisture from the new wound had formed into a fine layer over the thin veins that lay just under my skin.

He, her husband, Antonie, whimpered soundlessly.

'Just look what you can do! See your own power!'

She pulled, and I stumbled forward. Two steps closer to the bed. A third. And then she had pressed my wrist against his rotten lips and I felt fierce stabs, like dozens of little syringe needles.

'There now,' she said. She sounded content, like a cat who has just licked a saucer of milk clean. 'There now, my husband. My beloved.'

The rasping breath became more regular. The dilated pupils shrank again and – was it possible? – a fraction more flesh seemed to sit on his meager bones. But his facial expression was no less desperate, and I saw something else in it, something new, that I couldn't immediately place.

Only when he turned his head and fixed his gaze on mine did I recognize it.

Remorse.

'Drink a little tea, sweetie,' she said.

I did. It was as if my conscious brain was disabled, for I drank the tea with mechanical obedience, just as I had unprotestingly allowed my essence – exposed by the nails of a cat – to be administered to her husband.

The bitter liquid, with a hint of ginger, flowed through my mouth, rounded my tongue, and glided down my throat. The heat burned in my intestine and spread toward my stomach, throbbing and rippling through the capillaries of my system. I felt how my heartbeat slowed, how the diffuse light suddenly became bright as my pupils opened wide.

My muscles gave up the fight, my knees went weak. And as I fell and my cheek chafed against the rough carpet, I saw Dante's dented head in the door opening, behind the woman.

He looked at me with green-gold mirror eyes.

There was something in my mouth.

It was thick and slimy, as if I'd been to the dentist and the gel from the fluoride treatment was still stuck between my cheeks and jaws. And this tasted sweet, but not with the reassuring hint of mint or strawberry. This was instead sickly and warm. Mucky.

I moved my tongue, smacked my lips to get the substance away, but it seeped back in my mouth, slid down my throat. I coughed, retched in order to get my airways clear again. A breath filled my lungs but at the same time that sickly stuff filled my whole mouth and dripped down from the corners of my lips.

I tried to come upright, but the muscles in my arms, legs, and rear refused service. I heard a sound – soft squeaking like from a young kitten. It took a while before I realized that I was the one producing the sound.

Above me I discerned the bare rafters, as if I was in an attic. Beneath me irregular bulges like on an old mattress. My fingers lay on rough fabric. I felt tiny grains underneath my fingertips. The cat scratches on my arm throbbed slowly. Something warm dripped over my arm, while that . . . that *something* slipped back in my throat and immediately again rose from my bowels. I retched again in a reflex not to choke.

I squeaked, fought against muscles that didn't obey me. I gasped for breath while that foul sweetness oozed from my mouth, slimy tears dripped from my eyes, and my nose sniffled unpleasantly. I couldn't get any air, I could no longer see, I . . .

Felt hesitating hands being placed against my temples and gently pushing my head to the side. I saw the edge of the mattress now – gray-white with brown stripes – and a stainless steel bowl beside it.

With a dull *plop* a drop landed in the bowl and I experienced a bit of relief. Only a very little, for immediately a new wave of slime worked its way into my mouth.

Plop.

'Better now?' A thin voice. Man or woman? Boy or girl?

Movement. The figure walked around the mattress and squatted by the bowl. I saw sandals – not large. A child's size? Filthy socks, the edge of a sky-blue skirt. A girl then.

Christien Boomsma

I strained my blurry eyes to the utmost to be able to see her face.

Then the girl leaned farther forward and I would have recoiled had I been able. White blond hair, like only very young children have, was loosely stuck to a balding skull. The skin of her face was dark and rough, like willow bark. Fine veins crept through the off-white of her eyes, but they were grayish-black instead of red. A child, but no child. Not for a long time.

Along her narrow lips ran a yellowish-white trail that was almost dried up. Under her eyes were smears of the same.

'Crying or struggling makes it worse,' said the child. And then, her head tilted: 'But it gets better. Quickly.'

She took a piece of wood from her dress pocket. It was around ten centimeters long and spatula-shaped. The edges were smooth. Sanded or worn?

She brought it to my face and began to carefully scrape away the slush under my eyes and nose. She tossed it into the bowl with a vigorous motion. Then she repeated the movement over my cheeks and chin.

I opened my mouth. I *had* to ask it. 'Who are you? Where am I? What's going on?'

But I didn't get any further than a scratchy 'who' because once more my mouth filled with slime. The girl laid a hand on my head and her stick-like fingers pushed it a little lower.

Plop.

'I can't do any more,' said the girl. 'I'm used up.'

She seemed to contemplate.

'Her husband is really sick, you know? I help, and then he's better. But it's nice if someone else is going to do it. There's not much left.'

I closed my eyes while I tried to understand what she was saying. What did she mean by 'used up'? Who was she?

'Do you think mommy was angry?' the little girl asked. 'When I didn't come home, I mean?'

I didn't answer. I couldn't. My glance rested on the dried smears around her mouth. Then slid down to the bony hand that held the little piece of wood with which she had cleaned my face. A deep cat scratch on her arm. The edges of the wound were open, but there was no red bleeding through. Everything I saw was gray, dried-out flesh that the life had seeped out of.

Used up.

And then I understood it. My feverish brain made connections in the swirling stream of images and associations, of fear and of knowledge. It was . . . It must be . . .

I hadn't heard the door open, but I did feel the movement in the wood floor when she entered the room, and I heard her voice. 'That's the life streaming out of you, dearie. Your prana, your essence. The child is almost used up, but you . . . All that compassion, all that empathy . . . It drips out of you. Wouldn't it be a waste if someone didn't do something with it? A sin, almost?'

I wrestled the words out of my mouth. 'Let me go. Please . . .'

Movement beside me. The girl? She picked up the metal bowl. Gave it to her. Gottlieb . . . was that even really her name?

And then once more I felt her thin hands and the cool porcelain against my skin. 'It doesn't last long,' the girl's voice whispered.

Liquid between my lips. Black, bitter tea with a hint of ginger. I swallowed. Panted.

'Why?' I asked again.

Her voice, far away: 'Because I want to.'

This time it indeed didn't last as long. The panic, I mean.

Once again I awakened with the feeling I was choking, but I realized after a few seconds what was happening.

I managed to spit the slime out and air rattled into my lungs. There was no emaciated child beside me. No hollow, black eyes searching my face.

I tried to tell myself that this was progress, because the kid had scared me half to death. And I seemed now in any event to be able to use some muscles.

Where was the woman?

I lifted my head a little as I tried to move my fingers. My hand began to tremble and my index finger and middle finger came a little way off the ground.

My head slammed heavily back on the mattress. A new mouthful sought an outlet between my lips and dropped on the gray-striped cover. A yellow-gray puddle formed on the fabric. Transparent like a dead jellyfish on the beach.

I looked at it, my blurry eyes straining painfully as I tried to see it. I smelled it. Grim, poisonous, sweet. I . . .

. . . heard the footsteps on the stairs. The door of the room – it creaked a little – opening. I saw Mrs. Gottlieb – warm, old. But I smelled ash in her graying hair. I saw bones in her eyes. And I felt, knew suddenly, that she was more than just herself.

'Ah, good girl. Just a bit more.'

Despair spread through my body when I felt the cup against my lips.

Black tea.

I didn't choke any more when I woke for the third time.

The slime no longer forced its way out in great quantities from my mouth but oozed out the corners like drool at the dentist's office. I commanded my hand to wipe my mouth and it obeyed.

Now I tested my neck and back and buttocks. I fought my way upright.

The movement brought wafts of heavy sweat and stale tea and the room swayed around me. I waited till it was over and then looked carefully around the room, which I was finally able to really see.

It was an attic room, that was now certain. I felt cool air on my face: wind that was coming in through openings in the rafters. I saw two small, square attic windows, soiled by dust and spiderwebs. But in the middle the filth had been wiped away by thin fingers.

I managed to stand up and tottered in the direction of the little window. Looked out.

Below me I saw the neglected garden; behind that, between the branches and shrubs, the cobblestones of Appelstraat. A red Volkswagen Polo was making its way and I perked up.

Matt?

I stretched my neck, followed the car until it reached the bend where Dante had sat waiting, and felt my heart clench when he disappeared from view.

Dizzy, I let myself sink down along the wall. I wiped slime from the corners of my mouth and tried not to give in to the intense feeling of loss that washed over me. Maybe it hadn't even been Matt. Maybe not.

But I need you.

And then I saw the dark form in the nook by the rough shape of the chimney. I swallowed, spat, panted. I told myself that it couldn't be her, that it wasn't possible, couldn't be.

I crawled to the corner on all fours. I wiped my eyes, which kept clouding up, groped and left a little layer of sludge behind on the child's knee-high socks.

She hadn't gone home and her mother hadn't gotten angry. There would no longer be any home, not after all the many years that she must have been here.

Her skin was colored black and had become as stiff as parchment. Her flesh – hadn't it still been there when she'd sat beside me? – was rotted away until it looked like scraped asphalt. The black eyes stared upwards but no longer saw anything.

Used up.

I looked at my hands and the dried slime on my fingertips. Was my skin dryer than before? I wiped my knuckles along my slippery mouth. Were my lips thinner?

His voice in my head. *'Be a little kind to yourself.'*

I had to get out of there.

My trembling hands on the door handle. I fumbled at it, tried to pull it, but there was hardly any strength left in my body. It seeped out like a snail excreting slime to propel itself. But the door opened – had she forgotten to lock it? – and I saw the staircase, although it spun before my weary eyes.

I stepped. Stumbled. Fell.

My body crashed, thumped, clattered, knocked against the steps. My muscles screamed. I remained lying at the bottom of the stairs, fighting to get myself under control. Get up, Tara. Run!

But then she was there.

Had she always been so tall? And hadn't her eyes been cloudy blue instead of filled with dark fire? The woman who was approaching from the hall, who stood before me and towered over me, was Mrs. Gottlieb, but at the same time I felt someone else.

Mahabhaya, a voice whispered within me. It was a name, I knew; I recognized it with that deep human instinct with which we can fathom the unknowable.

'Get up, dearie,' she said.

It was as if the sound alone was enough to lift me up, and I rose until my face was the same height as hers. I saw the liver spots on her cheekbones and her forehead, the deep wrinkles that creased and folded every inch of her skin. The drooping eyelids, the fuzzy gray of her hair. And yet . . . yet there was power in this body, life in her eyes.

Prana.

'Kiss me,' she said.

She stretched her wrinkled hands out and I allowed her to place them on my cheeks. I smelled her breath and allowed it to fill my lungs. And then her lips closed over mine and licked the slime from my mouth. I let my life flow into hers, so that her body would not die.

She took my free will.

No . . . that's not right. My will is intact, but the ability to act on it is gone. How she did it still isn't clear to me. Maybe it's the figure that lives behind her eyes, that makes use of her voice: Mahabhaya, the Fearsome One.

She told me, after my prana had brought the light back in her eyes, after I had bent over her husband – Antonie – and he had drunk my life with unwilling gulps.

That as the wife of a missionary she had followed her beloved to a little village in the heart of India. That she'd had to watch as the devastating cholera took him within the span of a month. How his body rotted away and his piss turned black from the blood.

That was the moment she had turned away from the god who had chosen to take away her beloved before he had celebrated his thirtieth birthday. That was also the moment when the villagers introduced her to *their* divinity, which until then had lain hidden in the folds of her reality.

And there, concealed from the eyes of Westerners who think they know everything, she found Mahabhaya, the Fearsome One, who protects against old age, liberates from fear, and knows the secret of eternal life.

She had done what was necessary. She had recited Her name – Mahabhaya – ten thousand times, sitting on a mountain of bones and with the ash of countless cremations strewn on her head. And when She came, after hours and days, and granted mercy, she had greedily accepted.

But mercy has a price.

I am that price, the child was that price. Even Matt, who will never see me again, is part of that price. And in the end her beloved Antonie is too.

He too has been deprived of his will. In his eyes lives despair, in his hands a fatigue that is deeper than I can comprehend. His voice is regret.

I can't get him out of my head, that faltering supplication when I still had the strength to walk away, or to refuse. The desperate flutter of the dried-out wings against the bars of the cage.

The cat's eyes.

I turned back towards the attic room, obedient to a single look, a word. She is mighty, the Fearsome One, even if she looks through the eyes of an old woman.

Suddenly I wondered whether that was really her name, whether even for her eternity had already lasted longer than she had wanted.

Once out of her presence, my strength returned. I rattled on the shutters of the roof windows that were too narrow for a child to get through, let alone an adult, and I peered out, where I could see the road.

A car with the logo of the home care service. A tractor.

I fumbled at the door, banged on the wood. I pulled at the paneling around the fireplace in the hope of discovering an opening that would offer me a way out, any way whatsoever, onto the roof.

I shouted to the rafters and kicked at the walls. I was Tender Tara. I was the one who did volunteer work, who was socially minded, who fought to do what was *good* until my dying breath.

I sat motionless beside the desiccated remains that had once been a young girl and which now foretold my future. A future that I had to face alone.

I petted Dante, who had slipped upstairs with me. His aggressiveness had vanished. The bloody scab above his eye was nearly healed, but the look in his eyes was unchanged.

And then I heard the rumbling of a car on the road. A rattle that slowly grew louder and suddenly stopped.

I knew that rumble, that familiar rattling. Matt? Had he figured out where I was? Come to get me?

'Matt!'

At the beginning of the garden path stood Matt's red Volkswagen Polo. I heard his voice – urgent, though I couldn't understand what he was saying.

And I heard *her* voice, with the innocent tenacity of a very elderly person who has nothing left to lose.

Again I shrieked at the top of my lungs, but the sound died against the wall of silence that surrounded me. I cried, sobbed, when I heard the door shut, when I saw Matt, *my* Matt, walking down the path to his car.

I pounded on the window, banged with my fist. I . . .

Broke the window.

Shards on the ground. Sharp cuts on my hands. Blood on my fist. And again I screamed. 'Matt!'

I heard a little sound by my feet and saw Dante and those large, golden-green mirrors.

What are you trying to say?

Did he know how scared I was? Of loneliness? Silence? Judgment?

What do you mean?

In a cat's eyes you can read whatever you want. Compassion. Understanding.

I lifted him up to the window, which even he couldn't easily reach. I pressed him against me for a moment as I loosened the collar from his neck. I pushed him through the hole in the glass and it didn't matter that the glass cut into his fur. He wormed his way further, through the hole and up onto the roof.

By the road the car door slammed shut. An engine started.

A black bolt flashed down over the shingles, leapt into the tall alder by the house. Disappeared in the bushes underneath.

The Polo began to drive. Slowly. Then faster.

The black spot shot out from under the bushes and then towards the bend in the road.

Matt sped up. Dante did the same.

Then the sound. Screaming brakes. Dull thud.

And the outline of Matt, who hurried out of the car, knelt down on the cobblestones.

He remained sitting motionless for at least twenty heartbeats. Then he lifted the limp body from the cobblestones and laid it in the grass on the side of the road. Carefully. Lovingly.

He stepped back into his car, started the engine.

I closed my eyes, just for a moment. But I didn't see Dante's eyes anymore.

Translated from the Dutch by James D. Jenkins

Ariane Gélinas

Twin Shadows

For many years, the horror world in the French-speaking Canadian province of Quebec has been dominated by Patrick Senécal, a prolific novelist sometimes compared to Stephen King (though apparently only one of his novels has so far appeared in English). Recently, though, horror fiction in Quebec has begun to grow into more than just a one-man show, as evidenced by the 2017 anthology Horrifico-rama, *which features stories by fifteen Quebecois horror writers, including the one featured here. Multi-award-winning author* ARIANE GÉLINAS *(b. 1984) has published five novels and numerous short stories, some of the best of which, including the following tale, were collected in* Le sabbat des éphémères *(2013). The publisher of that volume describes Gélinas' work as existing at the crossroads of the Gothic and the fantastic, with forays into science fiction. The author's first publication in English, 'Twin Shadows' is an eerie tale that fits squarely into the Gothic tradition, a story about two sisters with a strange secret living in an isolated mansion. It will surely leave readers wanting to see more from this talented young author.*

TIME PASSES IN SLOW MOTION in the silence of the sleeping house. That's what I used to repeat to Floriane when we would talk, after dark. I grew used to these conversations, which broke the monotony of my anonymous existence. The rest of the time, I felt only the coldness of our vast residence, which had become familiar to me over the years. Only my sister deigned to look after me, often discerning my presence when I was hidden in the darkness of a hallway or lurking in a corner of her bedroom. And since we were identical twins, she possessed an innate ability to anticipate my intentions, predict my reactions.

Her devotion to me had been remarkable during our early youth. It is true that, unlike Floriane, I did not have the benefit of our parents' attention, nor anyone else's. Aside from their concern when they would catch her talking to me after midnight, they ignored me, letting me wander alone through the corridors of our centuries-old home, built well away from the city.

To keep me close to her, my twin decided, shortly before we turned five, to arrange her closet to suit me. Although I had always made do with only a little space, she insisted on removing her clothes from the closet, preferring to put them in her dressers. Our parents were surprised at first by this whim, which they came to consider as a simple child-ish caprice. Floriane kept only the metal rod, from which she had noticed I liked to hang, upside-down. She had laid several cushions on the floor, where she would come to lie beside me almost every night. She would wait until our parents had reached their room at the other end of the hall. She would then slip in to the back of the closet with a thick blanket to keep warm. I would let go of the bar to join her on the pillows, even though their comfort meant nothing to me. It was a different story with my sister's warmth, which aroused little tingling sensations in me. I knew it wasn't the same with my parents or their guests. Everyone except Flo-riane was impervious to me. I consoled myself going to sleep night after night in the arms of my twin, among the shadows of the closet.

I always awoke with the impression that time had stood still, that I had only just submerged myself in my sister's invigorating embrace. Unfortunately, for her part, it was time to get up and have breakfast at the family table, where three places had been set. I would close my hand one last time over her burning one, after she had assured me that she would come back to me as soon as the meal was finished. She would then hasten to get ready before closing the door of the wardrobe, where I would remain awaiting her return. During that time, I would invent quivering shapes on the walls or try to stick my fingers into the closet's partitions, which seemed to elude me when I tried to touch them. In any case, I had never liked to venture to the ground floor, which inspired a peculiar dread in me. I only felt safe upstairs, near my parents' bedroom, where Floriane and I had been born, or close to my twin, whose presence could always calm me. Outside seemed even worse to me, since everything there was a blinding white as far as the eye could see. So I was careful to stay away from the windows, whose formless brightness attacked me, like an immaculate grave, where I often felt the urge to destroy myself.

A diffuse light filtered through the slats of the wardrobe, illuminating the cushions and toys that Floriane had given me. So that I would feel less alone she had given me several stuffed animals as well as three of her dolls, which sat lined up against one of the walls, looking at me with their dead eyes. All of them had names, unlike me, which had always made me sad. Sometimes I would avenge myself on Floriane's dolls when the loneliness became too oppressive. A savage energy would take hold of me, pushing me to do violence on whatever was around me. Spurred on by anger, I would pick the toys up and shake them until their eyes rolled back in their heads and their joints threatened to break. Then I would cry for a long time in the darkness, hugging Olga, an old, worn-out plush toy whose eyes had been torn out and whose stuffing was coming out all over.

Every day I would relieve my boredom by long hours

of dancing in my twin's room. I had always loved moving gracefully, fluttering over the floor tiles after performing several ethereal twirls. I would sketch movements worthy of an elite ballerina, like our mother when she gave private classes in the dance studio that had been set up upstairs. I would imagine myself on a stage, like the dancing stars I loved to admire on my sister's television when she watched athletic competitions. Like them, I would be cheered, dressed in a shimmering leotard that made my supple body more beautiful.

I would whirl around the room until Floriane finally returned to take her turn dancing.

Around that time, my sister started taking classes with our mother. She was preparing a performance for school at the same time. When her teacher was busy, which was often the case, I would help her to practice her figures, to make her movements more wispy. Initially she had been rather awkward, heavy in her movements. Thanks to my good advice she had gradually improved into a remarkable ballerina, to the point that she had been offered one of the lead roles in the production. I was very proud of my twin, even if I would have liked more than anything to leap at her side, to blend our identical bodies in a choreography, joined in the classical music.

She was so lovely in her pink leotard, with her loose black hair down to her waist, her bangs falling over her big, deep-brown eyes. I would have loved to make her whirl on a stage, take off in my turn with a gossamer agility before landing again after a long flight. But I was aware that all I would be able to see of Floriane's performance would be her rehearsals with our mother in the dance studio, hidden behind the half-open door. On rare occasions, I would slip noiselessly in with them, hiding in the set decor. I was careful to be noticed by my sister, who didn't like me to appear unexpectedly. She had explained to me on several occasions that, despite our bond, my intrusion could be inappropriate and that she hated it when I startled her. She retained a bitter memory of the remonstrances she had brought on herself in her younger years when our parents caught her talking to me. So I was careful to respect her rules as much as possible and not to upset her.

After the performance, which enjoyed a certain success, Floriane came to visit me in the wardrobe less often at night, since, according to her, sleeping on the floor could hurt her back, which a dancer couldn't afford. I had suggested joining her in her bed, which was big enough for two, but she had flatly refused. That bed, she had made clear, was her reserved space, and she didn't have to share it. She had repeated to me that she was quite generous in offering me the wardrobe. I had gone back to shut myself up noiselessly in the darkness, to stir up the accumulated dust in the closet, which drew shapes like dead insects on the walls. On the floor, among the cushions, the toys were piled up. My sister would now store them here as she lost interest in them. Now almost a teen-ager, she no longer knew what to do with these objects. So I had to cohabitate with these baubles pell-mell in an already small space, where I endured the stoic looks of dozens of dolls reminding me cruelly of our shared past.

And yet, Floriane would still sometimes show me kind-ness, especially when loneliness weighed heavy on her and she felt the need to confide in someone. She would join me in the wardrobe like before, clearing herself a space between the abandoned objects. Then she would apologize while her tears poured out, my hands fondly smoothing her silky hair. I knew she liked the tingling sensations I inspired in her when I embraced her, that she enjoyed the fleeting contact of my lips when they brushed her skin. It was the same for me, and I hated to go too long without those embraces, which were the only thing that had the power to move me. The rest of the time, I was plunged into an icy lethargy, which evoked in me the image of a dying man caught prisoner in a frozen river from which, despite his efforts, he is unable to escape.

On our fourteenth birthday, Floriane gave me a birthday present for the first time. Touched, I opened the package, which was pierced with holes and on which she had written 'For my only sister'. I understood the purpose of the apertures when I discovered the kitten inside, which made its way curiously out from its prison. My twin set up a bed for it in the wardrobe, whose door she left ajar. The feline ruffled its fur at my touch, refused to let me come near it. Floriane argued that it would get used to me quickly, that from then on I would have a faithful companion to distract me during the day while she attended her classes. Yet the animal was constantly terrified of me and would curl up under my sister's bed every time I tried to pet it. It spent every night with her, nestled in the warm covers, purring. Bitterly, I would sometimes come out silently to watch them sleeping from my perch on the dressing table, while the kitten would half open its eyes suspiciously, on watch. After spying on them for a moment, I would return to my assigned space, where I would swing upside down on the rod, a stuffed animal in my arms. Sometimes I would catch myself laughing despite myself as I rocked. My fingers would then caress Olga's torn ears, sink into the orifices formed by her missing eyes.

I had had to beg Floriane to keep her from getting rid of this toy, of which I was especially fond, when she was re-doing her room. It all had a much too childish look to it, she had explained to me. So she had had it completely repainted and had gotten new furniture. Not to mention the posters she had stuck on the walls, depicting various stars. We would still dance sometimes, but she was distancing herself from ballet in favor of more current choreographies, in which I found little aesthetic interest. Nonetheless, her reputation was growing, and she had even been hired by a modern dance troupe to participate in a prestigious show.

Enviously I watched her perform the series of complicated movements with that grace that never left her. Yet her presentation lacked an ethereal lightness that I mastered much better than her, a lightness that I would have been honored to deploy before an audience, if I only had the opportunity. Alas, I remained in the shadows, contenting myself with helping my twin improve her movements. Swollen with pride, she would flaunt her body to me, that body that I considered perfect, simultaneously slender and solid, with discreet but sensual curves.

In the dance troupe she met Hector, a dancer around ten years older than her. He had spotted my sister quickly and would practice with her for hours. Floriane would tell me in detail about their budding love, their outings in the city, their daring embraces. Obsessed by her passion, she didn't seem to understand the pain it caused me, how I dreaded more each time to hear her secrets, which became increasingly explicit. I ended by closing myself up in the closet, where I threw myself against the walls. Furiously I would move the toys that were piled up there before hurling them against the walls. I would fall asleep a moment later, dizzy, with a great vertigo in my head that continuously sought to suck me up, to drag me into a permanent fog.

After two years of going out, Floriane decided to move in with Hector into an apartment downtown. She fixed her moving date for May and excitedly shared the news with me. She didn't seem to understand the coldness this announcement provoked in me, why I scowled before going to take refuge in the closet. From that moment on, I stopped obeying the rules she had always imposed on me, stopped returning to my hiding place every time she asked me to. On the contrary, I never missed a chance to disobey her, to startle her, especially at night when she struggled against insomnia. I would make a point of moving the objects in her room, as I'd often done with the toys in the wardrobe. I would switch her clothes and personal effects around, would take down one of the posters that decorated the walls, would hide insects I'd found in the wardrobe under her pillow. I also took a certain pleasure in tormenting the feline, which I would poke with hairpins.

Sometimes, I would make my way through the darkened room, my favorite stuffed toy held out at arm's length, and I would bring it close to Floriane's face. Her features contorted, she would beg me to stop. I would then exhaust myself in entreaties, kneeling on the floor, hoping that my insistence could keep her from putting her plan into execution.

During the days, distressed, I would hide the torn-out eyes of her old dolls, and she would cry out in terror when she discovered them. The only breaks I took were to dance among the boxes cluttering my twin's room, perched on the piled cardboard boxes, which I tried to make topple over, my plush toy in my arms. Only Olga escaped this methodical carnage, which I was careful to carry out in our parents' absence.

Hidden in the half-open wardrobe, I would revel at seeing our father, still dressed in his veterinarian's smock, looking with bewilderment at my sister, whose drawn features gave her face a pallid appearance. Out of his depth when faced with her anxiety, which was as sudden as it was inexplicable, he considered having her seen by a doctor. By his side, our mother, not quick to show her emotions, clenched her hands with their long, manicured nails. In order not to make things worse for herself, Floriane kept quiet about my misdeeds, for she didn't wish to increase our parents' worry, or, worse, raise concerns about her psychological balance.

Unfortunately for me, her nerves more and more tense, she moved her departure date up by a week. She left me without even a goodbye, her cat in her arms, abandoning me to loneliness. Deprived of all point of reference, the days ran together, identical, bringing only their set of fears and echoes that writhed on the walls like the slow streaming of blood. In Floriane's absence I wandered aimlessly in the room, which had been converted to a guest room, unused since her departure. I didn't recognize anything of her in this impersonal space, except my faithful Olga, whom I had managed to hide while our parents redecorated the room. It was just the two of us in the closet, which had been cleared of the other toys that cluttered it, just the two of us to swing on the rod, like the sickly needles of a defective clock.

I don't know how many days, how many weeks, passed before my twin returned to the family home. I had lost all pleasure in dancing long ago and continuously swung from the bar, murmuring secrets to Olga. At every moment the atmosphere of the house seemed more oppressive. Floriane's visit finally pulled me out of the torpor into which I had slid and awoke feelings in me that had been only partly swallowed up in oblivion.

As soon as she arrived, my sister rushed to the wardrobe to beg me to forgive her, I who had always remained faithful to her. Through her tears, I understood that she excused my childish behavior, which after all was only the mark of my attachment and the expression of my grief at her betrayal. I felt the extent of her sadness when she explained to me how Hector had cheated on her, how naive she had been to trust him.

When night fell, I slid into her bed as delicately as possible. This time, Floriane warmly invited me to sleep beside her. I inhaled her scent with delight, the smell of her bare neck, the dark strands scattered over it like the hair of Medusa. Then I placed my lips on hers in a long kiss. A feeling of rebirth spread through my breast at the same time as a sudden tingling sensation, while I continued to embrace her with a still unquenched desire. I felt her fitful breath, her wish to lose herself in our entanglement while our embraces continued. Around us the white sheets rose and fell, moved by a light breeze exhaled by invisible breaths. I saw one of them knotting around my sister's neck as she tried to free herself from the fabric that was squeezing her throat. The bottom of the sheet twisted around her ankles, pressing them together to keep her from moving. Her body arched as the cloth strengthened its hold, constricting her rib cage. The bedcover increased its pressure on her neck. Floriane's face grew more and more purple. My twin struggled, with disjointed movements. The sheets restrained her limbs once again. Then her muscles relaxed as she fell back on the bed, inert, her eyelids open. I finally moved away from her, admired her slender silhouette, her supple legs, perfect for dancing, her delicate arms, outstretched across the bed.

I didn't much care what our parents would think when they discovered Floriane's frozen body in the morning. All I desired at present was to spend one peaceful day after another waltzing through the room with my twin, performing ever more dizzying aerial movements in tandem. When night fell, we would return together to the wardrobe, where we would hang upside down from our shared perch, our hands caressing the worn-out body of the sleeping plush toy. For all that mattered now was that we were finally together again.

Translated from the French by James D. Jenkins

Anders Fager

Backstairs

Sweden's history of horror fiction dates back to Gothic tales and ghost stories published in the early 1800s. The first Gothic novel in Swedish was Hin Ondes Hus (1853) [The House of the Devil] *by Aurora Ljungstedt (1821-1908), who might be likened to a Swedish Sheridan Le Fanu. The writing of ghost stories and fantastic tales continued into the 20th century with writers like Selma Lagerlöf (1858-1940), the first woman to win a Nobel Prize in Literature, and Sven Chris-ter Swahn (1933-2005). Sweden has a active modern-day horror scene whose best-known representative is John Ajvide Lindqvist, author of* Let the Right One In (2004), *and which also includes short story writer Kristoffer Leandoer and novelist Mats Strandberg. However, one of the most interesting Swedish horror writers of recent years is* ANDERS FAGER *(b. 1964), who burst on the scene with his volume of Lovecraftian horror tales,* Svenska kulter [Swedish Cults], *in 2009. An expanded version, from which the following story is taken, appeared in 2011. Fager's collections have been translated into French and Italian, but he has had limited exposure to date in English. 'Backstairs' (the title is a 19th-century term for the servants' staircase in wealthy families' homes), is set in turn-of-the-century Stockholm, where a doctor's Freudian methods may be no match for the unspeak-able horror that haunts a girl's dreams. A note on the Swedish terms in the text: proper nouns ending in '–gatan' are street names; 'Stora Skuggan' (literally 'The Big Shadow') is a historic Stockholm park dating to the 18th century, and 'Fru' and 'Fröken' are the Swedish equivalents of 'Mrs.' and 'Miss', respectively.*

Elvira Wallin walks down the staircase. The long, narrow staircase down to the cellar under the house on Upplandsgatan. Walks slowly. She's dreaming. Knows she's dreaming, is wholly certain she's dreaming, and she goes down the stairs. Down into the damp and darkness. While a wind plays at her petticoat. Even though it can't be blowing in the cellar. But Elvira Wallin is dreaming, so crazy things can happen. Everyone knows that. For it is only in dreams that one walks down the stairs in only a corset, underwear, and petticoat. White chemise and bonnet. She should have stockings on. At the very least. After all she doesn't want to run around completely undressed. Not even when she goes down into the damp and darkness. Down the long staircase into the cellar on Upplandsgatan. Down under the house. Near Tegnérslunden. Which mother built with father's money.

Dr. Lohrman asks about her father. The major who became a timber baron. Was he a good father? Was he kind? Loving? Did he have time for you? Dr. Lohrman is that kind of doctor. A nosy, inquisitive little man with thick glasses, frock coat, a high cravat, and a well-groomed, pointed beard. A doctor who asks and asks and who always comes back to her dream.

'Do you dream the same dream every night?'

'Yes. Almost.'

'And have you dreamt the same dream for a long time?'

'I don't really know. A month or two.'

Dr. Lohrman says that he can cure her of the dreams. If she answers his questions. But Elvira Wallin wants medicine. Chloroform or tincture of opium. She wants to avoid Dr. Lohrman's questions. They're too prying. And he asks her to describe the dream carefully. Goes on and on about it. He 'wants to understand', he says. For he can only cure her through talking.

'What else do you dream about? Can you remember anything?'

'I dreamt a lot about papa when he died. That he came back from Sundsvall. That it was someone else who died in that accident.'

'Did you wish for that? That someone else had died in his place?'

'Naturally. Then my father would still be alive.'

'Of course.'

Dr. Lohrman doesn't say that she is selfish. Instead he keeps harping on about the dream.

'But now you dream exactly the same thing every time?'

'The past few weeks, yes. The same dream. Over and over again.'

'Are you certain? It doesn't change? It doesn't develop? Doesn't become worse or more frightening?'

Elvira Wallin thinks about it. There's a tickling at her belly. She thinks about walking down the stairs. Always dressed like a slut. Always in the damp and darkness. Over and over again. Until she awakes soaked in sweat and screams. And screams. And screams.

'I don't think so,' she says.

It's all a little peculiar, thinks Elvira Wallin. Talking with a doctor about a nightmare. She isn't very old and doesn't know anything about medicine. But a doctor who just talks? A person can't talk with someone to make their dreams stop, or make them sleep better. If you can't sleep, you drink some cognac, right? That's what mother does sometimes. Or maybe an opiate. Elvira Wallin has read about opiates. Oriental medicines that make you dream. That let you ride the dragon. That sounds exciting. Maybe she could ride the dragon down the stairs and her dragon would kill everything down there. Kill that horrid thing that waits for her in the cellar. Night after night. In the damp and darkness.

Elvira Wallin has lain down on Dr. Lohrman's chaise longue. In his consulting room on Drottninggatan. Two stories up, next to K.L. Lundberg's department store. The doctor has a nice place. And there's a housekeeper somewhere back in a kitchen. That feels important. That Elvira isn't alone with a man. Even if it's in broad daylight. And he's a doctor. Once a field surgeon in the guards. In father's company. And warmly recommended by Fru Sandell. They've exchanged greetings. Elvira Wallin has taken off her hat and cloak. Said 'no, thank you' to tea. She has lain down on the chaise longue and tries to lie still. But it feels strange to be lying down when he is sitting. And it itches. On her neck and on her back. On her legs. Everywhere. And she can't lie there on Dr. Lohrman's chaise longue and scratch herself like some flea-bitten dog. Elvira Wallin wonders. Is she hysterical, like Fru von Kantzow says? Or have her dreams simply settled into a bad habit? Like a cat chasing its tail. For in the dreams she's always walking down the stairs. In petticoat, corset, and underwear. It is midnight and she dreams that she is awake and stepping out of bed. It is quiet and everyone is asleep and nothing can be heard from the street and she must walk up and down the stairs. Every night.

'You don't walk in your sleep?' asks Dr. Lohrman when they have finished talking about the weather and traffic jams on Tegelbacken.

'I don't think I have ever walked in my sleep, Doctor.'

'How can you be sure?'

'I've never woken up walking on Upplandsgatan, if that's what you mean.'

'You never daydream?'

'Doesn't everyone?'

'Do you feel that time passes at different speeds? As if you'd missed some hours? That you're not sure whether you've really had lunch or not? That the day feels like you were reading a book and happened to skip a chapter?'

Elvira Wallin laughs that disarming sort of laugh that every eighteen-year-old girl has at hand. And shudders. 'Yes, Doctor,' she wants to say. 'It's like that all the time lately. I awaken in the morning and can't remember the evening before. I go out for a stroll and the very moment I come home I can't remember where I've been. I talk with mother but don't remember what about. I'm tired all the time. I hurt everywhere. Everything is like a dream except for the dream.' The dream about going down in the cellar.

But she keeps silent. Dr. Lohrman writes something. Scratch, scratch, says the pen. Elvira Wallin thinks about how it itches. On her thigh. She asked her mother if it's really proper to lie on the doctor's chaise longue in this way, but mother reassured her. Dr. Lohrman is a doctor. And just as you must show the doctor your leg if you twist your ankle, so must you lie down and relax if you're twisted in the head. That doesn't sound so nice. Although mother smiles when she says it.

Elvira Wallin thinks about how the dream at first smells like her bedroom. Stove. Lavender and soap. The warmth as she walks past the stove. Out in the hall. It's colder there. She doesn't have her nightgown on. Out on the staircase. Even colder. She gets goosebumps on her arms.

'Is the door open?' asks Dr. Lohrman.

'The front door?' Elvira Wallin has to think. Stretch her hand out in front of her. Pretend to touch the door. 'It's the kitchen door,' she says. Astonished by her own dream. 'To the backstairs.'

'Shouldn't that be locked?'

'Yes.'

'Didn't you know you were going down the backstairs?'

'I hadn't really thought about it before.'

'Did you think you were going down the main staircase?'

'Yes. I assumed so. That's where I go. When I'm awake.'

'In just your undergarments?'

'Yes.' Elvira Wallin feels herself blushing.

'And then underground?'

'Yes.'

'Not out into the courtyard?'

'No. Down in the cellar.'

'Through a cellar door?'

Elvira Wallin answers without thinking about it. 'Yes.
Mother gave me a key.'

Dr. Lohrman doesn't ask about mother. He writes a little
instead. Elvira Wallin wonders whether she really got the
key from her mother. In the dream. She is unsure. The chaise
longue feels uncomfortable. A horsehair tickles her neck.
And what is mother doing on the backstairs? Something
inside her left boot itches. Chafes.

'And you are certain that you have never really done this?'

'Done what?'

'You never go out late at night?'

'I've come home late before. From soirées or from the
theater. But I've never gone out in the middle of the night
like a ghost.'

'And never in your underclothing?'

'What do you think!' Elvira Wallin doesn't like that question.

'And not on the backstairs?'

'No.'

'Not even when you were a child?'

'We didn't live on Upplandsgatan then. We lived in the country.'

'The country? I thought your father had a flat on Stora Nygatan.'

'Yes, but he was the only one who lived there. Mother and I lived in Stureby.'

Dr. Lohrman falls silent. Elvira Wallin closes her eyes. She can see the stairs before her. Smells the odor of damp and mold. Her back itches from her corset. It itches. She wants to scratch.

'Do the backstairs in the dream look like the real stairs?'

'I think so. Maybe. I don't have any reason to go there.'

'Do you have to open another door?'

'Pardon?'

'When you walk down the backstairs and go down to the courtyard. Do you have to open a door to go down into the cellar? Was that the one your mother gave you a key to?'

'I don't know.' Behind her eyelids, Elvira Wallin looks around. Mother is standing there. She nods and gives her the key. And Elvira Wallin walks down the stairs. The long staircase down to the cellar under the house on Upplandsgatan. She dreams. Looks behind her eyelids. Feels a dream cold against her skin. Along her calves. The stone steps are cold. And she is barefoot. She thinks about how she knows the floor. The stone staircase. The dream is so real. There's some small stuff on the stairs. Gravel. And it grows damper the further down she goes.

'Is it the real cellar that you're going down into?'

'How should I know that? I've never been there.' Elvira Wallin wonders. Her corset itches. Her calf itches. Dr. Lohrman's office smells of tobacco.

'What do you think? Is the place something you remember from when you were little?'

'No.'

Elvira Wallin looks up at the ceiling. Sees the white-painted planks. She blinks. Doesn't want to say any more. It's so real. The mold and chill. As soon as she closes her eyes, she walks down the next flight of stairs. Stagnant water. The cold stone under the soles of her feet. A cold wind creeps up her legs. She knows precisely how the dream continues. What is going to happen. When it gets cold and it begins to move. When it hurts and when it becomes unbearable. She knows what she is luring out. From the first gust till the moment when she faints, sweating and screaming. And wakes up.

She sits up.

'I don't want to go down there.'

'But you do. What is it that compels you to dream the same thing over and over again?'

'I don't know!' Elvira Wallin almost screams. And is so ashamed that she blushes. And thinks that mother's friends are right after all. She's hysterical. She's hallucinating. They should send her to a hospital. And she knows what they do with hysterical girls at the hospital. They put them in ice water until they calm down. Lock them in small rooms. And big men hold the little misses tight and attach large leeches to their throats and breasts so the leeches will suck everything bad out of them.

'I don't want to!' screams Elvira Wallin. 'I don't want to!'

'Calm down.' Dr. Lohrman sounds calm. And very far away. The whole apartment smells of dampness. Her leg itches all over. Where the thing in the cellar usually touches her. Before it creeps up towards her belly.

'Lie down again.' Dr. Lohrman hasn't moved a muscle. 'If you'd be so kind.' Elvira Wallin blinks. Finally sees the doctor. Two steps away. Sitting in his armchair. His glasses shine so that you can't see his eyes. She didn't see him earlier. She didn't see anything. Not the desk. Not the green curtains. Not the paintings. A sailboat over by the window. Dancing elves directly opposite. They're dancing in the grass. Damp grass. A dark night. She thinks about something mother told her. About a dance at Stora Skuggan.

Elvira Wallin lies down slowly.

'Excuse me.'

'Don't worry. In these conversations sometimes strong feelings emerge. That's all right.'

'It's embarrassing.'

'Oh, no. What is it that you don't want?'

'I don't want to go to the hospital.'

'Has someone said you'll be sent to a hospital?'

Elvira Wallin is silent several moments. Someone calls out down on the street. A horse whinnies.

'No one is thinking of sending you to a hospital, Fröken Wallin. That's why we're here. Instead of the hospital.'

'So you're not thinking of putting leeches on me?' Elvira Wallin laughs at how stupid that sounds.

'No indeed.' Dr. Lohrman laughs with her. 'But I have a bucket of them in the kitchen. If you're obstinate.'

'You're joking?'

'Are you sure?'

'Almost.'

Elvira Wallin exhales. Concentrates on her corset. Her back itches. The edge of her right stocking is wrinkled.

'Do doctors really use leeches nowadays?'

'Occasionally perhaps. In any case to treat high blood pressure. Not for your sort of problem.'

'Thanks. I think.'

'Nowadays we use conversation. That is the latest scientific development.'

'It sounds crazy.'

'Think of it like the story about the troll. If one draws the nasty and troublesome things out in the daylight, they crack.'

'It sounds like a fairy tale.'

'It was a metaphor.'

'I understood.'

'We doctors have started having these conversations in recent years. And if conversation doesn't help then we use massage to treat nervous disorders. With a machine.'

Elvira Wallin looks at the doctor. Her blouse chafes at her neck. 'Machine?'

'Oh, yes. A mechanical contraption that massages women with nervous troubles. I can give you a demonstration.'

'Not on my account, thanks.'

'But then you must talk with me.'

'I promise.'

'So, where were we?'

Elvira Wallin doesn't answer. She closes her eyes. Concentrates on things that itch.

'Fröken Wallin?'

'Yes?'

'The staircase. The backstairs. Can you describe what you see?'

'It's cold. And damp. It smells bad.'

'Smells of what?'

'Moss, I think. Peat. Rotten vegetables. The floor is cold.'

'But what do you see?'

Elvira Wallin moves her head in astonishment. Looks around with her eyes shut. 'Nothing. It's dark.'

'Is there no light at all?'

'No, maybe a little from the staircase. But it's very long.'

'How can you see where you're stepping in the dark?'

'I walk carefully.' Elvira Wallin hesitates. 'And I'm holding someone's hand.' She gropes at the air in front of her. Without opening her eyes. Carefully grasps an invisible hand. Moves her legs. Tenses her abdomen. The chaise longue is small. Narrow. She extends her right wrist a little. Dr. Lohrman writes. Scratch, scratch.

'So that I won't fall,' continues Elvira Wallin. 'And won't go astray.' She sounds like someone who's trying to talk about one thing while she's reading about another. Absent. She looks around. Sees nothing in the darkness. Doesn't know whose hand it is. It smells worse now. More moss and mold. Hears those sounds. A rustling. Sounds like someone is dragging a sack over a floor.

'It's good you have company.' Dr. Lohrman talks very low. As if he's afraid of frightening her. Elvira Wallin nods guardedly. As if she in turn doesn't want to frighten the one holding her hand. She doesn't want to be left alone in the cellar. For she is not wholly certain that she's dreaming. About the damp and the darkness. About something playing in her undergarments. Stroking her foot.

'Yes,' she says at last.

The little room stinks so badly that she recoils. She gets dizzy. Things creep over her feet. Maybe rats. Eels. Up her calves. The hand she's holding feels strange. Like it's made of leather. A gloved hand that isn't really a hand. It's too narrow. Soft. She presses gently against it. Like one does when shaking hands. Fröken Wallin, how do you do. And the hand releases her hand and grips her wrist instead. Hard.

'The patient,' Dr. Lohrman wrote several hours later, *'then freezes. With her right hand in the air in front of her. As if she is holding someone's hand while she talks. She looks at her hand. With her eyes closed. All is calm and quiet and one hesitates to ask a new question that might interrupt the process going on within the patient. Then suddenly the patient is seized by the greatest confusion and horror. The patient feels as though she is falling and being embraced by some sort of monstrosity, and this delusion becomes so real to her that she falls off the chaise longue and tries to crawl backwards away*

from that imaginary attacker. At last I get Fru Hansson's help in holding the poor girl still until after several minutes' struggle she falls into a sort of light sleep. The whole time during the fit, the patient has her eyes wide open without seeing and is unreachable like someone in a hypnotic trance. The patient comes slowly to her senses, all the while complaining of severe paroxysms in her stomach, thigh, and lower abdomen. She thrashes with her body and kicks with her legs. The poor young woman's clothes end up in disarray and it takes all my and Fru Hansson's strength to prevent her from flailing her arms and clawing at the phantasms that besiege her.'

Dr. Lohrman and Fru Hansson laid Elvira Wallin on the chaise longue. Fru Hansson spoke to her reassuringly and straightened her clothes. Elvira Wallin leapt like a fish each time Fru Hansson touched her legs or hips.

Dr. Lohrman fetched laudanum. And the mechanical massage apparatus. He was unsure of what he should do. Was it more important for the girl to get rest, or that she get over the convulsions that were plaguing her? He needed to consult some colleagues. Talk with Dr. Sondén. Write a couple of letters to German colleagues. Lohrman was fairly certain that the girl's symptoms were mental. A compulsive dream that took on a physical manifestation. But it could also be something physical that Elvira Wallin couldn't explain and therefore wove into a dream. Anything whatsoever from colic to pregnancy. The massage apparatus could probably help there. Just in case.

Once Elvira Wallin has settled down, she has to answer questions about her body. Shameful questions. The doctor stands over by the window while he asks them. Looks at the traffic and tugs at his beard while he asks about her stomach. If she experiences pain when she passes water. If she is troubled by colic? Gas? That monthly thing. Has she gotten it? Does she drink wine? Does she eat a lot of cabbage? Onions?

Fru Hansson sits beside the sofa and looks at her. A stern, black-haired woman with chapped hands. She has narrow lips and could be twenty-five or fifty-five years old. Elvira Wallin answers truthfully. She has no problems with her stomach. Eats moderately. Almost never takes strong drink. The monthly business comes as it's supposed to.

Dr. Lohrman stuffs his pipe.

'And your maidenhead?'

'What about it? I'm not some servant girl who whores around in the rear house.'

'I really wasn't suggesting that.'

'Thanks.'

'But one's maidenhead can be damaged even without loose living. By one's youthful folly and curiosity. Or an accident. Or it can be weak from the beginning.'

Elvira Wallin blushes. Doesn't answer. Dr. Lohrman lights his pipe. Looks down at the people in the street. He tries to remember what it says in Hoffman's *Forensic Atlas*. Sometimes page after page about the womb. Could some defect in the womb trigger cramps? Does it secrete feminine seminal fluid and infect itself? The thought of having to examine Fröken Wallin in that way makes the doctor uneasy. And thank goodness there are more modern methods of treating women's diseases than going in and cutting their uterus out. Besides, it would be so repugnantly familiar. After all he's known the Wallins a long time. Remembers when her father offered him a cognac. Young Captain Wallin's wife had had a daughter. And Captain Wallin toasted with everyone he met. Of course the doctor would have a cognac with him. In the middle of a bright morning. 'Cheers, damn it. I'm so damned happy, Lohrman.' Those were the days.

'We must rule out purely physical causes. If you have a stone in your shoe, it doesn't help for us to talk about it. That won't make the stone disappear.'

'I have more than a stone in my shoe.'

'Stones don't give you any such nightmares,' says Fru Hansson. Elvira Wallin stares at her. As if surprised that she can even speak.

Dr. Lohrman puffs on his pipe. 'You'll have laudanum to help you sleep. You'll sleep soundly and won't dream. That will make you calmer. But first we'll try another thing that can help your body to relax. Many women have nervous syndromes connected with the lower parts of the abdomen. The female parts. Knots of tension seem to form there, which nature sometimes needs a little help in loosening up.'

He walks over to the desk. Unlocks the leather-covered case. Opens it. Elvira Wallin watches. Scared and curious. Fru Hansson watches Elvira Wallin. She smiles. Almost maliciously. Dr. Lohrman puts down his pipe. Takes out the massage machine. Inserts a crank in one end of it and begins to crank it. A faint ticking is heard.

'These days there are even electric versions of these machines. But they're not as reliable, and even if I think that as a doctor I should be open to the latest scientific discoveries, well, do we really know how electricity affects our bodies? There are experiments that show that plants die just from getting electric light. What does that mean for us? I'll stick to this device for the time being.'

Something clicks inside the machine. Dr. Lohrman removes the crank and lays it in the box. Picks up a piece of chamois leather.

'Now, then, Fröken Wallin. Can you place the leather on your belly, please. Below your navel and down over your thighs. It protects your clothing.'

'Is it going to hurt?'

'Oh, no. You may perceive a very strong stinging sensation just before the knot loosens, but that is completely normal.'

Elvira Wallin places the piece of leather over her belly. Stretches out. Takes a deep breath. Looks at the machine. Gleaming brass and wooden handle. The white contraption at the end looks like a ball of white skin. With long calluses on it. Seams. Fru Hansson grabs her hands. And Dr. Lohrman starts the machine. It buzzes like a mechanical toy.

It takes almost twenty minutes. Dr. Lohrman has to tighten his machine several times. Elvira Wallin loses count, sweats and tenses in a strange way. She presses against Fru Hansson's hands and feels how she too is sweating. She stares up at the ceiling. Closes her eyes. It flits. And flits. Elvira Wallin knows that she's not dreaming this time, and Dr. Lohrman's machine buzzes and rubs on the knots in her nerves. It's like being on a swing. Twirling around when you're dancing. Or when you lace a corset a little too tightly and you get breathless at the slightest movement. The machine sends thrills far down into her legs. It tickles, she wants to kick her legs and wriggle away. She presses herself against the machine's head. Twists her hips. Clenches her teeth. Breathes harder. Presses the nape of her neck against Fru Hansson's arm.

The machine does something that reminds her of her dream. But without clawing and tearing. As if the machine were making something nasty pleasant. And she would so like to take off some of her clothes, for it is so hot. Lie on the sofa in just her corset, underwear and petticoat, bonnet and chemise. Feel the wind blow and not let all that thick fabric in her skirts dampen the vibrations. Dream about the staircase. About Dr. Lohrman's stern look. The darkness of the cellar. About how the men tearing down the mill in Tegnérslunden stare at her. About Fru Hansson's strong hands. The smell of seaweed and putrid damp. About the two students who share a room high up in the rear house. Both of them are slender and lean. Light on their feet and quick to laugh. That which waits in the dark. Waits for her. In the smell of seaweed. She sweats. And sweats. The corset itches madly. One of the students has a little blond mustache. He must have tended to it with care. Maybe for her sake. She wants to swing on a swing. Kick. Scream out loud. The spasm makes her blush. Her breasts feel strange. The smell of the staircase. Mother's perfume. Cooking fumes in the kitchen. Soft, gloved hands. Up her leg. Over her belly. Over all of her.

'The paroxysm was exceptionally powerful,' writes Dr. Lohrman, *'and for a while plunged the young patient into an unreachable condition of the greatest exhaustion. She raves like a drunk and becomes weak in her limbs. She rests on the chaise longue, altogether heavy in that previously so tense body. Only a fit of speaking in tongues clears the released tension out of her body. The patient is given a glass of water to drink and slowly sits up, tired but her mind at ease. I explain to the patient that in all probability she will now be free from the tensions that caused the bad dreams, and that just to be on the safe side she will get a small dose of laudanum to take with her, to be taken at bedtime.'*

Fru Hansson led Elvira Wallin to a room with a washbasin. Let her wash her face. Accompanied her back to the doctor, who told her about the laudanum and followed her to the door.

'Are you sure you can walk on your own? Do your legs feel weak?'

'I'm fine. And I don't have far to walk. Mother and Fru Sandell are waiting at Café Petissan.'

'I can ask Fru Hansson to follow you.'

'I'll manage, thanks.' Elvira Wallin composes herself. The major's eldest daughter. She thinks about her father while she walks down the two sets of stairs to the street. That it's getting harder and harder to remember how he really was. He's becoming more and more the portrait in the living room and the stories mother tells. She misses him. Misses having two parents. A stern and strict mother, and a cheerful and boisterous father. There's more balance in life if there's a man to liven up the days a little.

She walks up to Café Petissan. Self-assured and elegant, a nice catch for a Lieutenant Sparre or an industrialist's son. Elvira Wallin knows French and German, can dance and dine, and knows her own worth. Boys watch her go by and she laughs inwardly. It's lovely to be alive. As soon as those stupid dreams are gone she'll really live. Go to the theater and help mother to manage father's shares.

Hedda Wallin is curious and inquisitive. She wants to know if she feels better. If the doctor's new methods really work. Elvira Wallin responds that they talked. Fru Sandell wonders about what. About dreams and why we dream them. She doesn't mention the machine or the strange spasm. But she assures them she feels more at ease. Less tense.

'And now you'll have a proper lunch,' says Hedda Wallin. 'So that both body and soul get what they need.'

It's a lovely walk home. Fru Sandell accompanies them. She's curious. And a little impertinent. She asks if her friend the doctor takes liberties? She has heard of doctors who do such things. Mesmerize their patients and unbutton their clothes. And if someone were going to unbutton your blouse, wouldn't it be nicer with someone other than Dr. Lohrman? Hedda Wallin rolls her eyes. Elvira Wallin laughs. Dr. Lohrman is so old. Probably forty. Mother rolls her eyes even more.

'Totally ancient, in other words?' Fru Sandell laughs. 'Do you know how old I am?'

'I didn't mean it like that.'

'Oh no, don't worry. But that beard of his. The man looks like a little billy goat.'

'Goat or not,' Elvira ventures to joke. Cheeky with the

adult women. 'He has his housekeeper there. It's all very respectable. A tailor is more intrusive.'

They laugh their way up Tegnérsgatan. Even mother laughs a little. That makes Elvira Wallin happy. Mother is often so weighed down with worry. Problems with money and stock shares. Karl and Margareta's studies. It's not easy being a single woman and having a hysterical daughter on top of things.

They eat. Vegetable soup and a small cutlet. Mother talks with Fru Sandell. They sit the whole evening and talk about the old times. When they were young and rushed off to dances with officers from the Life Guards. Mother loves talking about those times. How fun it was for her and her friends then. When the king was crowned and there were parties in Stockholm. Before the regiments moved out to the wilderness. They never talk about having fun nowadays. Instead, they get together, the same officers' wives, and complain. They crochet, help the poor and bake cakes. Talk about books. Zola and Fröding. Politics. Julius Mankell and the Suffrage Union. And they read coffee grounds, go to séances and visit churches. They crochet and embroider. Go to the theater. Go for strolls. Watch the parade of Guards. And have little secret gatherings. Like a secret society. The Göta Life Guards' Handcrafts Association, mother calls it. A little order of women with education and taste. And 'who get along fine without men'.

She takes the laudanum in her room. After she's brushed out her hair. Before she extinguishes the lamp. Two drops in a little glass of water. It tastes strong. Burns like brandy. She takes another dose. Just in case. Blows out the lamp. Lies a little while in the dark and listens for sounds in the house. She waits to get to ride the dragon. To take off in a colorful Chinese dream, but she gets extremely drowsy. She hears steps. Creaking. Distant voices. Elvira Wallin falls asleep to the sound of Dr. Lohrman's machine and with the bitter taste of laudanum on her tongue. The memory of the spasm creeps up and down her legs. Pulls at her. Tickles. And Elvira Wallin walks down the stairs. The long, narrow backstairs down into the cellar under the house on Upplandsgatan. She dreams. A special laudanum dream. Mother gives her the key there. And Fru Sandell and Fru von Kantzow and Fru Mosander are there too. They stand on the staircase and watch as she goes by. While a wind licks at all their white petticoats. She's lightheaded. Tired and feverish. She takes someone's hand. Thinks about the machine. That it was nice to drive the tension out of her body. She wants to try it directly against her skin. Where she can feel it more.

It's dark in the cellar. A hand is holding her wrist. Someone is standing behind her. Takes hold of her other wrist. Shoves her forward. Towards that which smells. Towards that which twists around her legs, which tears and claws and makes her think of Fru Hansson. Is she the one holding on to her? Elvira Wallin stumbles forward. And falls. She starts to scream in the dream. But doesn't wake up. It tears at her hair and her petticoat. Presses her down on the dirt floor. She hears Dr. Lohrman's voice far away. Thinks about Fru Hansson and mother and what she feels is a thousand times stronger than the doctor's machine. It buzzes and hisses and thrusts until everything goes black.

Elvira Wallin wakes up in the hallway outside her room. On the floor. In just her petticoat. She's sweaty and her whole body is shaking. Her hair is tangled and there is dirt under her fingernails. She doesn't cry. Doesn't scream. She just lies there. Waits out the spasms that shake her body. She thinks that she's had a fit. That she's drunk. That her stomach hurts. Her groin. She can't remember how she got out of bed. She can't remember where she's been.

She crawls into bed. Splashes a lot of laudanum in the water glass on the bedside table. A cup of water and opium. It tastes bad. And her head spins until she doesn't remember anything anymore.

Much later her mother comes in. She's worried. Elvira has slept too long. Mother found her corset in the kitchen. Does Elvira walk in her sleep? With her frail back, she should sleep tied down. She knows that. Mother goes for coffee. Fusses over her. Sends an errand boy to Dr. Lohrman.

The doctor comes at lunchtime. Elvira Wallin is still lying in bed. Tired and feverish. The maid Signe gave her honey water and wheat bread with butter. Helped her to comb her hair and change her undergarments. Elvira Wallin has long scratches on her legs. From her ankles all the way up around her hips. Thin, superficial wounds. As if a cat clawed her, says the maid. But she wouldn't have a cat under her skirt. Hedda Wallin orders her to cut Elvira's fingernails. So that she doesn't scratch herself like a dog.

'Do you remember what happened last night?' the doctor asks. He sits on a stool in the doorway to Elvira Wallin's bedroom. Fru Wallin and Signe stand in the hallway, silent and out of sight.

'I went down the stairs.'

'Again?'

'Yes.'

'And it was the same dream you usually have?'

'Yes. But yet it was so different.'

'Can you say what was different?'

'The dream was blurrier than ever before. It was so frightening. I think I'm going to need your machine, Doctor. I have knots of tension.' Elvira Wallin points at herself. 'There and there and there and there. It itches so.'

'Is that why you scratch yourself?'

'I'm not the one scratching me. They hold onto my hands and scratch me. It's driving me crazy.'

'Who scratches you? Is it one person or more than that?'

'I don't know. But there are many of them. I can't see. It's dark.'

Dr. Lohrman takes off his glasses. Tries not to look when Elvira Wallin scratches the inside of her thigh.

'I want massage and laudanum. Then I'll be quite well.'

'Do you promise to tell then? About what was different?'

'The patient promises to reveal the most painful and private details of her dream,' writes Dr. Lohrman. *'But as soon as she is brought to a strong paroxysm and has gotten her small dose of laudanum, she falls into a deep sleep. The patient giggles during the massage and her mother and the maid have to hold her so that the process can be performed correctly. The little maid who holds the patient's legs gets kicked in the face and her nose starts to bleed. The tumult attracts the housekeeper Andersson and Fru Wallin's other two children, who all three stand in the doorway and witness the procedure. The older child, a boy of fourteen, finds the procedure interesting, while his younger sister finds it frightening. When her older sister's giggles turn to screams, the little girl begins to cry. Fru Wallin reprimands the housekeeper and asks her to take the child away. As soon as the patient's paroxysm has passed and she has become limp and docile, Fru Wallin lets go of her and runs to see to her younger children.*

'A little later, when the patient is sleeping, I talk with the mother. She wants to know everything about her daughter's condition. She strikes me as both curious and concerned and tells me that when she was young she was afflicted by similar nightmares. Before she married and, however, not with the same intensity. It seems to me that it pains her to see her daughter suffering the same kind of torments as her. She is very inquisitive about my methods and conclusions and what I have learned about her daughter's dreams.'

'She says I give her a key?'

'Yes. To the cellar. It's common for family to be incorporated into dreams. The mind plays with the things it knows best.'

'How preposterous.'

It all soon becomes a habit. In the evenings, Elvira Wallin sleeps full of laudanum. At night, the nightmares come. In the daytime Elvira Wallin stays in bed. Slumbers for long periods. She drinks tea and eats biscuits. She is warm and languid. Pale but lucid. She reads the newspapers. The Family Journal. Magazines about art, news, and fashion. Bathes. Doesn't want to go out. Hedda Wallin is supported by her friends who come to visit. One and another two and two more. They look in and greet Elvira Wallin. Are worried, but encouraging. They sit in the parlor and talk with Hedda Wallin. Elvira Wallin hears them talking far away. But never about what. She wants to sit with them. To be grown up and talk about balls and theater and suffrage. Not to be sick and tired. To be hungry for something besides applesauce and laudanum. To be happy and not just want to scratch herself all over.

Dr. Lohrman comes every afternoon. With the machine in its case. Elvira Wallin wants massage. That makes her calm. Almost happy. Affectionate. One afternoon she asks little Signe to come and kiss her. She says terrible things when she refuses. That Signe too will surely be ridden by the dragon. As soon as it rides Elvira Wallin to death, then it will come straight for Signe.

'Are we merely alleviating the symptoms of something incurable?' Fru Wallin asks when the doctor is about to leave for the evening.

'Right now we are only alleviating the symptoms.'

'I'm very grateful to you for admitting that. And for

doing what you can. No one did as much for me when I was sick.'

'I hope I'll be able to get at more than just the symptoms.'

'You're very persistent. But sometimes maybe all we can do is just alleviate suffering. Until the problem resolves on its own.'

'Do you think it will resolve on its own?'

'My dreams stopped.'

'I want to understand. That is modern medicine. One understands the mind and cures it.'

Fru Wallin laughs. 'Understand the mind? Can one ever do that?'

'I think so. If one looks deep enough.'

'And you aren't afraid that the abyss will stare back at you?'

'Not really. It's another person's mind we're talking about. Not some kind of inferno.'

Dr. Lohrman asks Fru Wallin politely about her dreams. If she recognizes her daughter's nightmare. Whether she too scratched her legs. He doesn't dare ask about the worst details. If she also thought that snakes crept inside her. Fru Wallin doesn't want to answer. The dreams were dreadful and private. And they disappeared when she got pregnant. 'Maybe I was afraid of ending up an old maid,' she laughs.

But Elvira Wallin isn't pregnant. And she soon claims that she doesn't dream anymore about going down the stairs. She doesn't remember her dreams anymore. Dr. Lohrman is sure it's the laudanum that makes her not remember. He takes the matter up with Fru Wallin.

'Could it be something other than ghosts in your daughter's head?'

'What would it be?'

Dr. Lohrman wonders. Looks at Fru Wallin's hair. It's almost white. Simply but faultlessly done up. 'That someone is assaulting her here in her room and the dreams and all the theatrics are a defense against the trauma.'

'You and I both know that you're the only man who comes around here.'

'Besides the night-soil men.'

'But they only come for a little while every other day. And Andersson escorts them. One can't have such people running around loose in one's home.' She laughs. And looks tired. 'You can do better than that, Doctor.'

'Can she be meeting someone?'

'A boy, you mean?'

'Why not? I've seen both the youths who live in the rear house. Charming young men, to be sure.'

'Do you seriously think that my daughter runs out at night to cuddle with a poor student? And moreover that she's playing at being crazy in order to hide it?'

'It was a hypothesis.'

'Signe lives on the ground floor of the rear house. She keeps an eye on who's coming and going. It is after all my house.'

'And I suppose you've asked her if Elvira comes round there.'

'Naturally.' Fru Wallin sounds pleased. 'Signe sees who comes and goes. She may be young, but she's a shrewd girl with sharp eyes.'

Dr. Lohrman investigates the backstairs. One afternoon when Elvira Wallin is sleeping and her mother is entertaining two women from a handcrafts society. It's a narrow spiral staircase with narrow windows, one between each floor. It is barely wide enough for two people. Not more. Down at the courtyard there is a little landing. A door leads out to the yard. Unlocked. A door leads to the coal cellar. Locked. He asks the housekeeper Andersson who has the key. It's hanging on a hook by the stove. Where it always hangs. Where else would it hang?

He asks Elvira Wallin. Over and over again.

'What are you doing up at night?'

'I really don't know.'

'This morning your mother found you in the kitchen. And yesterday on the floor in your room. You were very scared when Fru Wallin woke you. What were you scared of?'

'I can't remember.'

'The same snakes we talked about before?'

'I don't know. I was just very tense.'

'Do you know why you were lying on the floor?'

'I had fallen out of bed?' Elvira Wallin giggles. It strikes Dr. Lohrman how impudent she's gotten the past few days. Pert. Disrespectful. It might be the laudanum talking. 'Maybe I dreamt I was in a shipwreck?'

He asks little Signe if she has seen Elvira Wallin in the yard. Or in the rear house.

'Never,' she answers in the Värmland dialect. 'I've never seen the young miss in the yard. Or in the house. What would she go there for?'

'And in the kitchen?'

'Almost never. Sometimes when the young children are there, maybe. The mistress and miss leave us to ourselves in here.' She gives Lohrman a look that says he should do the same. The household is full of stiff-necked women.

'And the backstairs?'

'What would she be doing there?'

'You see the staircase windows from your room, right?'

'Yes. But they're narrow windows.'

'Can you keep an eye on them tonight? For the young lady's sake. And if you don't say anything to your mistress, there's a copper for you as a reward.'

'Why shouldn't my mistress know?'

'Because she might unconsciously want to protect her daughter.' Signe nods. Pretends to understand, illiterate maid that she is.

'One wonders,' writes Dr. Lohrman, *'if the laudanum really has any effect other than to keep the girl's dreams and reality separate from one another? Can it be that the horrors that were previously played out in the theater of her dreams are now raging hidden behind the opium's curtain? And what kind of unforeseen effects can that have on the poor girl? Or can one safely ignore the little she perceives of the dreams? If the girl were still lying quietly in her bed and only her unconscious fantasies were running all over the place then it might be all right, but now she is walking in her sleep. The girl could hurt herself. Worse than the scratches she's already gotten. Realized today that Fru Wallin's shame over her daughter's sickness may be making her unconsciously hinder me in my work. Perhaps she is afraid she will be blamed for her daughter's condition.'*

Next evening. Dr. Lohrman sits by Elvira Wallin's bed. Silent. Thoughtful. Andersson found her in the kitchen this morning. And she can't remember anything. She scratches her thighs. Begs for massage. And laudanum. They bargain.

'You get massage if you talk.'

'Massage first.'

'Oh, no. I know what you're up to. Now tell me what you were doing in the kitchen.'

'I really don't know what I was doing in the kitchen.' She imitates Signe's dialect. Teases him. Dr. Lohrman realizes how much he dislikes her. 'What would I be doing there? Among the servants?'

'Maybe you were hungry?'

'Not really. I eat in the daytime. I don't have to run

around stealing things from the cupboard at night. Can I have massage now?'

Dr. Lohrman takes off his frock coat. Finds the machine. He's growing more and more doubtful that the machine is of any use. He hardly dares to look at Elvira Wallin during the treatment. Her reactions are getting stronger and stronger. Rhythmic spasms in her thighs and back. Shortness of breath. The girl blushes and moans. Presses herself against the apparatus. But maybe it's just that the nearer the tension comes to the surface, the more powerfully it reacts to one's efforts to get rid of it.

Elvira Wallin bites her blanket when the paroxysm comes. All grows quiet. Far off a piano is heard. Fru Wallin is teaching little Margareta to play. Preferably when her sister is being most noisy. Dr. Lohrman wipes his sweat from the machine. Slackens the spring. Dries his forehead and adjusts his cravat. And begins to ask again.

'Your mother says that she's found you in the kitchen several times. And in the servants' passage. You never go another way? Out in the rest of the residence? To the parlor or dining room or the other children's rooms. How come?'

'I really don't know. Sorry, doctor.'

'And the backstairs? What do you do there?'

'What would I be doing there?'

'I know you go there.'

'I dreamed about them before. We've talked about that.' Elvira Wallin rolls her eyes. 'Before I got the laudanum. And massage.'

Dr. Lohrman feels a kind of joy. Finally. He knows that the cheeky little ragdoll is lying. He looks at her. Without blushing. How she lies on the covers. In just her undergarments. The corset barely laced. Barefoot. Dirty feet. Dr. Lohrman can taste victory. His intellect over the sickness's lies. He studies Elvira Wallin's slender ankles. Sees one of those awful sores that run around her left leg. She is delicate, all over. Her throat and wrists. Looks at her straight, almost white hair. She's going to be a real beauty once he's freed her. A cool, ethereal beauty. He thinks about details. Mannerisms he has learned by heart. The little things in her way of moving. Of talking. The way she tilts her head to the side when she doesn't understand a question. Her mother does the same thing.

He plays out his triumph. 'Signe saw you on the staircase. Last night. You went down the stairs. And went back up again after about an hour. What were you doing in the cellar so long?'

Elvira looks at the ceiling. Her eyes tear up. Slowly. The tears run down her cheeks. She is completely quiet. The doctor smiles. A friendly smile, he hopes. He's broken through the wall. Reached a turning point in the therapy.

'I wish so badly that I could explain,' she says finally. 'I wish so badly.' Then she cries. Inconsolably. And Dr. Aaron Lohrman sits at her side. He's brought down his prey. But he doesn't know what to do with it. He can only sit there. Perplexed and speechless.

Elvira Wallin cries for a long time. Quietly. Without screaming or kicking up a fuss. She shudders sometimes. Shakes as if she's freezing. But never tries to dry her tears. They run down over her temples and drip on the pillow under her neck.

She thinks that she would like so much to tell the truth. If she only knew anything about it. Understood anything herself. She wants to make the doctor happy. Make mother happy. And she wants to sleep, she realizes finally. Just sleep. She asks for laudanum. With a feeble voice. The doctor gives her a weak dose. Far too weak. She wants to scream at him not to be such a stingy Jew. But he looks so stern.

Finally Elvira Wallin sinks into a light sleep. Dr. Lohrman

stands up. Puts on his frock coat and goes out into the parlor. Fru Wallin is just taking leave of three of her many girl-friends. A Kruse and a Sparre and a Something-hjelm. All equally elegant. Sophisticated and officious. Dr. Lohrman waits off to the side a little. He wonders about these women. How they seem to do nothing but visit each other. Drink coffee. Gossip and debate. Do needlework. Shouldn't such sensible people have better things to do than run around visiting one another all day?

The ladies go. Fru Wallin has Dr. Lohrman report as if he were an ensign. He's reached a breakthrough. We must discuss it. She walks slowly in a circle around the parlor. Straightens a tablecloth. Looks at the portrait of Major Wallin. Asks him to wait with Elvira while she talks with Andersson.

Dr. Lohrman sits for a long while watching Elvira Wallin sleep. He thinks about the next step. About his insights and what he should do with them. He has almost dozed off when Fru Wallin comes in the room. With her hair brushed out and wrapped in a large smoking jacket that must have belonged to the major. She looks like an adventuress. An explorer in some distant land. She should have one of those helmets the English wear in the tropics. And a carbine.

'Would you like anything to eat, Doctor?'

'Andersson fixed me a bit of ham and bread, thank you.'

Fru Wallin sits. Looks at her daughter. She looks sad.

'She goes down the stairs,' he says finally. 'In real life.'

Fru Wallin says nothing.

'Yes. She doesn't have a sweetheart,' he goes on. 'And I'm sure that she doesn't subconsciously want to run away from her family.'

'What do you think it's all about, Doctor?'

'She could be haunted by some kind of spirit.'

Fru Wallin laughs. Almost scornfully. 'Do you believe in such things?'

'Let us say that I find many things difficult to explain scientifically.'

'And you still want to cure my daughter with modern medicine?'

'The power of suggestion is strong.'

'Elvira hardly believes in God.'

'Honestly spoken, Fru Wallin. Does anyone believe more than hardly and out of respect these days?'

'I think it's funny that so many abandon God, but go to fortune tellers instead.'

'Undeniably. Séances are also said to be very popular, I've heard.'

Fru Wallin is silent a moment. Straightens her daughter's blanket. Stares at a point on the wall over the bed. She's making up her mind about something. 'I frequented séances when I was younger. And prayer meetings. And elf dances. The Guards' daughters danced in Stora Skuggan. You didn't think that about me?'

'I don't know how to answer that.'

'It was a fun time. Innocent. But some games become very serious with time. There are some things we should have left alone. You mustn't wake something up if you can't get it back to sleep again.'

Dr. Lohrman holds his breath. Fru Wallin is having a therapeutic conversation with him. Completely of her own accord.

'When Oskar died, Anna Lessander took me to a séance. Of the worst sort. The medium. That devil was some kind of ventriloquist. He pretended to be Oskar. And it was all wrong. He said the wrong things. Things that Oskar never would have said. You know how Oskar was, for God's sake. He was always happy and high-spirited. A boisterous man. He could see the funny side to anything. Even being crushed by falling timber. He would never moan like a ghost in *Hamlet*. I was furious.'

'Did you really think you would meet Oskar?'

'No.'

'But you went all the same?'

'Yes. I know that some things are in fact not governed by science. And I thought that man was one of them. Someone with some kind of insight. Stupid, isn't it?'

'Perhaps. But very human.'

Dr. Lohrman wonders. Where should he lead the conversation? Should he ask the critical question?

'I know that you know,' says Hedda Wallin at last. When she can't be bothered to wait on Dr. Lohrman any longer. 'Signe told me this morning. That she told you she saw Elvira and me on the stairs last night. She's loyal, that girl. Even if not very clever. If she had come to me first, she could have saved herself the trouble of sitting up last night.'

'Saved herself the trouble?'

'I could have shown you the door. Or asked her to lie.' Fru Wallin looks him in the eyes. Sternly. He understands how easy it was for Signe to choose sides. He can't measure up to this woman. 'Do you, the new kind of doctor, keep your patients' confidences? Whatever they may be? Like a confessor?'

'Of course. An intimate conversation would be impossible otherwise.'

'I thought I could handle this myself.'

'This?'

'What Elvira is going through. But it pains me to see her suffer. She is so weak. Not like me.' She falls silent. Notices that he doesn't know what to say.

'Consider yourself hired. As my family's doctor.'

'I'm not a medical doctor. You know that.'

'I know what an army doctor can do and what he can't. I know three pharmacists, and if you don't want to pull one of my teeth, I'll go to a smith in Kungsholmen. Do you understand? You shall help me to help Elvira get through something that I had to get through alone. And keep quiet about the business. Forever. You understand?'

Dr. Lohrman nods.

'Out of respect for my spouse. Your company commander.'

Dr. Lohrman nods again. Humbly.

'The slightest whisper about this to anyone and, well, you understand. I'll destroy your reputation as a doctor, you can count on it.' Fru Wallin smiles. Almost maliciously. They have nothing more to talk about. They wait. Dr. Lohrman leans back. Dozes with one eye open. Hedda Wallin knits. Without looking at what she's doing. When Hedda Wallin knits, it's always scarves. She doesn't know how to do anything else. Every Christmas the poorhouse gets a large bundle of scarves from the Wallin household.

It's midnight when Elvira Wallin gets out of bed. With unseeing eyes and her hands at shoulder height. She looks like someone walking in the dark. As if she's listening for something. In just her corset, underwear, and petticoat she walks down the hall towards the kitchen. Dr. Lohrman walks carefully behind her. Hedda Wallin walks in front. Fiddles with the key. The key to the door to the backstairs. Sets it in her daughter's hand.

Elvira Wallin fumbles. Unlocks the door. Goes down the stairs. The long, narrow staircase. Hedda Wallin walks in front of Dr. Lohrman. Holding a kerosene lamp in front of her. That's what Signe saw the previous night. They go down into the damp and darkness. Catch up with Elvira Wallin. Walk a step behind her. Without her noticing them.

They come to the cellar door. Dr. Lohrman sees. Hedda Wallin has put on gloves. Her daughter opens the door. With the same key. A wind comes up through the dark doorway.

It smells of seaweed. Hedda Wallin takes the key from her daughter. Takes her by the hand. Looks at Dr. Lohrman.

'One last chance,' she whispers. 'You can leave here now. And never speak with us again.'

Dr. Lohrman doesn't answer her. He only meets her gaze. She can't see his eyes behind the thick glasses, but she supposes he's trying to look brave. Ready to go down the stairs in the name of science. For its new methods and for his own curiosity's sake.

Hedda Wallin walks down the stairs with her daughter's hand in hers. Down into the damp and darkness. To atone for a mistake. To keep a promise. The dance in Stora Skuggan seems like something that happened a century ago. What was adventure and excitement then now just feels banal. Mundane and malevolent. Curiosity always has a price. She's known that for nearly twenty years. And now the doctor will learn it too.

The cellar at the foot of the stairs smells of peat and moisture. Seaweed and mold. The kerosene lamp shines on the coal and firewood. Empty bedpans. Empty room. Space to burn coal. If it comes to that.

They continue downwards. To the next floor. Blasted in the mountain. The lodge's room. No hall. No coats of arms. No seats where men sit and drink wine and pretend it's blood. Just a dirt floor. And an old bed. And an even older presence. The one that welcomes her. And which greedily wants its gift.

Hedda Wallin lets go of her daughter's hand. Lets the one twisted around Elvira Wallin's other wrist lead her further. Further towards that which is crawling over the bed. Further towards that which is covering the floor. That which is big and oily like piles of black rope. Black snares that tighten around Elvira Wallin's white clothing. Ensnare her arms.

Tear at her corset. She takes a faltering step forward. Mumbles a protest. Tries to break free. Weak like a kitten. The black snares creep up her legs. Tear her skin. Press her knees apart. Elvira Wallin whimpers.

Hedda Wallin turns her back. Walks out of the room. Dr. Lohrman remains there, hypnotized by the sight. Sees the girl fall forward among all that black. She screams for her mother. And the tentacles swoop over her. Tearing and pulling and clawing. They twist around Elvira Wallin, force themselves on her, and toss her to and fro.

Dr. Lohrman glimpses the girl's face. One last time before he flees for the stairs. Her eyes are open but empty. They shine with pain and bliss and madness. Her cries for her mother have turned into a gurgling, half-stifled scream.

Dr. Lohrman darts for the small staircase. Towards the kerosene lamp. Away from the unfathomable. Away from the inexplicable. He sees Hedda Wallin standing there. Calm, with her back against the stone wall. The lamp makes her skin look yellow. The light glints on glassy eyes. He knows she is forcing herself not to cover her ears.

The scream lingers in the air. It dies out. Replaced by a rhythmic panting. Hoarse and full of mumbled words. Dr. Lohrman stares at the woman beside him.

'What was I to do?' says Hedda Wallin. She doesn't sound apologetic. Not angry. 'It wants to breed. It wants offspring. Nineteen years ago it was me. Now it wants to meet its daughter.'

Translated from the Swedish by James D. Jenkins

Marko Hautala

Pale Toes

Reviewing a Finnish novel for NPR in 2016, a critic noted that 'Finland . . . has a thriving spec[ulative] fiction scene whose best writers rival those of the English-speaking world'. 'Finnish Weird' (or suomikumma in Finnish) is enough of a phenomenon that there's a whole website devoted to it – finnishweird.net – complete with free stories (in English) from leading Finnish weird fiction authors. Marko Hautala (b. 1973), by contrast, is more properly classified as a horror author than a weird fiction writer. With several volumes of fiction to his credit, and works translated into eight languages, including the novel The Black Tongue, *published in English in 2015, Hautala has been deemed the 'Finnish Stephen King'. 'Pale Toes' originally appeared in an anthology of Finnish horror fiction in 2015 and makes its first English appearance here.*

THEY FOUND A PLACE FOR THE NIGHT at the last minute. August had been a terrible time to travel, like Petri had said time and time again. Nina hadn't listened to him, and Petri hadn't cared to argue. Now, they'd exhausted and sweated themselves into a breakdown way too many times.

The B&B's receptionist dangled a key attached to a thin metal ring from the end of his index finger. Petri failed to take it at first. He just stared at the key like some foreign object, wondering how easily it could have fallen.

They carried their backpacks upstairs. A small nightstand separated the beds in the room. Neither of them suggested moving it out of the way and pushing the beds together. Nina flopped down on the thick mattress with a long sigh.

'I can't sleep here,' she said, finally breaking the silence.

Petri sat down on his bed. When they had stepped into the room, he had switched on the light and seen a cockroach scuttling away under the bathroom door, but that wasn't worth mentioning.

'There's a bar downstairs,' Petri said. 'We could get wasted. If you want to.'

Nina thought that was the first good idea in a week.

They chose a table by the window, although they couldn't see anything outside, only their own reflections in the uneven glass. Darkness had fallen during the thirty minutes they'd spent in their room.

'Where are we going?' Nina yawned.

All the other customers at the bar were men. They had barely glanced at Petri, but a few pairs of eyes had lingered on Nina, following her until they reached the table.

'Pezenas is next,' Petri said.

Nina did not react to this and only continued to stare at her own reflection in the window. Petri started to suspect that she might have meant something else by her question.

Where were they going? They had never needed to ask things like that before.

Petri watched Nina's profile. Her face was young, unfamiliar and pale. Petri thought about Pezenas and was terrified that it would not be enough for Nina.

'What are you thinking about?' Petri asked. Shame followed right after. That was not a question a grown man would ask.

'Nothing,' Nina sighed. 'My head's so tired it doesn't have anything to say.'

The girl brought her pint glass to her lips, quickly, and drank. She drank greedily until she gagged. She made no sound, but a jerk of her shoulders gave her away. Nina let the foam drip back into her glass.

'Is there something wrong with the beer?' Petri asked.

Nina wiped her mouth and leaned forward.

'What the fuck is wrong with you?' she asked.

She had tears in her eyes, but that was because of her gag reflex. Just a reaction without an emotion.

Petri had sacrificed so much for Nina. The kids would soon be at the age where they would know to blame the father who had left instead of themselves. They'd hear phrases like 'mid-life crisis'. They would block his calls and tear up all the birthday cards he sent them.

Last night, while waiting for sleep and for Nina to come back from buying a pack of smokes, Petri had realized that one of them had sacrificed nothing. Twenty-somethings have nothing to sacrifice.

When Petri looked into Nina's eyes, brimming with griefless tears, he knew that something would soon be said that could never be taken back. Here's where it would finally happen. In France, near the Spanish border, in some B&B the name of which Petri hadn't bothered to check.

Nina had just opened her mouth when someone dropped into the chair at the end of their table. The scent of soot, sweat and earth rolled over them.

'Want to see some cave paintings?' the man asked in English.

Unfamiliar accent. Matted, rust-brown beard. Still, the eyes revealed that the man was not that old. Thirty, at most.

'Fuck. Off.'

Nina's voice was icy, but the man pretended not to hear. He waved a hand at the bar and lifted up three fingers to the bartender.

'On me,' he said and pointed carelessly at Nina's and Petri's half-drunk glasses.

'Don't you understand what we're saying?'

Nina's eyes stayed on Petri.

'I'm not some useless tour guide,' the man said calmly, obviously used to objections. 'I know caves no one's ever even heard about. Unique chance. Take it or leave it.'

'We'll leave it,' Nina said. 'Get lost.'

The man tilted his head and thought for a while.

'Okay,' he said and gripped the table for support, about to rise.

'Wait,' Petri said.

'What the hell you are doing?' Nina whispered in Finnish.

'Tell us more,' Petri said.

The man sat down with a wide smile at Nina. The waiter brought their new glasses over and put them on the table.

The man explained that the area had many more prehistoric caves than the official records said. It sounded practiced, a routine speech, but Petri loved to listen. It was music that prevented Nina from saying something irrevocable.

'I've been to Font-de-Gaume.' Petri's voice was steady; the voice of a grown man who would not break down.

'Eh,' the man snorted and waved his hand. 'Boring. I can show you better ones. Practically untouched.'

The man told them about underground cave networks, hundreds of meters long, of ancient places of worship and ritualistic caves of shamans.

'Stop that,' Nina said to Petri in Finnish. 'We won't be going into any fucking caves.'

'I'm Alex,' the man said happily and offered his hand to Nina. A professional who knew who he needed to charm.

Nina kept her hands tightly under the table at first. She glanced at the man. Petri could tell that Nina wanted to smile. The short eye contact made her cheek muscles twitch slightly underneath her smooth skin. Petri had learned to register these things.

Nina put her hand out.

'There you go,' the man laughed. 'Life's too short to sulk.'

Petri and Nina told him their names. The man made them clink their glasses together.

'I've spent more time underground than any official guide,' Alex said and then leaned forward like he was about to share a state secret. 'A part of me is down there right now.'

The man waited for their reaction.

'Do you believe me?' he asked when they did not give him one.

'Maybe,' Petri said.

The man pushed his chair back, glanced over his shoulder toward the bar and then bent down to untie his left shoe. His sock came off with a scratching sound, like it had scraped off the man's leg hair. He looked over his shoulder again and then lifted his bare foot on the table.

The smell was so strong that Petri burst out laughing. Nina followed suit. And then, almost as one, they fell silent. They now saw what was wrong with the man's foot.

'What happened?' Petri asked.

The man's big toe looked unnaturally large. The hardened skin next to it looked like a yellowish tumor. Still, it was just a regular toe. It only looked huge because all the other toes were gone. The end of his foot was nothing but scarred skin.

'I don't know,' Alex said, obviously enjoying the shock he had caused.

They heard angry yelling from behind the bar. The bartender was waving his arms at them.

Alex threw a lazy apology over his shoulder and slid his foot off the table.

'I was exploring a cave alone about twenty kilometers from here,' he said, pulling the sock back on his foot. 'I slipped, lost consciousness. And when I woke up . . .'

He let out a strange whistling sound.

'Gone. Bye bye, toes.'

'Rats?' Petri suggested.

'Maybe. In any case, I left that cave faster than ever. Nearly got myself killed in the rush. I forgot the most important rule: never panic. Never.'

'Horrible,' Nina mumbled.

'Not really,' the man said. 'I made it to the doctor and shocked a few student nurses. The main thing is that I still have my big toe. That's the support pillar of the whole leg. Man's got to have a big toe or he won't be able to stand. You only need the other toes if you want to climb trees.'

'You have to know that this is the world's worst marketing speech,' Nina said.

'What do you mean?'

'If you want us to come into the cave with you.'

Alex laughed.

'Believe me, I learned from my mistake. I will never slip again. I will never panic again. And I will never go to a cave alone. If you follow those rules, it's just as safe as riding a bike. Safer, actually.'

The man bought them another round. Their tiredness had lifted. Petri was almost happy, even though he knew it was all just a sad game they were playing before the inevitable.

'A toe fairy!' Nina suddenly cried out.

Alex didn't get it.

'A toe fairy took your toes.'

They drank to that. They agreed on a price.

They would see some cave paintings.

'Is this your day job?' Nina asked when they walked out of the B&B.

'For now,' the man said and dug something out of his pocket. Car lights flashed in the shadows. 'Please,' Alex said, holding the back door open. Petri waited for Nina to climb in the back seat. Men in the front, women in the back. Petri was all for equality, but they were in a conservative region.

Alex held the door open and stared at the ground. Nina went around the car and stood by the front door.

Petri pointed questioningly at the back seat. Alex nodded and smiled, but avoided his gaze. Petri climbed into the back seat.

Alex drove along the side streets at such speeds that he must have known these alleyways through and through. The headlights showed them glimpses of cobbled streets and flashes of empty gardens.

'Did you train as a guide?' Nina asked Alex.

Petri had to lean toward them from the back seat like a toddler who wanted to hear what his parents were saying.

'No,' Alex said. 'I studied archaeology, but then well, things came up.'

'A woman?'

'Of course,' Alex said. 'And parties. And the whole world to see, with more women. And more. And more.'

Nina laughed. Petri only saw a part of her side profile through her hair. No eyes, just the tip of her nose and a mouth open in an unnatural laugh.

A sad game, before the inevitable.

After a twisting drive of more than an hour they arrived at their destination and stepped out of the car and into the cool night. It seemed they had driven uphill, as the lights of the village were far below them. Everything else was just darkness, rustling in the wind. A clear sky filled with stars above them.

Alex threw his backpack on, put on his headlamp, and told them to follow. They walked behind the bouncing beam of light, first on a path and then without one. Rotting branches crunched under their shoes. At some point, Alex turned his headlamp off and told Nina to grab onto his backpack and hold on. Petri didn't have time to catch Nina by her hood, so he had to stumble behind them, relying only on his ears until his eyes started to get used to the dark.

'We're here,' Alex soon said.

They were in a forest clearing. The calls of unfamiliar animals rang between the dark tree trunks.

'Give me a hand, Petri.'

Alex bent down and wrapped his hands around a large object on the ground. It was hard to see any details in the dark, but Petri assumed the intention was to move a boulder aside. He went to stand opposite Alex and tried to get a good grip with his fingers.

'Can you do it?' Alex asked.

Petri couldn't. Alex told him how to place his hands, and soon enough the boulder moved.

'Good,' Alex grunted. 'I can do the rest by myself.'

The boulder fell on its side with a hollow sound.

'Right,' Alex panted. 'I'll go first, if that's okay.'

He sat down on the ground, dragged his body forward and disappeared.

Petri and Nina stood under the stars and stared at the black hole in the ground.

'Follow me.'

Alex's voice echoed, like a sound in a container. He had switched his headlamp on. When Petri bent over the hole in the ground, he saw nothing but blinding light at first, then a hand that was reaching towards them.

Nina grabbed it before Petri could react.

'Sit down first,' Alex said in his echoing voice. 'Just like that. Then give me your hand. And the other.'

Nina's smiling face looked like a white sculpture when she disappeared underground.

A long silence followed. Petri saw a waving light in the hole, then nothing but darkness. He heard voices speaking, Nina's laughter. Then that disappeared, too. Petri stood still and tried to think about what could be delaying Alex. A strange thought came to him. Could he push the boulder back into place alone?

'All right, good sir,' Alex said. The light came back, revealing the rugged edges of the hole.

Petri sat down on the ground and put his legs in the hole.

'My hand's here,' Alex said.

'Just step away,' Petri said.

'Are you sure?'

'Yeah.'

The light stayed still for a moment and then disappeared.

Petri leaned his elbows on the ground and let his legs slide deeper into the darkness. Gravel scraped at his buttocks until gravity did its duty.

Petri came down legs first, but the drop made him stumble. Arms came around him right away. Petri tried to get a foothold on the slippery stones but had to lean on Alex for support.

'You okay?' the man asked.

'Perfect.'

That was not true. Petri was feeling confused. The heat of the last few weeks, the exhaustion and his dehydration all seemed to condense to the jumping beam of light that blinded him and painted afterimages on his retinas. Petri pulled away as politely as possible and sought Nina with his eyes. The waving light only showed him fragments of a strange woman, an alien that had filled his every thought for a year and a half.

'I'm here,' Nina said, right in front of Petri. 'Are you okay?'

'Of course,' Petri said.

Nina's arms suddenly wrapped around him. It was so sudden that Petri failed to return the gesture.

'All right, love birds,' Alex interrupted them.

Nina took a quick step away.

Alex gave them both their own headlamps. They placed them on their foreheads. When all the light beams were on, they could see how small the space they were standing in really was.

'Rule number one,' Alex said. 'Do everything like in a Mel Gibson movie.'

'Which means?' Nina asked, laughing.

'In slow motion.'

Alex showed them how to move. He took a deliberate step forward, bent down, placed his hand against the wall of the cave with exaggerated slow motions, then stepped forward again.

'Do you get it? Like Mel Gibson.'

Nina and Petri followed Alex. They walked forward with their backs bowed. Their clothes scraped against the walls.

'Look,' Alex soon said.

They stopped.

'The first greeting.'

Petri only saw Nina's heaving shoulders.

'Look at the protruding stone on your right side when you go past it. It has a carving of a mouth and a pair of eyes.'

When Petri came to the protrusion on the wall, he stopped to look at it. Yes, maybe there was a mouth. Perhaps eyes. Still, it was something nature could have done. Empty eye sockets, corners of the mouth twisted downward. A dead expression that came alive for a second when a beam of light moved and twisted the shadows.

Petri turned his head from side to side.

'Come on,' Nina said. She was whispering for some reason.

She was squatting less than five meters away, looking at Petri.

'Alex is already talking to himself up ahead.'

The passage grew narrower and narrower. When they reached Alex, he explained to them that the caves were made for much smaller people. Their diets were poorer and so on.

'But otherwise, they were just like us,' Alex said, a wild smile on his face, 'as you will soon see.'

They went deeper. Clothes scraped against the walls more and more. Breathing got heavier every moment. The relaxation created by the beers Alex had bought them started to evaporate. Petri had never been scared of tight spaces, but now he considered turning back. It was impossible to know how deep underground they were. The cave walls were so close at all times that it was impossible to find a spot where one shoulder wasn't touching stone. Petri realized that his breathing was shallow. Right then, he started hearing Nina's delighted calls.

'Come here, Petri,' the girl shouted in Finnish. 'You've got to see this!'

Petri pulled himself together and moved forward. When he reached Nina and Alex, it was a relief to see that they were in a slightly more spacious chamber. They could both stand up straight. Nina was looking at something on the wall, her hand covering her mouth. Alex was right behind the girl, so close that their shoulders were touching. Their light beams were connected, pointed at the images on the wall.

'Amazing,' Nina whispered.

Petri came to stand next to them. The space around them felt luxurious after the endless passageway. The light beam revealed handprints. Someone, or some people, had dipped their hands in dye and pressed their prints on the wall. The shapes looked black, but maybe the blue-gray glow of their headlamps distorted the color.

'Can I?' Nina asked, hovering her palm over one of the handprints without touching the wall.

'Of course,' Alex said. 'Maybe that's the reason they're here. Who knows?'

Nina placed her palm on one of the handprints. She did it slowly, as if the touch could have activated some ancient mechanism.

'An amazing feeling,' she whispered.

'At least thirty thousand years separate you,' Alex said. 'You and the person who made that print.'

'It feels like there's nothing between us.' Nina sounded rapturous. 'We have a connection.'

'Great to hear you say that,' Alex chuckled. 'I felt the same the first time I came here.'

He placed his hand on Nina's shoulder. The gesture was innocent, but Petri's eyes were nailed to it and he couldn't see anything else. No messages on the wall from thirty thousand years away.

There were only twenty-eight years and three months between Petri and Nina. Just a blink of an eye. But it was utter darkness, that fleeting moment.

Alex turned toward Petri.

'Come closer,' he said and removed his hand from Nina's shoulder.

Petri did as he was told and came to stand in front of the wall. Nina took hold of his wrist determinedly.

'Try for yourself.'

Petri's hand was in a fist when Nina pressed it against the wall. When he opened his hand, his fingers were in the wrong places. His hand and the dark stain in the stone formed a strange, ten-fingered pattern.

'Can you feel it?' Nina asked.

'I can,' Petri lied.

Just cold stone.

'And now, ladies and gentlemen,' Alex interrupted. 'A moment of choice.'

Petri wiped his hands on the hem of his coat.

'Tell us,' Nina whispered excitedly.

'The last cave,' Alex said. 'Do you want to see it?'

'Of course we do.'

Nina's voice was still husky with emotion.

'Very well,' Alex said without waiting for Petri's answer, 'but it's going to take some special measures.'

'What kind?'

Alex lifted his index finger, like a magician preparing for a trick, and took off his backpack. Then he took off his coat and shirt, yanking them over his head with one movement.

'What are you doing?' Petri asked when the man started to open his pants.

'A special measure,' Alex said and continued to undress himself. 'Like I said, our ancestors were smaller than us. The passage ahead is pretty narrow. Clothes could get stuck.'

Suddenly Alex stood naked before them, only his head-lamp remained.

'You can leave your underwear on, but I don't recommend it.'

Alex looked at them both in turn. He looked at Petri longer.

'What's wrong?' he asked, spreading his arms. 'You're from Finland. You bathe in the sauna with the whole village, right?'

Nina laughed at that and started to take her clothes off.

'Are you sure?' Petri asked in Finnish.

'We've come this far, so I want to see that cave,' Nina said. 'Don't you?'

'Good,' Alex said and dug out a plastic bottle from his backpack. He twisted the cap open and poured silky liquid on his shoulders and sides. The oil dripped down his chest when he spread it over his skin in quick movements.

'The stone is mostly smooth, so we will slip through in seconds with some oil on.'

'Are you serious?' Petri asked.

'Of course. Trust me. I've been there twenty-three times. No one has been left behind in the cave. I'll take care of that.'

Petri looked around, confused. A man oiling himself and Nina, who only had her bra on and was struggling with her shirt. Petri undid his belt quickly. He wanted to be naked before Nina. It would somehow make the situation more bearable.

Alex tossed the oil bottle to Petri and stood there watching when Petri took his underwear off. Petri didn't let that bother him. He poured some oil on his palms and started to slather it over his skin defiantly. He knew his skin was stretchy. He had gray in his pubes. Alex was probably wondering if he could get it up anymore.

Petri threw the bottle back to Alex. It slipped through the man's fingers and fell to the ground. Alex didn't bend down to pick it up but kicked the bottle in Nina's direction. She picked it up and started to oil herself. Alex stared at her shamelessly. It was obvious that Nina knew it.

Soon, they stood there naked and shiny, headlamps on, like in some weird ritual.

'Remember Mel Gibson,' Alex said. 'Move slowly, but determinedly.'

They nodded.

'Your body knows what to do, so trust your body. Just slither like snakes. And if you start to feel like you're getting stuck, just back up a few centimeters and try again, changing your position a little. Okay?'

A nod.

'Staying calm is the key. Remember, no one has gotten

stuck. Once, I took in this fat Chinese dude, who insisted on going, although I had some doubts about him. But this guy just popped out on the other side like a cork out of a champagne bottle. No problem at all.'

Nina laughed.

'Right,' Alex said and clapped his hands together. 'Follow me.'

They walked behind the man through a passage that was narrower than the ones before it. Nina had cut in front of Petri. Her shiny back glistened in the lamplight. Her hair was stuck to her skin.

Soon Alex stopped.

'Here it is. I'll go first, then you.'

He pointed at Nina.

'Put your arms against your sides, like this.'

Petri couldn't see because Nina was standing in front of him, but he understood what Alex meant.

'I know that you want to put your arms ahead, like you were about to dive, but that takes more space. Believe me. One time this Slovenian . . . Well, that went okay too, in the end. But yeah, arms to the sides and shoulders to the front, like this. Okay?'

In front of Petri, Nina nodded. Her shoulder blades bulged as she repeated the movement Alex was showing them.

'And remember that I'll be on the other side, waiting, and I'll help you if necessary. I'll pull you in by the head, like a midwife, okay?'

Petri, too, chuckled nervously at that.

'And here we go.'

Alex disappeared somewhere. Nina apparently saw where he had gone, as she bent down and then disappeared, too. Petri saw her white legs vanishing into a hole. He stooped down to feel its edges. Nina's legs were still visible, and then they were gone. He heard yelling and laughter at the end of the passage. Petri counted to three, put his arms against his hips and dove in.

Stone pressed against his skin, but Alex had been right: his body knew what to do. His anxiety disappeared. Even though he felt the pressure all around his body, the constricting sensation was not unpleasant. On the contrary. It was a carefree feeling, like being embraced by some large, benevolent creature. When Petri saw Nina's and Alex's headlamps, he was even a little disappointed. He could have stayed in the womb-like pressure longer.

'Well done, Mr. Gibson,' Alex said and slapped Petri on his oily back.

Petri turned around and hooted out loud. It was the pure joy of success. Like when he was a little boy and managed to score a winning goal in a soccer game.

Petri looked at the ceiling of the cave and saw a strange, phosphoric glow. Something in the stone reacted to the light of his lamp. It was like looking at a starry sky.

Petri sat up and looked over his shoulder.

Nina was standing in the middle of the cave, her back to him. She was naked, and glowing, and her black hair stuck to her shoulders and back. There was something primally beautiful in that sight. Petri wanted to fuck her right then and there. Press his old, stretchy skin against her smoothness and forget everything that had come between them.

Then his eyes moved to the wall. He realized what had Nina so enchanted.

'Unbelievable,' Petri heard himself muttering.

'Isn't it?' Alex said. Petri had spoken Finnish, but the man must have understood the tone of his voice.

Phosphoric crystals had formed an image on the wall in front of Nina.

Petri stood up and went to stand beside her.

'How can it glow like that?' the girl asked.

'No one knows,' Alex said from behind them. 'Like I said, this cave is not in any official records. No one has studied it.'

'Can I take a picture?' Nina asked.

'Go ahead,' Alex said.

They all laughed when Nina fumbled around her body before she realized she was naked and without a phone. Without the chance to communicate with the outside world, for once. Right now, when she finally saw something truly amazing.

'Is that a face?' Petri asked in Finnish.

Nina didn't answer him.

The glowing dots formed a large oval shape. Inside, there clearly were two eyes, a nose, a mouth. The expression on the face changed with the waves of their light beams. Like on that bulging stone Alex had called their first greeting.

'Some species of mold glow,' Alex said. 'Maybe our ancestors knew how to plant it on stone to make pictures. No one truly knows. But isn't it amazing?'

Petri moved his head from side to side slowly. The expressions on the face shifted with the light, but none of them looked pleasant. Petri's eyes started to hurt. He turned around. Alex stood smugly near the hole through which they had come to the cave. He had probably been watching Nina, but now he was smiling at Petri.

The beam of light revealed something else.

'What are those?' Petri asked.

His lamp pointed at the cave entrance. It was surrounded by dark, oblong tracks.

'Footprints,' Alex said.

Petri went closer. He bent down.

They were same the kinds of prints as in the previous cave, rough stains, but made with feet. They surrounded the hole. Most were on the sides, especially towards the bottom of it. Petri put his hand on one of the prints.

'There are toes missing,' he said.

'What do you mean?' Alex asked.

The light changed in a way that told Petri that the man was now standing behind him.

'Only the big toe is visible,' he said.

'That's normal,' Alex said. 'The big toe just leaves a clearer impression. Those black dots there are from other toes. See?'

Petri didn't, but the explanation sounded believable. He removed his hand from the footprint.

'Petri?'

Nina's voice was quiet and sleepy.

'Yeah?'

'I can't stop.'

Petri stood up and looked at Nina. Slumped shoulders. Arms flush against her hips. Glistening skin.

'Stop what?'

'Looking.'

Nina's whole body was bent forward.

'It's really . . . captivating,' Petri said.

He started to stare at the image again, too. It really was a captivating sight. The expression on the simplistic face changed with even the tiniest movement of light. Like the picture was trying to talk. His eyes started to hurt again; a sharp sensation behind his eyeballs, like unused capillaries were filling with blood again.

Petri made himself look away. He lifted his right hand in front of him, the one that had touched the footprint on the wall.

Blood. This close, the headlamp did not transform the color to black. The grooves of his palm were filled with bright red liquid.

'What the fu—'

The noise started gradually. At first, Petri thought that Alex had switched on some device, maybe a video camera or some other gadget that let out a broken, whining sound. He turned to Alex.

The man was standing against the wall. Almost as if he was waiting for something.

'What was that?' Petri asked.

Alex didn't answer him. Petri held out his palm to the man.

'Blood,' he said slowly. 'Fresh blood.'

It sounded like an accusation, but it wasn't. He only wanted an explanation.

Alex's expression was unreadable. Maybe fear, maybe excitement. A movement in his groin drew Petri's attention. A twitching movement. The man's member was swaying from side to side. Twitching to life.

'What the hell?' Petri said.

'Do not panic,' Alex said calmly. 'That will only make things worse. The most important rule.'

'Panic?'

The broken sound started again. It traveled along the stone. Alex did not react to it. Only his half-hard erection kept twitching expectantly.

'Nina?' Petri said.

No answer.

Petri turned to look. Nina was still staring at the image on the wall. Her shoulders were pointed forward, like she was diving in a cave again. Clear liquid ran along her inner thighs. It pooled around the girl's feet.

When the sound came for the third time, Alex finally reacted. He began to shout in a trembling voice. Petri didn't understand the words, but he did understand their meaning.

This way. We are here.

Petri's breathing grew shallow. Again, he felt how close the walls were. He felt all that stone and soil and the weight of eras that surrounded them. At least thirty thousand years. Handprints. Footprints. Holes in the walls. They were everywhere, identical to the ones they had come through.

Petri panicked. He chose to do it. Panic was a friend. Made him mad with rage. Showed him the rock on the ground.

When Petri hit Alex for the first time, the man didn't even try to dodge.

'Just give them what they want,' he said when Petri had already raised his arm. 'They won't ask for much.'

The blow hit him above his left ear. Alex's head jerked to the side, his expression distorted with pain. Then the same empty look returned.

'They basically live on handouts,' the man rushed to speak, 'even when people have taken everyth—'

The second blow landed directly on his nose. There was a crunch, blood spilled out on his pale chest. Only the third blow made Alex stop talking. He started to scream. The fourth one stopped that, too. There were splatters on the wall. A roar in Petri's head. Now there was blood on both of his hands. Alex had slumped into a sitting position. His head was lolling towards his chest, but he was still trying to climb back on his feet, like a wounded spider.

Petri dropped the rock and rushed towards Nina.

'We are getting out of here, right now,' he said, shaking Nina by her shoulder.

The girl looked at him, her face slack.

'I'll go first and pull you onto the other side,' Petri said. 'Like a midwife, right?'

'Okay.'

'You'll come right behind me. Do you understand?'

The screeching sound was closer now.

'Do you understand?' Petri yelled.

'Okay.'

Young, beautiful Nina.

Petri pulled her towards the hole and squatted beside it. He put his arms against his sides and dove.

'What is that?' Nina asked somewhere behind him.

Petri pushed himself deeper into the hole.

What is that?

Nina's shouts were dimmer now, as if muffled by cotton. Petri sped up, let his body twist and turn instinctively, allowed it to remember what it was like to be a fish or a snake.

When the constricting feeling started, Petri remembered what Alex had said: *just back up a few centimeters and try again, changing your position a little.* But Alex was a nutcase and a foreign perv who used Mel Gibson as his example. Nina was still in the cave, seeing something she didn't understand. Petri's heartbeat was ringing in his ears.

And so he kept pushing forward. Pushed even when he realized that his body didn't remember what being a fish or a snake felt like. Pushed because the fat Chinese man had gotten through, pushed until he was completely stuck.

Petri remained sensible about the situation, even when he realized he was screaming. He tried to move, although the stone squeezed his upper body harder and harder. His body tried to fix the situation with instinctive movements. Stupid, unnecessary, dangerous movements, constantly growing more violent. The beam of his headlamp swayed everywhere, but there was nothing but darkness there.

He heard a crunch.

Pain flooded through his left arm. All sensation of other limbs disappeared.

Petri screamed louder. The scream filled his head. It was a small space, his head. Small like the space he was in.

He had to think reasonably, but reason told him that some

big bone had just broken and that the spot would soon start to swell.

Swell and swell like a fat Chinese man.

Petri jerked his head from side to side, the only thing he was still capable of moving. His headlamp hit the wall and went out.

Swell and swell and—

Reason told him that everyone had gotten through this hole, and that everyone got to the surface and sent pictures to their friends and said that the experience was earth-shattering, but never again.

Swell and—

Dark and tight and dark.

This can't be happening, Petri thought, in some calm corner of his mind. *The world is not this evil.*

Not dark; darkness.

The point at which a fat Chinese man swells beyond all comprehensible limits.

Swells, and then, something pushing out, black sh—

Darkness comes.

The worst possible.

The darkness of a fat Chinese man.

—it.

Completely stuck.

Completely stuck and, in the darkness, it was difficult to say when he was conscious and when not. Sometimes, Petri fell through an endless space, sometimes nothing but choking pressure all around him, like sweaty skin.

Sometimes, he fell asleep.

Petri was in his childhood, in a movie theater. The scent of the red fitted carpet. The white screen glowed in the shadows. The breath of something huge snuffled and wheezed in the back row. Smacking sounds, like something was eating with great relish. Petri covered his ears with his hands and looked at the movie screen; it was like uneven glass, and there was night behind it and, in the night, flickering naked people or white reptiles in muddy water.

Petri forced his eyes closed, but in real life, he did the opposite. His eyes were open, he was conscious again and still helplessly stuck.

Petri started to scream and swing his head. No mercy; head against stone until it all fades away.

And finally it did.

Evening sun shining through the open balcony doors in some little Portuguese town, the name of which Petri couldn't remember. The balcony doors had wooden blinds; one of them was open. The sun was setting behind the mountains.

Nina's hair against the white pillow.

Look how beautiful, Petri said.

Nina didn't answer him. Petri took the girl by the shoulder and turned her around.

Her face was covered by hair. Petri moved it aside but could not find Nina's face. The hair would not end. Just when he thought he could see a glimpse of an eye or the tip of her nose, more hair appeared. The hair went on and on, tangled around his fingers, wrapped tightly around them, and there was something between all that hair, not eyes or tips of noses, but . . .

Small mouths angry rat mouths.

They greedily attacked the fingers tangled in hair, like this had been the plan from the very start, when Nina, whose name Petri did not yet know, had walked across that room at that party, so young and so beautiful and so sudden that everything changed, like waking up from a dream.

And Petri woke up.

He didn't scream this time. His shoulder was numb, but he felt something touching his feet. Petri held his breath and focused on the sensation like it was a quiet sound he was trying to listen for.

Fingers were exploring his toes. He could feel the tickles clearly. It was almost a pleasant feeling. The world was good, after all. The fingers separated his toes patiently, gently. Like an ape grooming its mate or a parent caressing the feet of their child.

When the pain came, it wasn't even that bad, all things considered.

It still left him unconscious.

Petri remembered the school festival at the end of first grade. He hadn't seen his father and mother anywhere. After the festival, he had run out and stood in the schoolyard, thinking that something bad had happened, that the world wanted to hurt him. The details of it remained hidden, like the details of some hostile, hiding, curled-up creature. Then his father and mother had stepped through the school doors. Familiar faces and smiles, and they asked why Petri had just run past them.

Petri couldn't explain. Maybe he had wanted to see the world as it was, without his father and mother, catch the world in the act before it curled up and hid.

Petri kept repeating the memory, absent-mindedly certain that it was something crucial, something he could not quite catch. Again and again, he focused on the moment in the empty schoolyard, when something had curled up to hide, had run underneath the bathroom door when he had flipped on the light.

Petri realized that his skin was free.

He was the cockroach that had gotten away.

Petri lifted his head. The motion felt like a luxury. To be allowed to move like that.

Only the skin of his back was touching stone. The darkness was still complete, but the tightness was gone.

Petri suspected that he was sleeping. The world wanted to hurt him, and it would not let go that easily.

He felt out his left shoulder. It was dislocated and broken. The pain was real. Petri pushed himself to sit up and groped at the ground around him. His hands touched fabric. His fingers explored the object until Petri realized that it was a backpack. Opening it one-handed was difficult. Inside, he felt the plastic shape of a cellphone.

A lucky cockroach, indeed.

When the screen woke up, it shone like the sun. It filled the cave. Petri hooted with joy and looked around. He saw the handprints covering the wall, the clothes on the ground. A miracle had happened. Petri did not understand how, but he accepted it. He illuminated the old cave, his old skin, the old childhood scar on his knee.

And his toes.

His legs were at the mouth of the passage leading to the last cave. Behind them, there was a darkness that the light could not reach.

The big toe was missing from his left leg. It was replaced by emptiness, and a rough wound with a bone peeking through. All the other toes were still there. Delicate, curling shapes, like a cluster of stunted mushrooms.

'Why?' Petri whispered.

The question sounded lonely and hollow in the cave's echoless space. Petri started to giggle, and his vision filled with tears.

'Why the big toe?' he asked the empty cave.

Petri realized that he was being stared at. The motion had been at the edge of his peripheral vision, but his mind was numb and slow to connect the dots.

The light of the screen went out just as he saw the silver dots of eyes at the end of the narrow passage. Petri dragged himself backwards and switched on the screen again.

The light did not reach far enough, but against the darkness he could discern faces as gray shapes around glowing pairs of eyes. Petri held his breath and listened. Scraping sounds, at the edge of his hearing. Like tired old men trying to saw timber at the same time. Ears that had grown up in the noise of traffic could just barely hear it. The sound was accompanied with lazy smacking sounds and frail sighs of pleasure.

They did not ask for much. They lived on handouts.

Something reached towards him from the darkness. A thin arm. Blue veins. One pair of eyes stooped closer. Petri leaned back but stayed where he was. For a fleeting moment, he saw a pale, hairless crown of a head. Shining eyes below it. Bloodstained fingers.

The arm jerked and something fell in front of Petri. Light, tingling sounds against the stone.

Petri lowered the cellphone light.

Two pieces of bone.

His big toe. Petri recognized it right away, even though the skin was gone. The pieces of bone were damp and shiny, maybe with spit. A few stains left by bloody fingers.

The eyes retreated back into the darkness. *Why?* Petri would have liked to ask. What was this grotesque trade all about? He had the right to know, but the sea of silver dots was like the starry sky. No use in asking. Maybe they were dead already.

Petri bowed forward and reached to take the pieces of bone with his left hand, even though pain was trying to tell him not to use that arm. He squeezed them in his fist. The lazy movement of his fingers made pain radiate all across his body.

The faces stayed still.

'Darling . . .'

A weak voice. A woman's voice. Petri stared at the pairs of eyes and tried to illuminate them better.

'You can talk?' he asked numbly.

The shape of a smaller face stood out amongst the figures, circled with black hair, without glowing eyes. Petri remembered Nina. How could he have forgotten the young, beautiful Nina?

'Are you okay?' Petri asked.

A long silence. Grunting breaths, smacking sounds. And then, one word:

'Go.'

Judging from her voice, Nina was very, very cold.

'No,' Petri said. 'You're coming with me.'

The hand that held the cellphone was shaking. The restless light made it hard to focus.

'I can't.'

'I got out, too,' Petri said. 'They let me go . . . pushed me out, I wouldn't have made it—'

'You're too old,' Nina interrupted him.

Petri tried to understand why his age suddenly mattered, in the middle of all this. Nina had never brought it up. Twenty-eight years and three months. A blink of an eye.

'Too old. They don't want you. Maybe they respect you. Alex told me before . . .'

'Alex is there?' Petri asked.

'Kind of.'

'I want to speak with him.'

'He's dead.'

'Are you sure?'

'Totally sure.'

He could hear Nina's teeth chattering through the creatures' smacking noises and dragging breaths. The girl had to be in shock. Petri thought about her naked, freezing body. About how Nina's skin touched the skin of the creatures with glowing eyes. The thought enraged him.

Petri found a loose rock on the ground. He squeezed it

inside his fist and started to crawl towards the hole, cursing and yelling.

'Don't.'

Petri stopped. The creatures had gone quiet. Not a sound. Only the chattering of Nina's teeth.

'You didn't see what they did,' Nina whispered.

She sounded like she wanted to cry but was too tired to do it. Nina, who had never sacrificed anything.

Petri's rage dulled as fast as it had awoken. Fear returned. It brought back the pain and exhaustion, the desire to breathe outside air. Petri lowered the hand that was holding the rock.

'I'll go back to the village and get some help,' he said.

'You do that.'

Nina sounded sleepy.

'We will come and get you really soon.'

'Good.'

'Don't let them take you anywhere.'

'I won't.'

Petri forced himself to stand up and started to collect some clothes. There was no time to be picky. He found his own pants, but the shirt was Nina's. It was too small and too tight around his injured shoulder, but it would have to do. The silver dots followed his every move when he put the pieces of bone into his trouser pocket.

'We will see each other soon,' Petri said, even though they both knew that this was the end.

Here's where it finally happened. In a nameless cave, deep underground, near the border between France and Spain.

Petri walked back along the same route they had followed, lighting the way with a cellphone. The stone scratched at his old, stretchy skin, tore wounds in the soles of his feet, which had been covered by shoes for too long.

When he came to the hole that led to the surface, he

looked up, breathed in the biting night air and felt alive for the first time in decades. Petri looked for protrusions in the wall that he could grab and use as footholds, started to climb towards freedom. It was a difficult task, maybe impossible. A dislocated shoulder, one of his supporting toes gone.

A lucky, wounded cockroach attempting to climb out of a glass bottle.

After falling for a third time, Petri lay on his back on the stony ground and panted. He cried a little and wondered if there was anything worth all this effort outside the cave. A sleeping village, disbelieving police officers who would never find Nina. The calls of unfamiliar animals, the meaning of which he did not understand. The blinking eyes of long-dead stars and a wind that blew around the shreds of torn birthday cards.

On an impulse, he took the two pieces of bone from his pocket. Twirled them around with his numb fingers. Put them in his mouth.

The bitterness of blood and strange saliva. He bit down with determination until something gave. Either a bone or a tooth. A musty, primal taste flooded his mouth. The taste of survival.

He forced himself on his feet and tried again.

Translated from the Finnish by Sanna Terho

Martin Steyn

Kira

One of South Africa's eleven official languages, Afrikaans is a relatively young one, a descendant of the Dutch spoken there by colonizing settlers and not recognized as a distinct language by the South African government until 1925. There is a long tradition of horror fiction and ghost stories in Afrikaans, dating back to the éminence grise of Afrikaans letters, poet C. J. Langenhoven (1873-1932), who published literary ghost stories, the best of which were collected in a 2015 volume in Afrikaans but await an English translation. Contemporary Afrikaans horror authors include François Bloemhof and Jaco Jacobs, both primarily writers for young readers, but whose horror stories for adults appeared in the 2016 anthology Skadustemme [Shadow Voices], *where they were featured along with our next story,* MARTIN STEYN's *'Kira'. Though predominantly an author of crime novels, one of which,* Dark Traces, *has appeared in English, Steyn grew up reading Stephen King and occasionally publishes a tale in the genres of horror or the supernatural, like this one, in which a man returns to his childhood home, where he experiences an otherworldly encounter.*

TAMASON.

I push the cabin's door open, Knysna Lake purling softly behind me. The stagnant odor hits me like an accusation. The dust must be at least two centimeters thick and I notice more than one thing scurrying.

I'm happy to be back. I've always seen Tamason as 'back'

and the apartment in Stellenbosch as 'away', although I spend my days in that student town. Here I always feel whole again.

That's why I've fled here.

I inherited Tamason from my parents. From the beginning there was a bond between me and the cabin; I was the one who gave it its name when I was little. We were sitting on the porch and my mom pointed out the sunset to me. When those red fingers, a woman's fingers without any doubt, drew silky stripes through the clouds, I said one word: 'Tamason'. What I tried to say was 'tomato sun', but at that stage, tomato was still either 'mato' or 'tama', depending on the sentence or my mood. And so was my beloved house christened.

It takes me the rest of the afternoon to make the house reasonably clean, 'every nook and cranny', as my mom was so fond of saying. In the process I discover all kinds of filthy creatures that had come to breed and mutate happily in mankind's absence, and everything gets summarily bugsprayed and massacred; I have no conscience when it comes to insects.

With the dust and corpses cleared away and my airways sneezed clean, I go and sit with a can of Castle on the porch swing. I look out over the water. The ripples look so calm, but the surface is a dark veil.

I start up a fire and grill a whole package of sausage. By the time it's ready there are three more empty beer cans beside the barbecue. I eat half of the sausage along with a roll and go sit down again on the swing, my second-to-last Castle in my hand.

I become conscious of hands. Soft hands, women's hands, touching my forehead carefully. I open my eyes, confused and disoriented and startled.

But she's already five steps away. Her eyes are large and dark like the lake, her cheeks dull white and smooth in the light of the gas lamp, her mouth slightly open. Dark hair hangs down to her shoulders. She has a loose white dress on, something that folds over her body almost like a sheet, and her bare feet are close together. She holds her hands in front of her.

I open my mouth to say something, but she is already gone.

Just gone. Like a drop of rain on the lake.

I rub my face and wonder if I'm awake. I still feel her cold fingertips against my skin.

I stand up and step on my empty beer can beside the swing, lose my balance and topple headlong.

It's one way of making sure you're awake. I remain lying on the wooden porch and wonder about her. Was she real? Or was it just a dream?

★

The morning sun is shining on the lake when I open the door. I walk into the mineral-rich water, swim out towards the depths and then back to shore. There are a lot of boats on the lake, some with sails, like paper flowers floating in a myriad of colors on the brownish water, others without sails but with powerful engines that cut through the silence. The lake feeds the village, and in a way the village feeds the lake.

Really in more than one way.

After breakfast I grab my guitar and go sit on the swing. It's somewhere during 'Polly' when I feel the clammy thing against my hip, where the T-shirt must have slid up. At first I'm startled, but then I see the animal who has pressed his muzzle against me, laughing and excited, low on his fore-paws, rear end in the air and tail wagging.

I can't resist the big golden retriever. I set the guitar down and sink onto my hands and knees, a mimic of the dog's posture. His mouth gives a bigger laugh and he shuffles closer. I slap on the plank, and when he jumps I push him to the left. He pulls back and comes again. I turn him away. So we try to outwit each other until he finally jumps around and licks my face. I push his head away but can't stop him from laughing.

When I finally stand up, I look around but don't see anyone. There's no collar on the dog's neck, but his fur is clean and it's obvious that he's well cared for.

'Where's your owner?'

He just laughs and sinks down again on his forepaws.

After lunch – we shared a can of Vienna sausages, mine with mustard, his without – I take him out onto the sand, in the hope that he'll head home. But he just sits and looks at me. He pays no heed to my encouragement. He follows me left and right along the lake. I try to chase him off, but he plays dumb and makes a game of it.

Finally I give up and walk back towards Tamason. I write my shadow's description and my address on a sheet of paper and walk towards the café. The dog is well trained too, because he doesn't go in with me.

Old Tolla is behind the counter and he smiles when he sees me. 'Hey, Tommie! Man, it's been a long time since I saw you last. How's it going?'

'Good, thanks.' Does it count as a lie if you don't think about the answer? 'And you?'

'Young man, if I complain, the wife says it's my own fault for wanting to sit and read the newspaper.' He holds up his hands and grins.

I used to come and buy sweets from Tolla when I was waist-high. He always let me have them at a discount. But old age has crept up on him; the gray has completely overtaken his lush forest of hair, the cracks around his eyes and the corners of his mouth are deeper and folds have appeared in the skin of his neck. Yet the lines on my forehead are deeper too.

'Are your parents here too?'

'No, they passed away.'

'Oh, no.'

'Yes, it's been almost two years.'

'So long?'

I nod. 'My mom had a stroke and two months later my father's heart went out. They could never make it without each other.'

'Oh, I'm sorry, man.'

'Thanks. Have you seen that dog before?' I motion to where the dog is sitting with its rear against the window.

'No. I thought it was yours.'

'No. He came sniffing around at Tamason. We played a little and ate and now he doesn't want to go home.'

Tolla laughed. 'That's what happens when you feed a dog.'

'Well, would you maybe hang this up somewhere?' I give him the paper.

'Sure thing.'

In the early evening I start another fire and meanwhile open a package of chips and a Castle. Sebastian comes to sit beside me – I've decided to give him a name, because how are we supposed to have a relationship if I think of him as The Dog? – and we watch the flames.

Sebastian snatches a couple of chips out of my hand when I make the mistake of holding it too low. After that he wants more and more. But he's not getting any beer. I found an old margarine tub in one of the kitchen cupboards and filled it with water.

After the meal, I'm back on the swing. Sebastian comes to

lie at my feet, buries his muzzle between his paws, closes his eyes and gives a contented sigh.

I look towards the lake. When the water is as still as it is this evening and it's a new moon, a person can almost forget it's there. But of course it's there.

Just like Deloris Mouton.

It's hard to run away from yourself.

Deloris Mouton, with her tidy hair and razor-sharp eyes. The devil in a skirt. Could I still save my soul, or had the transaction already gone through?

Before the faculty party she was Professor Mouton, the head of the Afrikaans-Dutch Department. And I was just a lecturer, new to the university. But that evening we really talked for the first time. When I'd gone outside to get some air. What a cliché. I thought it was a coincidence but of course she'd followed me.

As people do at such times, we shared our interests and quickly discovered that we both had a predilection for Romantic poetry. And it's hard not to enjoy the attention of a beautiful woman. The light touching started that evening.

It took her less than two weeks to seduce me. I was a willing victim. Her age didn't bother me; she was attractive, intelligent, self-confident. Available. And she could open doors at the university.

Then I found out she was married. The ring she always so deftly hid when we ran into each other on campus was actually not as great a shock as who had given it to her. The dean of the Faculty of Letters and Philosophy.

Yet I allowed her to convince me not to break off the relationship. And thus to weave me into her web.

And here I sit in Knysna, and it's already been a year that we've been going on like this.

I wake up with a start. Sebastian is barking. I stand up and walk carefully down the stairs. I had left the sliding door open a little in case he needed to go out. That was obviously not such a great idea.

Sebastian stands a little way back from the sliding door and growls, his body tense.

I look but don't see anything.

He walks a couple of steps closer to the door, barks, and trots towards me.

Whoever or whatever was there isn't there anymore.

I can't get back to sleep. I push the sheet off, pull it up, roll on my side, turn the pillow over, kick the sheet off my feet . . . give up, lie on my back and stare at the ceiling.

It's just before three.

I get up and creep down the stairs, over the tiles, and out the sliding door. The night air is delicious on my skin; I'm wearing only a pair of pajama pants.

I walk over the rough sand to the water. In the early morning hours it's just a large dark pool, a mysterious, opaque mass. A lake is different from the sea. There isn't the constant energy of the surf breaking on the shore, it's like something that breathes.

That waits.

When we were here ten years ago over the December holidays, a little girl drowned. Her name was Samantha and she was six. It was a particularly warm day and I recall how her mother's screams cut through the air, right through the laughter and buzz of vacation. I remember that little body on the sand. She was wearing a neon pink bikini. She lay there so still, her eyes half open.

And beside her was the lake.

The lake gives life and takes life. The lake feeds the village and the village feeds the lake.

But why a six-year-old child?

Goosebumps break out on my upper body and I fold my arms.

I become conscious of something to my left. She's standing there like a statue, looking out over the water. She has the same white dress on.

At first I just stare and then begin to step closer, slowly, like in a dream. 'Excuse me?'

She doesn't answer. It's as if she's not aware of me.

I look at the dark hair that covers her shoulders, the roundness of her cheek, and I want to reach out and touch her.

She turns and looks at me. Her eyes are dark and unfathomable. I can't look away. She begins to hum a little tune, soft and sweet, takes my hand and starts to dance with me. Slowly and dreamily we turn, her fingers cool. Beside us the lake murmurs. I drown in her eyes.

I feel her lips against my collarbone, cool and soft. Her mouth moves along my neck and I close my eyes. I put my hands on her hips and lose myself in her touch.

She takes a step back.

I open my eyes, reach for her. 'Wait. Don't go.'

She just looks at me.

'Who are you?'

She takes my hand and turns around. I follow her over the sand, alongside the lake. I don't care where she's leading me. I'm only aware of her fingers against mine.

She stops at the old hanging tree with the long misformed branches that touch the water. She turns around and I raise my hand to touch her cheek. I can't stop looking into her dark eyes. There's a heartache in there. I want to take it away.

'What's your name?' I whisper.

She holds her index finger against my lips, comes closer and presses her mouth against mine. Her lips are cool. Her mouth is cold. I taste the taste of the lake and then water, in my mouth, in my throat, in my lungs

(*kira*)
and I cough, bring the water up, and pant.
I look around, but she's just gone.

I'm awakened by someone licking my ear. I open my eyes and see it's Sebastian.

'Oh, no, man.' I push his head away.

And remember last night. Or did I dream it? I imagine the mineral taste of the lake in my mouth and feel even more confused.

Sebastian sits and looks at me with his head at an angle.

'Yeah, I'm going crazy.'

I shake my head and stand up. I go wash my face in the bathroom and look at my eyes.

And then at my neck.

At the red mark where she sucked on me.

I touch the mark gingerly.

It wasn't a dream.

I'm still smiling as I wash the breakfast dishes. My hands feel like they're charged with electricity. I can't wait to see her again.

The last time I felt like this was at university, when I met my first love. Mariska, a shy beauty with bright eyes, round cheeks and light brown hair that never wanted to stay behind her ears. It was she who taught me to appreciate Romantic poetry, to see the deeper beauty in it. In the afternoon we lay in bed and talked and laughed and drank. We read poems aloud to each other, discussed the words and emotions and fought over what the poet had meant. I traced her form with my finger

never before have i painted more beautifully than last night
i painted your whole back full of pictures
frolicking tangerines, guitars, and coins

We walked to class across the colored leaves and threw the leaves at each other on the way back. We stared out the window at the rain and wrote messages in the steam. Her name was the prettiest word I knew,

her figure is my coolness in the day
my brazier filled with red-hot coal in the night

We drank so much green tea that we couldn't stop giggling. We climbed under the covers with a bottle of red wine and talked about profound things. We forgot time and words and everything but each other. But

our love died with the dawn
and we buried it, pale and mute
tender grass and fragrant spring soil
cover it, unadorned by wreath and flower

And then came Deloris Mouton, not a second love, but a second-rate love, false, a trap, a fraud, a waste, like Langenhoven's moth . . . will the end of it be my ashes?

The long weekend is almost over.

You can run, but you always catch up to yourself.

The day doesn't want to end. Sebastian and I play on the sand and cool off in the lake. We eat and I play listlessly on my guitar. My thoughts are already on tonight, waiting anxiously for time to catch up.

After dinner I lie down on the bed in a T-shirt and jeans. I try to read but I keep having to flip back to find out what happened. A little after eleven Sebastian starts barking. I walk down the stairs to where Sebastian stands stiff-backed and growling.

She's standing outside, on the sand in front of the porch, barefoot in her white dress.

Sebastian growls again. I press my hand against his chest and hold him back while I slip out the opening in the sliding door. He forces his way towards me and I struggle to get the door closed. He stands up against the glass and barks.

I turn around.

She's still standing there. Her hair rises and falls in the wind. Her dress makes little waves over her body.

She takes a step back. Her eyes are large and haggard. She takes another step away from me.

'Don't be afraid.' She looks different tonight, so defenseless that I just want to put my arms around her. I want to feel her head against my shoulder and tell her that nothing else matters.

Slowly I go closer.

She turns around and runs.

I run after her. The sand shifts and grinds under my feet. I don't try to catch up with her. I know where she's going.

She's standing beside the old hanging tree. She's looking out over the dark water.

I grab her by the hair and turn her towards me. Her eyes are wet. I kiss the tears off her cheeks. It tastes like the lake.

(*kira*)

She turns around and I grasp her hand. She looks over her shoulder, her eyes large and sorrowful, and pulls her fingers slowly out from between mine.

Her feet are in the lake and the water foams against her ankles. She looks at it sadly and takes a step back.

'Don't go.'

The water bubbles hungrily around her legs, oozes into the material of the dress and sucks it tight against her skin.

'Stay with me.'

I can see she wants to, but she turns around and walks deeper into the lake. The water swirls around her waist. The white fabric clings to her body as if the lake is greedy to have her. The water spits up against the ends of her hair.

I walk after her. It's as if the water is holding me back. I use my hands and force my way ahead.

She looks around and her eyes beg me to go back. But I'm almost to her. She disappears under the water, as if something has grabbed her ankles and pulled her under.

I dive after her, search with my hands, but grab only water, cold and heavy. I run out of breath. I have to swim to the surface, but then I dive again and keep searching. I don't even know which side the shore is on anymore.

And then my fingers touch something. Material. I grab it, clutch it tightly. It's her. I get hold of her arm and pull, but she won't come to the surface. It's the lake. The lake doesn't want to let her go. My lungs burn, but I clutch her wrist firmly because if I let her go I'll never get her back again. My fingers hurt and at the same time start to go numb from the cold. The lake is too strong. I can't . . . Her arm slips between my fingers and I scream my last bit of oxygen away.

Something pulls me under. I flail my arms, but it has no effect. A weight presses against my chest. Panic takes over. I swallow water, the rich mineral taste of the lake

(*kira*)

see only black around me. My arms are too heavy and tired to flail. The burning in my lungs is far away. I just sink, slowly, down, down, down into the cold.

Pain cuts deep into my arm and something pulls me up. My head breaks through the surface and I pant and cough and choke. It takes a while for me to breathe normally again. And then I see the grayish object beside me. I see the teeth and the forepaws treading water.

Not an object. Sebastian. I grin back at him.

Around us the dark water is still.

I stand on the sand and watch the sun come up over the

lake. The rays can't penetrate its surface. The lake doesn't share her secrets easily.

Sebastian licks my fingers.

I smile and rub his head. 'Come on. You get a special breakfast today.'

I still don't know how Sebastian got out the sliding door last night. I don't think I had closed it all the way, but the space was too narrow for him to fit through.

Sebastian sits and watches me while I grill boerewors in a pan. I set his portion down in front of him and he devours it like it's the first time I've ever fed him.

While I tidy up a little, he jumps up, barks once and wags his tail. He looks towards the sliding door.

A little girl runs up to the door and starts to smile. 'Nemo!' Sebastian runs towards her and licks her face. She giggles and throws her arms around him.

A man appears behind her. He knocks on the sliding door.

He tells me how they've looked for Nemo everywhere and how many tears they've cried over him the past couple days. The thing that really strikes me is when I hear how far Sebastian came to find me.

I kneel down and rub his head for the last time. 'So, Nemo, then.' I smile and whisper in his ear: 'Thanks.'

I stand on the porch and watch them go. Sebastian looks back once and barks. Even if his teeth marks hadn't left scars on my left arm, I wouldn't ever forget him.

He presses his muzzle against the little girl to steer her farther from the water's edge.

I close the door to Tamason, the soft purling of the lake behind me. It's time to go back to Stellenbosch, to tell Deloris Mouton that it's over. And if that derails my career at Stellenbosch University, there are always other schools.

I walk across the sand to where the water begins. The

lake lies stretched out before me, shiny but opaque. I squat down, cup my hands and scoop some water. I suck it into my mouth, close my eyes, and I remember her

(*kira*)

fingers, light against my forehead that first evening, her

(*kira*)

mouth, cool against my neck, her

(*kira*)

cheek, soft and wet against my lips.

I let the last of the water drip back into the lake, stand up, and walk to the car.

Translated from the Afrikaans by James D. Jenkins

AUTHOR'S NOTE: The poetic excerpts are taken from the following poems in *Die Mooiste Afrikaanse Liefdesgedigte*, compiled by Fanie Oliver: Jeanne Goosen, 'Nog nooit het ek mooier geskilder', Rosa Keet, 'My pols sing 'n minnelied', and Elisabeth Eybers, 'Eerste liefde'.

Lars Ahn

Donation

Of the Scandinavian countries, Denmark probably has the most active contemporary horror scene, including a number of authors who have had at least some of their work appear in English, such as Steen Langstrup, Michael Kamp, A. Silvestri, and Teddy Vork. In fact, there's so much horror fiction being published in Denmark that there's even a Danish Horror Society (Dansk Horror Selskab) that gives out an award each year for the best work of Danish horror. The 2017 award went to a volume of short stories by our next author, Lars Ahn. In deeming Ahn's book 'a worthy winner of this year's award', the jury noted that the collection 'twists the horror genre's tools in surprising directions' and said the author 'manages to make a short story unfold like a novel and inspires re-reading'. He is the author of a novel, Rød Høst (Red Harvest), and his short stories have appeared in over thirty anthologies. He has also won the Niels Klim Prize for best Danish science fiction story twice. In 'Donation', Ahn gives us perhaps the most frightening monster in this book, in the unlikely form of a seemingly innocent young boy.

I T WAS THE LOVELIEST OF MORNINGS.
He couldn't remember the last time he had felt better. Everything had gone beyond expectations yesterday. She had said yes immediately and seemed genuinely surprised, and he amazed himself by shedding a tear when he realized how happy she looked.

I should have done it a long time ago, he thought, before they started calling friends and family.

They had spent the rest of the day talking and constantly touching each other, as if they wanted to assure themselves that it was actually real and not a dream. If they weren't holding hands, she was lying in his lap while he caressed her hair, and at regular intervals they broke out in laughter because they couldn't believe they were finally ready to do it after having talked about it for so long. After dinner and red wine, they rewatched their favorite film before taking their intimate contact to a new level in the bedroom.

He still felt a little sore as he sat there at the dining table checking the latest congratulations on his phone. He could hear her humming in the kitchen as she prepared their brunch. He had offered to help, but she had ordered him to stay seated and read the thick Sunday edition of the newspaper, which still lay unopened before him.

It was spring, the sun shone, birds sang – they didn't chirp, they *sang* – and green leaves had begun to appear on the trees. It was truly a lovely morning.

Then the doorbell rang.

Outside stood a little boy, who didn't appear to be more than nine or ten years old, though he had never been good at guessing people's ages. The first time he met her, he had thought she was three or four years younger than she turned out to be.

'Yes?' he said and wondered if he should recognize the boy. Several children lived on the street, but honestly he had a hard time telling them apart. She on the other hand had no problem with it and even knew the names of most of them.

'Hi, I'm here for the collection,' the boy said.

What collection? he almost asked, but he caught himself.

He seemed to vaguely remember that there was going to be some national collection drive or other today, or perhaps next Sunday? There were so many of them these days that it was hard to keep track, sort of like with the children on the street. He felt embarrassed at not being able to recall, since he always made a point to donate to such things if he was home.

So instead he said: 'Oh, yeah. One moment.'

It struck him as a bit odd that the boy wasn't accompanied by an adult. He thought children weren't allowed to walk around alone collecting money. He found his wallet in his jacket. There were only a few coins in it. Once again he had forgotten to withdraw cash.

'Honey, do we have any cash?' he said loudly.

'What for?'

'The collection.'

'What collection?'

'The . . . you know . . . the one from TV,' he said and grew a little irritated at having to waste time explaining while the boy was waiting. 'Do we have cash or not?'

'I think so,' she said and came out into the hall.

She caught sight of the boy.

'Hi,' she said. 'Who are you?'

Ok, so it's not one of the kids from the street.

'I'm here because of the collection,' said the boy.

'Who's it going to now?' she asked, as she looked for her wallet in her own jacket. 'It's a little embarrassing, but I simply can't remember.'

'The money goes to Neglected Victims,' the boy said.

'I don't think I've heard of them before. Is this their first collection?' he asked. He took a closer look at the logo on the boy's collection box. It was reminiscent of the logo of the Danish Cancer Society. A litigious attorney could definitely make a case out of it.

'I don't know,' said the boy. 'But I have a number here you can call, if . . .'

'Here it is,' she said and took out her wallet. She opened it. 'Yes, I have some cash.' She put the notes in the box.

The boy stared. 'Wow!' he burst out. 'That was really a lot. Have a good rest of your day.'

The boy made a move to go, but then stopped.

'Sorry,' he said, 'but could I please use your bathroom? I really need to . . .'

'Yes, of course,' she said, standing aside so the boy could come in.

He stepped over the threshold.

'It's just over here,' she said and showed him the bath-room.

'Thanks,' the boy said. 'I'll hurry.'

'Take all the time you need,' she said, and closed the front door behind him.

The boy walked to the bathroom door and slipped inside.

They looked at each other. He shook his head with a smile.

'What a polite young man,' he said.

'He must be doing more than just pee,' he said in the kitchen. 'He's been in there for almost ten minutes.'

'Really?' she said with her head halfway in the refrigerator.

'Something wrong?' He was surprised at her somewhat absent answer. Normally she would have said something sarcastic like, 'What, are you timing him?'

She sighed. 'I forgot the eggs while we were standing out there. Now they're hard-boiled.' They both preferred their eggs soft and runny.

'So cook some more.'

'Those were the last, so unless you feel like going out and buying . . .'

'We'll do without,' he said and kissed her on the cheek.

'Okay,' she said. 'Just go sit. I'll be right in.'

He found the boy sitting at the table in the living room.

'Are you finished?' he asked. He was so dumbfounded he didn't know what else to say.

'Yes, thanks, that was a relief,' said the boy.

'That's good,' he said and winced internally, because he knew very well how stupid it sounded.

The boy just smiled, but made no move to get up from the table.

He cleared his throat. 'Well, you'll need to be getting on with your route,' he said.

'No,' said the boy.

He thought at first he had heard wrong. 'What?'

The boy sniffed. 'Do I smell bacon?'

'Listen, you . . .'

'I did have breakfast, but I'm actually hungry again. You don't mind if I eat with you?'

He could feel his jaw physically drop. He blinked in a desperate hope that it would make the boy disappear, but the kid was still sitting there.

'All right, let's e—'

He turned around and saw her frozen in the doorway with a pitcher of fresh-squeezed orange juice in one hand and a plate of dry-cured ham in the other, while she tried to decipher the situation. Under other circumstances, he would have seen the comical side to it, but just now he only felt anger slowly rising within him.

'Oh . . . hi,' she said to the boy.

'Hi.'

'Are you finished?' she asked, and he could feel how his toes were about to curl.

'Yes, yes.'

'Aha . . .' she said and seemed as if she were at a loss for words.

He tried to come to her rescue. 'He'd like to eat with us.'

She stared in disbelief, first at him, then at the boy, and then at him again.

'Would you just come in the kitchen with me, dear? We're missing something,' she said sweetly.

'Did you invite him?' she asked.

He tried to gauge her tone of voice. She didn't sound angry so much as astonished.

He shook his head. 'I don't know what's going on. All of a sudden he was just sitting there. So it's more like he's invited himself.'

She leaned into the living room, still holding the ham and the pitcher of orange juice. 'What are we going to say to him?'

'That he has to go? He does have a route he's supposed to take care of.'

'Isn't that too rude? He does look a bit undernourished.'

Now it was his turn to look in. The boy still sat at the table, staring out into the air like a restaurant guest waiting on the server. He had to admit that the boy wasn't among the best fed, but on the other hand he didn't look like he was about to faint from hunger either.

'He looks healthy enough to me,' he said. 'Anyway, we only gave him permission to use the bathroom. We didn't say anything about him eating with us.'

'Yes, but all the same . . .' she said.

He groaned. 'Why are we even having this discussion? Neither of us asked him to be here, so I don't see any problem with asking him nicely to go on his way again. He has to be able to understand that. Otherwise there's something lacking in his upbringing.'

He could see that she was still hesitant.

'Let us flip the situation around,' he said. 'Neither of us

would ever go into a complete stranger's house and expect to get something to eat.'

'No,' she said. 'You're right. I just feel sorry for him.'

'That's okay, baby. You let your big heart get carried away.' That was one of the things about her he had originally fallen for. 'I'll just tell him,' he said and went into the living room, as she followed a little way behind.

He waited for her to set the juice and ham down before clearing his throat. 'Listen, we're going to have to ask you to go.'

The boy looked up at him. 'Why?'

'Why? Because you can't just go into the homes of people you don't know and expect to be waited on. We gave you permission to use our bathroom, but that was it. You must be able to understand that?'

'Not really,' said the boy. 'You seem to have tons of food.'

'Okay, party's over.' He leaned over the boy and sensed how she was holding her breath in the background. 'If you don't understand it in the normal way, then let's try this: What's your name, and where do you live? I'll call your parents and have them come get you.'

The boy shrugged his shoulders. 'If that's your plan, then why should I tell you?'

'Fine, then I'll call the police instead. No doubt they can convince you better than I can.'

'And what do you plan to tell them?'

'That a boy has forced his way into our home and won't leave.'

'You invited me in yourselves,' the boy pointed out.

'Yes, but under false pretenses. Is there even a national collection drive today, and does Neglected Victims even exist? It's illegal to make fake collections.'

'I don't know what collection you're talking about.'

'But – ' He looked around for the boy's collection box,

but he couldn't catch sight of it. 'We gave you money,' he said.

'I don't know anything about that.'

'You've stolen from us!'

The boy frowned. 'I still don't know what you're talking about. But it can't possibly be theft, if you yourself gave the money away.'

He had never been closer to hitting a child before and had to find hitherto unknown strength to restrain himself. He took a deep breath and counted slowly to twenty. Backwards.

'For the last time,' he said. 'Give us our money back and leave our home. Then we'll forget the rest.'

The boy shook his head. 'I haven't taken your money. Check for yourself.'

He looked at her.

'Just a second,' she said and went out to the hall. He heard her rummage around out there and open first one door and then another and finally the front door. Then she came back. From her astonished facial expression he already knew what she was going to say before she opened her mouth.

'All the bills were there?' he said.

She nodded.

'What about the box?'

'I didn't see it anywhere.'

He gaped and stared at the boy, who looked back at him with an innocent expression.

'How?'

'You know, the food's getting cold,' said the boy.

The boy wiped his mouth with the back side of his hand.

'Thanks for the food,' he said. 'It tasted delicious.'

'You're welcome,' she said automatically.

They all three sat at the table, but only the boy had eaten.

He had launched himself at the food with an appetite that had almost frightened them and for a moment made them consider whether he really had been starving. Their compassion evaporated, though, just as quickly as it had come, when he began to smack loudly and dip his fingers in the strawberry jam. Not once had he used the cutlery, with the result that he had bits of food around his mouth and there was a flood of crumbs, blobs, crusts, and peels on the table and the floor. That was enough to make them lose their own appetites.

The whole time he had sat and stared the boy down, but apparently without effect.

'Now you've got what you came for. Will you be so good as to go home to your parents?'

The boy belched. 'I can't do that.'

'Why not?'

'I don't have parents or a home.'

'You must live somewhere.'

'Yes, but it's not home to me.'

'All right, then bugger off back to the institution you escaped from, and don't bother us anymore.'

'Honey,' she said.

'What?'

'You can't talk like that. He's only a child.'

He blinked. 'What do you mean?' Then it dawned on him. 'Oh no, say it's not true . . . you couldn't possibly.'

'What?' she said.

'You're starting to feel sorry for him again, aren't you? Even after all this bullshit . . . it's so typically you.'

'What's that supposed to mean?'

'Dear, I love you, but you've got this thing about letting other people take advantage of you.'

'What nonsense. I do not.'

'No? Just look over there.' He pointed over to the sofa

table. 'Why do we have three copies of the new issue of *Street News* lying there? Who the hell buys the same issue three times, and what's more, twice from the same homeless guy?'

'It's not like it cost very much.'

'No, but it's the principle of the thing. Like how you always choose to donate the refund on the bottle deposits.'

'And what's wrong with that?'

'Nothing, but you just do it without us ever talking about it.'

'You've never complained about it.'

'No, but you've never asked either.'

'Hmm,' she said. 'There's a word for this kind of thing: empathy. Ever heard of it, dear?'

He shook his head. 'Drop it. You know better than anyone that I always give to a good cause when someone asks.'

'And this coming from someone who only signed up for Unicef to get out of talking to their street fundraisers. Super, dear.'

'So you're calling me a hypocrite?'

'Come on, we all are. We pay so that we can feel saintly and not have to think too much about the unpleasant reality. I'm just honest about it, unlike you. And didn't you say that you loved me because of my, quote, "big heart"? Or was that just a pick-up line?'

'Of course it wasn't. I meant it, and I mean it still. That is one of the things I love about you, but frankly, your IQ drops several points when you have somebody disadvantaged standing in front of you.'

'You should know all about that, since I said yes to you yesterday.'

'Are you saying you've changed your mind?'

'No, but sometimes you are just so . . .'

'Yeah? I'm waiting anxiously to hear the end of that sentence.'

She made a dismissive gesture. 'Forget it. I won't bother.'

'No? You were just about to tell me some vital new information about myself.'

'Honey, stop it now.'

He could see she was on the verge of crying, and all at once it was like all the anger seeped out of him. That was the effect her tears usually had. They might have their arguments, but they were seldom mad at each other for long. He stood up and walked over to her. He pulled her to him as he kissed her on the back of her head.

'Sorry, baby,' he said. 'Sometimes I'm a big idiot.'

She laughed and kissed him in return. 'And I'm looking forward to being Mrs. Big Idiot.'

The boy cleared his throat. Until that moment he had kept silent during their whole discussion. They both turned towards him.

'Might I make a suggestion?' he said.

'I understand that you're getting married?' the boy said, sounding as though he'd just laid his eyes on all the presents under the Christmas tree.

'Yes, and . . . ?' he said.

'Convince me.'

'Of what?'

'Convince me that it really should be the two of you till death do you part. That you're made for each other. The perfect couple. Soulmates. Each other's best friends. If you can do that, then I'll leave.'

'But what for?' she said.

'Just because,' said the boy.

He had had just about enough. He stood beside the boy and looked down at him. 'Listen here, my little friend. I can't really see what our relationship has to do with you. So my suggestion is that you get up quickly from that seat and find your way out of here. Otherwise I'll help you out the door.'

The boy smiled. 'So you'd lay a hand on me? That will be tough to explain to the police. They'd love another child abuse case.'

'Honey,' she said in her irritatingly effective 'let's-be-sensible-now-voice'. 'Don't do that. If you hit him, he's won.'

'What?'

'Can't you see what he's up to?' she said. 'He's trying to play us against each other, and he was about to succeed just now.'

He stared back at the boy in disbelief. 'Is that true? Is that really what you're after?'

The boy scratched at his nose. 'She said it, I didn't. I just want to be sure that you're making the right decision.'

'But why us? And why today?'

'Why not?' said the boy.

It was the almost indifferent way the boy said it that caused the reaction. He could feel his legs quivering, and it was only force of will that prevented him from collapsing. Instead he clung to the tabletop. He was at his wits' end and looked confusedly at her for help.

She sat with her arms crossed and looked at the boy. 'Fine,' she said. 'We'll do it.'

We will? He didn't trust his own voice just then and kept quiet.

The boy clapped his hands excitedly. 'Fantastic! This will be fun.'

'Darling?' he tried.

She looked at him with a determined glance. There was still a tinge of red in her eyes.

'We can do this,' she said decidedly.

He nodded and could tell that now it was he who was on the verge of crying. Instead, he moved his chair so that he was sitting beside her. They grasped each other's hands. He took a deep breath.

'Okay,' he said. 'We're ready.'

'Tell me how you met. Was it love at first sight?'

They looked at each other.

'Not exactly,' he said.

'It's a little complicated,' she said.

'We were friends, before we were lovers,' he said.

'He was going out with one of my friends,' she said.

The boy tilted his head at an angle. 'You don't say.'

She waved this off. 'I didn't know her that well. We were in the same study group, but I was closer to some of the others.'

'I had broken up with her when we met,' he added.

The boy frowned. 'Wait a minute, there's something I don't understand. You said you were friends before you were lovers, but how could you be friends if you didn't know each other better?'

'Okay, "friends" was maybe the wrong word to use. It would probably be more accurate to say we were close acquaintances,' he said.

'We would meet at the same parties, and we used to have nice conversations. We had good chemistry, but it wasn't any more than that because we were going out with other people,' she said.

'So how did *you* get together, if I may ask?' said the boy.

He laughed, a little too loudly. 'Ha! That's actually a really funny story.'

'It happened online,' she said.

'We hadn't seen each other for a while but were still friends on Facebook, and then she commented on one of my posts and I replied and it just went on from there,' he said.

'How very modern,' the boy said. 'What did you post?'

'Just some lame joke that only we understood. We still have the whole thread on our profiles,' he said.

'Yes, let's print it out and have someone turn it into a wedding song,' she said with a smile.

They laughed quietly together. The boy watched them with an unfathomable look. 'That actually wasn't a particularly funny story.'

He snorted. 'Sorry, kid. But sometimes people just love each other, without having to go all Hollywood about it.'

'Okay,' the boy said. 'But when did you realize you loved each other?'

'That's hard to say,' he said. 'In my case, it was something that happened gradually.' He turned towards her. 'I just know that suddenly I couldn't stop thinking about you, and I was all happy inside every time I saw you.'

She smiled. 'That says it all, doesn't it?'

'Very touching,' said the boy. 'But what about you? When was the flash of lightning? Or did it just sneak up on you too?'

She shook her head. 'No, I know precisely when it happened.'

'Really?' he said. 'You've never said anything about that. When was it then?'

She cleared her throat and looked over at the boy. 'Isn't there something else you'd rather ask us about? I have a hard time seeing what this will prove.'

'On the contrary,' said the boy. 'Your unwillingness to answer a simple question is just making this more interesting. I think your fiancé feels the same way?'

'Honey?' he said.

She sighed. 'It was that evening when we'd been to the movies to see *Sex and the City 2*, even though the World Cup was on, and I got sick after eating a shawarma and threw up on the train. You held my hair and on the way back you took my bag, which was full of vomit, and carried it the whole way home. It was then that I realized I loved you.'

'But . . .' he said. 'That wasn't even two years ago.'

'And how long is it that you've been a couple?' asked the boy.

'F-four years,' he said.

'So if I've calculated right, that means that . . .'

'SHUT UP!!!' He rose from his seat so the chair toppled over with a bang, and bent down over the boy. 'One more word, you little shit, and I swear . . .'

She reached out towards him. 'Darling, please . . .'

He pulled away from her touch. 'And you,' he said and pointed at her. 'Don't you get started either. What the hell was that shit just now? And to say it to *him*.'

All the color had vanished from his face, and he took a deep breath and tried not to start crying.

'Darling, let me explain,' she said.

'Fuck you,' he said and left the room.

She expected to hear the front door slam, but instead it was the door to the bathroom that was opened and closed. She sank back down in the chair and took her head in her hands.

'Shit,' she said.

'You were just being honest,' the boy said.

She shot daggers at him. 'I'm going to him now, no matter what you say, and I don't give a shit if it goes against your rules.'

The boy shrugged. 'It's a free country, and there are no rules. You can do what you want, as long as you manage to convince me that you two should be together. Right now I have my doubts.'

She got up from the chair.

'This isn't over yet,' she said.

*

'Honey?' she knocked carefully on the door.

No answer. But she could hear him inside. It sounded as if he were hyperventilating, but she knew that it was his struggling to hold back tears. She tried the door handle. It was locked.

'Honey, won't you open up?'

Still no answer.

'Talk to me, baby,' she said. 'I'm sorry about what I said in there, but we have to talk about it if we're going to have a chance.'

She could hear him mumble something half-stifled.

'What did you say? I couldn't hear you.'

'Leave me alone,' he said.

'Honey,' her voice cracked, and she could feel the tears welling up. She leaned against the door. 'Forgive me. You know how much I love you. I have the whole time, but that evening was the first time I was 100% sure.'

The door opened and she nearly fell in.

He looked at her with an empty expression in his eyes, which scared her more than anything else. 'Two years,' he said tonelessly. 'We were together for two years without your really knowing whether you loved me.'

'Listen to me, baby,' she said. 'Of course I did, otherwise we wouldn't have stayed together. But it wasn't until that night when I realized how much you can love another person. Suddenly I could see the rest of my life crystal clear before me, and you were with me the whole way.'

He frowned. 'Fuck you,' he whispered, but he smiled when he said it. 'You know I can't be angry with you when you cry.'

She raised her hand up to her face and found that her cheeks were wet. She hadn't even realized she had cried.

He stroked her gently over her cheek. 'I lied in there,' he said.

'When?'

'When I said that I didn't know when I fell in love with you.'

'But . . .'

'I already loved you the first time we saw each other. You had had a study group meeting and I was coming to pick up Julie, but instead we all decided to go to a café, and we wound up sitting beside each other. *That's* where I fell for you. I tried not to, but it just got worse every time we met, and that was one of the reasons why it didn't work out between me and Julie.'

'Why have you never told me that?'

'Because I felt so damn guilty about Julie, and that didn't exactly make me stand out as the best boyfriend material.'

She laughed. 'You might be right about that, but right now you're Mr. Perfect compared to me.'

'Yes, who would have thought it would come to this?' he said and pulled her to him.

They remained standing like that until she dried her eyes and pulled loose. 'What do you say? Shall we go in and throw that little brat out on his ass? Right now I don't give a damn if he reports us to the police or his parents, whoever they are.'

He shook his head. 'No, you had it right before. If we touch him, he's won. We can only beat him by standing together. We're behind on points, but I know we can do it.'

She kissed him. 'Okay,' she said, 'but afterwards we trash the little bastard.'

The boy glowed like a sun when they sat down again.

'Outstanding,' he said. 'That's what I call fighting spirit. Shall we continue?'

'Do your worst,' she said.

'Good. Tell me, what is your worst fear about each other?'

They exchanged glances.

'That he doesn't want to have children,' she said.

'That I love her more than she loves me,' he said.

'What?' she said.

'Interesting,' the boy replied.

'Did you say that because I just . . .'

'No,' he interrupted her. 'I've felt it the whole time. Since we started going out, I've feared that one day you'd realize you can do better, so when you said that other thing a little earlier, you confirmed my worst suspicions.'

'Oh, no,' she said. 'You have to forgive me, baby. That wasn't what I meant.'

'I know,' he said. 'But what do you mean that I don't want to have children? There's nothing I want more than to have a family with you.'

She threw up her hands. 'It's just that whenever we're around children, I don't get the impression that you're wildly excited about them.'

'In what way?'

'You don't really talk to them, and you're not interested in what they do.'

'They're children. What should I talk to them about? Tax regulations? Teletubbies?'

'That's what I mean. You don't even make the attempt. If you can't do it with other people's kids, what about our own?'

'Whoa, whoa,' he said. 'Just because I don't find our friends' children intellectually stimulating, that doesn't mean that I wouldn't be there 100% for our kids. And your brother's girls and my sister's boys seem happy with me.'

'Yes, but I've also seen how when we babysit you can't wait for them to be picked up again so we can be by ourselves. I don't doubt that you love them, but you'd rather be with them in small doses.'

'You yourself have to admit that it can be a little exhausting to be with them for a long time, and you said yourself that you felt totally worn out after we'd watched the boys for a whole weekend last time. They're great kids, but you'd think they had Duracell batteries in their bloodstream.'

'Your nieces aren't much better. When they run amok, it's like watching a children's edition of *Bridezillas*,' she said.

'Let me reiterate: they are not our children,' he said. 'There's a bloody difference how one treats his own children and other people's children. So you can't just transfer my behavior and say that's how I'd be as a father. If I did the same thing with you, I'd have good grounds for being seriously worried.'

'And what's that supposed to mean?'

He took his head in his hands. 'Forget it. I shouldn't have said that.'

'No, no,' she said coolly. 'Go on and say it. I'm really interested in hearing what opinions you have of my skills as a mother.'

'Honey, nothing good is going to come of this.' He looked over at the boy. 'Can't you see, we're doing it again.'

Her eyes shot icicles. 'The damage is already done, so come out with it.'

He rubbed his neck. 'I think,' he said slowly, 'that you're a little too indulgent when you're with kids. It's probably me there's something wrong with, but you let them get away with too much, and you let them run circles around you.'

'Like you yourself said: there's a difference between if it's one's own kids or someone else's that one's dealing with. I can't start teaching good manners to kids that aren't mine.'

'You're right, dear,' he said. 'Forget what I said. That was stupid of me.'

She snorted irritatedly. 'Oh, for fuck's sake. Why don't you grow a pair of balls?'

'What the hell?!'

'Now it's you who's too indulgent.'

'And is there something wrong with that?'

'Yeah, who wants a pussy-whipped man for a husband?'

'There are apparently a lot of women who do. Just look at the sorry excuses for men some of your girlfriends have picked.'

She laughed. 'You're one to talk. Your brother-in-law can hardly walk three steps in a straight line because your sister has him grabbed so hard by the balls.'

'Your brother . . .' he began.

'What about my brother?' she said.

They stared at each other.

'Fuck,' he burst out and banged a clenched fist on the tabletop so that it shook.

She smiled sadly. 'This isn't going so well, is it?' she said.

'No,' he admitted.

The boy raised a finger.

'Might I point out something?' he said.

It happened so fast that he didn't have time to react.

'You,' she sneered at the boy, and suddenly she had the bread knife in her hand and was standing behind him, with a firm grip on his hair and the serrated blade against his bare throat.

He gaped. 'Dear, what the fuck are you doing?'

'I swear,' she said to the boy in a voice that no longer sounded like her own. 'One more word from you, and I'll cut your throat. Understood? Don't say anything. Just nod.'

The boy nodded. The self-assured attitude was all gone, and now he just looked like a scared little boy.

'Honey.' He got up slowly from his chair and reached his hand out. 'Honey, give me the knife.'

She trembled. Not just her head, but her whole body, and he was afraid she'd wind up cutting the boy.

'I . . . can't . . . take . . . any . . . more,' she said.

'I understand that,' he said. 'But this isn't the right way.'

'Why not?' she said. 'One little slice, and the whole thing is over.'

The boy whined.

'Quiet!' she hissed and pressed the blade tighter against his skin.

'Believe me, I've considered the possibility myself,' he said. 'But it will only do more harm than good. What would we do with the body? How do we get rid of it without the neighbors seeing it? What about all the blood?'

She broke into a loud laugh. 'Just listen to yourself. Your fiancée, the woman you love, and whom you want to marry and have kids with, is threatening to slit a child's throat and your first thought is how you can clean up after her.'

He looked at her in disbelief. 'Tell me, are you bluffing?'

'Only partly,' she said. 'I still feel really tempted, but it was interesting to hear your reaction.'

He blinked. 'Sorry, but just who is it standing there with the knife? I mean, I'm the one with more reason to be concerned.'

She looked at him with a pained expression on her face. 'I just want all this to stop.'

'So do I,' he said.

'So we agree? Can you forgive me?'

'Always,' he said.

'Good,' she said and laid the knife down.

The boy turned around in the doorway. He hadn't said anything since he got up from the table and went out into the entryway.

'Thanks,' he said.

'For what?' she said.

'Your generous contribution.'

Neither of them had any desire to know what he meant by that.

'The pleasure was all yours,' he said to the boy.

That was meant as a sarcastic comment, an 'I-got-the-last-word' reply, but he could himself hear how lame it sounded.

'Farewell,' she said.

The boy just smiled and went down the garden path. They remained standing in the doorway and watched him go, as if to assure themselves that he had entirely disappeared from their life. Only when they could no longer see him did they close the door and lock it.

They looked at each other.

'Did we win?' she asked.

'I hope so,' he said.

Translated from the Danish by James D. Jenkins

Solange Rodríguez Pappe

Tiny Women

Born in Guayaquil, Ecuador in 1976, Solange Rodríguez Pappe is a professor and an award-winning writer whose work often incorporates elements of the supernatural, strange, or macabre, usually mixed with a dose of quirky or offbeat humor. 'Tiny Women' originally appeared in her 2018 collection La primera vez que vi un fantasma (The First Time I Saw a Ghost) *and was also selected for inclusion in the 2019 anthology* Insólitas, *which collected the best fantastic tales by contemporary women writers from Spain and Latin America. We fell in love with this odd little story the first time we read it, and though it's perhaps not a 'horror' story in the traditional sense, we nonetheless thought it was a perfect fit for this volume, and we're confident our readers will enjoy it as much as we did.*

A S I FILLED BOX AFTER BOX with rubbish taken out of my parents' house, I saw the first tiny woman run to the sofa and scamper away under its legs with a shout of euphoric joy. Nor did it surprise me overly much to stumble upon her. Being the daughter of a couple of hoarders who had done nothing else their whole life except stockpile empty paper bags, plastic containers and porcelain bugs increases the possibility that, if you make a thorough exploration, you'll run across very strange things hidden in your childhood home.

One of my favorite activities during my boring childhood was rummaging through the contents of boxes, but challenging myself to leave things exactly as I had found them. Thus, I came across a collection of keychains from the Second World War, some pornographic coasters, and the silver dagger that my father guarded jealously underneath the slats of the bed. 'You've been messing with things!' my mother would shout if she noticed some slight rearrangement of one of the hundreds of collected objects. Then she would give me some good open-handed slaps or a stroke of her belt across my palms. 'Learn from your brother, who never gives us any trouble.' Obviously, since for as long as I could remember Joaquín had spent all his time playing in the street, with his toy cars, his bicycle, his skates, his gang, his little girlfriends. He had always refused to be one of the many gadgets in my mother's collection.

Once they were in the retirement home, my parents wouldn't need anything more than what was essential, so I had spent almost a week separating into piles what I would donate to charity, what I would give away, sell and auction at a good price, and also what I was going to hold onto. But first I had to get rid of all the filth. Amidst all the junk in the kitchen I found several lizards, a rat, and even a dead bat. If I thought about it carefully, the rat even appeared to be the corpse of an old hamster we lost in my childhood. As I was chasing some spiders with a shoe, I saw the tiny naked woman cross the living room in full war cry. Between all the odd things I was discovering there, a wild little woman running around didn't seem all that incredible.

I looked under the seat and, just as I had imagined, there was an entire civilization of diminutive women making their life. Some were seated in groups close together, combing each other's hair, telling each other things and laughing; some others were reclining, smoking pieces of leaves torn from a fern near the sofa; and others were entwined in wars of pleasure, licking each other's genitals and breasts by turns, as they bit the fingers of each other's little hands or let out sharp groans of delight. These exercises I'm telling you about, they did them in general view of the entire population without shame or modesty. I didn't see children or pregnancies among the tiny women, who were all young and slender. All of which seemed rather hedonistic to me, not to say indecent.

In mid-afternoon the phone rang. I answered with a mixture of courage and dismay at the tiny women who were now making my cleaning of the room difficult. It was my brother Joaquín, who was asking me for a place at the house to spend the night because his wife had thrown him out again.

'She figured out that I hadn't broken things off with Pamela like I promised her. You know that Mom always gave me a hand with this kind of thing and let me sleep on the sofa.'

'I'm tidying up the house, everything's a mess and covered in dust. But if you think you can stand it, then come.'

'Thanks,' he said. 'I don't know what it is about that sofa, but it always makes me sleep well.' Then I felt a shiver go up my spine.

Armed with a broom I went to sweep the tiny women's city. With the strength of my few kilos, I turned over the seat and, when it was upside down, with swipes of the broom like an expert housewife killing crawling insects, I dispersed, shook up, and killed those that I could. It wasn't easy. They stood their ground and they had sharp little teeth; but in less than an hour I had evicted them from the sofa. One or two fled towards the bedrooms, but I was sure that it had only been a small number in comparison with those I had eliminated. Just when I had replaced the piece of furniture in its original position, the doorbell rang. Joaquín smiled at me charmingly like Clark Gable from the other side of the peephole. Together we put the trash bags full of tiny women out on the curb so that the garbage truck could collect them.

We made a quick dinner out of some leftover soup. From time to time my glance would turn towards the floor to see the occasional tiny woman running around as she pulled her hair or wept with her mouth open, wandering aimlessly. But I managed to ignore them while my brother recounted for me the details of his sophisticated life as adviser to a politician, about the trips he was taking, the people he knew, while I discreetly kicked at the tiny women who were trying to climb up my leg.

'I don't want to have to choose any one woman because the impression I have is that they would rather me choose so they'll have an excuse to start a fight. For women, men are just one more motive for their war, and no: I refuse to play that game. I'm happy with the two, the three, with the four women in my life,' and I feigned an itch on my leg to scare a tiny woman who was vengefully sticking an arrow into my knee. Yes, Joaquín was awful, he had taken a philosophic stance towards his persistent infidelity. I thought that, I didn't say it. Instead I smiled at him with an expression much like pleasure. Like Mom used to.

Before going to bed, as I was carrying the trash to the kitchen, I saw him take off his clothes in the twilight of the living room, lit only by the electric light from the street. My brother was a very handsome man. Tall, a muscular frame, with a solid Adam's apple visible in his strong neck, and a pair of vigorous arms forged in the gym and in arm-wrestling contests with other men as competitive as he was. While he was throwing himself on the sofa, half undressed, ready to enter the world of dreams, hoping to continue there his conquest of places and females, the surviving tiny women huddled on the floor and plotted a defense strategy.

One of them boldly scaled the sofa and explored my

brother's body with curiosity. I don't know if there were tiny men in their world, but coming upon one so large had her fascinated: she sniffed and bit his skin while Joaquín scratched here and there. More tiny women managed to climb up and stopped at his hairy chest, crouching and rolling around among the hair; and others inspected the bulge that could be discerned in his pants. You could see they were comfortable in this new world they had discovered.

Before going out, I left the kitchen light on. I silently approached Joaquín, who was breathing with a heavy rhythm while a number of armed little women insisted on clambering noisily between his legs. He displayed an impudent smile of pleasure that came from the depths of his satisfied male brain. I felt a deep disgust. Without making any noise, I took his car keys from the table as more and more fierce and disheveled little women arrived to check out the state of their new colony. When I closed the door and double-locked the exit, I wondered if my brother's groans, which I could hear from the other side of the threshold, were of pain or pleasure.

Translated from the Spanish by James D. Jenkins

Elisenda Solsona

Mechanisms

Most of us know Barcelona, the capital of Catalonia, as a popular tourist destination. But Catalonia as a place in its own right, separate from Spain, wasn't on many Americans' radar until October 2017, when the region voted to declare independence from Spain. Catalonia is distinct from the rest of Spain not only in its language (Catalan, a Romance language in some respects closer to French or Italian than Spanish) but also in its culture and literary traditions. Catalan lit-erature has a long history of horror and fantastic fiction, the best of which was collected in the massive, 700-page Els altres mons de la literatura catalana [The Other Worlds of Catalan Literature] (2004). *The doyenne of Catalan letters, Mercè Rodoreda, wrote a number of horror stories, and renowned writers Manuel de Pedrolo (author of the post-apocalyptic* Typescript of the Second Origin) *and Joan Perucho (author of the classic vampire novel* Natural His-tory) *are among those who have made important contributions to Catalan speculative fiction.* ELISENDA SOLSONA *is a young writer who follows in their tradition. Her award-winning 2019 collection* Satèl·lits [Satellites] *features weird tales that all take place on the same night, a night when the moon has inexplicably disappeared. 'Mechanisms' is the first story from that collection and the first — but we're sure not the last — appearance of Solsona's writing in English.*

M ANEL TURNS OFF THE FLASHLIGHT, clicks his tongue, and lowers the hood of the rental car. Slowly, with gentle movements, he wipes his large hands on his pants and turns. The tenuous orange glow of the lights on the narrow mountain road allow him to see Òscar silhouetted in the distance, taking photos of the ski lift.

A long silhouette, making sinuous arm movements to find the perfect position. The precise angle. Carefully planting the tripod.

And shooting.

Manel can even make out his curly blond hair he says he wants to cut before the opening of his photographic exhibition.

Is that what he noticed first about him? The lock of curly, almost white hair that covered Òscar's right eye?

He sits in the car and turns the key hanging from a ring in the shape of a wheel with the logo of the rental car company. Will it start? He has no idea what could be wrong with the engine. The car's been stalled for half an hour and they're only a few yards from the hotel. He scratches his thick black beard. He turns the key again. It seems like the engine is responding now, but with a slight wheeze.

As if coughing, wearily.

The car had broken down close to the abandoned ski station, the landscape Òscar had chosen for the final photograph in his series, and he decided to do a first shooting session while Manel checked the engine.

The setting didn't disappoint him. It's exactly like the photos he'd seen.

He squeezes his right eye firmly and looks through the viewfinder with his left, lifting his lips slightly. He focuses on the chairs. No, on the cables. And the forest that climbs along with the chairlift up the mountain.

His pupil moves frantically in the viewfinder. The landscape is too dark. The lights on the road give off a very faint glow.

He blinks.

In the background, he hears the engine of the car they rented at the airport. Manel must have already fixed it, but he wants to take one more photo before they leave. His first contact, his first caress of that landscape.

Why had they shut down the ski resort? He read that it'd been closed for eighteen years, but if he knew why, if he knew the reasons behind it, maybe he could capture its essence in a photograph.

The photograph.

The abysm.

The laughter and the friction of skis against snow, the shouting, the instructors' advice, the music in the background with the latest hit songs. Would he be able to capture all those absent sounds in a photograph?

The abysm: dead defense mechanisms against death.

Suddenly, Manel places a hand on his shoulder and kisses his neck.

Òscar spins around coldly, to shake him off.

'Just a minute, shit, I was in the middle of a long exposure!'

Manel opens his mouth a little and lowers his eyelids a millimeter. He swallows air that, as always, turns into tension, rapidly snaking into his stomach in the shape of an S.

As if he were swallowing Òscar's curly locks.

Another gulp.

And another.

One more and his tone of voice will be normal again.

He's digesting all the tension in his stomach, but his voice will be normal again.

'I don't know how, but it looks like I fixed it. Come on, it's getting really late, Òscar. We should go.'

Òscar lets his camera slide down to the height of his chest, held by the red strap Manel gave him for his birthday. He lifts his chin and looks at the sky. The wind lifts his hair. He furrows his brow, pushes aside that lock of curls, and looks at Manel.

'I don't get it. You said there'd be a full moon. I need it for the photos. I can't take them without it.'

A tango comes through the speakers of the car. It smells of new car and lemon air freshener. Manel drives in silence along a very sharp curve, ten kilometers an hour and with his head glued to the windshield. Every once in a while he blows up on his glossy black bangs. The engine seems to be making a muffled whine again, but he's pretty sure they can make it to the hotel.

A three-minute drive.

He can't remember the distance, but he calculated it that morning at the airport, while they were waiting to board. A three-minute drive from the hotel to the ski resort.

From the ski resort to the hotel.

How many times will they make that trip during their five days of vacation? Will he find the right moment to bring up the subject again?

According to the map, after the ski resort comes a straight stretch, then a big sharp curve and, just as it ends, you should see the hotel. Manel wiggles his fingers a little because he's feeling the cold make its way into his joints.

Òscar, riding shotgun, studies the three long-exposure photographs he made, cycling through them slowly.

He gently presses the button.

They're dark. All three of them are too dark.

He pauses at the last photograph. He lifts his thumb off the button and strokes the fingerprint-covered screen.

He brings the camera to his face as he feels his biceps throbbing.

There is a shadow in the trees.

A big, curved shadow. It's in profile, but it seems to be looking at him.

Manel glances sidelong at Òscar. The light coming off the camera screen illuminates his intensely blue eyes and his wrinkled brow. What if he brought it up now? Is now a good time? They have five days ahead of them, but maybe now ... No, it's better to wait until they're in the hot tub, after a bottle of cava, after he's rubbed him down with the foamy pink soap he bought this morning. One that's really foamy, please. He inhales. He hasn't brought it up in three months, not since the last argument. He has to be subtle, speak calmly. He's got it all planned. He blows on his bangs again. He has to tell him. Òscar, Wednesday is the information session at the adoption center, they haven't held one in a long time. He needs to emphasize that: it's just a first informational meeting. That will be enough for him to see if Òscar's changed his mind.

Òscar zooms in on the photograph.

He zooms in more.

But the pixels are already huge. He can't make out anything.

He closes the camera, puts it in its case, and looks out the window, chin in hand.

'Why'd they shut down the ski resort, Manel?'

'I have no idea. But that's not important, is it? I mean, you keep focusing on that but you can still take the photographs, without knowing why it closed.'

Òscar turns and stares at him.

'Actually, no. I want to know what happened. I want to understand the landscape.'

When Òscar came up with the idea that the final photo of his *Abysms* series could be an abandoned ski station, he spent a week searching on the web before finding this one: small and near a town hidden in a valley, and with a hotel nearby where he could stay. He'd have to fly in and then rent a car to get there.

He searched for more information, but all he found out was that it'd been shut down for eighteen years. He looked at the photographs again.

It was perfect.

He had found the place to finish *Abysms*.

The car's headlights reveal an enormous gray square building, seven stories high. Two gilded columns ascend to an arch over the revolving door reached along a grand marble staircase.

'We're here.' Manel looks through the windshield at the hotel's dark windows. 'And I was right: I think we'll be the only ones here.' He swallows and contemplates the hotel. 'Maybe it will be more inviting in the daylight.'

Weeks ago, after Òscar explained that he'd found the location for his final photograph and showed him the map online, Manel called the hotel from his office at the architectural firm, and made a reservation. Òscar had said that the most important thing was that it was during the full moon, in case he wanted to make some night shots. Manel spoke directly with the manager. He had a deep, hoarse voice, as if his vocal cords hadn't vibrated in years and his saliva had solidified. Manel asked for a room with a hot tub. They were already spending their vacation working on Òscar's photographic project, and he wanted to feel that he was making some decisions. At least one.

They get out of the car. Manel rubs his arms. He looks around and smiles at Òscar.

'This is all fine, right?'

Òscar shrugs.

'Should we go in? I want to download the photos.'

Manel sees someone pulling aside the red curtain on the window closest to the door. Òscar puts his camera case carefully on his shoulder. Manel opens the trunk and pulls out their red suitcase. They hear a creak. The revolving door starts to move and out of it comes a tall man, slightly hunched over and with wrinkled, yellow skin. He walks toward them.

'I was expecting you earlier.'

The man's voice, in person, sounds even deeper to Manel.

The manager shakes first Manel's hand and then Òscar's. He's maybe sixty years old.

'Welcome, I'm Sam.'

Sam positions himself behind the long black reception desk. Manel puts down the suitcase. Òscar looks around him. On the right-hand side of the lobby there is a waiting room with armchairs and sofas upholstered in red and white flowers, with gilt legs. In one corner there is a small bar and a gramophone.

Sam opens up a thick, square notebook, with hard brown covers. Its pages are yellowed. He removes the cap on a fountain pen.

'I'll need your IDs.'

He writes their names slowly, pressing hard with the pen and making flourishes on each letter.

'There is no one else staying at the hotel.' He shakes his head and contemplates the empty room. 'This used to be full of life. This will most likely be the last year I stay open. If you need anything,' he turns and points to a door behind him, 'this is my room.'

Sam closes the notebook, turns, rummages around in some small drawers and grabs a keyring that he then gives to Manel.

Òscar contemplates the paintings of forests that decorate the walls.

Manel takes the key and realizes that, hanging right below the paintings, there's a shotgun.

The room smells musty and stale, like thick fusty blankets covered in dust. The walls are covered in peeling wallpaper patterned with brown- and ochre-colored round shapes. The floor has red carpeting and a grayish cloud lifts at each step.

Òscar, stretched out on the bed, connects his camera to the computer and transfers the photos as he chews off a piece of skin on his lip.

The bathroom is small, but the tub is big and round. Manel takes off his clothes, folds them carefully and places them on the stool. He lays out two towels that smell like an old closet. He turns on the hot water faucet and grabs the bottle of soap. He pours it into the water and stirs. A nice, relaxing atmosphere to bring up the subject again, to very tactfully say, Òscar, next Wednesday there's an initial information session at the adoption center. He runs through the list of papers in his head:

His pay stub.

The lease.

Medical records.

Marriage certificate.

It's just an initial meeting, but he wants to make a good impression and show the documents that he knows they'll ask for at some point in the future, to prove they meet all the requirements.

They'll be good parents.

And Òscar will take beautiful black-and-white photos of the three of them, and they'll hang them in the dining room in golden frames.

Suddenly an engine is heard. He looks out the bathroom window. A brown off-road vehicle parks beside his rental car, brakes hard and raises a cloud of dust. He brings his head closer to the pane. He steams it up.

The driver gets out of the car, violently slams the door, and then opens the trunk.

'I want to go back.'

Manel turns suddenly with a start.

Òscar is drumming his fingers on the bathroom's doorframe. He's wearing a yellow raincoat and his red wool cap.

'I want to go back, Manel. Take the photos again. The ones I took before are too dark. I could try it with the flash I bought. I don't think it'll look good, but it's worth a try . . .'

Manel shakes his head, lifts his eyebrows, takes a deep breath, and sits on the edge of the tub. The marble is cold and he feels strangely ridiculous, so naked, with so much skin, so fat. He crosses his legs to try to impose a little seriousness and blows on his bangs. He lets one arm drop.

'It's midnight, Òscar . . . I wanted us to have a soak after dinner. We still have five days. All for you.' He rubs his bangs. 'All for you.'

Òscar can feel the tension between his eyebrows, and his stomach hard.

He needs the last photo for his series.

The photo.

It won't be easy to get one that concludes the entire project.

The abysm.

Manel straightens up his back and crosses his legs with some difficulty. He has to convince him. No more working tonight. This is their vacation.

Òscar takes in a breath, looks at the small window in the bathroom, then looks at him.

'Manel, the sooner I send a good photo to Quique, the better. We'll all be more relaxed.'

'All of us?'

'Oh, so you could care less? Sure, you're already relaxed, you're on vacation! I knew I should've come here alone. I knew it.'

Manel's neck muscles get so tight he has to put his head back and lift his shoulders.

'Come on, Òscar, it's time to get some rest, tomorrow is . . .'

Always redirecting the situation.

Always that role.

His stomach digesting gulps of tension.

Manel stands up and walks over to him, rubs his sleeve and then caresses his cheek. Òscar looks at the floor.

'It's true, Manel. You're the one who wanted to come with me, OK? I'm working, this is my job.'

Manel realizes that the hat he gave Òscar for his birthday is too small. His forehead still has a mark from when he wore it earlier. Rows of small triangles from ear to ear. Maybe he should buy him a new one.

'Come on . . . You need to relax, Òscar. All this pressure won't make for good photos.' He gently squeezes his shoulder and strokes his ear. 'And I think I'll buy you a new hat.'

Òscar looks at him with his brow furrowed, and scratches his neck.

'Come on, don't act like my daddy.'

Daddy.

Daddy. Òscar goes through phases. When they fight he uses the same defense for months. Lately it's this daddy thing. Coincidentally, ever since Manel started to say he wanted to have a child.

Daddy.

Daddy.

Every daddy is a dart between the ribs, or into his navel.

But it doesn't matter. Redirect the situation.

His stomach filled to bursting, swollen.

Manel takes him by the hand and, with some effort, leads him toward the tub.

'Come on, I'll give you a massage. It'll do you good.'

Òscar resists, but nods in agreement. He takes off his hat. He purses his lips, turns and disappears into the room as he takes off his raincoat. The sound of the zipper relaxes Manel's neck muscles, and he lifts his arms to fully shake off the tension. He smiles and gets into the tub. That's it. Situation redirected.

'I'm in, just waiting for you!' He sits down. It's very nice. They'll fit perfectly. 'The water's just right. Bring the cava!'

But just as the last 'a' comes out of his mouth, an abrupt door slam makes him close his eyes.

Silence.

Only the sound of the water when he moves his legs.

'Òscar?'

He extends his neck to peer through the slit between the bathroom door and the frame. Nothing.

'Òscar?'

He gets up and grabs one of the enormous towels he'd left on the sink and wraps himself in it. It isn't soft at all. He presses his arms against his ribs.

He leaves the bathroom. The red carpeting brushes the bottom of his feet. Òscar's cell phone rests on the bed.

An intermittent sound makes him turn.

Click, click, click, click. The beat slows.

It's the little sign they'd found on the bed that evening when they entered the room. It's long and has a hole that fits over the doorknob. DO NOT DISTURB. Manel had hung it on the knob, but facing into the room.

So they would see it themselves.

Do not disturb.

Safewords, like the couples therapist suggested they use to break the spell of arguments.

Do not disturb.

It is still gently swaying.

Right and left. Left and right.

Increasingly slower.

He approaches the door and opens it. At the end of the hallway, he can hear the sound of footsteps heading off.

He closes the door again, hard. The sign shakes violently.

Do not disturb, do not disturb, do not disturb, do not disturb.

His hand slides down the railing, his palm hot from the friction. His palm and his brain getting hotter with each passing floor. Òscar takes the stairs two by two. He needs to go back. Shoot a good photograph. Capture the murmur of the leaves, the creak of the chairlift. The darkness. Nature climbing the lift's pylon.

And perhaps, the shadow.

Who is hiding behind the trees?

He passes the empty reception area. The sound of two deep voices blended in an argument makes him stop. He turns to the left, toward the manager's room. He can hear the conversation clearly:

'Don't be rash, Tom, please, calm down.'

'It's back, Sam. It's back!'

Òscar grips his camera tightly and looks at the stairs, then at the elevator.

He looks back at the door to the manager's room.

'Please, wait. Let's see, there has to be some solution, Tom.'

'I'm this close to losing it, Sam.'

Now the voice is calmer. He hears footsteps. His back rigid. What is he doing? He has to go back to the ski resort.

Completely naked, stepping over the towel with long

strides, Manel approaches the rectangular window that goes from one side of the room to the other. He rests his forehead on the glass and a second later it's steamed up. Seven floors down, in the hotel parking lot, beside the brown off-road vehicle, he sees Òscar lighting a cigarette and looking up. He has his camera equipment hanging around his neck.

Òscar. What are you doing?

Their gazes intersect at some point between them.

Manel looks down hastily, supplicant; Òscar looks up defiant, harsh.

Their gazes meet at the second floor. Manel sticks a palm to the glass and tries to transmit to Òscar that he shouldn't take another step, that he's coming down now and they'll take all the photos he wants to. Òscar takes another drag. He looks at the car. He can't wait to get his driver's license.

Manel watches Òscar's silhouette disappear around the bend, swallowed up by the night. He grabs the window handle and pulls it to the right. The glass moves, with a piercing shriek. Bitter cold air comes in, freezing his uvula.

'Òscar! Òscar! Don't walk there! Come back!'

His shouts dissipate. Some snowflakes dance hesitantly and slip in through the window. He follows them with his gaze. They move slowly. The white snow melts amid the hairs of the red carpet, turning into a slight cloud of smoke. Is it snowing?

Òscar hears his name in the distance. He tosses the cigarette. He needs the photo. Quique, the curator of the exhibition, warned him: the last image has to be powerful. They had to impress the museum director. What's more, Òscar, I've noticed that your work is losing intensity. You have to recover your energy.

You are losing intensity.

Intensity.

The intensity you used to have.

What was that shadow?

Òscar adjusts the camera strap. Manel doesn't understand anything, he doesn't understand my rhythm. His pace is set by working in an office. If he hadn't desperately sought out work as an architect and focused on the comic he had finally started, maybe he'd understand me better. And now, he still wants a kid. Isn't it enough that they're married?

He turns. He looks at the hotel. Claustrophobia. He turns back and advances more quickly. You won't keep me locked up here, I need the photo.

To recover my intensity.

His pants are getting damp because he didn't dry himself off well. Manel throws the towel on the carpet. He'll get the car, catch up with him halfway there, open up the door and say, come on, let's go take all the photos you want.

Redirect the situation again.

They can't discuss the subject tonight, but if he can manage to reduce the tension, maybe they can talk about it tomorrow. He sits down on the bed and ties his sneakers.

A child, for both of them.

The scent of Òscar.

There's a gentle knock on the door. Three times. Manel stands up and feels his muscles relaxing again. He came back. Sometimes he does that. Not often, but sometimes. He leaves and comes back. In a bad mood. But he comes back.

Relaxed muscles, tension, relaxed muscles, tension.

Now he'll hug him very, very tight. He's anxious to smell his scent.

He opens the door.

Sam, hunched over, observes him, with a bunch of papers in his hand. Manel feels his stomach getting hard and small.

'I'm sorry to disturb you. I'm gathering signatures.'

'Sorry, I'm in a rush.'

Manel closes the door. He takes in a breath. He tightens his lips. He takes a step back, grabs the other sneaker and balances as he puts it on. Who cares if he was rude.

Tense muscles. He needs the smell of Òscar.

There's a knock at the door again. Harder this time. What the . . . ? He finishes tying his shoelace and opens it.

'I'm sorry to disturb you. But I need the signatures.' Sam rubs his forehead, his right hand trembles. 'I've been collecting signatures for years. It's so they'll take the bear to a shelter.'

Sam holds out the papers to him.

Manel looks at the yellowed, slightly wrinkled pages divided into rectangles, each containing a signature. He wants to hug Òscar very, very tight. He's starting to get jittery.

'What bear?'

'The bear that lives in the forests above the ski station. My brother is very nervous. He's here, downstairs, in my room, and he is very nervous today. The signatures are to have the bear taken to a shelter. I need the signatures. Tom says that two sheep have disappeared from his flock and he found blood on the grass above where they graze. I already told him not to worry, that we'll gather more signatures, that they'll finally pay attention to us. That for once and for all . . . they'll pay attention to us.'

Sam hands the fountain pen to Manel.

Manel opens his eyes wide. His nostrils have become thin, fine ducts.

'But is this bear dangerous? You didn't mention it when I made the reservation.'

Sam shakes his head, with a sad expression.

'Not at all. Don't worry. I swear.'

Manel takes Sam's fountain pen. He lifts his leg and places

the pages on his left thigh. He signs quickly and hands them back. Sam stands there, staring at him.

'It's snowing a lot. Hard to believe. I haven't seen it snow like this in many years. And with this heat . . .'

Manel turns and looks through the window of his hotel room. The snowflakes plummet into the night.

White on black.

Suddenly, a car engine is heard. Sam turns, looks at the hallway and shouts, 'No! Tom!'

He runs off, Manel glances around the hotel room, grabs his car keys from the bedside table, closes the door and follows him. They rush down the stairs and when they reach the lobby Sam lets out a sigh, places his hands on his nape.

'No! No! No! No!'

Manel sees where Sam is looking. On the lobby's wall, beneath the paintings, there is only the dusty outline of the shotgun.

The windshield wipers move at the rhythm of his heartbeats. Manel drives at twenty kilometers per hour with his chin pressed tight to the steering wheel, following the footprints Òscar left in the snow. Beside him, Sam looks nervously out the window and just keeps repeating in a whisper: he's crazy, he's crazy . . .

The temperature is plummeting. He turns on the brights. The darkness is absolute. Outside, everything is blackness. Sam asked Manel to drive him to the ski station, he's sure that's where his brother is headed. To the upper part. To the forests. Manel finds it all crazy, but he has no time to argue. He needs to find and hug Òscar.

Relax his muscles.

He should have gone with him. He had five long, beautiful days to calmly tell him about the meeting.

Five days.

Manel should have waited until Òscar had at least one good photo. The coordinator at the center, months ago, gave him just one piece of advice over the phone: you have to cultivate patience, adoption is a long process.

Patience.

Manel chews his lip. He forgot to breathe and inhales suddenly through his nose and is overcome with an immense desire to cry. Òscar had been saving up months for that flash.

Almost there, almost there. A long, tight curve. A straight stretch and I'll be there. And I'll hug you, Òscar.

Redirecting the situation, as always. Swallowing the tension.

Daddy.

Sam keeps repeating: he's crazy, he's crazy.

The snow piles up on Òscar's shoulders as he walks along the side of the road, slightly hunched over because it's getting colder and colder. And he looks at the ground, at the snow, at his new boots. Manel, as they sat on benches in the airport, had assured him the weather would be good, that there would be no clouds and that the full moon would give off plenty of light. Didn't he check carefully? Did he not know how to read the lunar calendar? Or maybe he just didn't say anything, because that way they would stay in the hotel room, no excuses, holed up.

While it snowed.

It's pretty obvious he lied to him on purpose.

He pats the camera case. It's soaked. He opens up his coat and hides it inside. It must be fifteen more minutes of walking before he gets to the ski station. He's not sure if the case will keep the camera dry.

Suddenly he hears the sound of skidding wheels on the road. That's it. He always ends up coming looking for him. Can't he just leave him be? He turns and is dazzled by the car's headlights. He places a hand on his forehead as a visor. He feels the camera lens sticking in his chest. Now he'll say, come on, Òscar, let's go, let's go take the photos. Of course. It's his work, he isn't here on vacation. He stands in the middle of the road so he'll see him and he lifts his arms, lowering his chin slightly so the car's lights don't pierce his retinas. The car brakes, the wheels skate on the virgin snow. Òscar looks up and feels a shiver at the back of his neck.

The car in front of him is not the one they rented earlier that day.

It must not smell of lemon or new car and it must not be Manel's hand resting on the gear shift, about to stroke his thigh.

Òscar squints his eyes, the headlights reduce to two yellow spots, but he still can't identify the driver. He hears barking. The car is not moving. Snow is dropping onto the hood. Òscar approaches without taking his eyes off the windshield. The driver lowers his window. Is that Sam?

'Where are you going?'

'To the ski station.'

The driver nods to his right. Is he telling him to get in? He makes the same gesture, this time with his forehead furrowed. Òscar nods and walks around the car and opens the passenger side door. In the back seat there are two dogs, their eyes filled with rage.

'Don't mind them. They're not dangerous. Not to you.'

'Did you leave the hotel unattended?'

The driver smiles with one side of his mouth and looks at him.

'I'm not Sam, I'm his twin brother. My name is Tom.'

'Did you have a fight?'

Manel is driving, keeping his eyes on Òscar's footprints,

which are already disappearing, covered by snow. He notices Sam's gaze.

'No.'

Sam looks out the window again.

Manel glances at him out of the corner of his eye. The hotel manager has thin, white hair. His coat seems to be from some other time period and smells of wood, and ash. He chews on his lips.

'And why did you fight with your brother?'

Sam doesn't look away from the window. He sees his Adam's apple going up and down. He wipes his nose.

'Over the bear.'

Manel changes gears.

'What?'

'The bear doesn't exist. I've been trying to convince him that this bear legend is absurd, ever since we were little. The adults in town would tell it to us. A mother bear that lived in the forests behind the town.' He sighs loudly. 'My brother has never been able to tell the difference between fantasy and reality. Never.'

Manel notices that Sam's voice has started to crack, and it's getting worse and worse. He shifts gears again and looks at him. Sam has put a hand on his forehead and is making a sound with his nose.

'My brother is a loner, he hallucinates. But for years now he's been doing fine . . . as a shepherd.'

'And why are you gathering signatures?'

Sam shrugs.

'I started the petition to show him that I believed him. When he suffered more intense paranoid episodes, that would calm him down.' He takes in air in uneven gulps. 'When the ski station and the hotel started to fail, he said it was the bear's fault, that she was scaring off the skiers.' He shakes his head and points to the black sky. 'And it was the snow. It was the snow. It's been snowing less and less. You know how many years it's been since I've seen it snow here?'

The snow.

He wants to hug Òscar and tell him, you know what? The ski station closed because there wasn't enough snow. That's it, nothing more. Sometimes things are simple, Òscar. Try to capture that.

'Yesterday he was hysterical over the disappearance of two of his sheep. Well they escaped and that's all, Tom!' Sam gives the car window a light punch. 'That's all!'

Sometimes things are simple, Òscar. I want us to be parents. What are you afraid of?

The engine coughs three times and the car stops.

One of the dogs keeps scratching at the glass and the sound of its nails hitting the window is making Òscar nervous, and he keeps turning around. The animal's mouth is full of saliva as it reveals its sharp, dirty fangs. Between the two dogs he glimpses the shotgun.

'He's nervous, wants to get out.'

Tom's voice is just as deep as Sam's. Òscar nods and grips the door handle tightly.

'Yeah.'

'So what are you doing here, at the ski station?'

Òscar unzips his jacket and strokes the still damp camera case.

'I have to take photos. I'm a photographer.'

Tom scratches his nose compulsively. Òscar takes a long hard look at him. Maybe he doesn't look that much like his brother. Tom's eyes are more almond-shaped and his jaw more square.

'Of a ski station that's been shut down for years?'

Òscar looks straight ahead. He can already see the chairlift.

'It's for a photographic project on abandoned spaces.'

One of the dogs starts barking. Tom looks into the rear-view mirror.

'It used to be full of skiers. Full. My brother made a ton of money, with the ski station and the hotel. Look at it now. Empty.'

Caress the landscape. Merge with it. Understand its language.

'What happened?'

Tom shifts gears, looks at him, looks back at the road. He lowers his chin and furrows his brow.

'He never believed there was a bear.'

Òscar grabs his camera. Tom looks at him sidelong. His eyes are gleaming.

'Skiers would disappear.' He lifts his arm slowly and points to the road with his index finger. 'They went up in the chairlift and never came back down. Sometimes, there was growling. He was totally money crazy and didn't say a word. He kept quiet and didn't do a thing.' He falls silent. He swallows hard and drums his fingers on the steering wheel. 'Towards the end he was halfway round the bend, and he started a petition, but of course,' he shrugs, 'by then, nobody was coming anymore.'

'And that's why it closed?'

Tom nods.

'People were afraid.'

Òscar strokes his camera and realizes his heart is beating fast. His right leg starts moving and he gnaws on the cuticle of his index finger. The chairlift is getting closer and closer.

A bear.

They shut it down because of a bear. Nature versus culture. The perfect photo to conclude his series. The fear of death.

Recovering intensity.

'I was never able to prove it to my brother. Never.' He extends his right hand to Òscar and lifts two fingers. 'But today two of my sheep disappeared. The bear took away my brother's livelihood, and he didn't know how to stop her.' He bangs his fist against his chest. 'I won't let her do that to me!'

Òscar turns on the camera and looks at the last photograph he took. He zooms in and studies the shadow. He glances into the mirror on the passenger side. Where's Manel? Isn't he going to come looking for him? Suddenly, he feels a stab in his left nipple.

Manel and Sam are walking along the road. It's been five minutes since they pushed the car to the shoulder. After studying the engine and trying to start it three times, they gave up and continued on foot. There aren't many lights, but they have no problem following the road. Sam is not dressed very warmly, and keeps rubbing his arms. It's not snowing anymore, but the temperature is dropping. Manel has the flashlight and keeps nervously pressing the on/off button, his eyes on Òscar's footprints.

'Why did your friend leave?' Sam's voice is getting hoarse.

'He wanted to take photos. And he's more than a friend.'

Manel looks at the sky. Yes. He's sure. He checked and double checked, and then checked again. The moon should be full, starting today. He spins around. There are some clouds, but he can see plenty of stars. Where is the moon?

Sam approaches, hastening his step.

'What are you doing?'

Manel lifts his chin skyward.

'There should be a full moon. I checked before booking the trip. It's . . . it's as if it's disappeared!'

Barking is heard. Sam looks at the road.

'We have to keep going!'

Manel starts to walk, following Òscar's enormous foot-prints. Size 12. A large foot. Size 12. Òscar's big boots. The snow boots he bought two weeks ago downtown. Manel was antsy about how long they were in the store. Òscar couldn't make up his mind. He didn't like any of them.

'These ones make me taller, right?'

Manel looked at the boots through the mirror that leaned against a column and then looked at his face. Tense.

'Yes, they make you even taller. In the end I'll have a stiff neck from looking up at you. Those ones seem good.'

'They're expensive . . .'

'But the ones you have are destroyed.'

Did Òscar know Manel's shoe size? And whether he needed new sneakers or not? Did he know? He pressed on Òscar's toes to see if the boots fit.

'Aren't they a little small?'

'Oh, man! Stop acting like my daddy!'

Manel quickly withdrew his hand.

'Don't call me daddy again, Òscar. This is important to me. Let's not go there with this subject, OK? Please. You should get those ones, they're nice. Let me get them for you.'

Òscar shrugged and sat down to untie them.

'Yeah, they are nice.'

Manel stops. The footprints change direction, four more and the last few are in the middle of the road. As if he'd been abducted. As if he'd disappeared. Him and the moon.

'We did fight, goddamnit! We did have a fight!'

Tom pulls the hand brake and looks at Òscar.

'See you later.'

Òscar grips the door handle.

'Where are you headed now?'

'Up a path that leads to the woods above the station.'

'You aren't going to kill the bear, are you?'

Tom tightens his lips.

Òscar leaps from the car. He observes how the dogs are watching him through the glass. They steam it up. Tom starts the car and the dogs begin to bark. Òscar is left standing there, stock-still, watching the off-road vehicle head into the distance. He lifts his chin and looks out at the black night. There are no longer any clouds, and the stars shine much more intensely without the moon.

He jumps over the fence, passes by the small lodge and heads decisively to the ski lift. The freezing wind moves the rusty chairs.

They creak.

A lament amid the white silence.

He looks around him.

A mother bear. This stillness is a mother bear's fault.

Fear's fault. The fear of death. The same engine behind the building of a ski station is what causes it be abandoned. The fear of dying makes us build devices to distract ourselves, Manel, and then, abandon them. That's the subject of *Abysms*. My new project. You like it?

He looks to right and left and approaches one of the chairlift's pylons, its paint peeling.

When he finds the perfect spot, he pulls out his camera.

The flash lights up one of the chairs. Its sound travels through the mountains and comes back to his eardrums, like a boomerang. He quickly puts the camera in his coat so it doesn't get wet and then looks at the photograph.

There's too much snow. It doesn't look like an abandoned ski station. It doesn't have the effect he wants.

What if it snows every day they're here? What will they do? Stay warm in the room. Soak in the tub. Massages.

He wants to try to take the photograph from another angle that shows the cable of the chairlift merging with the pine trees at the top of the mountain. He'll try to not show the snow. He could focus just on the tree trunks. He pulls out his camera quickly and adjusts his hood so it covers it a little bit.

He looks through the viewfinder. He tries to imagine the chairlift working. Families laughing. Colorful anoraks. What are you afraid of, Òscar?

He shoots.

From the distance comes the sound of high-spirited barking.

He lets go of the camera. He turns and looks at the completely snow-covered road.

And where is Manel anyway? It would have been so simple for him to have just come with him. Manel could have stood behind him, watching him take the photos, saying this one is good, that one's not. Like when they selected the images for his exhibition on evictions, stretched out on the floor of the dining room. Manel wanted a few to trace for the comic book project he'd been envisioning. That was when he was still on unemployment and was taking that illustration course, before the idea of adopting a kid flooded his entire brain, swallowing up the comic, the photo selecting, the this one is good, that one's not.

Adopting.

Òscar, I found out that in Ethiopia it would take us three years. In Vietnam it seems like it'd be faster. And Òscar, alone looking through the photos. Losing intensity. This one's good, that one's not. Look, Manel, maybe this one could work for the cover of your comic?

My comic? Pfff . . . don't know when I'll get around to it, with all the work I have in the office right now! But you had the whole plot figured out! You had it all perfectly figured out before you found a job!

Òscar contemplates the chairlift. Immobile. Are you soaking in the tub, Manel? Did you know there's no full moon? But I guess it's okay. In the distance, the dogs bark more furiously. A few seconds later, Òscar feels another, more intense stab in the nipple of his left breast.

They can already see the chairlift's enormous pylons. It seems it's not snowing as hard. Manel walks behind Sam, who hasn't said anything in a while. He feels his socks wet and a shiver climbing his legs, moving through his entire spine up to his neck. He looks at his old sneakers. Do you know my shoe size, Òscar? Do you know it? Do you know whether I need new sneakers because these ones are super old? They're nice; let me get them for you. Oh, man! Stop acting like my daddy!

Daddy.

He should have stood up and thrown it all to the floor. Every boot on the shelf. Every single one of those boots for the photo expedition to the abandoned ski station. The hotel stay they would pay for with his salary, the salary he earns working at the architecture firm. The trip he would meticulously prepare: the rental car, the hotel, the flights. OK, he didn't know there would be no full moon. That's the only thing Òscar can reproach him for, but he could have taken care of all the arrangements himself. But, of course, he is the artist. All Òscar can think about are landscapes and positioning the lens. Oh, and on insisting about his comic. Manel, innocently, had defended himself: the comic's just a hobby.

A hobby? But you love it, you even had an editor interested.

Òscar, please, it's a tiny publishing house.

So? That's a start.

Yeah, right, and how would we pay the bills then, with your exhibitions? Maybe you should start thinking of your photography as a hobby, too, and look for a real job!

Sam stops, turns, looks at him and places his index finger on his ear.

'Did you hear that?'

The cold has made its way into Òscar's coat and he's been shivering, and he still hasn't got a decent photo.

The best.

Abysms.

Exhibition: *Abysms*, by Òscar Torres.

You need a more powerful photo, Òscar, your work is losing its strength. What do you think about an abandoned ski station, Quique? I found one. Far away. I'd have to fly there but I think it's a good idea. Sure, give it a try.

Òscar exhales loudly. Manel, I'm going to go on a trip to an abandoned ski station. I think I've found the idea for the last photo of the abysm. Manel was annoyed that he'd planned the vacation. By yourself? I don't know . . . You want to come with me? Yes, but it's not that, Òscar, it's not that. Two days later Manel showed him the page he'd printed. It's the hotel reservation, we'll spend our vacation there. We'll take a plane and then we'll rent a car. It's all paid for. You'll have five days to find the photo you're searching for.

Suddenly, another stab in his left nipple. It feels like it's burning. He approaches the chairlift and sits in the seat closest to the ground. He props up his boots on the footrest. He rubs his nipple. He folds forward and that seems to lessen the pain. The dogs have stopped barking.

He hears a shot in the distance. The sharp sound spreads along the ski slope. The chairs sway and it seems they're howling. Òscar turns and his gaze runs up the cable that leads into the forest.

Frightened, Manel looks at Sam, who turns and observes the mountain. His eyes are gleaming.

'It's Tom.'

He starts to run and Manel follows him. They hop the fence. Sam pulls a set of keys from his coat pocket and opens the door to the ski station's little hut. Manel contemplates the landscape. He doesn't see Òscar anywhere. He's having trouble breathing. He looks inside the hut. Sam turns on some lights.

'What are you doing?'

'I have to go up.'

Sam lifts a wood panel and presses a button.

Suddenly, the spotlights on the chairlift switch on. Òscar puts his right arm in front of his eyes. The stab in his nipple pierces his guts and reaches his back. He shakes his right leg compulsively. Who turned on the spotlights?

He hears a deafening screech followed by a cadenced hum.

The chairs swing and start to move.

Òscar grips the frozen bar and rams his feet into the footrest.

And he starts to ascend.

He wants to scream, but his voice is trapped in his throat. The pain in his nipple is sharp and he doubles over again. He bites his lips. His eyes are beginning to get used to the light, he looks down and feels a dizziness that runs through his neck and sinks into his eardrums. It's too late to jump, he's too high up.

Sam moves Manel away from the door and starts to run toward the chairlift. Manel takes two steps and observes the ascending seats. What is that? What is that shadow on the chairlift? He takes two more steps and notices Òscar's yellow raincoat. Òscar? He opens his mouth slightly. Òscar? His mouth turns dry and he feels a scraping in his brain.

'Òscar!'

He takes a running start and is off.

Running.

Running.

His old sneakers sink into the snow.

Running.

His socks wet.

Òscar doesn't move, he can't even see his face. He's doubled over.

What is he doing? Is he looking at the photos in his camera?

'Jump!'

Another shot is heard. A few birds fly out of the fir trees and scatter into the black night. The sound of their wings blends into the sound of the chairlift.

'Òscar!'

He reaches the chairlift, his esophagus burned by the cold. He jumps into the damp seat. He looks forward, backward. Where is Sam?

Òscar hugs his camera. He hears Manel's voice. Is he calling him? He's afraid to look down, but he tries to open his left eye and turn his head a little. The voice is coming from a chair. He's here. He came looking for him. The two of them are heading up into the forest. Together.

What did he make him do?

They would be soaking in the tub right now. No. Now they'd be naked in the bed, covered in soap, tipsy. With the cava's sparks exploding in their heads. The photo. The abysm. The exhibition that would make his reputation. Give him a little more prestige. It's not a hobby, Manel. Maybe feel more confidence. It's not a hobby, Manel. Feel sure of himself. At home, and beyond.

I'm a photographer.

Oh, really? Is that how you earn your living?

To be able to say: The abysm. I'm a father and I'm a photographer.

That's how I earn my living, support a family.

Father.

Father.

Manel grips the railing hard. Why isn't he answering? Is it possible he doesn't hear him? Does he not hear him? Is he not answering because he's still angry? Why? He's the one who wasted all his fucking vacation days last year on this project that . . .

'Òscar! It was the snow! They closed because it didn't snow! You hear me?'

Ever since the summer, since the first photo of the *Abysms* project, at the abandoned water park. That was where he wanted to tell him, for the first time, that he wanted to be a father. They had snuck into the park after lunch at a beachside bar. Òscar saw from the very first moment the photo he needed: a rusty row of seven slides with deflated flotation devices at the bottom. He took it from different angles while Manel observed him. Then they dropped down, tired, into one of those blue floaties covered in dirt and roasted ants, big enough to hold four or five people. Òscar lit a cigarette. Manel rubbed his shoulder. How did you come up with this idea for the project? Òscar exhaled smoke. I love these places. Places of premeditated leisure, filled with laughing people. Infrastructures we create to have fun and avoid thinking about death. And now, look, nature is devouring these rusty old objects designed as our saviors from the abysm, from having to think about the void.

Òscar, do you really think people come to water slides to escape thinking about their mortality? Are you sure it's not you who's depressed?

Òscar shrugged his wide, tanned shoulders and his expression grew sad.

I have been, but I'm much better now.

Manel never found the right time to tell him about the desire growing inside of him, they talked until it got dark about all the periods of depression that Òscar had suffered since his teenage years.

You have to have patience, it's a long process. And how do you measure patience anyway? And since when did he have to start being patient?

Manel bites down hard on his lower lip. It can't be. He'll adopt on his own. He doesn't need Òscar, not for anything. Actually, he would hold up the process. He would raise flags. No salary, a freelancer, with a history of depression. Manel can be a father on his own.

Father.

The papers: pay stub, lease, marriage certificate, are you divorced?

Is he divorced?

If he were a widower . . .

The chairlift is now reaching the top, in three seconds it will make a small turn and descend. In three seconds Òscar will have the ground just a few centimeters from his feet.

One.

Two.

Three.

Òscar grips his camera and jumps. He is trembling. It's colder up here. Suddenly, he hears a howl of pain.

And silence.

Terrified, he looks to his left. A few meters away, amid the trees, there is a shadow on the ground. He rubs his nipple and slowly walks toward it. He extends his neck. He squints his eyes. His heart makes a jolt so hard his ribs shake.

It's the mother bear. Enormous, furry.

She's on the ground in the middle of a puddle of blood that blends into the snow. His knees grow weak. The piercing pain in his nipple intensifies and expands to surround the areola. He throws his head back. He opens his mouth. He can feel his guts twisting. He throws his head further back, but he takes a step. And another. He contracts his shoulders and now throws his head forward. The camera sways gently on his chest. The puddle of bear blood is spreading. A force he does not comprehend leads him forward.

A step.

Another.

An intense stab in his nipple. He curves over a little. He struggles to breathe.

The sound of footsteps makes him lift his head, fearful. His heart beats faster, which makes his nipple hurt even more.

From among the trees, a bear cub comes toward him, scared.

Òscar feels a cramp in his belly and he kneels down.

The little bear springs forward until it is at his knees. It sniffs him. Its snout is damp.

Tears.

Snot.

Snow.

Òscar lets out a smile when he exhales and strokes the cub's back with a trembling hand, leans over and kisses its head. He feels his nipple boiling. Again he strokes the cub, who is now nestled against his thighs. It is rubbing its back against his belly. Suddenly, Òscar feels a burning in his pubis, a fiery scratching that travels from his belly to his thorax. He feels his heart melting and his nipple opening as if it were a camera shutter. He unzips his coat, lifts his sweater.

A stream of milk burbles from his left nipple and floods his belly button. The pain instantly disappears.

The cub moves into position, licks the liquid, smells it, rests its paws on Òscar's belly and sucks on Òscar's nipple. With each slurp, Òscar's belly clenches, like it did when he took his first photo and his parents framed it in the dining room.

You'll be a good photographer, my son.

Manel's chair reaches the top and with a quick jump he hits the ground on his knees. Why did Òscar jump? Where is he?

He hears a whimper.

He looks to his right and sees a man's body laid out on the ground. Encircled by a puddle of blood. Manel approaches him slowly. One step, another. The man has a giant scratch on his back that opened his coat, his sweater and his skin. Manel kneels beside him. The man is dying. Suddenly, his eyes widen and he stops breathing. His right hand limply holds a shotgun. Is it Sam's brother? Manel takes the weapon with trembling hands. It weighs less than he imagined.

Milk keeps bubbling from Òscar's nipple. The cub moves its back paws as it nurses with devotion. Òscar, suddenly, hears footsteps behind him. He turns his head as far as he can and sees Manel a few meters away. He doesn't want to move. He doesn't want to disturb the cub.

'Manel!'

Manel turns abruptly and sees Òscar near the trees, on his knees with his back to him, but with his head turned, looking at him.

'Manel, come here! You have to take a photo of me. This will be the final one!'

A photo? Òscar is still thinking about photos? About the abysm.

The abysm.

Abysms.

The marriage certificate. Is he divorced? That will make things complicated.

Òscar, gripping the cub with his right arm, pulls out the camera with his left hand and without moving extends it behind him to Manel, who is already approaching.

'Here, stand in front of me, Manel. You have to see this. You'll be the one to shoot the last photograph in the series. The perfect photograph, Manel. And it will be you. You'll be the one to shoot it.'

Manel takes two more steps, grabs the camera. He stops. Òscar turns his head again and kisses the cub's head.

'Stand in front of me, Manel. You have to see this. The perfect photograph. Now I understand, Manel.'

Manel contemplates Òscar's back, his wide shoulders, his head lowered, probably looking at the photos he took, as usual.

He looks at the shotgun in his left hand.

He looks at the camera in his right hand.

He again contemplates Òscar's back. His bowed head. His curly blond hair.

And he shoots.

Translated from the Catalan by Mara Faye Lethem

Bathie Ngoye Thiam

The House of Leuk Dawour

Located on the west coast of Africa, Senegal has a long tradition of storytelling; many of these stories involve the rab *(evil spirits),* djinn *(powerful supernatural creatures), and* deum *(considered capable of draining a person's life force). While frightening stories involving these beings are well known to most Senegalese, they have histori-cally existed primarily in oral, rather than written, form.* BATHIE NGOYE THIAM, *in his* Nouvelles fantastiques sénégalaises *(2005), adapted many of these oral traditions into modern-day fan-tastic or horror tales, including the following story, which deals in part with a* rab *called Leuk Dawour. The author informed the editors that even today many in Senegal's capital city of Dakar refrain from mentioning Leuk Dawour's name for fear of attracting his attention. Indeed, when he was in the process of publishing his collection of tales, the author's mother told him he should write stories about love or societal problems instead and warned him to leave the djinns and rabs alone. Fortunately for us he didn't heed her advice!*

IS THERE ANYONE FROM SENEGAL, especially from Dakar, who has never heard of Leuk Dawour Mbaye?

Leuk Dawour is the *rab* of Dakar, just as Ndoumbé Diop is Diourbel's *rab*, Mame Coumba Lamba is Rufisque's, and Mbossé is Kaolack's . . .

It is well known that a town doesn't belong to the humans who are busy there in the daytime, but to a *rab* (spirit) who prowls it at night. Woe to anyone who finds himself in its path. They say that Ndoumbé Diop appears in the form of a hen accompanied by her chicks. Seeing that hen after midnight means instant death or incurable madness. Mbossé, on the other hand, takes the form of a monitor lizard. There is one they say waits until you are in the middle of a street; he then transforms into two thundering barrels which shoot out from opposite ends of the roadway, roll at great speed, and come to crush you. Ask our ancestors, they will tell you many such stories. Those who happen to remain on the streets until undue hours risk unpleasant encounters. They are found the next day, dried out and inert like chunks of wood or, in the best case scenario, with their mouth in the back of their head. Naturally I couldn't swallow such nonsense. Yet . . .

Let me catch my breath before continuing . . .

It all started the night before the 'disappearance' of Bakary, my husband. My mother uses that word, *disappearance*. As for the others, they never stop telling me he's dead, which I can't bring myself to believe. Bakary couldn't leave me like that . . . Without even saying goodbye . . . There are also rumors that I killed him . . . What twisted minds! How could anyone imagine that? . . . No, I'm not whining. There's no reason to. I'm not worried either, I know he will return. He's just gone to visit his family in Mbour. His car probably broke down . . .

We met, I'll always remember it, at a Senegalese party on the university campus, in Paris. We had an instant connection. Love at first sight, as they say. Since then we've never been apart. We got married in France, since my father couldn't accept someone from another caste, and especially from a low social class, as a son-in-law. Me, I had found the man of my life and I wasn't going to let him go for anything in the world.

Bakary was a musician, a talented percussionist. In fact,

he played a little of everything. Gifted at everything, he often composed pretty ballads just for me. However, what I liked best about him – besides the love and respect he showed towards me – was his great sensitivity, which was both his weakness and his strength. He was true to himself in all circumstances. Just like me, he rejected almost all social conventions and led his life as seemed best to him. But, unlike me, he came (as I said earlier) from a very modest background, from poor parents in other words.

As for me, as you might suspect, I am, you might say, from high up in Senegal. I'm not boasting of it, but I'm not ashamed either. You have to be born somewhere, right? My mother is well known in the business world, and my father has important responsibilities in the administration. I'm the youngest of four siblings. The only daughter in the family. Let the indigent take comfort in listening to my story! Princesses often envy Cinderellas. I was raised in luxury, but I felt like I was in prison.

I was brought up with good manners, for in that society the image you project is the most important thing. I was stuffed full of good manners, stuffed to the point of vomiting. Ugh! Good manners! 'Dress like this . . . Walk like that . . . Talk this way . . . Don't look over there . . . What are you doing at such an hour? . . . Who is that boy who called? . . . You're not going out this week . . . You have to have a chaperone . . . Watch out for thugs . . . There's an invitation . . . There's a reception . . .' Whoa! Whoa! That way of life disgusted me. Yet I had to play the game, pretend . . . It was the only way to gain my parents' confidence and convince them to send me to pursue my studies in Paris.

I even forced myself to smile and be friendly with Matar, the minister's son to whom they'd introduced me and whom they invited over at the slightest occasion.

'How charming that boy is!' Mother would exclaim.

'He's got a good head on his shoulders! The country needs young people like him,' Father would one-up her.

The hell with the country! The hell with Matar's head! (The poor guy! He didn't understand a thing. Whenever my parents left me alone with him, wanting to encourage a certain intimacy, I would tell him to get lost.)

At last I was in Paris! Mother, who had made the journey with me, had stayed in my apartment almost two months just to make sure everything was going well. She cooked my meals, did my laundry, and made my bed. It's true that at the time I wasn't even capable of making coffee or cooking an egg. Everything was done for me. Rich people don't leave their children without safeguards. I was kept away from fire and all danger. Even when I went to the preschool directly across from our house, someone always had to bring me across the road. What can I say? You can't choose your parents. Mother, who intercepted my mail, gave me the letters that Matar would send me almost every day. Some very clumsy declarations of love, only good for filling trash bags with. All the same, I continued playing the game until my progenitor's departure, which let me breathe such a sigh of relief!

I had enrolled in the fine arts. Ah! I remember father's face. Oh! Oh! You should have seen him, my old man! I had categorically refused the boring law studies he had suggested ... Damn it! A person has the right to decide for herself, doesn't she?

For pocket money, my parents sent me practically a yuppie's salary. I've never known what a 'yuppie' was, but well, it's as good an expression as any. In any case, I had enough money to get into trouble with.

I was, to tell the truth, a naive and slightly capricious bourgeois girl who was finally escaping from her golden cage. I wanted to discover the world and swallow it whole. I went out when I wanted and with whom I wanted. I dressed according to my moods and came home when I felt like it. I couldn't begin tell you what a good time I had. In the beginning, I let myself be taken advantage of often. That served me well, experience being a strong asset. I learned to know my nature and my limits.

It was then that Bakary came into my life. He was the breath of fresh air I so needed. I discovered love and the happiness that comes with it. I no longer wanted but one thing: to spend the rest of my life with him. In fact, I don't believe it was even a decision, it just went without saying.

My parents, informed by I don't know what blabbermouth, were caught off guard. As usual! But I can tell you, you'd better not mess with me! Good Lord! Just leave me alone! My life is all I've got, and it's mine to manage as I see fit. Even God can't control it. My father, whose job didn't allow him to travel much, nearly had a heart attack more than once on the telephone. As for mother, she often took a plane to try to reclaim her daughter who was lost in the clutches of some loser. I stood up to my father, and she tried to smooth ruffled feathers, as they say. She cried or whined, caught between the hammer and the anvil. Nothing to be done. It pained me, but what did they expect? What could I do? Sacrifice my life to make them happy? Well, no! No, no and no! No, mom and dad, you are how you are, so let me be too! My self-respect drove me to find a part-time job. Cashier in a supermarket. My parents could keep their pennies for their old age. From then on, the bridges were burned. I had kept the apartment though. They had bought it and put it in my name. The last straw was when I lived there with Bakary. That really showed them!

When we returned to Dakar, we crashed in an apartment a friend had rented us. Bakary had found work as a radio DJ and was looking for musicians to form a group. His salary wasn't very high, and my sculptures didn't exactly sell like hot cakes. We had just enough to survive on without touching our savings.

We bought a little house by the sea. The whole story starts with that house. For thirteen years no one had lived in it. The man who had built it died a week after he moved in, preceding his wife by only a few days. It was rented subsequently to two other people who died one after the other, deaths you might call rather mysterious. No one dared to live there because it was, supposedly, haunted. It was called 'The House of Leuk Dawour'. Rumor had it that it was the *rab* who caused this series of deaths. No one slept there for longer than twenty days. These rumors, far from discouraging us, helped us to buy it at a very reasonable price. We started by renovating it.

I must point out, however, that the first time I saw that house, it presented a very somber appearance that unnerved me a little. On the walls, dilapidated and frightfully veined with strange fissures, I perceived the deep traces of a rather sinister mystery. A cold and oppressive sense of loneliness reigned there. It was the only house whose back was turned towards the ocean to open onto a cul-de-sac. There was a balcony, however, where attentive eyes and ears could follow the discourse of the waves sweeping the rocky beach. The sea freshness entered the four bedrooms, two of which were on the ground floor. The kitchen was spacious, as was the bathroom. It certainly wasn't a beautiful villa, but it suited us. I just wanted 'my place'. The days were long past when I used to complain over the slightest lack of comfort. I had finally turned my back on the sordid bourgeoisie.

While the construction work followed its course, I ventured to visit our future residence alone one night. In fact, I was really seeking refuge there. Bakary and I had had a fight. One of those fights that are part of any couple's life.

You know, living with other people isn't easy. Even with the one you love with all your heart, sometimes you need a little alone time, to just be one-on-one with yourself. At these moments, the other person's presence can become irritating, unbearable, and then anything can give rise to a conflict . . . In short, I just needed a little air.

I had rolled some joints carefully saved in my handbag, where there was also a packet of Camelia Sport (my favorite cigarettes), a bottle of whisky, and pepper spray in case any little thugs hassled me. It was, I think, two o'clock in the morning, maybe even three. It was my first time going to those premises at such a late hour. I had parked my car in front of the gate.

Alone in the courtyard, leaning against a wall, my joint of Lopito in one hand, my Johnny Walker in the other, I thought about some things and about others. Simply put, I daydreamed. I was chilled out.

At a given moment, something extraordinary took place. A wind of an unheard-of force burst into the house. Everything started shaking, and me along with it. Although there was a full moon, the sky found a way of putting on its darkest cloak and the agitation of the earth started to compete with that of the sea. Everything moved around me, even the piece of cardboard on which I was sitting. The wind materialized and took on shapes and colors so marvelous that I was sorry I hadn't brought my camera. I was surprised, astonished and fascinated, but I wasn't scared. I was stoned, and I calmly attended the spectacle that was presented to me. The wind let out insane howls that covered the deafening groans of the kamikaze waves crashing against the rocks. It entered the building, making the doors and windows slam shut, then returned to whirl furiously in the courtyard. Finally it took on a distinct shape before my eyes: the silhouette of a horse. More than a silhouette, it was a very real horse, an all-white horse whose shiny coat gleamed as brightly as its blood-red eyes. It had only one leg beneath its torso and it moved with little hops. No question, it was Leuk Dawour Mbaye, just as the old people described him. My grandmother used to tell me that in her youth she would huddle up in bed at night, frozen with fear, for she heard the 'Clop! Clop! Clop!' of Leuk Dawour patrolling the streets.

I was in the presence of the one and undeniable master of Dakar, he who, since time immemorial, had had a stranglehold on the city. I was seized with fright, paralyzed. I didn't dare to make any movement, not even to blink, despite all the dust there was in the courtyard. I sweated in my T-shirt and torn jeans to the point where you'd have said I had taken a shower fully dressed. Cold sweat. I watched Leuk Dawour rise up towards the sky and loom over my head in an enormous and impressive firework display. Suddenly, I heard a whinnying quite near me that made me jump. I turned around. There was nothing but a wooden ladder placed against the cracking wall. It had seemed to me, however, that the whinnying came from that ladder. I didn't have time to recover from my astonishment. I saw the ladder shake, as if under the influence of an electrical shock, and sink slowly into the earth, provoking horrible sounds like bones cracking. If I'd had the courage, I would have pinched myself to assure myself that I wasn't dreaming. I saw the ladder descend until it was completely swallowed up by the earth. Leuk Dawour also disappeared. Then, nothing. It became calm once more, a calm disturbed intermittently by the sorrowful cries of the dying waves.

'Bizarre! Bizarre!' I said to myself. I stumbled out of the courtyard. I was sober enough for anything, except driving a car. I went to a main street to hail a taxi. And if Leuk Dawour had disguised himself as a cab driver? I had all the anxiety in the world, but I didn't have a choice. Everything came out all right, fortunately. Nonetheless, I was sure that the *rab* of Dakar wasn't going to let me go so easily. I felt his gaze at my back. He was following me . . .

Bakary was sleeping. I undressed and lay down beside him. I had never squeezed him so tight in my arms as on that night. He had woken up several times to ask if I was all right. I responded, 'Yes.' I didn't want to tell him . . . Anyway, he would have told me that I had hallucinated. For some time, he hadn't stopped telling me I smoked too many joints and drank too much . . . Ah! I was 'in a state' (pregnant), as they say here. Two months pregnant.

When I woke up the next day, Bakary wasn't beside me. He had left word on the table to say that he was going to visit his family in Mbour and would probably return late that night. I had known about this trip for a long time. But what he really wanted to say in the message was in the final words: 'Have a good day. A big hug from me. I love you.'

I took the bus to see the 'premises' again. The workers hadn't yet arrived. They didn't have set hours. They began when they wanted, which is to say late. I made a tour of the house. Nothing seemed out of the ordinary. Everything was in order. Even the ladder was in its place. I saw my nearly empty bottle and my stubs stuck in the sand. I took my car and returned home, totally confused.

I didn't feel well. I was nauseous and had terrible stomach pains and discharges. My fetus wound up in the toilet. It was clearly a blow from Leuk Dawour. How was I going to tell Bakary? Oh what a day!

I felt so bad that I had to disconnect my telephone and go to bed very early, after having chugged a bottle of whisky and lit several joints. I needed a pick-me-up.

The terrifying image of the one-legged horse haunted me. I was tormented by the *rab* of Dakar. Why had he left me alive? When was he going to show up again? To reassure myself, I had gotten into bed with a little pistol under my pillow. It was a Raven 25 semi-automatic that my father, worried about my safety, had given me. I slept, my finger on the trigger. Let's just say I dozed off . . .

I couldn't tell you what time it was. All I remember is that at a given moment I felt Leuk Dawour's gaze upon me. He pushed his muzzle towards my face. Smoke came from his nostrils. But before he could touch me, I had fired. He collapsed at the foot of the bed, giving an inhuman cry. Blood flowed onto the floor as a cigarette burned my sheets. I had just eliminated the *rab* of Dakar . . .

Since that night, I haven't stopped repeating to the psychiatrist, every time I'm sitting across from him, looking him straight in the eyes: 'Yes, I killed Leuk Dawour Mbaye, but it was in self defense.'

Translated from the French by James D. Jenkins

Frithjof Spalder

The White Cormorant

Unlike its Scandinavian neighbors Sweden, Finland, Denmark, and even to a small extent Iceland, Norway apparently has no contemporary horror scene to speak of, seemingly eschewing the supernatural in favor of crime novels by writers like Jo Nesbø and Karin Fossum. But excellent horror stories and supernatural tales do exist in Norwegian literature – if you're willing to dig a little bit to find them. As discussed in the foreword, the Norwegian thriller writer André Bjerke (who dabbled a little in the supernatural himself, as in his novel De dødes tjern *[The Lake of the Dead], which reads like a Norwegian episode of* Scooby-Doo*) unearthed nearly two dozen rare Norwegian ghost and horror stories from the 19th and 20th centuries. In our opinion, the best of them was the following tale by* FRITHJOF SPALDER (*b. 1933*), originally published in 1971 in the collection* Jernjomfruen *[The Iron Maiden], named after the medieval torture device. Though Spalder's tales were received with appreciation by connoisseurs of the genre, they seem not to have found a wide public, perhaps because they were so different from anything else being published in Norwegian literature at the time. 'The White Cormorant' is an elegant, perfectly constructed little tale that we're delighted to present to a wider audience of readers.*

IT WAS EVENING BY THE TIME I CAME OUT OF THE TAVERN and went down the dusty road that led to the harbor where our boats were. It was almost dark, and it had started to drizzle. I could smell the wet dust from the road filling the air. I began to walk slowly downhill, a little tipsy from the beer I had drunk. Fortunately I had brought my jacket with me, and I put it on and turned the collar up to my ears. It was not particularly cold, but it is nice to walk with your collar like that, especially if it is a good collar, like this one, and if you have something to think about. And I had something to think about.

Our village, Ballyheigue, is small and lies on the west coast of Ireland, nestled in a narrow bay. It consists of twelve or thirteen small cottages and a tavern, a road that goes inwards toward the countryside, and one that leads down to the harbor. There is nothing else. Almost all of us make our living from the sea.

A couple miles further south lies the great cliff named Sybil Point. It is a high, steep cliff of weathered black granite that lies like a clenched fist out in the sea, connected to the mainland by a low, narrow ridge where some scraggly grass and windblown bushes grow, like a hairy wrist.

Sybil Point.

I remember well that one of the old, bearded chaps at the tavern, after having gotten good and drunk on the strong beer, had coughed and said anyone who sailed round the cliff must be either one hell of a sailor or else downright mad, and the others had nodded, mumbling. He had grabbed my scarf with large, clenched fists and pressed my face down to his own so that I could smell the beery stench from his sagging mouth and see how blurry his watery blue eyes were.

'Listen here, my boy,' he had said in a drunkard's voice. 'I'll tell you something. There isn't a single man here who manages to travel past Sybil Point unless he's one hell of a sailor – or downright mad!'

He looked at me for a long time after saying this, long enough for me to feel uncomfortable. The others remained quiet. He swayed before me and stared as though he expected a challenge on the spot. I kept completely silent and merely looked intently into his darkening eyes. Then he released his grip, which by the way was solid enough, and turned away with a contemptuous sound.

It was that contemptuous sound I thought of as I walked, kicking at the stones on the way to the harbor. Well, all right. He had been drunk. What are a drunkard's words? Lies or truth? Maybe the only truth. I stood on the wet planks of the pier and looked out over the forest of masts that tilted and pitched up and down before me in the weak swells. It had grown dark, mostly because of the woolly gray clouds that hung over the sea to the west and which now silently sent their fine drizzle down over the harbor. Out at the jetty where the lighthouse was, I could see a strip of lighter cloud-cover. It was possible there would be fine weather tomorrow. And if it was fine weather . . .

Why not?

I was young and strong and full of daring. Why shouldn't it go well for me? Who was to say that I wouldn't manage it? Now I suddenly saw a challenge in it, that challenge I had hesitated to answer up at the tavern. This was the only proper course. A quiet, deliberate decision, taken alone, without provocation. Decisions made under pressure are almost always worthless.

I went over to my own large sailboat where it was moored with the sail taken down and the gaff tied to the boom, as is the custom here. It was a spacious but slender sea boat, thirty-two feet long, built for rough and stormy seas. I bent down and pulled a little at the mooring rope. Tightened it, felt the movement in the boat. It answered with some small gurgles from the bow where beneath the nailed boards the dark water lay.

I stood on the wharf for a long time and stared out

towards the shiny sea surface that lay there like molten lead, and the stars emerged one by one in the steel-blue heavens.

I was up very early the next morning to get the equipment ready for the trip. A sense of anticipation made my skin tingle as I got dressed. The sun was about to break through the foliage over the forest-clad ridge behind the cottage. I went out on the steps, took a breath of the fresh morning air and saw the harbor far below like a big U, with boats lying along the protruding wharfs.

It was completely silent.

Down at the tavern and the cottages behind it, smoke had begun to emerge from the first chimneys. I took my watch from my pants pocket and flipped open the thin silver cover. Quarter to four. Soon the crews of the lobster boats would set out after their traps. I went in and made breakfast, packed some rations in my bag and pulled out what clothes I had for stormy weather.

The grass was still wet and the air clear and pleasant to inhale after the previous day's rain. I sang to myself as I walked rather quickly down the slope to the harbor, which the sun had now tinged with a reddish glow.

I had almost reached the wharf, where the large granite rocks meet the planks, when I stopped. In the glistening wet grass to my left, halfway down in a ditch, sat a man. He sat so motionless that he almost blended in with the ground. It was the drunk from the night before at the tavern. He sat and looked straight ahead, didn't move. He didn't seem to have seen me. I walked away and stopped above and opposite him so that he could not avoid catching sight of me. He sat with his legs astride, his hands on the ground. I could see that he was as drunk as the night before, if not more so.

'Hello!' I called out. He sat totally motionless. I called again, a little louder, 'Hello!'

It was as if he shivered a little just then, his face tensed up, and he ran his tongue over his lips. Then he saw me.

'I hear you,' he said with a tongue that was thick and stiff. His eyes widened and then contracted. 'I recognize you . . .' He squinted up at me with dull eyes. 'And now you're going to sail to Sybil – to Sybil Point!' His mouth drew into a twisted grin, his chest heaved as though he were going to vomit, but then I realized he was sitting there laughing, laughing with a hoarse, objectionable sound that quickly turned into a violent cough. My sack had suddenly become heavy to hold, and I let it fall onto the road with a thud. The old man's breath came out in squeaks between coughs. Then he pointed a bony finger at me and called hoarsely – 'You're going to Sybil . . . to Sybil . . . she . . .'

She?

I took a step forward and bent down.

'What's that you say, old man? She who?'

His voice grew weak from fatigue, and he tilted his head back as he looked at me and whispered:

'Sybil . . .'

'Who is Sybil?' I said. 'There's no one by that name here. Sybil Point is a place.'

He coughed and drew a creaking breath.

'Beware . . . the cormorants . . .'

His eyes closed again and his voice died away.

I realized I had gotten worked up by what he had said. My blood pulsed faster, and I felt a strange shiver run down my back. I tried to shake him to wake him up. It was useless. He lay there reclining in the wet grass with his legs spread out to the side and his head leaning backward. It was impossible to get any more out of him.

I got up and walked over to the boathouse, where I had hung the sail out to dry. It was rough and thick and I half dragged it with me over the wharf down to the boat. There

I secured it. Afterwards I found an old sack in the boathouse, which I laid over the sleeping drunk in the ditch. Then I untied the mooring ropes, set the tiller in place, and rowed the heavy sailboat out of the mooring place and out of the harbor, past the jetty. There I raised the square gaff sail and remained adrift, waiting on the breeze that always comes from the west at that time of day.

After a while it filled the gray-white sail, and the sea began to wash along the bow.

I sat good and deep down in the steering hatch and held the tiller with one hand. I had lashed the mainsail, for now a brisk side wind was blowing that made the craft keel, with the boom and the gaff hanging out over the gunwale. I had brought a bag of apples with my provisions and I picked one up and began to eat.

I could not help thinking again about the old drunkard. It was the second time I had bumped into him, and both times he had talked about Sybil Point. Or rather – hadn't he talked about a 'her'? A woman? He had said something else too:

'Beware . . .'

It goes without saying of course that his mind wasn't altogether sound.

It had gotten colder, and the fog had drifted in from the sea. I could hardly see land out there.

The sun had traveled half its arc over the sky and hung like a yellow paper disk in the mist, when I noticed that the sail flapped weakly a couple of times and finally hung dead from the gaff. A whirlwind sketched a dark ripple over the sea. I noticed too that the swells had become bigger and stronger. I craned my neck and scouted ahead. Far up ahead, as at the oceanfront, I could see a dark clump formed against the colorless sky, like a knot on the horizon. That had to be it – the cliff.

The sky above me had all at once gone gray and dark like an arched vault. The seagulls, which had followed in my wake since I set out, had disappeared. I looked back. The horizon could no longer be seen. The swells bobbed me up and down like a cork on the sea, and the water was dark and smooth like oil. The wind was totally dead here, and the sail hung heavy and quiet. But I was born and raised on the sea and I knew what that meant.

I locked the rudder and climbed up to the mainsail. I had barely got the halyard lowered when it broke loose. The first gust almost sent me overboard, but I hooked myself securely in the stays as the wind ripped and tore at my clothes, and with rapid movements I made the ropes secure. Then the wind came howling over me.

The little boat tossed wildly, quivering under the violent wind pressure and keeling until the gunwale was all the way down to the water's surface. The sun had completely disappeared. Breaking waves heaved over the deck, and wind and sea and rain and salt spray were like a violent whirlwind around me. A mighty bolt of lightning ripped the sky into a network of blue fire, larger and more intense than I had ever seen before, and the thunder came almost simultaneously, a deafening bang like God's own voice, and the whole time the whistling and howling of the wind, which sent the boat like a sliver of wood along the lashing sea. I sat stiff-legged pressed up against the bulkhead and held onto the rudder with all my strength. I was soaking wet and almost breathless from the wind and breaking waves, and the oiled wood of the rudder was wet and slippery. My leg muscles trembled and my arms had begun to cramp.

Then I saw it.

I had gotten there before I had realized it. The boat suddenly careened more than usual, and I saw now that I hadn't spotted it before because the sail had been in the way the whole time.

Before me rose a giant of a granite block, dark, worn and gnarled by erosion. It went steeply down into the sea opposite me. Down in the foaming surf I could make out sharp and jagged stones that time had broken loose from the cliff wall. The sea was white at the foot of the mountain, and the water broke with a thunderous sound. In a flash I thought about why the pointed stones hadn't been worn smooth by the water, why they rose like sharp knives towards the sky though they were certainly hundreds of years old, and that was the only thing I had time to think, for suddenly I discovered, with a growing sense of fear, that I was too close – I was far too close!

I was headed at whirlwind speed straight towards the granite cliff!

I tugged like a madman at the tiller. I had the wind from the starboard tack, the boat had spun off a little because I hadn't had time to slacken the jib; it was way too big. I tried to go against the wind. The thundering from the cliff wall was deafening and the breaking waves tossed crushingly against the sharp stones. All at once I recalled the drunkard's words:

'A hell of a sailor – or downright mad . . .'

I felt the cold sweat drip off me. It had gotten dark like in a cellar. The granite wall rose up higher and higher as I was mercilessly pushed towards the diabolical stone teeth, and I cried out in the storm, cried out in fear when I looked death in the eyes among the crashing breakers. A prayer poured from my lips. Then the bow fell off. There was a violent strain on the leaden sail, and the whole boat trembled during the maneuver. I pulled at the rudder with all my strength, my muscles were like knots under the oilskin. There was a cracking in the rigging.

Then!

It banged like a rifle shot when the turnbuckle on one of the starboard stays snapped like a violin string. There was a crunching sound in the mast and I watched open-mouthed and in fear as the timber split and splintered, saw the storm pull sail and mast and rigging overboard as if it had been a handful of leaves. I was almost blind from the rain and saltwater, but I knew what I had to do and grabbed the ax from the steering hatch and tried to cut through what was left of the rigging. It was too late. A mighty wave seized the boat and sent it sidelong against the cliff, and I sat and waited for the impact that I knew must come.

There was a crushing sound like the jaws of a wild beast against thin bone. The shock knocked me almost senseless, and I hung with my torso over the gunwale as I struggled to keep myself onboard. Then another impact, and it was as if a giant's hand gripped me and whirled me round and round – it was all just froth and foam and sea, smashed bits of wood and rope. I felt a powerful blow to my head that half deprived me of consciousness at the same time as I felt something clutching my wrist. In my half-conscious condition I thought I had gotten my hand caught in some rope and struggled desperately to get it loose. The grip only grew tighter. Everything was going black. Red and white figures danced and whirled before my eyes, and I was drawn into a maelstrom of water and light and darkness. I only hoped that death would come quickly . . .

I was past the breakers. They were behind me, and I was lying on my back in a calm eddy. Above me the sky was yellow. Bewildered, I tried to find firm ground underneath me and discovered I could manage to stand. The wind was no longer blowing. The surf went thundering towards the stones, and I could see the white foam over the serrated rocks, but where I stood it was still. I tottered shakily up onto some flat stones up on the beach and lay down exhausted with my head resting on my arms.

I do not know how long I lay there on the rocks. It was still twilight when I opened my eyes, and the sea was just as heavy out there. It might have been a couple of hours, or a minute. I got up stiff and sore and tried to make out the wreckage. It wasn't to be seen. I suddenly noticed that I was frozen and shivering. I turned to go further around the cliffside and try to make my way inland, and it was then that I saw her.

She stood only a few meters from me, barefoot on the smooth stones. Totally still. Her face was white, and her hair, which was long and shiny and black like a raven's wing, waved lightly in the weak breeze. She was wearing a dress that looked as though it were made of white linen. I stood motionless, without making a sound. Then I felt my legs beginning to move of their own accord, and I walked, but with steps that were not my own, up to where she stood. I could now see her face quite clearly.

Her face was almond-shaped. The dark eyes shone as with an inner glow, as if her head were translucent, and they stared right at me. Her mouth was pale but had a softness that I had never seen before, and which is not common among our women.

'Come,' she said in a low, melodic voice as she extended her hand toward me. I took it, almost without knowing it. It was warm and soft. She turned halfway around and signaled that she wanted to go upwards toward the cliff wall. I followed her, for I had no will, and the grip on my hand was firm and determined. Together we went upwards along a path that wound along the cliffside in a steep ascent. She walked beside me, upright, with her head raised and that black hair waving and fluttering behind her. I looked at her from the side as we went up, and she turned her face toward me and smiled. It was a peculiar smile. It was half as though she were crying, but at the same time the smile reflected a thousand years of happiness, as if she were seeing something she had always sought . . . and found. Her eyes glittered, and it was again as though I could see straight through them and out into the starry sky on the other side. In the same moment I knew that I belonged to her.

We had come high up the cliff wall. The path, which was sufficiently broad for us both, was a mountain ledge, and below me I could see the surf thundering against the rocks. Further out the sea was rough and turbulent. The sky was still yellow, with a golden tinge. I was surprised that I wasn't dizzy. It was equally odd, I didn't understand it, but up here where we were walking I couldn't feel any wind. The air was still, the only thing that revealed we were in motion was her black hair fluttering like a mane across her pale face. I asked:

'Why doesn't the wind blow up here?'

She turned towards me again.

'Haven't you had enough wind for today?' she said with that low, slightly hoarse voice. I could see the gleam of her white teeth. I nodded.

'Yes.' I noticed that she hadn't answered my question, but I didn't ask again, without knowing why.

She stopped suddenly. In the cliff wall, with an opening as tall as a full-grown man, was a cavern. She motioned to me to continue inwards, and half senseless I stepped in through that archway that was formed of granite and time itself. She let go of my hand for a moment and walked over to the cliff wall, which rose dark and close in front of us. She moved her hand, and it was as though blue flames came forth and illuminated the walls – small points of light – like with St. Elmo's fire. I stood spellbound and saw her delicate body walk in between the rough walls, while lights were lit where she touched the mountain with her hands. Her whole white figure was surrounded with a bluish aura, and a few times it looked as though she were transparent.

There was no roof, nor any walls or floor, it was just her and me and the blue lights around us that twinkled and shone weakly, flickered and faded away, only to emerge again from the depths.

Then she came towards me, and I could see her face, which was pale like a moonbeam, and her eyes were like fire from an inner world when she invited me to lie down on a bed of woven rushes on the floor.

She was mine that night in the granite cave. Who she was and what she was doing there were beyond my thoughts, all I know is that she gave herself to me on a carpet of soft reeds, woven by fingers that also were caressing my neck. All at once I understood what love was, what I had lost by not having known it before, and what I knew I had always longed for. I loved her from the depths of my young heart. She was mine. I gave her all the youthful affection I had, there in that cave, as the lights sparkled and flickered. I could barely see her face, a pale surface with two dark openings into eternity. Her eyes were like the night itself. I knew at once what her name was . . .

She was my Sybil.

Was she Sybil? Was it possible that a person of that name really existed? I don't know. But for me she was Sybil. And I loved her.

It was morning. The air was gray and cold outside the cave entrance. Far off I could hear the whisper of the surf. I felt cold and wet, and my head was heavy after the night's sleep. I turned my head to look at my beloved.

There was no one there.

My hand lay on the woven grass, which was cold from the morning dew that drifted into the cave.

I got up slowly, trembling, still stiff and lightheaded after the shipwreck, and tottered dizzily towards the exit. I remembered vaguely the dream I had had just before waking. It was clearly etched in my brain like a relief sculpture under the sun. A swarm of cormorants, a sailing, flying, flapping flock of black birds. And one of them had been white, it had stood on the edge of the precipice at the cave opening and stretched its wings out broadly and fallen – fallen towards the sea surface, and in its fall I had seen that it was my Sybil . . .

I stood in the opening and felt the moist air drawn into my lungs as I shivered with cold. I bent over, looked over the edge and downwards.

In the same moment I felt my chest tighten around my heart and a wild pain of anguish shot through my body. My eyes glimpsed something white on the surface of the water; there was a white garment washing in towards the rock wall.

My lungs brought forth a scream that rose up in my throat and dissolved in the fog beyond.

'Sybil!'

My hands got cut and scraped as I clung to the rough stones in a desperate attempt to get down to the water quickly. My feet stumbled on countless protrusions and the whole time I was whispering her name, over and over again, as I hoped – hoped by all that was holy – that I had been mistaken.

It took some time nonetheless before I reached sea level at the mountain wall. Meanwhile the tidewater had done its work. The white thing had drifted farther out, almost all the way out among the sharp cliff rocks, I could barely see it when it came up to the surface several times. Finally it was totally gone.

I stood with my empty hands stretched out before me, staring at that point between the rocks. The fog rolled in waves towards me.

I heard my own scream echo from the granite wall and hover tremblingly in the air where the cormorants sailed on black wings. And I swung at them when they came over me, around me, and behind me. They sat along the path up on the mountain wall, packed tightly together, and highest up, in the middle of the cave's opening, sat the largest of them all, and it was only its head that was black like the others', for the rest of the bird was white like the whitest garment. It lifted off with a heavy beating of its wings and sailed around up there until its wings filled the sky, then came lower and closer and stretched out until the tips of its white arms touched the horizon, and the whole time its eyes were on me, clear, dark – eyes of crystal, it was as if I could see right through them and out into the gray fog on the other side.

I don't know from which direction I came home. Did I wander past Dingle and Kerry over to Ballyheigue? That's what I must have done. I remember I saw hills and mountains that at first seemed to be quite near, while in the next moment they were far off, and then again close to me. I registered that I was walking, that my feet were carrying me forward, but several times I was tired and lay down on the ground and stretched my arms out to catch the rain that fell gently and softly down over me. One time I lay my cheek against a flower, because it was there and I was there, down on the slope where the moisture from the grass soaked in through my clothes and lay like cold fingers around my shoulders.

The old drunkard from the tavern has disappeared. I never

see him anymore. They say that in his intoxication he walked off the pier one night as the sea was foaming white and the rain was whipping against our windows. If that's true, it's unfortunate. He was my friend. We were often at the tavern together. It also happened sometimes that we would wake up together in the morning in some ditch or other, arm in arm like two lovers. Now and then – it was quite strange – I had the feeling that we were of the same age. And now he's gone. I'm alone. But the beer is good here, and I have a great thirst to quench.

A young man came here one evening. He boasted that he wanted to sail around Sybil Point. The silly little fool. He's full of youthful stupidity. I warned him that night. It didn't help.

I saw him early today too. He was coming down along the road towards the wharf with a sack in his hand. It was bright and clear and the sun had just risen. I had sat in the tavern all night, and the intoxication hadn't totally worn off yet, and I was sitting in the grass down by the sea when he came towards me.

Translated from the Norwegian by James D. Jenkins

Yvette Tan

All the Birds

There is quite a bit of Filipino horror fiction being published in both English and Tagalog, probably not surprising given the over 500 often horrific creatures that have been documented in Philippine mythology, from the shapeshifting aswang to the hideous, vampire-like manananggal to the terrifying half-man, half-horse tikbalang. YVETTE TAN, one of the Philippines' most popular and successful modern-day horror writers, has published stories in both Tagalog and English, with most of the latter collected in Waking the Dead and other Horror Stories *(2009). The following story first appeared in the anthology of Filipino horror* All That Darkness Allows *in 2016. Like many of Tan's stories, it incorporates elements from Filipino mythology and folklore, exploiting the frightening possibilities of those legends to craft an unsettling modern-day horror story.*

ANNE CAUGHT ME OUTSIDE THE HUT, fiddling with my phone, trying to get a decent signal.

'You're up early,' she said, arms crossed tight against her robe, almost straining at the fabric.

'Just telling Tim I'm okay,' I said. 'Signal sucks here.'

She made a face. 'Of course you're okay. You're here. Why wouldn't you be?'

The signal held. I sent my SMS. I looked up at her. 'You shouldn't be out here.'

'You weren't inside when I woke. I got worried.'

There was a caw. A crow had joined the birds gathered in the front yard. There were a few when I arrived – birds have always been a fixture in these parts – but their number had swelled over the course of my visit, almost tripling by the time the crow arrived. They sat on nearby branches, nestled in the yard, worried at the bushes. There were different kinds. Maya birds, mynah birds, swallows, shrikes, kites. Others I didn't recognize. It was chaos some of the time, the flurry of feathers and the squawking as they chased each other around in play. But most of the time, they were silent. They didn't seem to be preying on each other, which unnerved me almost just as much as their being there in the first place.

The other birds made space for the noisy newcomer, who, after a few more caws, settled in.

We watched the whole thing in silence. I got up and gently nudged her back inside. 'I'll make breakfast.'

I have been here for a week now. I came as soon as I could, after I got the letter. Anne is sick, it said. What it meant was, Anne is dying.

And so I went on leave from work, kissed my fiancé goodbye, and traveled back to the place I grew up in, to see the friend who thinks I abandoned her.

Anne lives in her family home a ways from the barrio. It is small and neat and smells of dried leaves. We used to hang out here a lot. I practically grew up here. My parents worked abroad. My aunt took care of me, but you could tell that she would rather go to the salon or go on dates than watch over her sister's kid. Anne's aunt didn't mind having me over, as long as we were quiet because, 'The plants don't like noise.'

Anne and I learned a lot from her aunt. How to cultivate a garden, how to tell which plants were edible, which herbs cured what. Anne and I were inseparable. I don't blame her when she took it very badly when my parents offered to send me to college in Manila and I said yes.

We wrote each other at first. Always snail mail, because Anne wasn't comfortable with technology. Their hut didn't even have electricity, even though it had been available in the barrio forever. They were weird like that. But my letters got shorter and her replies got more bitter until we stopped writing altogether. Tim and I had just started dating then, so I didn't think much of it when I should have. I wasn't much of a friend.

Turned out she had been ill for a while. She had always been sickly, but she got steadily worse after her aunt passed away and she tried to keep pace with responsibilities. At first she could, and then she couldn't. It was my mom, now retired, who found her sprawled at the foot of her hut. She refused to go to a hospital. She asked for me.

Breakfast is instant coffee and champorado. We had salted duck eggs and rice the day before, and were now craving something salty-sweet. I pour evaporated milk into my, by regular standards, extremely sweet coffee before adding some to my chocolate porridge as well.

Anne wrinkles her nose distastefully at the amount of sugar and dairy I mix into my coffee.

'What do you want for lunch?' I ask as I mix my champorado, cooling it as fast as I can so I can eat it right away.

She laughs. 'How Pinoy of you to be talking about the next meal even before you've eaten this one.'

Times like this, she doesn't seem sick. Times like this, when her eyes sparkle as she laughs from her belly, I tell myself that she isn't really sick, that I am just visiting, that I will go home when she is better, back to Tim, back to work, back to my life far, far away from here.

But nowadays, one laugh is all it takes before she doubles up, coughing, hacking, trying to expel something, the demon that lives within, the one that courses through her veins and consumes her from the inside. I catch her as she bends over the table.

We eat in silence.

'I don't want to die.'

The words were uttered under her breath as we sat on the edge of the hut, watching the birds. There was almost a ridiculous amount of them in the yard now. It was almost funny.

I take her hand and squeeze it. She traces her other hand down my face.

'They're waiting, you know,' she said. 'For me.'

'Don't you think they're overdoing it just a little?'

'I know you're here because you pity me.'

I take my hand away, hurt, angry. 'You don't get to talk to me like that,' I say. 'You don't get to push me away.' I get up and go inside.

There is always something to do at Anne's. Picking herbs, drying herbs, preparing tinctures, preparing teas. Seeing to the vegetable garden, seeing to the chickens, gathering firewood and water, the general upkeep of a hut that's slowly falling apart as if it was a reflection of its owner, who was slowly wasting away.

Out here, in the middle of nowhere, it is as easy to keep busy as it is to do nothing.

And there is always food. Anne and I, we're eaters. We eat when we're stressed, we eat when we're bored. We eat when we want to avoid things. I distract myself by cooking, which I have to do anyway. I munch on some cashews as I make dinner. I've been eating a lot lately. I'm always hungry, always reaching for a meal, a snack. Anne, meanwhile, has lost some appetite, but not enough so that it's alarming.

When we're not keeping house or making sure herbs are stocked, we're making food. She chops, I cook. It's a rhythm we developed by accident, because neither of us can stand being still. It also helps fill the silences when we argue, an occurrence that has become alarming in its frequency.

We don't talk until after dinner, when she takes my hand and says she is sorry. We hug. She gives me a peck on the lips; I let her. We lie beside each other, and I stroke her hair until she falls asleep. Then I go out to send Tim an SMS.

'Tao po!'

The call comes at about five in the morning. Manong Albert, the baker.

Tao po. I'm a person. I'm not a beast or bird or monster. I am a person. I am a baker. Are you home? I need your help.

I check to see if the noise has woken Anne, but she is sleeping soundly. I put on a jacket and see to the visitor.

Five a.m. is still dark in these parts. The air is chilly and has yet to warm up. I find Manong at the entrance of the gate, battery operated lantern in hand, eyeing the yard full of birds warily. Most of the birds are asleep; you can hear them snoring very softly. The few that are awake are silent. They watch the intruder from their places on the ground, their perches on the trees.

Manong is visibly glad to see me. He calls out my name in relief. 'Avery!'

'Good morning, Manong.' I walk towards the gate.

He looks worried. 'I know Anne's sick but – '

'I'm filling in for her for a while. What do you need?'

'George, you remember my youngest boy? He has a toothache. It's been bothering him all night.'

I give him a disapproving look. 'We have a dentist in the barangay, you know.'

'Ay, it's not the same,' he says good-naturedly. 'You know

that. Don't let working in Manila make you think otherwise.'

I sigh. 'Let me get something for him. Want to wait inside?'

He eyes the birds. 'I'll wait out here.'

It doesn't take long to find what he needs. I wrap it up and hand it over. 'Take Selo to the dentist as soon as you can, okay?'

Manong smiles. 'Hay, ija. They don't know what Anne does. What you do.'

'I'm only here on vacation. I leave as soon as Anne's better.'

'I know, ija.' He hands me two paper bags. One of them is comfortably warm. 'For your breakfast,' he says. 'Thank you for your help.'

We have the pan de sal and Star margarine Manong Albert brought for breakfast. Anne was surprised.

'I can't believe I slept through that,' she says miserably.

'It wasn't anything I couldn't handle.'

'I know. It's just that I used to wake at the littlest sound. Now I sleep through everything.'

'You need to rest to get better.'

'I know,' she sighs. 'It's just that I'm asleep longer and longer each day. I'm afraid that one day, I'll just forget to wake up.'

The birds come when Anne's asleep. They fly in softly and never leave. You'd think that this would result in a dirty, bloody mess, but the yard is clean. They eat and hunt and shit elsewhere. They pick the air clean of insects, and I swear – swear – that they keep the outside of the hut clean as well. They are usually silent. It is the newcomers who are noisy at first, but they calm down eventually. They learn to wait.

Dinner is steamed vegetables – okra, eggplant, string beans – with bagoong and steamed white rice. We have Coke because Anne is feeling celebratory at not having coughed all day, at not having buckled.

'Do you love him?'

The question comes out of the blue, though I've been dreading it ever since I arrived. Anne had never brought up Tim until now.

'What kind of question is that?'

She shrugs.

I don't answer.

Anne and I, we have this thing. She likes to hold my hand and bury her face in my hair – things friends don't normally do. Sometimes I let her, but sometimes, I pull my hand away, move my head, even though I want to keep them there, even though it is comfortable, even though it feels right. I like to think that we would have made a good pair, but I had things I wanted to do in life, and I knew that I would have to leave home to do them, something that Anne was never willing to do.

The barrio had always been good to me, but growing up, I felt that we had nothing to offer each other, that my calling lay elsewhere. I wasn't built for a small town. I wasn't sure what I was going to do, only that whatever it was, it wouldn't be here.

I look away, willing a change in subject. She is still staring at me when I look back.

'What's it to you?' I ask, meeting her gaze.

'Nothing,' she mumbles. 'Just making conversation.'

'Dr. Vera is coming by tomorrow,' I say. 'He says he may know what's making you sick.'

Anne smirks. 'We all know what's making me sick.'

'No, we don't.'

'Yes, we do. Everyone does, even though they won't say it.'

'This isn't some ancient family curse, Anne.'
She looks hurt. 'It isn't a curse.'
'I'm sorry.'
We don't talk the whole night after.

I really like Dr. Vera. He's smart and funny and really enjoys his work, even if it sometimes means trekking through the forest to see out-of-the-way patients like Anne. He grew up in the barrio. He's older, old enough that by the time we were kids he had gone off to med school, so we weren't familiar enough to call him by his first name when he returned.

He'd been here a couple of times before I arrived, administering tests, trying to get Anne to take medicine, trying to tell her that there shouldn't be anything wrong with her, that it's all in her head. He doesn't understand it, how she can be ill. All her vital signs are normal; there is nothing wrong with her. He does not understand how a perfectly healthy person can be wasting away in front of him, coughing hard, throwing up black bile. He wants to study her, publish her case in a journal. He knows none of us will let him.

He speaks to me outside the hut. The birds watch us, watch him.

'I'm sorry,' he says. He is confused. 'I don't know what's going on. I don't know what to do. If only she'd let herself be checked into a –'

'We both know they won't be able to find anything, either,' I say.

He nods, numb. I wonder what kind of a doctor he is, unable to grasp the idea that someone is going to die from something no one understands. He struggles to say something. I wait until he finally finds the words.

'It's true what they say about her family,' he says. 'Only

back then, it was her aunt. I was about seven when I caught a fever. My parents brought me here – to her. I don't remember what she did. I should be dead. That's why I became a doctor. I want to do what she did. I want to thank her by saving lives.' He looks at me. 'And now Anne is sick, and I can't save her.'

It is easy to make someone's pain about yourself. You feel helpless, you internalize their discomfort, make it your drama. You are stealing their thunder; suddenly, you have a venue to attract the attention you did not know you were seeking. I understand Dr. Vera's frustration, but I also think that he should have known better.

I am very careful not to make Anne's pain mine. I am very particular about making sure that my pain is my own, and I have to remind myself that whatever frustration I feel is nothing compared to Anne's. I have to remind myself that I am not the one who is dying. I have to remind myself that this is not my story. But sometimes, in the middle of the night, when I wake suddenly, either from a dream or the sound of an errant bird or from a flash of blind fear, I wonder if really, this is a story about me, too.

It is not hard to care for Anne when she's in a good mood. And I know she tries to be, for the most part, for my sake. But sometimes, she can be difficult. Sometimes, most of the time, she wants me to leave.

'Bitch,' she says one day, throwing her plate across the room, fish and rice flying.

'Stop it,' I say. We are not fighting. We are not fighting.

'You left when I told you not to. Why are you here now? Because you feel guilty? I don't need your charity.'

I clean up her mess. I do not say anything.

'Why are you here?' she asks.

I do not answer, not because I don't want to engage her, but because I don't know the answer to that myself.

The birds are particularly noisy the morning I call Tim. Even he can hear them on the other end of the line, a cacophony of shrills and shrieks, of caws and calls.

'What the hell is going on there?' he asks through a choppy signal.

'It's the birds,' I say. Tim knows all about the birds. 'They're crazy today. I don't know why.'

'When are you coming home?'

The question makes me feel guilty. There I was, in the middle of a life I had left behind a long time ago, while the life I had wanted, the life I had made for myself, was put on hold. A crow dive-bombs me before I can answer. I duck instinctively, almost dropping my phone. The bird calls become louder, more agitated, until it feels like they encompass the whole forest.

'I'll call you as soon as I can,' I scream into the phone. 'I love you.'

I barely finish the sentence when another bird comes for me, and I have to run into the safety of the hut.

I close the door, waking Anne with my short, loud gasps. She looks more pained than usual. Her skin has taken on a pallor just this side of gray. Her eyes have lost their sheen. She looks weak, spent. Outside, the birds continue their assault, calling at each other, attacking the hut, engaging in aerial warfare.

She looks at me. I take her in my arms. We hold on tightly to each other until the clamor dies down.

We don't fall asleep, even after the birds calm down. It is comfortable, holding Anne and being held by her. It had taken us a while to get back to this level of familiarity, the week I had been here starting out with our just staring at each other; then a hand carelessly alighting on an arm, to be pulled away self-consciously at first, but to stay on with a soft squeeze later. And then we were holding hands again, running fingers through each other's hair, holding each other through the night. This time, when she puts her head on my shoulder, I let her. When she presses her lips to my cheek, I do not pull away. Sometimes, I kiss her back. While it is true that the dying get away with many things, I believe that the ones who know they will be left behind take many liberties as well.

I don't know how long it has been since the birds stopped, how long it has been since the only thing we can hear is the sound of our breath, and underneath, the thud of our heart-beats. Anne is warm against me. She hugs me, pulling me in tight before letting her arms go slightly limp, her hands slowly, deliberately, sliding up and down my back. I rest my head on her clavicle, snuggling close. There's a small rumble in my belly. Idly, I think that I would like a snack. But this, I like this more. I tilt my head up. Our eyes meet, and then our lips, and it is the most delicious thing in the world. We move slowly, but with a feverishness running underneath, the years of holding back behind us, unbelieving, wanting things to move faster, wanting this first moment to last for-ever. I take her nightshirt off and kiss her breasts. She does the same to me. We fuck, both of us afraid to say anything, both of us worried that this might not be real. When morn-ing wakes us, we are wrapped around each other, naked, and happy.

Things seem easier after that. We stop arguing, almost. We laugh more. Anne regains some color, though the cough is still there, and she still throws up sometimes. But now I can hold her hand and squeeze it and kiss her, and she can kiss me back and play with my hair and snake her hand up my shirt to touch my breasts and I can, in turn, dip my hand inside her underwear and then we are fucking again, sometimes loudly, sometimes in silence, sometimes schoolgirl giggly. We baptize her hut with our juices, our laughter, our love. Times like this, Anne does not seem sick at all. Times like this, when she is whispering my name, asking me to go faster, slower, deeper, I wonder what it would have been like if I hadn't left the barrio, what our life would have been like together. But, in the wee hours of the morning, when I am awake and Anne is sleeping, I tell myself I know the answer to that question: no matter what I would have chosen in the past, it would always end like this, here in this hut, with Anne dying.

The days seem shorter now. We spend them picking and drying herbs, preparing tinctures and poultices, seeing to the people who occasionally drop by. Most of the time, they bring things to barter for our services: rice, fish, chicken, snacks. Sometimes, they visit just because. Anne would meet them when she felt that she was strong enough, but lately, it seems to be more and more just me.

'You have a knack for this,' Aling Bebang, the grocer, said once.

'I'm only here until Anne gets better,' I reply.

I had been there a month by then.

'When are you coming home?' Tim asks, the question more and more frequent now.

'Soon,' I say. 'Soon.'

The birds go crazy only one other time, and that is the night Anne died.

It was just before dinner. We were lying in bed, talking, when Anne seized into the fetal position, clutching her abdomen. She was trying to cough and breathe at the same time, her breaths coming out in short wheezes punctuated by the shaking of her small, frail body. I tried to pull away so I could reach for medicine, but she held me close, with a surprising strength I didn't know she had.

'I can't do this anymore,' she said.

Outside, the birds began to stir, then began to call, soft chirping giving way to screeches and caws, the shapes of flying raptors turning the night darker, more sinister. Anne began to dry heave, each spasm a wave of pain, each gasp a choke that ended with air and a little saliva, black around the edges.

'Please,' she said. 'Help me.'

I have thought long and hard about this moment. I had been thinking about it even before I left the barrio, even before I let Anne disappear from my life, before I got her letter, before I returned. I was unsure and resentful when I first arrived, but the last month has helped me make peace with what must be done. People say that everybody has a choice, and this is true. But sometimes, the choices are moot, skewed, unfair, irrelevant. I knew that I had a choice not to open that letter. I knew that I had a choice not to return. I knew that I had a choice to leave.

I also knew that, deep in my heart of hearts, I didn't.

Tim knows this. I made sure to tell him everything, to have his consent before I left. He is a good man, and I am lucky to have him.

I gently lifted Anne so that we were both sitting. She held my face, tracing my jawline with her thumbs, our eyes never leaving each other. She brought her lips to mine. Anne's kisses are usually sweet, her tongue electric. This time, it felt as if she was devouring me, and I felt a hunger I had never sensed before. Her grip on my face became stronger, but still gentle. She started hacking, dry heaving, but would not let go, her mouth still on mine. I panicked, trying to push myself away, but Anne held on tight. We heard it before we felt it, a soft pop. Something had come up Anne's throat and was pushed into my mouth. It felt small and slick and wrong. I jerked back on impulse, spit it out. It fell to the floor, making tiny sounds of distress.

Outside, the cacophony continued to rise, more and more birds joining in, the sound confusing and deafening. We heard something thud against the hut, and then another, and another. The birds were dive-bombing the hut again, the normally docile birds attacking us, trying to get inside.

The thing that had come out of Anne's mouth shifted, its cries almost lost in the sounds from outside. It looked strange in the gaslight, a tiny newborn chick, smaller than usual, midnight black from beak to claw. It was slick with bile and blood and saliva. Anne was slumped in pain beside it, her mouth opening and closing, no words coming out. I looked at the chick. Its eyes were held closed by a thin keloid that made them look as if they were sewn shut with irregular dark thread. It mewled angrily at me, an un-chick sound, surprisingly loud, coming from such a diminutive creature. It was vile and disgusting, but it was also what was keeping my friend from dying.

Like I said, there are many choices I could have made. I could have not answered the letter, or come to see Anne, or stayed for so long, but I did, even though I knew what it would eventually lead to, because I could not bear to see my friend suffer.

I held out a hand. The chick hopped onto it. It was half the size of my palm, and it stank, its feathers slick from Anne's insides. I shuddered. I could hear the birds trying to get at it from outside. I could feel my belly rumbling, clamoring for this new source of nourishment. The birds stabbed their beaks into the thatched roof and bamboo walls, but the house held. I tried not to let their cries distract me. I closed my eyes and put the chick in my mouth.

It slid down my throat effortlessly, leaving behind a not unpleasant aftertaste much like cotton candy. I felt it move inside me, through me, weaving through passageways impossible to define by conventional anatomy, until it settled in the pit of my stomach, a calm, quiet presence. Anne took my hand, weakly.

'Thank you,' she said.

I moved towards her and held her, listening as her breathing became softer and more shallow, until her breath disappeared altogether.

When I leave for the barrio the next day, the birds are gone, and – I realize with a start – I am not hungry anymore.

José María Latorre

Snapshots

We opened this book on a high note and wanted to end it with a bang as well. So, last but certainly not least (indeed, it was the first story we selected for the book), we're pleased to offer this delightfully macabre tale by JOSÉ MARÍA LATORRE *(1945-2014), a prolific writer of fiction and nonfiction best known in his native Spain for his film criticism, but who also published a number of fine horror tales. This story was previously selected for a 2011 anthology of the best contemporary horror stories from Spain and has also been published in Polish and Italian, but makes its first English appearance here.*

THE FLASH FROM THE PHOTO MECHANISM hidden in the bowels of the machine dazzled him more than usual when it shot its four successive lightning flashes in his face. Then he seemed to vaguely remember that one of the times he had squinted or frowned, but that didn't justify the fact that the four photos proffered to him on a still-wet strip of cheap cardstock, literally vomited from one of the machine's openings, showed the face of a different man: he did not recognize himself either in the facial features, or the gray hair, or the terrified expression of the person in the photos. Nor did it explain the unpleasant sensation, a mixture of disgust, anxiety, and fear, that he had experienced when he sat down on the stool and rotated it to adjust his tall stature to the height of the black arrow that had been marked beside the instructions for how to use the machine. Nor the strange, revolting odor that had assailed him when he entered the booth and had unsettled him just like, he thought, one is unsettled by the smell of a room opened after its having been closed up for several years, and the peculiar odor of cemeteries in summer. It smelled the way he figured old mausoleums and crypts must smell. An absurd, inexplicable smell since the interior of that instant photo booth was continuously ventilated, for it was insulated only by a small black cloth curtain and because it was not summer, but winter. He almost smiled at thinking that he wasn't in a cemetery either, or a crypt, or a mausoleum. But it smelled musty, a smell of accumulated dust and decomposing organic matter. And the four photographs the machine had given him after a sort of growling sound were not his. The only possible explanation was that they belonged to the previous user, since in those automatic machines the photos were delayed a certain time in coming out, sometimes several minutes even: it had happened to him once years ago; a defect in the machine, they told him. Maybe the previous user, the owner of that aged, frightened face, had gone off, tired of waiting for photographs he wasn't receiving and thinking that he would have to contact the name and telephone number indicated on a small metal plaque and demand a refund. There are machines that are faulty and others that are out of order, thought Elias, and this was one of them, which could mean that his photos would not come out or, in the best case scenario, would be delayed several more minutes in emerging. He would wait; he was in no hurry. For a few moments, the situation struck him as funny, thinking about the possibility that because of some defect or malfunction the machine was daily bestowing on some customers the photographs of others.

The booth was located in the entrance to a street next to the Plaza Mayor, usually well frequented, beside a newspaper and magazine kiosk that at this hour had already closed its shutter, just as the bar across from it was also closed. Hadn't it closed earlier than usual? It was colder than on the previous nights: that might be why Elias didn't see anyone else around; cars, yes, the automobiles circulated at almost suicidal speeds, taking advantage of the scant traffic. While he kept his eyes fixed on the slot through which – if all went well – his photos would fall out, expelled from the guts of the machine, Elias thought that he shouldn't have yielded to the temptation of having his photos taken that night, and specifically in that booth, since in reality he didn't need them until the following day. He lit a cigarette, nervous, waiting on the sound that would indicate the arrival of the developed photos that were genuinely his, and threw the others on the floor. Ten minutes later he was convinced that the machine really was out of order. His first reaction was to leave; yet he didn't. He pushed the curtain aside, and, conquering with difficulty his unease at the foul odor, he again performed the same operation as before, beginning with inserting the required coins in the slot. Waiting for the burst of the flash, he was startled at not recognizing himself in the mirror: his eyes were more sunken in their sockets and had bags under them; his hair was whitish and the features he saw reflected were not his. He could feel a tightness in his chest, which always happened when his nerves got the better of him, and he hurriedly left the booth once the four flashes indicated the new photographic operation was underway. His hands trembled; a pair of wrinkled hands with long, yellowish nails. It was colder than before, and, surprisingly, even the cars had stopped traveling through the street, which was now submerged in silence. Nonetheless, in the neighboring Plaza Mayor, the traffic seemed normal, judging from the sound of the vehicles. There could be no doubt that he had been the victim of an optical illusion; the four photographs would drop down shortly, they would be his, he would pick them up and get away from this place, forgetting the disagreeable incident. The anxiety was almost making it difficult to breathe.

The strip of cardstock came out right away. He went on trembling as he picked it up: the individual in the photograph was not him, but it closely resembled the face he had just seen in the mirror. 'What a lot of nonsense!' he said aloud, as if trying to justify himself before an invisible witness. 'The mirror couldn't reflect any face but mine. I was the occupant of the booth, and I was also the one looking at myself.' Yes, he had been the model for the photo, but the man photographed was a stranger. The silence that reigned in the street began to weigh on him; not even the traffic from Plaza Mayor reached his ears. What should he do? Get out of there and look for another mirror somewhere else to verify stupidly that he was still the same? Phone one of his friends to come to the photo booth and be witness to such an abnormal occurrence or else confirm that it was just a hallucination? The street had grown dark; the streetlamps were off and not a single light emerged from the houses, as if silence and darkness had conspired to plunge this fragment of the urban landscape into nothingness. He did not even glimpse a weak slit of light coming from a courtyard or a window, nor the flickering of a television in a half-lit bedroom. Despite the insufficient streetlight, from where Elias was standing the Plaza Mayor seemed a movie set illuminated by the strong spotlights of a film team doing a nighttime shoot. 'That's all I needed, to have to deal with a power outage now,' he thought to calm himself. He could understand a power outage, just as he could understand that he had been using a machine that was out of order, but why were no vehicles passing in the street? And above all, why did the light in the booth continue to glow when everything around it was shrouded in a mantle of darkness?

A strong gust of cold wind impelled Elias to take shelter in the booth. From within, holding his breath at times because of the unbearable stench, he heard the whistling of the wind as it kicked up such a racket that it seemed it would drag every sort of object along in its path. He closed his eyes to avoid falling into the temptation of looking at his reflection again, but he couldn't resist the insane attraction the mirror exerted upon him. What he saw horrified him: the man he saw in the mirror was even older than before; his hair had fallen out, his eyes were sunken, scored with red veins and framed in black circles; his wrinkled face had taken on the same tone as the bags under his eyes. Elias looked at his hands: they were more wrinkled; the nails were long and yellowish. Running his fingers across his face, he noticed the rough feel of the withered skin. In the mirror, the elderly stranger repeated his same gestures, like a sad caricature in a distorting carnival mirror. Was there really such a thing as mirror creatures? Meanwhile the wind had intensified, its concert of malignant whistles growing more acute. Elias, paralyzed by fear, remained for a while listening to the onslaught of the gale against the photo booth. Later he peeked out, pushing the little curtain to the side, but the intense cold made him take refuge again within. Nevertheless, he was sweating, he could feel his clothes sticking to his body.

Mechanically he inserted more coins into the slot, moved by a morbid curiosity, by a strange desire to see the image he had seen reflected in the mirror reproduced in the cardstock, by an urge to abnegate himself in the horror. Then he had to grab hold of the curtain, both he and it whipped by the wind, while he awaited the mechanical delivery of the quadruplicate photo. A sound even stronger than the wind surged from the bowels of the machine and the photo strip was subsequently deposited in the expected place. Unlike the other times, it had fallen upside down, exposing its sickly, provocative whiteness to Elias's view. And although the wind was very strong, the card did not move a single millimeter from where it had fallen, as if it were held by unseen hands. He turned it over. The photos belonged to the same man as before, deformed by advancing age, but still recognizable despite everything. It was like a vision of what his own old age might be, a light illuminating death's waiting room. The wind ceased then as suddenly as it had risen, and Elias, although gasping, was able to stand outside the booth. He breathed with difficulty, he must have a fever; his forehead and cheeks felt warm, but when he tried to check by raising his hand to them, the touch of the dry skin grinding against his wrinkled fingers produced in him such a sensation of horror and disgust that he wanted to scream. From his throat no scream came, only a death rattle. He pinched one of his hands so that the pain would pull him out of this bad dream; he hurt himself, but he didn't wake up from any nightmare; he was awake and he could tell he was dying.

The street was still immersed in darkness. Near the spot where Elias stood, the streetlamps of Plaza Mayor spread their light over the familiar place, over vehicles, stoplights, and houses, but for him the distance seemed to have been multiplied a hundredfold. And though he knew that wasn't the case, neither was he going to start walking towards the Plaza: he had to have one more photograph taken, to prove to himself that none of what he was experiencing was real, or to demonstrate to the perverse monster in the machine that he wasn't afraid of it. When he entered the booth once more, he couldn't remember his name nor did he know why he was there at that late hour, having instant photos taken of himself. He still had some loose coins to insert in the machine. The last ones. He sat on the stool adjusted for his height and looked bravely ahead at the figure in the mirror, almost a skeleton with bones covered by ashen skin and clothed in a suit that hung off him as though he were a coat hanger, like a terrifying mannequin. This time the four flashes fired off by the machine produced a kind of blindness. He could hardly stand, and he had to catch hold of the curtain in order to emerge from the booth. Thus, clutching the rough cloth, he waited for the photos to come out, preceded by the usual noisy din. He strained to pick them up with one hand, without loosening his hold on the curtain with the other, and examined them in the interior light: the four photos were identical, there was no nuance to distinguish one from another, and they consisted of snapshots of a skull, with empty eye sockets and a hollow nasal cavity, its mouth open in a stupid, lipless grin. Elias fell to the ground before he was able to look at himself in the mirror again. The traffic had resumed, not heavy but still noisy. The last thing he saw were the bones of his right hand, which had ended up twisted into a grotesque posture only a few inches from his face, and he dedicated his final thought to imagining the newspaper headline announcing the strange appearance of a skeleton dressed in fashionable clothing inside an instant photo booth.

Translated from the Spanish by James D. Jenkins

About the Authors

LARS AHN is a Danish author and journalist. He has published one novel and two short story collections in Danish and has won two Niels Klim Awards for best Danish science fiction short stories. He was born in South Korea but was adopted as an infant and grew up in Denmark. His translated stories can be found in the anthologies *Sky City* and *Unconventional Fantasy: Forty Years of the World Fantasy Convention*.

FLAVIUS ARDELEAN is a writer of fantasy and horror for adults and children. He is the author of six novels and three short story collections, for which he has received multiple awards and nominations in his home country. He has an MA in Publishing from Oxford with a dissertation on the field of international horror publishing and is an affiliate member of the Horror Writers Association. He occasionally speaks about, coaches, and teaches on creativity, creative writing, and storytelling.

CHRISTIEN BOOMSMA (b. 1969) has been writing since she learned her first letters, but her career as a professional writer didn't begin in earnest until she won the Paul Harland Prize for Dutch-language fantastic literature in 2004 and 2006. She focuses on works for young readers, with titles like *Schaduwloper* [*Shadow Walker*] (2014) and *Vuurdoop* [*Baptism of Fire*] (2015). Her love for horror started in 2006 when she wrote a ghost story for her own children. She became intrigued by the interplay of darkness and evil, slowly and inexorably creeping closer. That finally resulted in the collection of twelve modern ghost stories *Spookbeeld* [*Spectre*] (2012) and a number of horror stories for adults. 'The Bones in Her Eyes' came about after she ran over a cat one night. She was struck by the strange, clear look in the cat's eyes – even though it was already dead. A look that even now is still fresh in her mind and has caused her its share of nightmares.

BERNARDO ESQUINCA's fiction is characterized by a fusion of the genres of the supernatural and the crime novel. Born in Guadalajara in 1972, he is the author of several novels and story collections, including one translated into English, *The Owls Are Not What They Seem* (2014). He has also co-edited two anthologies of fantastic tales from Mexico City from the 19th-21st centuries. He has been a member of the Sistema Nacional de Creadores de Arte and in 2017 won the Premio Nacional de Novela Negra. He has also written screenplays and audio series. He lives in Mexico City with his daughter Pía and his Xoloitzcuintle dog, Ramona.

ANDERS FAGER was born in 1964 in Stockholm. After a career as an army officer and game designer he turned to writing full time in 2009, when he released his first volume of Lovecraftian short stories, *Svenska kulter* [*Swedish Cults*]. The book was a critical success and a hit with readers and led to an expanded version, *Samlade Svenska kulter* [*Collected Swedish Cults*] in 2011. He has written several novels, a children's book, a graphic novel, and has also worked with movie scripts, games, and other kinds of storytelling. His works have been published in Finland, Italy, and France, where he became the only Swedish writer ever to have been nominated twice for the Grand Prix de l'Imaginaire. He lives in Stockholm with a tank full of fish and is very happily married.

CRISTINA FERNÁNDEZ CUBAS was born in Arenys de Mar, Barcelona, in 1945. Since the publication of her first volume of short stories in 1980, she has become an undeniable point of reference for the generations of short story writers to have followed. She has been translated into eight languages. Her complete stories were published recently by Tusquets, paying homage to her literary career, for which she received the Premio Ciudad de Barcelona and the Premio Salambó for the best book published in Spanish in 2008. Her most recent collection of stories, *La habitación de Nona*, once again proved her mastery in this genre, winning both the prestigious National Book Prize in Spain and the equally prestigious Premio de la Crítica, among other noteworthy prizes.

ARIANE GÉLINAS is the literary director of the journal *Le Sabord* as well as the artistic director of *Brins d'éternité*. She also edits reviews and columns on speculative fiction in *Lettres québécoises* and *Les libraires*. She is the author of *Les villages assoupis* (Prix Jacques-Brossard, Arts Excellence and Aurora/Boréal) and the collection *Le sabbat des éphémères*. Her novels *Les cendres de Sedna* (Prix Arts Excellence and Aurora/Boréal) and *Quelques battements d'ailes avant la nuit* appeared in 2016 and 2019 respectively.

MARKO HAUTALA is a Finnish writer of literary horror whose work has been translated into eight different languages, including the novel *The Black Tongue*, published in English in 2015. One of his novels was recently optioned for a film. In his native Finland, Hautala has received the Tiiliskivi Prize, Kalevi Jäntti Literary Prize and has been nominated for the Young Aleksis Kivi Prize.

FLORE HAZOUMÉ was born in Brazzaville, Congo, the daughter of a Beninese father and a Congolese mother. She grew up in France and is now a citizen of Ivory Coast, where she has lived for more than thirty years. Enriched by these different cultures, she considers herself above all a citizen of the world. She is the author of ten books, including novels, story collections, and works for young adults. Her writing deals with themes connected to African societies, contemporary history, and family. She is at present head of the nongovernmental organization Audace-C, which works in the fields of art, culture and education, and she is the founder of *Scrib Magazine*.

JOSÉ MARÍA LATORRE was born in Zaragoza in 1945. He was a celebrated film critic in his native Spain as well as a prolific author of some thirty books and an award-winning screenwriter. His best macabre stories have been collected in *La noche de Cagliostro y otros relatos de terror* [*Cagliostro's Night and Other Tales of Terror*] (2006) and *Música muerta y otros relatos* [*Dead Music and Other Tales*] (2014). He died in 2014.

LUIGI MUSOLINO was born in 1982 in the province of Torino, Italy, where he still lives and works. A specialist in Italian folklore, he is the author of several collections of short stories in the areas of weird fiction, horror, and rural Gothic: *Bialere* (2012), *Oscure Regioni* [*Dark Regions*] (2 vols., 2014-15), and *Uironda* (2018). In 2019 his first novel, *Eredità di carne* [*Legacy of Flesh*] appeared. He has translated into Italian works by Brian Keene, Lisa Mannetti, Michael Laimo, and the autobiographical writings of H. P. Lovecraft. His stories have been published in Italy, the United States, Ireland, and South Africa.

PILAR PEDRAZA (Toledo, 1951), has combined a career as a professor at the University of Valencia with a prolific writing career, producing an extensive body of work that includes stories, novels, columns, articles, and essays. As a fiction writer, she is the author of many novels and story collections, including *La fase del rubí*, *La pequeña pasión*, *Arcano trece*, *La perra de Alejandría*, *Lobas de Tesalia*, and *El amante germano*. As a researcher, she has devoted various essays to cinema (*Metropolis*, *Cat People*, Federico Fellini, Agustí Villaronga and Jean Cocteau) and to the construction of the feminine in literature and cinema of the fantastic, with works such as *Máquinas de amar* and *Espectra*. She has received many awards throughout her career, including the Ignotus, Nocte, Sheridan Le Fanu, Gabriel, and Celsius Awards.

MICHAEL ROCH is a science fiction writer and scriptwriter born in 1987 in France. He is also the creator and director of the literature channel *La Brigade du Livre* on Youtube and is part of the video label Pandora. His first fantastic and horrific short stories were published in various underground fanzines before joining Walrus Editions with two science fiction novels: *Twelve* and *Mortal Derby X*. His novel *Moi, Peter Pan* (MU Editions, 2017), was longlisted for the Grand Prix de l'Imaginaire in 2018. Since he returned to his native West Indies in 2015, he has conducted several creative writing workshops on the theme of Afrofuturism – a literary movement developing afrocentered counter-dystopias – in prison and university environments. His latest novel, *Le livre jaune* [*The Yellow Book*], at the crossroads of Lovecraftian influences and the Astroblackness movement, is published by MU Editions (2019).

SOLANGE RODRÍGUEZ PAPPE was born in Guayaquil, Ecuador in 1976. With seven volumes of fiction to her credit, she explores the genres of weird and fantastic fiction, horror, and science fiction. She has won the Joaquín Gallegos Lara Prize for best story collection in 2010 (for *Balas perdidas* [*Lost Bullets*]) and 2019 (*La primera vez que vi un fantasma* [*The First Time I Saw a Ghost*]). She has worked as a Professor of Literary Arts and a coordinator of creative writing workshops since 2005. In 2014 she earned her MA with a study on Latin American apocalyptic literature and the possible destruction of her city. Her predictions are starting to come true.

ELISENDA SOLSONA (Olesa de Montserrat, 1984) is a writer and secondary school teacher. She has a degree in Humanities and Audiovisual Communication and a master's in Film Writing. She has published the collection of flash fiction, *Cirurgies* [*Surgeries*] (Voliana Editions, 2016) and a volume of short stories, *Satèl·lits* [*Satellites*] (Editorial Males Herbes, 2019). The latter book was a substantial success in Catalonia and won the Premi Imperdible for best Catalan book in the realm of fantastic literature.

FRITHJOF SPALDER was born in 1933, the son of a well-known Norwegian composer of the same name. He is the author of a collection of macabre tales, *Jernjomfruen* [*The Iron Maiden*] (1971) and a novel, *Dødningerittet* (1976) and has also translated books from English to Norwegian and worked as an animator. He is a trained designer and illustrator in black & white, watercolor, airbrush, and acrylic. He lives in Oslo.

MARTIN STEYN fell in love with words when he discovered Stephen King, and it wasn't long before he took up a pencil and wrote a horror story of his own. Serial killers would later seduce him into crime and, armed with degrees in Psychology and Criminology, he's been writing police procedurals and psychological thrillers set in Cape Town, South Africa, the first published in 2014. But the short story still holds a special place in his heart and every year a few appear in local magazines. Whenever he can get away with it, he slips a bit of horror in as well. Read more about Martin and his books at www.martinsteyn.com.

YVETTE TAN is one of the Philippines' most celebrated horror writers. Works in the genre include two collections, one in English and the other in Tagalog, and a full-length film. She's written for TV, magazines, and the web, and is currently agriculture editor of one of the Philippines' leading newspapers. She's commonly asked how horror is related to agriculture, and her answer is that they both involve keeping the apocalypse at bay. Follow her on Twitter and Instagram at @yvette_tan and on yvettetan.com.

BATHIE NGOYE THIAM was born and raised in Baol (Senegal). He has lived for many years in Europe but remains attached to his country of birth. An architect by training, he expresses himself more through painting, writing, and on stage as an actor or storyteller. He has published two novels, a volume of plays, and a collection of fantastic tales based in part on Senegalese folklore.

TANYA TYNJÄLA was born in 1963 in Callao, Peru. She is the author of five books in the genres of fantasy and science fiction and is also a freelance journalist and a teacher of French and Spanish. Her short stories have been widely anthologized internationally, including in Argentina, Spain, Bulgaria, and Finland, among other places. She lives in Finland.

ATTILA VERES (b. 1985) is a Hungarian writer of horror and weird fiction. His first novel *Odakint sötétebb* [*Darker Outside*] (2017) was a surprise success in his native country, and was followed by the short story collection *Éjféli iskolák* [*Midnight Schools*] (2018). His short fiction appears regularly in *Black Aether*, a magazine dedicated to Hungarian cosmic horror, as well as in literary magazines. As a screenwriter he wrote several short and feature length films all over Europe, and he won the Best Television Screenplay award at the 2020 Hungarian Film Awards for the TV feature *Lives Recurring*. He is originally from Nyíregyháza but currently lives in Budapest. He collects books, vinyl, and memories of strange encounters. He is currently working on his new novel. 'The Time Remaining' is his first English publication.

CPSIA information can be obtained
at www.ICGtesting.com
Printed in the USA
LVHW041654231120
672481LV00006B/1371